MY COUSIN
RACHEL

Daphne du Maurier

With an Introduction
by Roger Michell

Virago

Virago

This edition published by Virago Press in 2017
Published by Virago Press in 2003

First published in 1951 by Victor Gollancz Ltd

3 5 7 9 10 8 6 4 2

A CIP catalogue record for this book
is available from the British Library.

ISBN 978 0 349 00985 8

Typeset by Palimpsest Book Production Limited,
Falkirk, Stirlingshire
Printed and bound in Great Britain by
Clays Ltd, St Ives plc

Papers used by Virago are from well-managed forests
and other responsible sources.

MIX
Paper from
responsible sources
FSC® C104740

Virago Press
An imprint of
Little, Brown Book Group
Carmelite House
50 Victoria Embankment
London EC4Y 0DZ

An Hachette UK Company
www.hachette.co.uk

www.virago.co.uk

Introduction

Three years ago I reached up to a high shelf for an old paperback copy of *My Cousin Rachel*. My mother had signed and dated it 1963, twelve years after its first publication, and I vaguely remembered her being a fan. On the cover was a windswept figure in dodgy period gear with plunging neckline: a bodice-ripper. I was searching for something light and effortless to lead me to sleep, but found myself, within a couple of pages, beguiled. What I'd idly suspected as fifties chick-lit with a dash of melodrama proved to be complex, dark, mysterious, and full of erotic, brooding disquiet . . . all underscored by the rumbling sound of surf on shingle.

Rachel is a chimera: 'rather sinister', as the author wrote of her, 'and you will never really know whether the woman is an angel or a devil'. She, and the book, are shrouded in ambiguity: when is it set? Exactly where? How old is she? How did the protagonist's parents die? Why have all the mothers in the book been consigned to the grave or the absurd? Why is Ambrose a woman-hater? What really went on in Italy, and with whom? Rachel wears a perpetual Mona Lisa smile; part poisoner, part prisoner, far more alive than those around her, yet hard and closed-up and secret and forever dressed in black. A post-Freudian heroine parachuted by her besotted author into a sort of Cornish *Mansfield Park*: alive to and unashamed of her sexuality, as exotic as a glass of iced prosecco, as sweet as panettone, as dangerous as a stiletto.

For I'm sure Daphne du Maurier, like her readers, absolutely fell for Rachel, choosing to write the book in the first person through the dewy, ever-widening eyes of her boy protagonist. Like poor Philip, that confused and wet-nosed puppy, we can feel du Maurier's addiction start to grow: Rachel's so very unItalian ivory skin, shrouded by veil; her delicate hands framed by white lace; those dark, sparkling eyes, brimming with tears or obscuring some vivid inner life; fashionable mourning in tight-fitting taffeta, ('Mourning certainly does not appear drab on her,' comments Louise); the riding gear that makes every man on the farm stop to stare; the sudden, without-warning kisses in the candle's shadow. And then, the sexual current swinging between child and adult, between mother and son, between lovers whose desire is ramped up by a sense of its wrongness. 'In the writing of the novel,' she says, 'I turned myself so completely into Philip, I was beguiled, and she could have poisoned the entire world and I would not have minded.'

Daphne wanted to be a boy when she was growing up, even creating a male alter ego for herself. By the time she started writing *My Cousin Rachel* in her little hut at the bottom of the garden at Menabilly, in the bitter winter of 1950, she was middle-aged, often alone, unsure of her marriage, confused by her 'Venetian' (a version of Wilde's 'Uranian'?) feelings for two very different women: Gertrude Lawrence, who was, like du Maurier's father, an actor; and Ellen Doubleday, the wife of her American publisher. The latter, dark, sophisticated and abroad, was by some accounts a model for Rachel. Even her surname seems a clue. 'What is strongest in you comes out in the middle years,' du Maurier wrote, and it's hard to avoid the sensation that what was coming out in her were strong and conflicted feelings about herself.

Did she? Didn't she? Was she? Wasn't she? This simple device fuels the novel's spectacular slalom ride of unclarity. It's a brilliant trick played out with smoke and mirrors: candles, fires, moonlight, low light, back-light, characters moving up and out and into the darkness. Du Maurier lights her scenes like Caravaggio and writes them like Hitchcock: half-conscious of camera angles, close-ups, cutting points. Chapters end on cliff-edges: doubt is dripped into the story like poison into tea with a cool hand and calibrated precision. There's just enough to make you feel a bit weird, but not so much for you to know you're being duped. For all the sometimes ill-concealed craft, it never feels like B-movie hack work, and even though now and then the gears creak a bit, and the reader is thrown into uncomfortable G-force by yet another impossible narrative hair-pin, the book is held by a second, hidden, inner tension. Perhaps the writer's thrilling indecision about her leading character (an indecision which she once confessed outlasted the writing of the novel) is part of a more profound and buried indecision about herself.

Is Rachel bad or good? Innocent or guilty, carnal or 'pure'? Or does the truth lie somewhere else? Is she an anachronism, full of life, possessed of sound mind and spirit, enjoying her sexuality as and where and with whomsoever she might wish, a woman in a man's world, determined to escape from the limitations of both the period when the book is ostensibly set and those of when it was written?

And as for poor, stunted, desperate Philip, that most stolid and priggish of unreliable narrators: did he really think he had bought her?

In the spirit of the novel's wilful ambiguity, I chose to set the film somewhere in the 1840s (between Austen and Dickens: between canals and railways), with costumes to fit (between the high-waists of Empire and the burgeoning of crinoline), and somewhere in the west of England (between Wessex and the recently rather over-oiled contours of Poldarkshire).

In short, wherever possible, I have scrupulously avoided exactitude.

Any attempt to adapt a novel can only result in a version. The novel itself remains unheeding and unharmed, high on a shelf. And any such version is fated, however attentive the film-makers, to bear a strong imprint of the era in which it is made, an imprint which becomes more obvious with the passing of the years. Every generation recreates its own favourite version of the past and this film is no different in reflecting, intentionally or otherwise, the spirit of its own age.

I hope my version gives pleasure to those who know nothing

of the book and enhances the experience for those who do. Of course, the best version of all, perfectly cast, impeccably lit and designed, with the greatest soundscape, most dizzying score, infinite budget and cast of thousands, will always be the one projected into the keen reader's imagination as she or he turns the pages that follow.

Roger Michell
February 2017

1

They used to hang men at Four Turnings in the old days. Not any more, though. Now, when a murderer pays the penalty for his crime, he does so up at Bodmin, after fair trial at the Assizes. That is, if the law convicts him, before his own conscience kills him. It is better so. Like a surgical operation. And the body has decent burial, though a nameless grave. When I was a child it was otherwise. I can remember as a little lad seeing a fellow hang in chains where the four roads meet. His face and body were blackened with tar for preservation. He hung there for five weeks before they cut him down, and it was the fourth week that I saw him.

He swung between earth and sky upon his gibbet, or, as my cousin Ambrose told me, betwixt heaven and hell. Heaven he would never achieve, and the hell that he had known was lost to him. Ambrose prodded at the body with his stick. I can see it now, moving with the wind like a weather-vane on a rusty pivot, a poor scarecrow of what had been a man. The rain had rotted his breeches, if not his body, and strips of worsted drooped from his swollen limbs like pulpy paper.

It was winter, and some passing joker had placed a sprig of holly in the torn vest for celebration. Somehow, at seven years old, that seemed to me the final outrage, but I said nothing. Ambrose must have taken me there for a purpose, perhaps to test my nerve, to see if I would run away, or laugh, or cry. As my guardian, father, brother, counsellor, as in fact my whole world, he was forever testing me. We walked around the gibbet, I remember, with Ambrose prodding and poking with his stick; and then he paused and lit his pipe, and laid his hand upon my shoulder.

'There you are, Philip,' he said, 'it's what we all come to in the end. Some upon a battlefield, some in bed, others according to their destiny. There's no escape. You can't learn the lesson too young. But this is how a felon dies. A warning to you and me to lead the sober life.' We stood there side by side, watching the body swing, as though we were on a jaunt to Bodmin fair, and the corpse was old Sally to be hit for coconuts. 'See what a moment of passion can bring upon a fellow,' said Ambrose. 'Here is Tom Jenkyn, honest and dull, except when he drank too much. It's true his wife was a scold, but that was no excuse to kill her. If we killed women for their tongues all men would be murderers.'

I wished he had not named the man. Up to that moment the body had been a dead thing, without identity. It would come into my dreams, lifeless and horrible, I knew that very well from the first instant I had set my eyes upon the gibbet. Now it would have connection with reality, and with the man with watery eyes who sold lobsters on the town quay. He used to stand by the steps in the summer months, his basket beside him, and he would set his live lobsters to crawl along the quay in a fantastic race, to make the children laugh. It was not so long ago that I had seen him.

'Well,' said Ambrose, watching my face, 'what do you make of him?'

I shrugged my shoulders, and kicked the base of the gibbet with my foot. Ambrose must never know I cared, that I felt sick at heart, and terrified. He would despise me. Ambrose at twenty-seven was god of all creation, certainly god of my own narrow world, and the whole object of my life was to resemble him.

'Tom had a brighter face when I saw him last,' I answered. 'Now he isn't fresh enough to become bait for his own lobsters.'

Ambrose laughed, and pulled my ears. 'That's my boy,' he said. 'Spoken like a true philosopher.' And then he added, with a sudden flash of perception, 'If you feel squeamish, go and be sick behind the hedge there, and remember I have not seen you.'

He turned his back upon the gibbet and the four roads, and went striding away down the new avenue he was planting at the time, which cut through the woods and was to serve as a second carriage-way to the house. I was glad to see him go because I did not reach the hedge in time. I felt better afterwards, though my teeth chattered and I was very cold. Tom Jenkyn lost identity again, and became a lifeless thing, like an old sack. He was even a target for the stone I threw. Greatly daring, I watched to see the body move. But nothing happened. The stone hit the sodden clothing with a plonk, then shied away. Ashamed of my action I sped off down the new avenue in search of Ambrose.

Well, that was all of eighteen years ago, and to the best of my recollection I have not thought much of it since. Until these last few days. It is strange how in moments of great crisis the mind whips back to childhood. Somehow I keep thinking of poor Tom, and how he hung there in his chains. I never heard his story, and few people would remember it now. He killed his wife, so Ambrose said. And that was all. She was a scold, but that was no excuse for murder. Possibly, being over-fond of drink, he killed her in his cups. But how? And with what weapon? With a knife, or with his bare hands? Perhaps Tom staggered forth from the inn upon the quay, that winter's night, all lit with love and fever. And the tide was high, splashing upon the steps, and the moon was also full, shining on the water. Who knows what dreams of conquest filled his unquiet mind, what sudden burst of fantasy?

He may have groped his way home to his cottage behind the church, a pale rheumy-eyed fellow stinking of lobster, and his wife lashed out at him for bringing his damp feet inside the door, which broke his dream, and so he killed her. That well might be his story. If there is survival after death, as we are taught to believe, I shall seek out poor Tom and question him. We will dream in purgatory together. But he was a middle-aged man of some sixty years or more, and I am five-and-twenty. Our dreams would not be the same. So go back into your shadows, Tom, and leave me some measure of peace. That gibbet has long since gone, and you with it. I threw a stone at you in ignorance. Forgive me.

The point is, life has to be endured, and lived. But how to

live it is the problem. The work of day by day presents no diffi-culties. I shall become a Justice of the Peace, as Ambrose was, and also be returned, one day, to Parliament. I shall continue to be honoured and respected, like all my family before me. Farm the land well, look after the people. No one will ever guess the burden of blame I carry on my shoulders; nor will they know that every day, haunted still by doubt, I ask myself a question which I cannot answer. Was Rachel innocent or guilty? Maybe I shall learn that too, in purgatory.

How soft and gentle her name sounds when I whisper it. It lingers on the tongue, insidious and slow, almost like poison, which is apt indeed. It passes from the tongue to the parched lips, and from the lips back to the heart. And the heart controls the body, and the mind also. Shall I be free of it one day? In forty, in fifty years? Or will some lingering trace of matter in the brain stay pallid and diseased? Some minuscule cell in the blood stream fail to race with its fellows to the fountain heart? Perhaps, when all is said and done, I shall have no wish to be free. As yet, I cannot tell.

I still have the house to cherish, which Ambrose would have me do. I can reface the walls where the damp enters, and keep all sound and well and in repair. Continue to plant trees and shrubs, cover the bare hills where the wind comes roaring from the east. Leave some legacy of beauty when I go, if nothing else. But a lonely man is an unnatural man, and soon comes to perplexity. From perplexity to fantasy. From fantasy to madness. And so I swing back again to Tom Jenkyn, hanging in his chains. Perhaps he suffered too.

Ambrose, those eighteen years ago, went striding down the avenue, and I in wake of him. He may well have worn the jacket I am wearing now. This old green shooting jacket, with the leather padding on the elbows. I have become so like him that I might be his ghost. My eyes are his eyes, my features his features. The man who whistled to his dogs and turned his back upon the four roads and the gibbet could be myself. Well, it was what I always wanted. To be like him. To have his height, his shoulders, his way of stooping, even his long arms, his rather clumsy looking hands, his sudden smile, his shyness at first meeting with a stranger, his dislike of fuss, of ceremony. His ease of manner with those who served and loved him – they flatter me, who say I have that too. And the strength which proved to be illusion, so that we fell into the same disaster. I have wondered lately if, when he died, his mind clouded and tortured by doubt and fear, feeling himself forsaken and alone in that damned villa where I could not reach him, whether his spirit left his body and came home here to mine, taking possession, so that he lived again in me, repeating his own mistakes, caught the disease once more and perished twice. It may be so. All I know is that my likeness to him, of which I was so proud, proved my undoing. Because of it, there came defeat. Had I been another man, agile and quick, with a deft tongue and a shrewd head for business, the past year would have been no more than another twelve months come and gone. I should be settling down to a brisk contented future. To marriage, possibly, and to a young family.

But I was none of these things, nor was Ambrose. We were dreamers, both of us, unpractical, reserved, full of great theories never put to test, and, like all dreamers, asleep to the waking world. Disliking our fellow men, we craved affection; but shyness kept impulse dormant until the heart was touched. When that happened the heavens opened, and we felt, the pair of us, that we had the whole wealth of the universe to give. We would have both survived, had we been other men. Rachel would have come here just the same. Spent a night or two, and gone her way. Matters of business would have been discussed, some settlement arranged, the will read formally with lawyers round a table, and I – summing up the position in a glance – have given her an annuity for life, and so been quit of her.

It did not happen that way because I looked like Ambrose. It did not happen that way because I felt like Ambrose. When I went up to her room, that first evening she arrived, and after knocking stood within the door, my head bent slightly because of the low lintel, and she got up from the chair where she had been sitting by the window and looked up at me, I should have known then, from the glance of recognition in her eyes, that it was not I she saw, but Ambrose. Not Philip, but a phantom. She should have gone then. Packed up her trunks and left. Travelled back to the place where she belonged, back to that shuttered villa, musty with memories, the formal terraced garden and the dripping fountain in the little court. Returned to her own country, parched in mid-summer and hazy with heat, austere in winter under the cold and brilliant sky. Some instinct should have warned her that to stay with me would bring destruction, not only to the phantom she encountered, but finally to her also.

Did she, I wonder, when she saw me standing there diffident and awkward, smarting with sullen resentment at her presence yet hotly conscious of being host and master, and all too angrily aware of my big feet and arms and legs, sprawling, angular, an unbroken colt – did she, I wonder, think swiftly to herself, 'Ambrose must have been thus when he was young. Before my time. I did not know him when he looked like this' – and therefore stayed?

Perhaps that was the reason why, when I had that brief meeting with Rainaldi, the Italian, for the first time also, he too looked at me with the same shock of recognition quickly veiled, and playing with a pen upon his desk thought for a moment, and then softly said to me, 'You have only arrived to-day? Then your cousin Rachel has not seen you.' Instinct had warned him also. But too late.

There is no going back in life. There is no return. No second chance. I cannot call back the spoken word or the accomplished deed, sitting here, alive and in my own home, any more than poor Tom Jenkyn could, swinging in his chains.

It was my godfather Nick Kendall who, in his bluff straight-forward fashion, said to me on the eve of my twenty-fifth birthday – a few months ago only, yet God! how long in time – 'There are some women, Philip, good women very possibly, who through no fault of their own impel disaster. Whatever they touch somehow turns to tragedy. I don't know why I say this to you,

6

but I feel I must.' And then he witnessed my signature on the document that I had put before him.

No, there is no return. The boy who stood under her window on his birthday eve, the boy who stood within the doorway of her room the evening that she came, he has gone, just as the child has gone who threw a stone at a dead man on a gibbet to give himself false courage. Tom Jenkyn, battered specimen of humanity, unrecognisable and unlamented, did you, all those years ago, stare after me in pity as I went running down the woods into the future?

Had I looked back at you, over my shoulder, I should not have seen you swinging in your chains, but my own shadow.

2

I had no sense of foreboding, when we sat talking together that last evening, before Ambrose set out on his final journey. No premonition that we would never be together again. It was now the third autumn that the doctors had ordered him to winter abroad, and I had become used to his absence and to looking after the estate while he was away. The first winter that he went I had been up at Oxford still, so his going had made very little difference to me, but the second winter I came down for good and remained the whole time at home, which was what he wanted me to do. I did not miss the gregarious life at Oxford, in fact I was glad to be quit of it.

I never had any desire to be anywhere but at home. Apart from my schooldays at Harrow, and afterwards at Oxford, I had never lived in any place but this house, where I had come at the age of eighteen months after my young parents died. Ambrose, in his queer generous way, was seized with pity for his small orphaned cousin, and so brought me up himself, as he might have done a puppy, or a kitten, or any frail and lonely thing needing protection.

Ours was a strange sort of household from the first. He sent my nurse packing when I was three years old, because she smacked my bottom with a hairbrush. I don't remember the incident, but he told me later.

'It made me so damnably angry,' he said to me, 'to see that woman belabouring your small person with her great coarse hands for some trifling misdemeanour that she was too unintelligent to comprehend. After that, I corrected you myself.'

I never had reason to regret it. There could not be a man more fair, more just, more lovable, more full of understanding.

He taught me my alphabet in the simplest possible way by using the initial letters of every swearword – twenty-six of them took some finding, but he achieved it somehow, and warned me at the same time not to use the words in company. Although invariably courteous he was shy of women, and mistrustful too, saying they made mischief in a household. Therefore he would employ only menservants, and the tribe was controlled by old Seecombe, who had been my uncle's steward.

Eccentric perhaps, unorthodox – the west country has always been known for its odd characters – but despite his idiosyncratic opinions on women, and the upbringing of small boys, Ambrose was no crank. He was liked and respected by his neighbours, and loved by his tenants. He shot and hunted in the winter, before rheumatism got a grip on him, fished in the summer from a small sailing boat he kept anchored in the estuary, dined out and entertained when he had the mind to do so, went twice to church on a Sunday even though he did pull a face at me across the family pew when the sermon was too long, and endeavoured to induce in me his passion for the planting of rare shrubs.

'It's a form of creation,' he used to say, 'like anything else. Some men go in for breeding. I prefer growing things from the soil. It takes less out of you, and the result is far more satisfying.'

It shocked my godfather, Nick Kendall, and Hubert Pascoe, the vicar, and others of his friends who used to urge him to settle down to domestic bliss and rear a family instead of rhododendrons.

'I've reared one cub,' he would make reply, pulling my ears, 'and that has taken twenty years off my span of life, or put them on, whichever way I care to look at it. Philip is a ready-made heir, what's more, so there is no question of having to do my duty. He'll do it for me when the time comes. And now sit back in your chairs and be comfortable, gentlemen. As there is no woman in the house we can put our boots on the table and spit on the carpet.'

Naturally we did no such thing. Ambrose was nothing if not

fastidious, but it delighted him to make these remarks before the new vicar, hen-pecked, poor fellow, with a great tribe of daughters, and round the dining-room table would go the port after Sunday dinner, with Ambrose winking at me from his end of the table.

I can see him now, half hunched, half sprawling in his chair – I caught the habit from him – shaking with silent laughter when the vicar made his timid ineffectual remonstrance, and then, fearing he might have hurt the man's feelings, intuitively changing the tone of the conversation, passing on to matters where the vicar would be at ease, and putting himself to the utmost trouble to make the little fellow feel at home. I came to appreciate his qualities the more when I went to Harrow. The holidays passed all too swiftly, as I compared his manners and his company with the urchins who were my schoolmates, and the masters, stiff and sober, lacking to my mind all humanity.

'Never mind,' he used to say, patting my shoulder before I started off, white-faced, a trifle tearful, to catch the coach to London. 'It's just a training process, like breaking in a horse; we have to face it. Once your schooldays are behind you, and they will be before you've even counted, I'll bring you home here for good, and train you myself.'

'Train me for what?' I asked.

'Well, you're my heir, aren't you? That's a profession in itself.'

And away I would go, driven by Wellington the coachman to pick up the London coach at Bodmin, turning for a last glimpse of Ambrose as he stood leaning on his stick with the dogs beside him, his eyes wrinkled in sure and certain understanding, his thick curling hair already turning grey; and as he whistled to the dogs and went back into the house I would swallow the lump in my throat and feel the carriage wheels bear me away, inevitably and fatally, along the crunching gravel drive across the park and through the white gate, past the lodge, to school and separation.

He reckoned without his health, though, and when school and university lay behind me it was then his turn to go.

'They tell me if I spend another winter being rained on every day I shall end my days crippled in a bath-chair,' he said to me. 'I must go off and search for the sun. The shores of Spain or Egypt, anywhere on the Mediterranean where it is dry, and warm. I don't particularly want to go, but on the other hand I'm damned if I'll end my life a cripple. There is one advantage in the plan. I shall bring back plants that nobody else has got. We'll see how the demons thrive in Cornish soil.'

The first winter came and went, likewise the second. He enjoyed himself well enough, and I don't think he was lonely. He returned with heaven knows how many trees, shrubs, flowers, plants of every form and colour. Camellias were his passion. We started a plantation for them alone, and whether he had green fingers or a wizard's touch I do not know, but they flourished from the first, and we lost none of them.

So the months passed, until the third winter. This time he had decided upon Italy. He wanted to see some of the gardens in Florence and Rome. Neither town would be warm in winter, but that did not worry him. Someone had assured him that the air would be dry, if cold, and that he need not have any fear of rain. We talked late, that evening. He was never one for early bed, and often we would sit together in the library until one or two in the morning, sometimes silent, sometimes talking, both of us with our long legs stretched out before the fire, the dogs curled round our feet. I have said before that I felt no premonition, but now I wonder, thinking back, if it was otherwise for him. He kept looking at me in a puzzled, reflective sort of way, and from me to the panelled walls of the room and the familiar pictures, and so to the fire, and from the fire to the sleeping dogs.

'I wish you were coming with me,' he said suddenly.

'It wouldn't take me long to pack,' I answered.

He shook his head, and smiled. 'No,' he said, 'I was joking. We can't both be away for months at a time. It's a responsibility, you know, being a landowner, though not everybody feels as I do.'

'I could travel with you down to Rome,' I said, excited at the idea. 'Then, granting the weather did not hold me back, I'd still be home by Christmas.'

'No,' he said slowly, 'no, it was just a whim. Forget it.'

'You're feeling well enough, aren't you?' I said. 'No aches or pains?'

'Good God, no,' he laughed, 'what do you take me for, an invalid? I haven't had a twinge of rheumatism for months. The trouble is, Philip boy, I'm too much of a fool about my home. When you reach my age, perhaps you'll feel about it the way I do.'

He got up from his chair and went over to the window. He drew back the heavy curtains and stood for a few moments, staring out across the grass. It was a quiet, still evening. The jackdaws had gone to roost, and for once even the owls were silent.

'I'm glad we did away with the paths and brought the turf close to the house,' he said. 'It would look better still if the grass went sloping right to the end there, by the pony's paddock. One day you must cut away the undergrowth to give a view of the sea.'

'How do you mean,' I said, '*I* must do it? Why not you?'

He did not answer at once. 'Same thing,' he said at last, 'same thing. It makes no odds. Remember though.'

My old retriever, Don, raised his head and looked across at him. He had seen the corded boxes in the hall, and sensed departure. He struggled to his feet, and went and stood beside Ambrose, his tail drooping. I called softly to him, but he did not come to me. I knocked out the ashes of my pipe into the hearth. The clock in the belfry struck the hour. From the servants' quarters I could hear Seecombe's grumbling voice scolding the pantry boy.

'Ambrose,' I said, 'Ambrose, let me come with you.'

'Don't be a damn fool, Philip, go to bed,' he answered.

That was all. We did not discuss the matter any more. Next morning at breakfast he gave me some last instructions about the spring planting, and various things he had in mind for me to do before his return. He had a sudden fancy to make a small pool where the ground was marshy in the park by the entrance to the east drive, and this would have to be cut out and banked if we got some passable weather in the winter months. The time for departure came all too soon. Breakfast was over by seven, for he was obliged to make an early start. He would pass the night at Plymouth, and sail from there on the morning tide. The vessel, a trader, would take him to Marseilles, and from there he would travel into Italy at his leisure; he enjoyed a long sea trip. It was a raw damp morning. Wellington brought the carriage to the door, and it was soon piled high with baggage. The horses were restless and eager to be off. Ambrose turned to me, and laid his hand upon my shoulder. 'Take care of things,' he said, 'don't fail me.'

'That's a hit below the belt,' I answered. 'I've never failed you yet.'

'You're very young,' he said. 'I put a great deal on your shoulders. Anyway, everything I have is yours, you know that.'

I believe then if I had pressed the matter he would have let me go with him. But I said nothing. Seecombe and I put him in the carriage with his rugs and sticks, and he smiled at us from the open window.

'All right, Wellington,' he said, 'drive on.'

And they went away down the drive just as the rain began.

The weeks passed much as they had done during the two previous winters. I missed him as I always did, but there was plenty to occupy me. If I wished for company I rode over to visit my godfather, Nick Kendall, whose only daughter, Louise, was a few years younger than myself, and a playmate from childhood days. She was a staunch girl, with no fancy ways, and pretty enough. Ambrose used to jest at times and say she would make me a wife one day, but I confess I never thought of her as such.

It was mid-November when his first letter came, brought back in the same vessel that had landed him at Marseilles. The voyage had been uneventful, the weather good, despite a bit of a tossing in the Bay of Biscay. He was well, and in good spirits, and looking forward to the journey into Italy. He was not trusting himself to a diligence, which would have meant going up to Lyons anyway, but had hired himself horses and a conveyance, and proposed driving along the coast into Italy, and then turning towards Florence. Wellington shook his head at the news, and foretold an accident. He was of the firm opinion that no Frenchman could drive, and that all Italians were robbers. Ambrose survived, however, and the next letter came from Florence. I kept all his letters, and I have the bunch of them before me now. How often I read them during the next months; they were thumbed, and turned, and read again, as though by the very pressure of my hands upon them more could be gleaned from the pages than the written words gave of themselves.

It was towards the close of this first letter from Florence, where he had apparently spent Christmas, that he first spoke of cousin Rachel.

'I have made the acquaintance of a connection of ours,' he wrote. 'You have heard me talk about the Coryns, who used to have a place on the Tamar, now sold up and changed to other hands. A Coryn married an Ashley two generations ago, as you will find on the family tree. A descendant of that branch was born and brought up in Italy by an impecunious father and an Italian mother, and married off at an early age to an Italian nobleman called Sangalletti, who departed this life by fighting a duel, it appears, when half-seas over, leaving his wife with a load of debts and a great empty villa. No children. The Contessa Sangalletti, or, as she insists on calling herself, my cousin Rachel, is a sensible woman, good company, and has taken it upon her shoulders to show me the gardens in Florence, and in Rome later, as we shall both be there at the same time.'

I was glad that Ambrose had found a friend, and someone who could share his passion for gardens. Knowing nothing of Florentine or Roman society, I had feared English acquaintances would be few, but here at least was a person whose family had hailed from Cornwall in the first place, so they would have that in common too.

14

The next letter consisted almost entirely of lists of gardens, which, though not at their best at this season in the year, seemed to have made a great impression upon Ambrose. So had our relative.

'I am beginning to have a real regard for our cousin Rachel,' wrote Ambrose in early spring, 'and feel quite distressed to think what she must have suffered from that fellow Sangalletti. These Italians are treacherous blackguards, there's no denying it. She is just as English as you or I in her ways and outlook, and might have been living beside the Tamar yesterday. Can't hear enough about home and all I have to tell her. She is extremely intelligent but, thank the Lord, knows when to hold her tongue. None of that endless yattering, so common in women. She has found me excellent rooms in Fiesole, not far from her own villa, and as the weather becomes milder I shall spend a good deal of my time at her place, sitting on the terrace, or pottering in the gardens which are famous, it seems, for their design, and for the statuary, which I don't know much about. How she exists I hardly know, but I gather she has had to sell much of the valuable stuff in the villa to pay off the husband's debts.'

I asked my godfather, Nick Kendall, if he remembered the Coryns. He did, and had not much opinion of them. 'They were a feckless lot, when I was a boy,' he said. 'Gambled away their money and estates, and now the house, on Tamar-side, is nothing much more than a tumbled-down farm. Fell into decay some forty years ago. This woman's father must have been Alexander Coryn – I believe he did disappear to the continent. He was second son of a second son. Don't know what happened to him though. Does Ambrose give this Contessa's age?'

'No,' I said, 'he only told me she had been married very young, but he did not say how long ago. I suppose she is middle-aged.'

'She must be very charming for Mr Ashley to take notice of her,' remarked Louise. 'I have never heard him admire a woman yet.'

'That's probably the secret,' I said. 'She's plain and homely, and he doesn't feel forced to pay her compliments. I'm delighted.'

One or two more letters came, scrappy, without much news. He was just back from dining with our cousin Rachel, or on his way there to dinner. He said how few people there were in Florence amongst her friends who could really give her disinterested advice on her affairs. He flattered himself, he said, that he could do this. And she was so very grateful. In spite of her many interests, she seemed strangely lonely. She could never have had anything in common with Sangalletti, and confessed she had been hungry all her life for English friends. 'I feel I have accomplished something,' he said, 'besides acquiring hundreds of new plants to bring back home with me.'

Then came a space of time. He had said nothing of the date of his return, but it was usually towards the end of April. Winter had seemed long with us, and frost, seldom keen in the west country, unexpectedly severe. Some of his young camellias had been affected by it, and I hoped he would not return too soon and find hard winds and driving rains with us still.

Shortly after Easter his letter came. 'Dear boy,' he said, 'you will wonder at my silence. The truth is, I never thought I should, one day, write such a letter to you. Providence works in strange ways. You have always been so close to me that possibly you have guessed something of the turmoil that has been going on in my mind during the past weeks. Turmoil is the wrong word. Perhaps I should say happy bewilderment, turning to certainty. I have made no quick decision. As you know, I am too much a man of habit to change my way of living for a whim. But I knew; some weeks back, that no other course was possible. I had found something I had never found before, and did not think existed. Even now, I can hardly believe it has happened. My thoughts have gone to you very often, but somehow I have not felt calm and steady enough to write, until today. You must know that your cousin Rachel and I were married a fortnight ago. We are now together in Naples, on our honeymoon, and intend returning to Florence shortly. Further than that I cannot say. We have made no plans, and neither of us have any wish, at the present time, to live beyond the moment.

16

'One day, Philip, not too far distant, I hope, you will know her. I could write much of personal description that would weary you, and of her goodness too, her real and loving tenderness. These things you will see for yourself. Why she has chosen me of all men, a crusty cynical woman-hater if ever there was one, I cannot say. She teases me about it, and I admit defeat. To be defeated by someone like herself is, in a sense, a victory. I might call myself victor, not vanquished, if it were not so damnably conceited a statement.

'Break the news to everyone, give them all my blessings, and hers too, and remember, my dearest boy and pup, that this marriage, late in life, cannot belittle one jot my deep affection for you, rather it will increase it, and now that I think of myself as the happiest of men I shall endeavour to do more for you than ever before, and will have her to help me. Write soon, and if you can bring yourself to do so add a word of welcome to your cousin Rachel.

'Always, your devoted Ambrose.'

The letter came about half-past five, just after I had dined. Luckily, I was alone. Seecombe had brought in the post-bag, and left it with me. I put the letter in my pocket and walked out across the fields down to the sea. Seecombe's nephew, who had the mill cottage on the beach, said good-day to me. He had his nets spread on the stone wall, drying in the last of the sun. I barely answered him, and he must have thought me curt. I climbed over the rocks to a narrow ledge, jutting into the little bay, where I used to swim in summer. Ambrose would anchor some fifty yards out in his boat, and I would swim to him. I sat down, and taking the letter from my pocket read it again. If I could have felt one spark of sympathy, of gladness, one single ray of warmth towards those two who were sharing happiness together down in Naples, it would have eased my conscience. Ashamed of myself, bitterly angry at my selfishness, I could raise no feeling in my heart at all. I sat there, numb with misery, staring at the flat calm sea. I had just turned twenty-three, and yet I felt as lonely and as lost as I had done years before, sitting on a bench in Fourth Form, at Harrow, with no one to befriend me, and nothing before me, only a new world of strange experience that I did not want.

3

I think what shamed me most was the delight of his friends, their real pleasure and true thought for his welfare. Congratulations were showered upon me, as a sort of messenger to Ambrose, and in the midst of it all I had to smile, and nod my head, and make out to them that I had known it would happen all along. I felt double-faced, a traitor. Ambrose had so tutored me to hate falsity, in man or beast, that suddenly to find myself pretending to be other than I was came near to agony.

'The best thing that could have happened.' How often I heard the words and had to echo them. I began to shun my neighbours, and skulk at home around the woods, rather than meet the eager faces and the wagging tongues. If I rode out about the farmlands, or into town, there was no escape. Tenants on the estate, or acquaintances from here and there, had but to catch a glimpse of me and I was doomed to conversation. An indifferent actor, I forced a smile on to my face, feeling the skin stretch in protest as I did so, and was obliged to answer questions with a kind of heartiness I hated, a heartiness that the world expects when there is mention of a wedding. 'When will they be coming home?' For this there was one answer. 'I don't know. Ambrose has not told me.'

There would be much speculation upon the looks, the age, the general appearance of his bride, to which I would make reply, 'She is a widow, and she shares his love for gardens.'

Very suitable, the heads would nod, could not be better, the very thing for Ambrose. And then would follow jocularity, and jesting, and much amusement at the breaking in of a confirmed bachelor to wedlock. That shrew Mrs Pascoe, the vicar's lady, ground away upon this subject as if by doing so she won revenge for past insults upon the holy state.

'What a change there will be now, Mr Ashley,' she said on every possible occasion. 'No more go-as-you-please for *your* household. And a very good thing too. Some organisation will at last be brought to bear upon the servants, and I don't imagine Seecombe being too well pleased. He has had things his own way long enough.'

In this she spoke the truth. I think Seecombe was my one ally, but I was careful not to side with him, and stopped him when he tried to feel his way with me.

'I don't know what to say, Mr Philip,' he murmured, gloomy and resigned. 'A mistress in the house will have everything upside down, and we shan't know where we are. There will first be one thing, then another, and probably no pleasing the lady whatever is done for her. I think the time has come for me to retire and give way to a younger man. Perhaps you had better mention the matter to Mr Ambrose when you write.'

I told him not to be foolish, and that Ambrose and I would be lost without him, but he shook his head and continued to go about the place with a long face, and never let an opportunity pass without making some sad allusion to the future, how the hours of the meals would no doubt be changed, the furniture altered, and an interminable cleaning be ordered from dawn till dusk with no repose for anybody, and, as a final thrust, even the poor dogs destroyed. This prophecy, uttered in sepulchral tones, brought back to me some measure of my own lost sense of humour, and I laughed for the first time since reading Ambrose's letter.

What a picture Seecombe painted! I had a vision of a regiment of serving girls with mops, sweeping the house free from cobwebs, and the old steward, his underlip jutting in the familiar way, watching them in stony disapproval. His gloom amused me, but when much the same thing was foretold by others – even by Louise Kendall, who knowing me well might have had perception enough to hold her tongue – the remarks brought irritation.

'Thank goodness you will have fresh covers in the library,' she said gaily. 'They have gone quite grey with age and wear, but I dare say you never noticed it. And flowers in the house, what an improvement! The drawingroom will come into its own at last. I always thought it a waste that it was not used. Mrs Ashley will furnish it, no doubt, with books and pictures from her Italian villa.'

She ran on and on, going over in her mind a whole list of improvements, until I lost patience with her and said roughly, 'For heaven's sake, Louise, leave the subject alone. I'm sick and tired of it.'

She stopped short then, and looked at me shrewdly.

'You aren't jealous, are you, by any chance?' she said.

'Don't be a fool,' I told her.

It was an ugly thing to call her, but we knew each other so well that I thought of her as a younger sister, and had small respect for her.

After that she was silent, and I noticed when the well-worn theme came up again in conversation she glanced across at me, and tried to change it. I was grateful, and liked her the more.

It was my godfather and her father, Nick Kendall, who made the final thrust, unaware of course that he was doing so, and speaking bluntly in his plain straightforward way.

'Have you made any plans for the future, Philip?' he said to me one evening, after I had ridden over to take dinner with them.

'Plans, sir? No,' I said, uncertain of his meaning.

'Early yet, of course,' he answered, 'and I suppose you cannot very well do so until Ambrose and his wife return home. I wondered whether you had considered looking around the neighbourhood for some small property of your own.'

I was slow to grasp his meaning. 'Why should I do that?' I asked.

'Well, the position is somewhat changed, isn't it?' he said in matter-of-fact tones. 'Ambrose and his wife will want most naturally to be together. And if there should be a family, a son, things won't be the same for you, will they? I am certain Ambrose won't let you suffer from the change, and will buy you any property you fancy. Of course it is possible they will have no children, but on the other hand there is no reason to suppose they won't. You might prefer to build. It is sometimes more satisfactory to build your own place than take over a property for sale.'

He continued talking, mentioning places within twenty miles or so of home that I might care to own, and I was thankful that he did not seem to expect a reply to anything he said. The fact was that my heart was too full to answer him. What he suggested was so new and unexpected that I could barely think straight, and shortly afterwards made an excuse to go. Jealous, yes. Louise was right about that, I supposed. The jealousy of a child who must suddenly share the one person in his life with a stranger.

Like Seecombe, I had seen myself doing my utmost to settle down to new uncomfortable ways. Putting out my pipe, rising to my feet, making an effort at conversation, drilling myself to the rigours and tedium of feminine society. And watching Ambrose, my god, behaving like a ninny, so that I should have to leave the room from sheer embarrassment. I had never once seen myself an outcast. No longer wanted, put out of my home and pensioned like a servant. A child arriving, who would call Ambrose father, so that I should be no longer needed.

Had it been Mrs Pascoe who had drawn my attention to this possibility I should have put it down as malice, and forgotten it. But my own godfather, quiet and calm, making a statement of fact, was different. I rode home, sick with uncertainty and sadness. I hardly knew what to do, or how to act. Should I make plans, as my godfather had said? Find myself a home? Make preparations for departure? I did not want to live anywhere else, or possess another property. Ambrose had brought me up and trained me for this one alone. It was mine. It was his. It belonged to both of us. But now no longer, everything had changed. I can remember wandering about the house, when I came home from visiting the Kendalls, looking upon it with new eyes, and the dogs, seeing my restlessness, followed me, as uneasy as myself. My old nursery, uninhabited for so long, and now the room where Seecombe's niece came once a week to mend and sort the linen, took on new meaning. I saw it freshly painted, and my small cricket bat that still stood, cobweb-covered on a shelf amongst a pile of dusty books, thrown out for rubbish. I had not thought before what memories the room held for me, going in and out of it once in two months perhaps, with a shirt to be repaired, or socks to be darned. Now I wanted it for my own again, a haven of refuge from the outer world. Instead of which it would become an alien place, stuffy, smelling of boiled milk and blankets put to dry, like the living-rooms of cottages that I so often visited, where there lived young children. In my imagination I could see them crawling with fretful cries upon the floor, forever bumping heads or bruising elbows; or worse, dragging themselves up upon one's knees, their faces puckering like monkeys if denied. Oh God, was all this in store for Ambrose?

Hitherto, when I had thought of my cousin Rachel – which I did but sparingly, brushing her name from my mind as one does all things unpleasant – I had pictured to myself a woman resembling Mrs Pascoe, only more so. Large-featured and angular, with a hawk's eyes for dust as Seecombe prophesied, and far too loud a laugh when there was company for dinner, so that one winced for Ambrose. Now she took on new proportions. One moment monstrous, like poor Molly Bate at the West Lodge, obliging one to avert the eyes from sheer delicacy, and the next pale and drawn, shawl-covered in a chair, with an invalidish petulance about her, while a nurse hovered in the background, mixing medicines with a spoon. One moment middle-aged and forceful, the next simpering and younger than Louise, my cousin Rachel had a dozen personalities or more and each one more hateful than the last. I saw her forcing Ambrose to his knees to play at bears, the children astride his back, and Ambrose consenting with a humble grace, having lost all dignity. Yet again, decked out in muslin, with a ribbon in her hair, I saw her pout and toss her curls, a curving mass of affection, while Ambrose sat back in his chair surveying her, the bland smile of an idiot on his face.

When in mid-May the letter came, saying that after all they had decided to remain abroad throughout the summer, my relief

23

was so intense that I could have shouted aloud. I felt more traitorous than ever, but I could not help it.

'Your cousin Rachel is still so bothered by the tangle of business that must be settled before coming to England,' wrote Ambrose, 'that we have decided, although with bitter disappointment, as you may imagine, to defer our return home for the present. I do the best I can, but Italian law is one thing and ours another, and it's the deuce of a job to reconcile the two. I seem to be spending a mint of money, but it's in a good cause and I don't begrudge it. We talk of you often, dear boy, and I wish you could be with us.' And so on to enquiries about the work at home and the state of the gardens, with his usual fervour of interest, so that it seemed to me I must be mad to have thought for a moment he could change.

Disappointment was of course intense throughout the neighbourhood that they would not be home this summer.

'Perhaps,' said Mrs Pascoe, with a meaning smile, 'Mrs Ashley's state of health forbids her travelling?'

'As to that I cannot say,' I answered. 'Ambrose mentioned in his letter that they had spent a week in Venice, and both of them came back with rheumatism.'

Her face fell. 'Rheumatism? His wife also?' she said. 'How very unfortunate.' And then, reflectively: 'She must be older than I thought.'

Vacuous woman, her mind running upon one single train of thought. I had rheumatics in my knees at two years old. Growing pains, my elders told me. Sometimes, after rain, I have them still. For all that, there was some similarity between my mind and Mrs Pascoe's. My cousin Rachel aged some twenty years. She had grey hair once more, she even leant upon a stick, and I saw her, when she wasn't planting roses in that Italian garden which I could not picture, seated at a table, thumping with her stick on the floor, surrounded by some half-dozen lawyers all jabbering Italian, while my poor Ambrose sat patient at her side.

Why did he not come home and leave her to it?

My spirits rose, though, as the simpering bride gave place to

24

the ageing matron, racked with lumbago where it catches most. The nursery receded, and I saw the drawing-room become a lady's boudoir, hedged about with screens, huge fires burning even in midsummer, and someone calling to Seecombe in a testy voice to bring more coal, the draught was killing her. I took to singing once again when I went riding, urged the dogs after young rabbits, swam before breakfast, sailed Ambrose's little boat about the estuary when the wind favoured, and teased Louise about the London fashions when she went to spend the season there. At twenty-three it takes very little to make the spirits soar. My home was still my home. No one had taken it from me.

Then, in the winter, the tone of his letters changed. Imperceptible at first, I scarcely noticed it, yet on re-reading his words I became aware of a sense of strain in all he said, some underlying note of anxiety creeping in upon him. Nostalgia for home in part, I could see that. A longing for his own country and his own possessions, but above all a kind of loneliness that struck me as strange in a man but ten months married. He admitted that the long summer and autumn had been very trying, and now the winter was unusually close. Although the villa was high, there was no air in it; he said he used to move about from room to room like a dog before a thunderstorm, but no thunder came. There was no clearing of the air, and he would have given his soul for drenching rain, even if it crippled him. 'I was never one for headaches,' he said, 'but now I have them frequently. Almost blinding at times. I am sick of the sight of the sun. I miss you more than I can say. So much to talk about, difficult in a letter. My wife is in town today, hence my opportunity to write.' It was the first time that he had used the words 'my wife'. Always before he had said Rachel or 'your cousin Rachel', and the words 'my wife' looked formal to me, and cold.

In these winter letters there was no talk of coming home, but always a passionate desire to know the news, and he would comment upon any little trifle I had told him in my letters, as though he held no other interest.

Nothing came at Easter, or at Whitsun, and I grew worried. I told my godfather, who said no doubt the weather was holding up the mails. Late snow was reported in Europe, and I could not expect to hear from Florence before the end of May. It was over a year now since Ambrose had been married, eighteen months since he had been home. My first relief at his absence, after his marriage, turned to anxiety that he would not return at all. One summer had obviously tried his health. What would a second do? At last, in July, a letter came, short and incoherent, totally unlike himself. Even his writing, usually so clear, sprawled across the page as if he had had difficulty in holding his pen.

'All is not well with me,' he said, 'you must have seen that when I wrote you last. Better keep silent though. She watches me all the time. I have written to you several times, but there is no one I can trust, and unless I can get out myself to mail the letters they may not reach you. Since my illness I have not been able to go far. As for the doctors, I have no belief in any of them. They are liars, the whole bunch. The new one, recommended by Rainaldi, is a cut-throat, but then he would be, coming from that quarter. However, they have taken on a dangerous proposition with me, and I will beat them yet.' Then there was a gap, and something scratched out which I could not decipher, followed by his signature.

I had the groom saddle my horse and rode over to my godfather to show him the letter. He was as much concerned as I was myself. 'Sounds like a mental breakdown,' he said at once. 'I don't like it at all. That's not the letter of a man in his right senses. I hope to heaven . . .' He broke off, and pursed his lips.

'Hope what?' I asked.

'Your uncle Philip, Ambrose's father, died of a tumour on the brain. You know that, don't you?' he said shortly.

I had never heard it before, and told him so.

'Before you were born, of course,' he said. 'It was never a matter much discussed in the family. Whether these things are hereditary or not I can't say, nor can the doctors. Medical science isn't far enough advanced.' He read the letter again, putting on his spectacles to do so. 'There is, of course, another possibility, extremely unlikely, but which I would prefer,' he said.

'And that is?'

'That Ambrose was drunk when he wrote the letter.'

If he had not been over sixty years, and my godfather, I would have hit him for the bare suggestion.

'I have never seen Ambrose drunk in my life,' I told him.

'Nor I either,' he said drily. 'I am merely trying to choose the better of two evils. I think you had better make up your mind to go to Italy.'

'That,' I remarked, 'I had already decided upon before I came to see you,' and I rode home again, without the remotest idea how to set about the journey.

There was no vessel sailing from Plymouth that would help me. I was obliged to travel up to London, and thence to Dover, catch the packet to Boulogne, and then cross France into Italy by the usual diligence. Granted no delay, I should be in Florence within three weeks or so. My French was poor, my Italian non-existent, but none of this bothered me as long as I could get to Ambrose. I bade a short farewell to Seecombe and the servants, telling them only that I intended paying a hurried visit to their master but saying nothing of his illness, and so set forth for London on a fine morning in July, with the prospect of nearly three weeks' travelling in a strange country ahead of me.

As the carriage turned on to the Bodmin road I saw the groom riding towards us with the post-bag. I told Wellington to rein the horses, and the boy handed me the bag. The chance was one in a thousand that there would be a further letter from Ambrose, but it so happened that the chance was there. I took the envelope from the bag and sent the boy on home. As Wellington whipped up the horses I drew out the scrap of paper and held it to the window for light.

The words were scrawled, almost illegible.

'For God's sake come to me quickly. She has done for me at last, Rachel my torment. If you delay, it may be too late. Ambrose.'

That was all. There was no date upon the paper, no mark upon the envelope, which was sealed with his own ring.

I sat in the carriage, the scrap of paper in my hand, knowing that no power on heaven or earth could bring me to him before mid-August.

4

When the conveyance brought me and the other passengers to Florence and dumped us down at the hostelry beside the Arno, I felt I had been a lifetime upon the road. It was now the fifteenth of August. No traveller, setting his foot upon the continent of Europe for the first time, was ever less impressed than I. The roads we traversed, the hills and valleys, the cities, French or Italian, where we halted for the night, seemed all alike to me. Everywhere was dirty, verminous, and I was nearly deafened by the noise. Used to the silence of a well-nigh empty house – for the servants slept away in their own quarters beneath the clock tower – where I heard no sound at night but the wind in the trees and the lash of rain when it blew from the south-west, the ceaseless clatter and turmoil of foreign cities came near to stupefying me.

I slept, yes, who does not sleep at twenty-four, after long hours upon the road, but into my dreams came all the alien sounds; the banging of doors, the screech of voices, footsteps beneath the window, cart-wheels on the cobbled stones, and always, every quarter, the chime of a church bell. Perhaps, had I come abroad upon some other errand, it would have been different. Then, I might have leant from my window in the early mornings with a lighter heart, watched the bare-footed children playing in the gutter and thrown coins to them, heard all the new sounds and voices with fascination, wandered at night amongst the narrow twisting streets and come to like them. As it was, I looked upon what I saw with indifference, passing to hostility. My need was to reach Ambrose, and because I knew him to be ill in a foreign country my anxiety turned to loathing of all things alien, even of the very soil itself.

It grew hotter every day. The sky was a glazed hard blue, and it seemed to me, twisting and turning along those dusty roads in Tuscany, that the sun had drawn all moisture from the land. The valleys were baked brown, and the little villages hung parched and yellow on the hills with the haze of heat upon them. Oxen lumbered by, thin-looking, bony, searching for water, goats scuffed by the wayside, tended by little children who screamed and shouted as the coach rolled by, and it seemed to me, in my anxiety and fear for Ambrose, that all living things were thirsty in this country, and when water was denied they fell into decay and died.

My first instinct, on climbing from the coach in Florence, as the dusty baggage was unloaded and carried within the hostelry, was to cross the cobbled street and stand beside the river. I was travel-stained and weary, covered from head to foot with dust. For the past two days I had sat beside the driver rather than die from suffocation within, and like the poor beasts upon the road I longed for water. There it was before me. Not the blue estuary of home, rippling, and salty fresh, whipped with sea spray, but a slow-moving turgid stream, brown like the river bed beneath it, oozing and sucking its way under the arches of the bridge, and ever and again its flat smooth surface breaking into bubbles. Waste matter was borne away upon this river, wisps of straw, and vege-tation, yet to my imagination, fevered almost with fatigue and thirst, it was something to be tasted, swallowed, poured down the throat as one might pour a draught of poison.

I stood watching the moving water, fascinated, and the sun beat down upon the bridge, and suddenly, from behind me in the city, a great bell chimed four o'clock, deep-sounding, solemn. The chime was taken up by other bells from other churches, and the sound mingled with the surging river as it passed, brown and slimy, over the stones.

A woman stood by my side, a whimpering child in her arms, another dragging at her torn skirt, and she stretched out her hand to me for alms, her dark eyes lifted to mine in supplication. I gave her a coin and turned away, but she continued to touch my

elbow, whispering, until one of the passengers, still standing by
the coach, let forth a string of words at her in Italian, and she
shrank back again to the corner of the bridge whence she had
come. She was young, not more than nineteen or so, but the
expression on her face was ageless, haunting, as though she
possessed in her lithe body an old soul that could not die; centuries
in time looked out from those two eyes, she had contemplated
life so long it had become indifferent to her. Later, when I had
mounted to the room they showed me, and stood out upon the
little balcony that gave upon the square, I saw her creep away
between the horses and the carrozzas waiting there, stealthy as a
cat that slinks by night, its belly to the ground.

I washed and changed my clothes with a strange apathy. Now
that I had reached my journey's end a sort of dullness came upon
me, and the self which had set forth upon his journey excited,
keyed to a high pitch and ready for any battle, existed no longer.
In his place a stranger stood, dispirited and weary. Excitement
had long since vanished. Even the reality of the torn scrap of
paper in my pocket had lost substance. It had been written many
weeks ago; so much could have happened since. She might have
taken him away from Florence; they might have gone to Rome,
to Venice, and I saw myself dragged back to that lumbering coach
again, in their wake. Swaying through city after city, traversing
the length and breadth of the accursed country, and never finding
them, always defeated by time and the hot dusty roads.

Or yet again, the whole thing might be an error, the letters
scribbled as a crazy jest, one of those leg-pulls loved by Ambrose
in days gone by, when as a child I would fall into some trap he
set for me. And I might go now to seek him at the villa and
find some celebration, dinner in progress, guests invited, lights
and music; and I would be shown in upon the company with
no excuse to offer, Ambrose in good health turning astounded
eyes upon me.

I went downstairs and out into the square. The carrozzas that
had been waiting there had driven off. The siesta hour was over,
and the streets were crowded once again. I plunged into them

and was lost at once. About me were dark courts and alleyways, tall houses touching one another, jutting balconies, and as I walked, and turned, and walked again, faces peered at me from the doorways, passing figures paused and stared, all wearing upon them that same age-old look of suffering and passion long since spent which I had first noticed on the beggar girl. Some of them followed me, whispering as she had done, stretching out their hands, and when I spoke roughly, remembering my fellow passenger from the coach, they drew back again, flattening themselves against the walls of the tall houses, and watched me pass on, with a strange smouldering pride. The church bells began to clamour once again, and I came to a great piazza where the people stood thickly, clustered together in groups, talking, gesticulating, having, so it seemed to my alien eyes, no connection with the buildings fringing the square, austere and beautiful, nor with the statues remotely staring with blind eyes upon them, nor with the sound of the bells themselves, echoing loud and fateful to the sky.

I hailed a passing carrozza, and when I said doubtfully the words 'Villa Sangalletti' the driver answered something which I could not understand, but I caught the word 'Fiesole' as he nodded and pointed with his whip. We drove through the narrow crowded streets, and he shouted to the horse, the reins jingling, the people falling back from us as we passed amongst them. The bells ceased and died away, yet the echo seemed to sound still in my ears, solemn, sonorous, tolling not for my mission, insignificant and small, nor for the lives of the people in the streets, but for the souls of men and women long since dead, and for eternity.

We climbed a long twisting road towards the distant hills, and Florence lay behind us. The buildings fell away. It was peaceful, silent, and the hot staring sun that had beaten down upon the city all day, glazing the sky, turned gentle suddenly, and soft. The glare was gone. The yellow houses and the yellow walls, even the brown dust itself, were not so parched as they had been before. Colour came back to the houses, faded perhaps, subdued, but with an afterglow more tender now that the full force of the sun was spent. Cypress trees, shrouded and still, turned inky green.

The driver drew up his carrozza before a closed gate set in a long high wall. He turned in his seat and looked down at me over his shoulder. 'Villa Sangalletti,' he said. The end of my journey.

I made signs to him to wait, and, getting out, walked up to the gate and pulled at the bell that hung there on the wall. I could hear it jangle from within. My driver coaxed his horse into the side of the road, and climbing from his seat stood by the ditch, waving the flies away from his face with his hat. The horse drooped, poor half-starved brute, between his shafts; he had not spirit enough after his climb to crop the wayside, and dozed, with twitching ears. There was no sound from within the gate, and I rang the bell again. This time there was a muffled barking of a dog, becoming suddenly louder as some door was opened; the fretful cry of a child was hushed shrilly, with irritation, by a woman's voice, and I could hear footsteps approaching the gate from the other side. There was a heavy dragging sound of bolts being withdrawn, and then the grind of the gate itself, as it scraped the stone beneath and was opened. A peasant woman stood peering at me. Advancing upon her, I said: 'Villa Sangalletti? Signor Ashley?'

The dog, chained inside the lodge where the woman lived, barked more furiously than before. An avenue stretched in front of me, and at the far end I could see the villa itself, shuttered and lifeless. The woman made as though to shut the gate against me, as the dog continued barking and the child cried. Her face was puffed and swollen on one side, as though with toothache, and she kept the fringe of her shawl to it to ease the pain.

I pushed past her through the gate and repeated the words 'Signor Ashley.' This time she started, as though for the first time she saw my features, and began to talk rapidly, with a sort of nervous agitation, gesturing with her hands towards the villa. Then she turned swiftly and called over her shoulder, to the lodge. A man, presumably her husband, appeared at the open door, a child on his shoulder. He silenced the dog and came towards me, questioning his wife. She continued her torrent of words to him, and

I caught the words 'Ashley,' and then 'Inglese,' and now it was his turn to stand and stare at me. He looked a better type than the woman, cleaner, with honest eyes, and as he stared at me an expression of deep concern came upon his face and he murmured a few words to his wife, who withdrew with the child to the entrance of the lodge and stood watching us, her shawl still held to her swollen face.

'I speak a little English, signore,' he said. 'Can I help you?'

'I have come to see Mr Ashley,' I said. 'Are he and Mrs Ashley at the villa?'

The concern on his face became greater. He swallowed nervously. 'You are Mr Ashley's son, signore?' he said.

'No,' I said impatiently, 'his cousin. Are they at home?'

He shook his head, distressed. 'You have come from England then, signore, and have not heard the news? What can I say? It is very sad, I do not know what to say. Signor Ashley, he died three weeks ago. Very sudden. Very sad. As soon as he is buried, the contessa she shut up the villa, she went away. Nearly two weeks she has been gone. We do not know if she will come back again.'

The dog began to bark again and he turned to quieten it.

I felt all the colour drain away from my face. I stood there, stunned. The man watched me, in sympathy, and said something to his wife, who dragged forward a stool, and he placed it beside me.

'Sit, signore,' he said. 'I am sorry. So very sorry.'

I shook my head. I could not speak. There was nothing I could say. The man, distressed, spoke roughly to his wife to relieve his feelings. Then he turned again to me. 'Signore,' he said, 'if you would like to go to the villa I will open it for you. You can see where the signor Ashley died.' I did not care where I went or what I did. My mind was still too numbed to concentrate. He began to walk up the drive, drawing some keys from his pocket, and I walked beside him, my legs heavy suddenly, like lead. The woman and the child followed behind us.

The cypress trees closed in upon us, and the shuttered villa, like a sepulchre, waited at the further end. As we drew closer I saw that it was large, with many windows, all of them blank and closed, and before the entrance the drive swept in a circle, for carriages to turn. Statues, on their pedestals, stood between the shrouded cypresses. The man opened the huge door with his key, and motioned me inside. The woman and the child came too, and the pair of them began to fling open the shutters, letting the daylight into the silent hall. They went before me, passing from room to room, opening the shutters as they did so, believing, in the goodness of their hearts, that by doing this they somehow eased my pain. The rooms all led into each other, large and sparse, with frescoed ceilings and stone floors, and the air was heavy with a medieval musty smell. In some of the rooms the walls were plain, in others tapestried, and in one, darker and more oppressive than the rest, there was a long refectory table flanked with carved monastic chairs, and great wrought iron candlesticks stood on either end.

'The villa Sangalletti very beautiful, signore, very old,' said the man. 'The signor Ashley, this is where he would sit, when the sun was too strong for him outside. This was his chair.'

He pointed, almost with reverence, to a tall high-backed chair beside the table. I watched him in a dream. None of this held reality. I could not see Ambrose in this house, or in this room. He could never have walked here with familiar tread, whistling, talking, throwing his stick down beside this chair, this table. Relentlessly, monotonously, the pair went round the room, throwing wide the shutters. Outside was a little court, a sort of cloistered quadrangle, open to the sky but shaded from the sun. In the centre of the court stood a fountain, and the bronze statue of a boy, holding a shell in his two hands. Beyond the fountain a laburnum tree grew between the paving stones, making its own canopy of shade. The golden flowers had long since drooped and died, and now the pods lay scattered on the ground, dusty and grey. The man whispered to the woman, and she went to a corner of the quadrangle and turned a handle. Slowly, gently, the water trickled from the shell between the bronze boy's hands. It fell down and splashed into the pool beneath.

'The signor Ashley,' said the man, 'he sat here every day, watching the fountain. He liked to see the water. He sat there, under the tree. It is very beautiful, in spring. The contessa, she would call down to him from her room above.'

He pointed to the stone columns of the balustrade. The woman disappeared within the house, and after a moment or two appeared on the balcony where he had pointed, throwing open the shutters of the room. The water went on dripping from the shell. Never fast, never flowing, just splashing softly into the little pool.

'In summer, always they sit here,' went on the man, 'signor Ashley and the contessa. They take their meals, they hear the fountain play. I wait upon them, you understand. I bring out two trays and set them here, on this table.' He pointed to the stone table and two chairs that stood there still. 'They take their tisana here after dinner,' he continued, 'day after day, always the same.'

He paused, and touched the chair with his hand. A sense of oppression grew upon me. It was cool in the quadrangle, cold almost as a grave, and yet the air was stagnant like the shuttered rooms before he opened them.

I thought of Ambrose as he had been at home. He would walk about the grounds in summer time without a coat, an old straw hat upon his head against the sun. I could see the hat now, tilted forward over his face, and I could see him, his shirtsleeves rolled above the elbow, standing in his boat, pointing at something far away at sea. I remembered how he would reach down with his long arms, and pull me into the boat when I swam alongside.

'Yes,' said the man, as though speaking to himself, 'the signor Ashley sat in the chair here, looking at the water.'

The woman came back and, crossing the quadrangle, turned the handle. The dripping ceased. The bronze boy looked down at an empty shell. Everything was silent, still. The child, who had stared with round eyes at the fountain, bent suddenly to the ground and began grubbing amongst the paving stones, picking up the laburnum pods in his small hands and throwing them into the pool. The woman scolded him, pushing him back against the wall, and seizing a broom that stood there began to sweep the court. Her action broke the stillness, and her husband touched my arm.

'Do you wish to see the room where the signore died?' he said softly.

Possessed with the same sense of unreality, I followed him up the wide stairway to the landing above. We passed through rooms more sparsely furnished than the apartments below, and one, looking northwards over the avenue of cypress trees, was plain and bare like a monk's cell. A simple iron bedstead was pushed against the wall. There was a pitcher, a ewer, and a screen beside the bed. Tapestries hung over the fireplace, and in a niche in the wall was the small statuette of a kneeling madonna, her hands clasped in prayer.

I looked at the bed. The blankets were folded neatly at the foot. Two pillows, stripped of their linen, were placed on top of one another at the head.

'The end,' said the man in a hushed voice, 'was very sudden, you understand. He was weak, yes, very weak from the fever, but even the day before he had dragged himself down to sit by the fountain. No, no, said the contessa, you will become more ill, you must rest, but he is very obstinate, he will not listen to her. And there is coming and going all the time with the doctors. Signor Rainaldi, he is here too, talking, persuading, but never will he listen, he shouts, he is violent, and then, like a little child, falls silent. It was pitiful, to see a strong man so. Then, in the early morning, the contessa she comes quickly to my room, calling for me. I was sleeping in the house, signore. She says, her face white as the wall there, "He is dying, Giuseppe, I know it, he is dying," and I follow her to his room, and there he is, lying in bed, his eyes closed, breathing still, but heavily, you understand, not a true sleep. We send away for the doctor, but the signor Ashley he never wakes again, it was the coma, the sleep of death. I myself lit the candles with the contessa, and when the nuns had been I came to look at him. The violence had all gone, he had a peaceful face. I wish you could have seen it, signore.'

Tears stood in the fellow's eyes. I looked away from him, back to the empty bed. Somehow I felt nothing. The numbness had passed away, leaving me cold and hard.

'What do you mean,' I said, 'by violence?'

'The violence that came with the fever,' said the man. 'Twice, three times I had to hold him down in bed, after his attacks. And with the violence came the weakness inside, here.' He pressed his hand against his stomach. 'He suffered much with pain. And when the pain went he would be dazed and heavy, his mind wandering. I tell you, signore, it was pitiful. Pitiful, to see so large a man helpless.'

I turned away from that bare room like an empty tomb, and I heard the man close the shutters once again, and close the door. 'Why was nothing done?' I said. 'The doctors, could they not ease the pain? And Mrs Ashley, did she just let him die?'

He looked puzzled. 'Please, signore?' he said.

'What was this illness, how long did it last?' I asked.

'I have told you, at the end, very sudden,' said the man, 'but one, two attacks before then. And all winter the signore not so well, sad somehow, not himself. Very different from the year before. When the signor Ashley first came to the villa, he was happy, gay.'

He threw open more windows as he spoke, and we walked outside on to a great terrace, spaced here and there with statues. At the far end a long stone balustrade. We crossed the terrace and stood by the balustrade, looking down upon a lower garden, clipped and formal, from which the scent of roses came, and summer jasmine, and in the distance was another fountain, and yet another, wide stone steps leading to each garden, the whole laid out, tier upon tier, until at the far end came that same high wall flanked with cypress trees, surrounding the whole property.

We looked westward towards the setting sun, and there was a glow upon the terrace and the hushed gardens; even the statues were held in the one rose-coloured light, and it seemed to me, standing there with my hand upon the balustrade, that a strange serenity had come upon the place that was not there before.

The stone was still warm under my hand, and a lizard ran away from a crevice and wriggled down on to the wall below.

'On a still evening,' said the man, standing a pace or so behind me, as though in deference, 'it is very beautiful, signore, here in the gardens of the villa Sangalletti. Sometimes the contessa gave orders for the fountains to be played, and when the moon was full she and the signor Ashley used to come out on to the terrace here, after dinner. Last year, before his illness.'

I went on standing there, looking down upon the fountains, and the pools beneath them with the water lilies.

'I think,' said the man slowly, 'that the contessa will not come back again. Too sad for her. Too many memories. Signor Rainaldi told us that the villa is to be let, possibly sold.'

His words jerked me back into reality. The spell of the hushed garden had held me for a brief moment only, the scent of roses and the glow of the setting sun, but it was over now.

'Who is Signor Rainaldi?' I asked.

The man turned back with me towards the villa. 'The signor Rainaldi he arrange all things for the contessa,' he answered, 'matters of business, matters of money, many things. He knows the contessa a long time.' He frowned, and waved his hand at his wife who with the child in her arms was walking on the terrace. The sight offended him, it was not right for them to be there. She disappeared within the villa, and began fastening the shutters.

'I want to see him, Signor Rainaldi,' I said.

'I give you his address,' he answered. 'He speak English very well.'

We went back into the villa, and as I passed through the rooms to the hall the shutters were closed, one by one, behind me. I felt in my pockets for some money. I might have been anyone, a casual traveller upon the continent, visiting a villa from curiosity with a view to purchase. Not myself. Not looking for the first and last time on the place where Ambrose had lived and died.

'Thank you for all you did for Mr Ashley,' I said, putting the coins into the fellow's hand.

Once again the tears came in his eyes. 'I am so sorry, signore,' he said, 'so very sorry.'

The last shutters were closed. The woman and the child stood beside us in the hall, and the archway to the empty rooms beyond and to the stairway grew dark again, like the entrance to a vault.

'What happened to his clothes,' I asked, 'his belongings, his books, his papers?'

The man looked troubled. He turned to his wife, and they spoke to one another for a moment. Questions and answers passed between them. Her face went blank, she shrugged her shoulders.

'Signore,' said the man, 'my wife gave some help to the contessa when she went away. But she says the contessa took everything. All the signor Ashley's clothes were put in a big trunk, all his books, everything was packed. Nothing left behind.'

I looked into both their eyes. They did not falter. I knew they were speaking the truth. 'And you have no idea,' I asked, 'where Mrs Ashley went?'

The man shook his head. 'She has left Florence, that is all we know,' he said. 'The day after the funeral, the contessa went away.'

He opened the heavy front door and I stepped outside.

'Where is he buried?' I asked, impersonal, a stranger.

'In Florence, signore, in the new Protestant cemetery. Many English buried there. Signor Ashley, he is not alone.'

It was as if he wished to reassure me that Ambrose would have company, and that in the dark world beyond the grave his own countrymen would bring him consolation.

For the first time I could not bear to meet the fellow's eyes. They were like a dog's eyes, honest and devoted.

I turned away, and as I did so I heard the woman exclaim suddenly to her husband, and before he had time to shut the door she had darted back into the villa once again, and opened a great oak chest that was standing against the wall. She came back carrying something in her hand which she gave to her husband, and he in turn to me. His puckered face relaxed, broadening to relief.

'The contessa,' he said, 'one thing she has forgotten. Take it with you, signore, it is for you alone.'

It was Ambrose's hat, wide-brimmed and bent. The hat that he used to wear at home against the sun. It would never fit any other man, it was too big. I could feel their anxious eyes upon me, waiting for me to say something, as I turned the hat over and over in my hands.

5

I remember nothing of the return drive to Florence except that the sun had set and it grew quickly dark. There was no twilight as we had at home. From the ditches by the wayside insects, crickets maybe, set up their monotonous chanting, and now and again barefooted peasants passed us, carrying baskets on their backs.

When we came into the city we lost the cooler cleaner air of the surrounding hills, and it was hot once more. Not like the day-time, burning and dusty white, but the flat stale heat of evening, buried too many hours in the walls and roofs of houses. The lassitude of noon, and the activity of those hours between siesta and sunset, had given place to a deeper animation, more alive, more tense. The men and women who thronged the piazzas and the narrow streets strolled with another purpose, as if all day they had lain hidden, sleeping, in their silent houses, and now came out like cats to prowl the town. The market-stalls were lit by flares and candles and besieged by customers, delving with questing hands amongst the proffered goods. Shawled women pressed one another, chattering, scolding, and vendors shouted their wares to make their voices heard. The clanging bells began again, and it seemed to me this time that their clamour was more personal. The doors of the churches were pushed open so that I could see the candlelight within, and the groups of people broke up a little, scattered, and pressed inside at the summons of the bells.

I paid off my driver in the piazza by the cathedral, and the sound of that great bell, compelling, insistent, rang like a challenge in the still and vapid air. Scarcely aware of what I did, I passed into the cathedral with the people, and straining my eyes into the gloom stood for a brief moment by a column. An old lame peasant stood beside me, leaning on a crutch. He turned one sightless eye towards the altar, his lips moving, his hands trembling, while about me and before me knelt women, shawled and secret, intoning with shrill voices after the priest, their gnarled hands busy with their beads.

I still held Ambrose's hat in my left hand, and as I stood there in the great cathedral, dwarfed into insignificance, a stranger in that city of cold beauty and spilt blood, seeing the priest's obeisance to the altar, hearing his lips intone words, centuries old and solemn, that I could not understand, I realised suddenly and sharply the full measure of my loss. Ambrose was dead. I would never see him again. He was gone from me forever. Never more that smile, that chuckle, those hands upon my shoulder. Never more his strength, his understanding. Never more that known figure, honoured and loved, hunched in his library chair, or standing, leaning on his stick, looking down towards the sea. I thought of the bare room where he had died, in the villa Sangalletti, and of the madonna in her niche; and something told me that when he went he was not part of that room, or of that house, or of this country, but that his spirit went back where it belonged, to be amongst his own hills and his own woods, in the garden that he loved, within sound of the sea.

I turned and went out of the cathedral and on to the piazza, and looking up at that great dome and the tower beside me, remote and slender, carved against the sky, I remembered for the first time, with the sudden recollection that comes after great shock and stress, that I had not eaten for the day. I turned my thoughts away from the dead, back to the living; and having found a place to eat and drink, close to the cathedral, I went, with hunger satisfied, in search of Signor Rainaldi. The good servant at the villa had written down his address for me, and after one or two enquiries, pointing at the piece of paper and struggling lamely with the pronunciation, I found his house, over the bridge from my hostelry, on the left bank of the Arno. This side of the river was darker and more silent than in the heart of

Florence. Few people wandered in the streets. Doors were closed and windows shuttered. Even my footsteps sounded hollow on the cobbled stones.

I came at last to the house, and rang the bell. A servant opened the door within a moment, and without enquiring my name led me upstairs and along a passage, and knocking upon a door showed me into a room. I stood blinking at the sudden light, and saw a man seated in a chair beside a table, looking through a pile of papers. He rose as I came into the room, and stared at me. He was a little less than my own height, and of some forty years perhaps, with a pale, almost colourless face, and lean aquiline features. There was something proud, disdainful about his cast of countenance, like that of someone who would have small mercy for fools, or for his enemies; but I think I noticed most his eyes, dark and deep-set, which at first sight of me startled into a flash of recognition that in one second vanished.

'Signor Rainaldi?' I said. 'My name is Ashley. Philip Ashley.'

'Yes,' he said, 'will you sit down?'

His voice had a cold hard quality, and his Italian accent was not strongly marked. He pushed forward a chair for me.

'You are surprised to see me, no doubt?' I said, watching him carefully. 'You were not aware I was in Florence?'

'No,' he answered. 'No, I was not aware that you were here.'

The words were guarded, but it may have been that his command of the English language was small, so that he spoke carefully.

'You know who I am?' I asked.

'I think I am clear as to the exact relationship,' he said. 'You are cousin, are you not, or nephew to the late Ambrose Ashley?'

'Cousin,' I said, 'and heir.'

He took up a pen between his fingers, and tapped with it on the table, as if he played for time, or for distraction.

'I have been to the villa Sangalletti,' I said, 'I have seen the room where he died. The servant Giuseppe was very helpful. He gave me all the details, but referred me to you.'

Was it my fancy, or did a veiled look come over those dark eyes?

'How long have you been in Florence?' he asked.

'A few hours. Since afternoon.'

'You have only arrived to-day? Then your cousin Rachel has not seen you.' The hand that held the pen relaxed.

'No,' I said, 'the servant at the villa gave me to understand that she had left Florence the day after the funeral.'

'She left the villa Sangalletti,' he said, 'she did not leave Florence.'

'Is she still here, in the city?'

'No,' he said, 'no, she has now gone away. She wishes me to let the villa. Sell it possibly.'

His manner was oddly stiff and unbending, as if any inform-ation that he gave me must be considered first, and sorted in his mind.

'Do you know where she is now?' I asked.

'I am afraid not,' he said. 'She left very suddenly, she had made no plans. She told me she would write, when she had come to some decision about the future.'

'She is with friends perhaps?' I ventured.

'Perhaps,' he said. 'I do not think so.'

I had the feeling that only to-day, or even yesterday, she had been with him in this room, that he knew much more than he admitted.

'You will understand, Signor Rainaldi,' I said, 'that this sudden hearing of my cousin's death, from the lips of servants, was a very great shock to me. The whole thing has been like a nightmare. What happened? Why was I not informed that he was ill?'

He watched me carefully, he did not take his eyes from my face. 'Your cousin's death was sudden too,' he said, 'it was a great shock to us all. He had been ill, yes, but not, as we thought, dangerously so. The usual fever that attacks many foreigners here in the summer had brought about a certain weakness, and he complained too of a violent headache. The contessa – I should say Mrs Ashley – was much concerned, but he was not an easy patient. He took an instant dislike to our doctors, for what reason it was hard to discover. Every day Mrs Ashley hoped for some improvement, and certainly she had no desire to make you and his friends in England anxious.'

'But we were anxious,' I said, 'that was why I came to Florence. I received these letters from him.'

It was a bold move perhaps, and reckless, but I did not care. I handed across the table the two last letters Ambrose had written me. He read them carefully. His expression did not change. Then he passed them back to me.

'Yes,' he said, his voice quite calm, without surprise, 'Mrs Ashley feared he might have written something of the sort. It was not until those last weeks, when he became so secretive and strange, that the doctors feared the worst, and warned her.'

'Warned her?' I said. 'Warned her of what?'

'That there might be something pressing on his brain,' he answered, 'a tumour, or growth, of rapidly increasing size, which would account for his condition.'

A lost feeling came over me. A tumour? Then my godfather's surmise was right after all. First uncle Philip, and then Ambrose. And yet . . . Why did this Italian watch my eyes?

'Did the doctors say that it was a tumour that killed him?'

'Unquestionably,' he answered. 'That, and a certain flare-up of after-fever weakness. There were two doctors present. My own, and another. I can send for them, and you can ask any question you care to put. One speaks a little English.'

'No,' I said slowly, 'no, it is not necessary.'

He opened a drawer and pulled out a piece of paper.

'I have here a copy of the certificate of death,' he said, 'signed by them both. Read it. One copy has already been posted to you in Cornwall, and a second to the trustee of your cousin's will, Mr Nicholas Kendall, near Lostwithiel, in Cornwall.'

I looked down at the certificate. I did not bother to read it.

'How did you know,' I asked, 'that Nicholas Kendall is trustee to my cousin's will?'

'Because your cousin Ambrose had a copy of the will with

him,' replied Signor Rainaldi. 'I read it many times.'

'You read my cousin's will?' I asked, incredulous.

'Naturally,' he replied. 'As trustee myself to the contessa, to Mrs Ashley, it was my business to see her husband's will. There is nothing strange about it. Your cousin showed me the will himself, soon after they were married. I have a copy of it, in fact. But it is not my business to show it to you. It is the business of your guardian, Mr Kendall. No doubt he will do so, on your return home.'

He knew my godfather was my guardian also, which was more than I did. Unless he spoke in error. Surely no man past twenty-one possessed a guardian, and I was twenty-four? This did not matter, though. What mattered was Ambrose and his illness, Ambrose and his death.

'These two letters,' I said stubbornly, 'are not the letters of a sick man, of a person ill. They are the letters of a man who has enemies, who is surrounded by people he cannot trust.'

Signor Rainaldi watched me steadily.

'They are the letters of a man who was sick in mind, Mr Ashley,' he answered me. 'Forgive my bluntness, but I saw him those last weeks, and you did not. The experience was not a pleasant one for any of us, least of all for his wife. You see what he says in the first letter there, that she did not leave him. I can vouchsafe for that. She did not leave him night or day. Another woman would have had nuns to tend him. She nursed him alone, she spared herself nothing.'

'Yet it did not help him,' I said. 'Look at the letters, and this last line, "She has done for me at last, Rachel my torment . . ." What do you make of that, Signor Rainaldi?'

I suppose I had raised my voice in my excitement. He got up from his chair, and pulled a bell. When his servant appeared he gave an order, and the man returned with a glass, and some wine and water. He poured some out for me, but I did not want it.

'Well?' I said.

He did not go back to his seat. He went over to the side of the room where books lined the wall and took down a volume.

47

'Are you any sort of a student of medical history, Mr Ashley?' he asked.

'No,' I said.

'You will find it here,' he said, 'the sort of information you are seeking, or you can question those doctors, whose address I am only too willing to give you. There is a particular affliction of the brain, present above all when there is a growth, or tumour, when the sufferer becomes troubled by delusions. He fancies, for instance, that he is being watched. That the person nearest to him, such as a wife, has either turned against him, or is unfaithful, or seeks to take his money. No amount of love or persuasion can allay this suspicion, once it takes hold. If you don't believe me, or the doctors here, ask your own countrymen, or read this book.'

How plausible he was, how cold, how confident. I thought of Ambrose lying on that iron bedstead in the villa Sangalletti, tortured, bewildered, with this man observing him, analysing his symptoms one by one, watching perhaps from over that three-fold screen. Whether he was right or wrong I did not know. All I knew was that I hated Rainaldi.

'Why didn't she send for me?' I asked. 'If Ambrose had lost faith in her, why not send for me? I knew him best.'

Rainaldi closed the book with a snap, and replaced it on the shelf.

'You are very young, are you not, Mr Ashley?' he said.

I stared at him. I did not know what he meant.

'What do you mean by that?' I asked.

'A woman of feeling does not easily give way,' he said. 'You may call it pride, or tenacity, call it what you will. In spite of all evidence to the contrary, their emotions are more primitive than ours. They hold to the thing they want, and never surrender. We have our wars and battles, Mr Ashley. But women can fight too.'

He looked at me, with his cold deep-set eyes, and I knew I had no more to say to him.

'If I had been here,' I said, 'he would not have died.'

I rose from my chair and went towards the door. Once again

Rainaldi pulled the bell, and the servant came to show me out.

'I have written,' he said, 'to your guardian, Mr Kendall. I have explained to him very fully, in great detail, everything that has happened. Is there anything more I can do for you? Will you be staying long in Florence?'

'No,' I said, 'why should I stay? There is nothing to keep me.'

'If you wish to see the grave,' he said, 'I will give you a note to the guardian, in the Protestant cemetery. The site is quite simple and plain. No stone as yet, of course. That will be erected presently.'

He turned to the table, and scribbled a note which he gave me.

'What will be written on the stone?' I said.

He paused a moment, as though reflecting, while the servant waiting by the open door handed me Ambrose's hat.

'I believe,' he said, 'that my instructions were to put "In Memory of Ambrose Ashley, beloved husband of Rachel Coryn Ashley", and then of course the date.'

I knew then that I did not want to go to the cemetery or visit the grave. That I had no wish to see the place where they had buried him. They could put up the stone, and later take flowers there if they wished, but Ambrose would never know, and never care. He would be with me in that west country, under his own soil, in his own land.

'When Mrs Ashley returns,' I said slowly, 'tell her that I came to Florence. That I went to the villa Sangalletti, and that I saw where Ambrose died. You can tell her too about the letters Ambrose wrote to me.'

He held out his hand to me, cold and hard like himself, and still he watched me with those veiled, deep-set eyes.

'Your cousin Rachel is a woman of impulse,' he said. 'When she left Florence she took all her possessions with her. I very much fear that she will never return.'

I left the house and went out into the dark street. It was almost as if his eyes still followed me from behind his shuttered windows.

I walked back along the cobbled streets and crossed the bridge, and before turning into the hostelry to seek what sleep I could before the morning I went and stood once more beside the Arno.

The city slept. I was the only loiterer. Even the solemn bells were silent, and the only sound was the river, sucking its way under the bridge. It ran more swiftly now, it seemed, than in the day, as though the water had been pent up and idle during the long hours of heat and sun and now, because of night, because of silence, found release.

I stared down at the river, watching it surge and flow and lose itself in the darkness, and by the single flickering lantern light upon the bridge I saw the bubbles forming, frothy brown. Then borne upon the current, stiff and slowly turning, with its four legs in the air, came the body of a dog. It passed under the bridge and went its way.

I made a vow there, to myself, beside the Arno.

I swore that, whatever it had cost Ambrose in pain and suffering before he died, I would return it, in full measure, upon the woman who had caused it. Because I did not believe Rainaldi's story. I believed in the truth of those two letters that I held in my right hand. The last Ambrose had ever written to me.

Someday, somehow, I would repay my cousin Rachel.

6

I arrived home the first week in September. The news had
preceded me – the Italian had not lied when he told me
he had written to Nick Kendall. My godfather had broken
the news to the servants and to the tenants on the estate.
Wellington was waiting for me at Bodmin with the carriage. The
horses were decked in crepe, as were Wellington and the groom,
their faces long and solemn.

My relief at being back in my own country was so great
that for the moment grief was dormant, or possibly that long
homeward trek across Europe had dulled all feeling; but I
remember my first instinct was to smile at sight of Wellington
and the boy, to pat the horses, to enquire if all was well. It was
almost as though I were a lad again, returned from school. The
old coachman's manner was stiff, however, with a new formality,
and the young groom opened the carriage door to me with
deference. 'A sad home-coming, Mr Philip,' said Wellington, and
when I asked after Seecombe and the household he shook his
head and told me that they and all the tenants were sorely
grieved. The whole neighbourhood, he said, had talked of
nothing else since the news became known. The church had
been draped in black all Sunday, likewise the chapel on the
estate, but the greatest blow of all, Wellington said, was when
Mr Kendall told them that the master had been buried in Italy
and would not be brought home to lie in the vault amongst
his family.

'It doesn't seem right to any of us, Mr Philip,' he said, 'and
we don't think Mr Ashley would have liked it either.'

There was nothing I could say in answer. I got into the carriage
and let them drive me home.

It was strange how the emotion and the fatigue of the past weeks vanished at sight of the house. All sense of strain left me, and in spite of the long hours on the road I felt rested and at peace. It was afternoon, and the sun shone on the windows of the west wing, and on the grey walls, as the carriage passed through the second gate up the slope to the house. The dogs were there, waiting to greet me, and poor Seecombe, wearing a crepe band on his arm like the rest of the servants, broke down when I wrung him by the hand.

'It's been so long, Mr Philip,' he said, 'so very long. And how were we to know that you might not take the fever too, like Mr Ashley?'

He waited upon me while I dined, solicitous, anxious for my welfare, and I was thankful that he did not press me with questions about my journey or about his master's illness and death, but was full of the effect upon himself and the household; how the bells had tolled for a whole day, how the vicar had spoken, how wreaths had been brought in offering. And all his words were punctuated with a new formality of address. I was 'Mr' Philip. No longer 'Master' Philip. I had noticed the same with the coachman and the groom. It was unexpected, yet strangely warming to the heart.

When I had dined I went up to my room and looked about me, and then down into the library, and so out into the grounds, and I was filled with a queer feeling of happiness that I had not thought ever to possess with Ambrose dead; for when I left Florence I had reached the lowest ebb of loneliness, and hoped for nothing. Across Italy and France I was possessed with images which I could not drive away. I saw Ambrose sitting in that shaded court of the villa Sangalletti, beside the laburnum tree, watching the dripping fountain. I saw him in that bare monk's cell above, propped on two pillows, struggling for breath. And always within earshot, always within sight, was the shadowy hated figure of that woman I had never seen. She had so many faces, so many guises, and that name contessa, used by the servant Giuseppe and by Rainaldi too, in preference for Mrs Ashley, gave to her a kind of aura she had never had with me at first, when I had seen her as another Mrs Pascoe.

Since my journey to the villa she had become a monster, larger than life itself. Her eyes were black as sloes, her features aquiline like Rainaldi's, and she moved about those musty villa rooms sinuous and silent, like a snake. I saw her, when there was no longer breath left in his body, packing his clothes in trunks, reaching for his books, his last possessions, and then creeping away, thin-lipped, to Rome perhaps, to Naples, or even lying concealed in that house beside the Arno, smiling, behind the shutters. These images remained with me until I crossed the sea and came to Dover. And now, now that I had returned home, they vanished as nightmares do at break of day. My bitterness went too. Ambrose was with me once again and he was not tortured, he no longer suffered. He had never been to Florence or to Italy at all. It was as though he had died here, in his own home, and lay buried with his father and his mother and my own parents, and my grief was now something I could overcome; sorrow was with me still, but not tragedy. I too was back where I belonged, and the smell of home was all about me.

I went out across the fields, and the men were harvesting. The shocks of corn were being lifted into the waggons. They ceased work at the sight of me, and I went and spoke to all of them. Old Billy Rowe, who had been tenant of the Barton ever since I could remember and had never called me anything but Master Philip, touched his forehead when I came up to him, and his wife and daughter, helping with the rest of the men, dropped me a curtsey. 'We've missed you, sir,' he said, 'it hasn't seemed right to start carrying the corn without you. We're glad you're home.' A year ago I would have rolled up my sleeves like the rest of the hinds, and seized a fork, but something stayed me now, a realisation that they would not think it fit.

'I'm glad to be home,' I said. 'Mr Ashley's death has been a great sadness to me, and to you too, but now we all have to carry on as he would have wished us to do.'

'Yes, sir,' he said, and touched his forelock once again.

I stayed a few moments talking, then called to the dogs and went my way. He waited until I reached the hedge before telling the men to resume their work. When I came to the pony paddock, midway between the house and the sloping fields, I paused and looked back over the sunken fence. The waggons were silhouetted on the further hill, and the waiting horses and the moving figures black dots on the skyline. The shocks of corn were golden in the last rays of the sun. The sea was very blue, almost purple where it covered the rocks, and had that deep full look about it that always comes with the flood tide. The fishing fleet had put out, and were standing eastward to catch the shore breeze. Back at home the house was in shadow now, only the weathervane on the top of the clock tower catching a loose shaft of light. I walked slowly across the grass to the open door.

The windows were still unshuttered, for Seecombe had not yet sent the servants to close them down. There was something welcome in the sight of those raised sashes, with the curtains softly moving, and the thought of all the rooms behind the windows, known to me and loved. The smoke rose from the chimneys, tall and straight. Old Don, the retriever, too ancient and stiff to walk with me and the younger dogs, scratched on the gravel under the library windows, and then turning his head towards me slowly wagged his tail as I drew near.

It came upon me strongly and with force, and for the first time since I had learnt of Ambrose's death, that everything I now saw and looked upon belonged to me. I need never share it with anyone living. Those walls and windows, that roof, the bell that struck seven as I approached, the whole living entity of the house was mine, and mine alone. The grass beneath my feet, the trees surrounding me, the hills behind me, the meadows, the woods, even the men and women farming the land yonder, were all part of my inheritance; they all belonged.

I went indoors and stood in the library, my back to the open fireplace, my hands in my pockets. The dogs came in as was their custom, and lay down at my feet. Seecombe came to ask me if there were any orders for Wellington, for the morning. Did I want the horses and the carriage, or should he saddle Gypsy for me? No, I told him, I would give no orders to-night. I would see Wellington myself after breakfast. I wished to be called at my usual time. He answered, 'Yes, sir,' and left the room. Master Philip had gone forever. Mr Ashley had come home. It was a strange feeling. In a sense it made me humble, and at the same time oddly proud. I was aware of a sort of confidence and of a strength that I had not known before, and a new elation. It seemed to me that I felt as a soldier might feel on being given command of a battalion; this sense of ownership, of pride, and of possession too, came to me, as it might do to a senior major, after having deputised for many months and years in second place. But, unlike a soldier, I would never have to give up my command. It was mine for life. I believe that when I had this realisation, standing there before the library fire, I knew a moment of happiness that I have never had in life, before or since. Like all such moments it came swiftly, and as swiftly passed again. Some sound of day by day broke the spell: perhaps a dog stirred, an ember fell from the fire, or a servant moved overhead as he went to close the windows – I don't remember what it was. All I remember is the feeling of confidence which I had that night, as though something long sleeping had stirred inside me and now come to life. I went early to bed, and slept without once dreaming.

My godfather, Nick Kendall, came over the following day, bringing Louise with him. As there were no close relatives to summon, and only bequests to Seecombe and the other servants, with the customary donations to the poor in the parish, the widows, and the orphans, and the whole of his estate and property was left to me, Nick Kendall read the will alone to me, in the library. Louise took herself off for a walk in the grounds. In spite of the legal language, the business seemed simple and straightforward. Except for one thing. The Italian Rainaldi had been right. Nick Kendall *was* appointed my guardian, because the estate did not become virtually mine until I was twenty-five.

'It was a belief of Ambrose's,' said my godfather, taking off his spectacles as he handed me the document to read for myself, 'that no young man knows his own mind until he turns twenty-five. You might have grown up with a weakness for drink or gambling or women, and this twenty-five-year clause made a safeguard. I helped him to draw the will when you were still at Harrow, and though we both knew that none of these tendencies had developed yet Ambrose preferred to keep the clause. "It can't hurt Philip," he always said, "and will teach him caution." Well, there we are, and there's nothing to be done about it. In point of fact it won't affect you, except that you will have to call upon me for money, as you always have done, for the estate accounts and for your personal use, for a further seven months. Your birthday is in April, isn't it?'

'You should know,' I said, 'you were my sponsor.'

'A funny little worm you were too,' he said with a smile, 'staring with puzzled eyes at the parson. Ambrose was just down from Oxford. He pinched your nose to make you cry, shocking his aunt, your mother. Afterwards he challenged your poor father to a pulling race, and they rowed from the castle to Lostwithiel, getting drenched to the skin the pair of them. Ever felt the lack of parents, Philip? It's been hard on you, I often think, without your mother.'

'I don't know,' I said, 'I've never thought about it much. I never wanted anyone but Ambrose.'

'It was wrong, all the same,' he said. 'I used to tell Ambrose so, but he never listened to me. There should have been someone in the house, a housekeeper, a distant relative, anyone. You have grown up ignorant of women, and if you ever marry it will be hard on your wife. I was saying so to Louise at breakfast.'

He broke off then, looking – if my godfather could look such a thing – a little uncomfortable, as if he said more than he meant.

'That's all right,' I said, 'my wife can take care of all the difficulties when the time comes. If it ever does come, which is unlikely. I think I am too much like Ambrose, and I know now what marriage must have done to him.'

My godfather was silent. Then I told him of my visit to the villa and of my meeting with Rainaldi, and he showed me in turn the letter that the Italian had written him. It was much as I expected, giving in cold stilted words his story of Ambrose's illness and death, of his own personal regret, and of the shock and grief to the widow, who was, according to Rainaldi, inconsolable.

'So inconsolable,' I said to my godfather, 'that the day after the funeral she goes off, like a thief, taking all Ambrose's possessions with her, except his old hat, which she forgot. Because, no doubt, it was torn and had no value.'

My godfather coughed. His bushy eyebrows knitted.

'Surely,' he said, 'you don't begrudge her the books and clothes? Hang it all, Philip, it's all she has.'

'How do you mean,' I asked, 'it's all she has?'

'Well, I've read the will to you,' he answered, 'and there it is before you. It's the same will that I drew up ten years ago. No codicil, you know, upon his marriage. There is no provision in it for a wife. All this past year I rather expected word from him, at some time or other, about a settlement at least. It's usual. But I suppose his absence abroad made him neglectful of such a necessity, and he kept hoping to return. Then his illness put a stop to any business. I am a little surprised that this Italian, Signor Rainaldi, whom you seem so much to dislike, makes no mention of any sort of claim on the part of Mrs Ashley. It shows great delicacy on his part.'

'Claim?' I said. 'Good God, you talk of a claim when we know perfectly well she drove him to his death?'

'We don't know anything of the sort,' returned my godfather, 'and if that is the way you are going to talk about your cousin's widow I don't care to listen.' He got up and began to put his papers together.

'So you believe the story of the tumour?' I said.

'Naturally I believe it,' he replied. 'Here is the letter from this Italian, Rainaldi, and the death certificate, signed by two doctors. I remember your uncle Philip's death, which you do not. The symptoms were very similar. It is exactly what I feared, when the letter came from Ambrose and you left for Florence. The fact that you arrived too late to be of any assistance is one of those

57

calamities that nobody can help. It is possible, now I think of it, that it was not a calamity after all, but a mercy. You would not have wished to see him suffer.'

I could have hit him, the old fool, for being so obstinate, so blind.

'You never saw the second letter,' I said, 'the note that came the morning I went away. Look at this.'

I had it still. I kept it always in my breast pocket. I gave it to him. He put on his spectacles again, and read it.

'I'm sorry, Philip,' he said, 'but even that poor heartbreak of a scribble cannot alter my opinion. You must face facts. You loved Ambrose, so did I. When he died I lost my greatest friend. I am as distressed as you when I think of his mental suffering, perhaps even more so, because I have seen it in another. Your trouble is that you will not reconcile yourself to the fact that the man we knew and admired and loved was not his true self before he died. He was mentally and physically sick, and not responsible for what he wrote or said.'

'I don't believe it,' I said. 'I can't believe it.'

'You mean you won't believe it,' said my godfather, 'in which case there is nothing more to be said. But for Ambrose's sake, and for the sake of everybody who knew and loved him, here on the estate and in the county, I must ask you not to spread your views to others. It would cause distress and pain to all of them, and if such a whisper ever got to his widow, wherever she may be, you would cut a miserable figure in her eyes, and she would be well within her rights to bring a case against you for slander. If I were her man of business, as that Italian seems to be, I would not hesitate to do so.'

I had never heard my godfather speak with such force. He was right in saying there was no more to be said on the subject. I had learnt my lesson. I would not broach it again.

'Shall we call Louise?' I said pointedly. 'I think she has been wandering about the gardens long enough. You had both better stay and dine with me.'

My godfather was silent during dinner. I could tell he was

still shocked by what I had said to him. Louise questioned me about my travels, what had I thought of Paris, the French countryside, the Alps and Florence itself, and my very inadequate replies filled up the gaps in conversation. She was quick-witted, though, and saw something was wrong. And after dinner, when my godfather summoned Seecombe and the servants to tell them of the various bequests, I went and sat with her in the drawing-room.

'My godfather is displeased with me,' I said, and told her the story. She watched me in that rather critical enquiring way she always had, to which I was well accustomed, her head a little on one side, her chin lifted. 'You know,' she said, when I had finished, 'I think you are probably right. I dare say poor Mr Ashley and his wife were not happy, and he was too proud to write and tell you so before he fell ill, and then perhaps they had a quarrel, and everything happened at once, and so he wrote you those letters. What did those servants say about her? Was she young, was she old?'

'I never asked,' I said. 'I don't see that it matters. The only thing that matters is that he did not trust her when he died.'

She nodded. 'That was terrible,' she agreed, 'he must have felt so lonely.' My heart warmed to Louise. Perhaps it was because she was young, my own age, that she seemed to have so much more perception than her father. He was getting old, I thought to myself, losing his judgement. 'You should have asked that Italian, Rainaldi, what she looked like,' said Louise. 'I should have done. It would have been my first question. And what had happened to the Count, her first husband. Didn't you tell me once he had been killed in a duel? You see, that speaks badly for her, too. She probably had several lovers.'

This aspect of my cousin Rachel had not occurred to me. I only saw her as malevolent, like a spider. In spite of my hatred, I could not help smiling. 'How like a girl,' I said to Louise, 'to picture lovers. Stilettos in a shadowed doorway. Secret staircases. I ought to have taken you to Florence with me. You would have learnt much more than I did.'

She flushed deeply when I said this, and I thought how odd girls were; even Louise, whom I had known my whole life, failed to understand a joke. 'At any rate,' I said, 'whether that woman had a hundred lovers or not doesn't concern me. She can lie low in Rome or Naples or wherever she is for the present. But one day I shall hunt her out, and she'll be sorry for it.'

At that moment my godfather came to find us, and I said no more. He seemed in a better humour. No doubt Seecombe and Wellington and the others had been grateful for their little bequests and he, in benign fashion, felt himself in part the author of them.

'Ride over and see me soon,' I told Louise, as I helped her into the dog-cart beside her father. 'You're good for me. I like your company.' And she flushed again, silly girl, glancing up at her father to see how he would take it, as though we had not ridden backwards and forwards visiting one another before, times without number. Perhaps she also was impressed by my new status, and before I knew where I was I would become Mr Ashley to her too, instead of Philip. I went back into the house, smiling at the idea of Louise Kendall, whose hair I used to pull only a few years back, now looking upon me with respect, and the next instant I forgot her, and my godfather as well, for on coming home there was much to do after two months' absence.

I did not think to see my godfather again for at least a fortnight, what with the harvest and other things upon my hands; but scarcely a week had passed before his groom rode over one morning, soon after midday, with a verbal message from his master, asking me to go and see him; he was unable to come himself, he was confined to the house with a slight chill, but he had news for me.

I did not think the matter urgent – we carried the last of the corn that day – and the following afternoon I rode to see him.

I found him in his study, alone. Louise was absent somewhere. He had a curious look upon his face, baffled, ill at ease. I could see he was disturbed.

'Well,' he said, 'now something has got to be done, and you have to decide exactly what, and when. She has arrived by boat in Plymouth.'

'Who has arrived?' I asked. But I think I knew.

He showed me a piece of paper in his hand.

'I have a letter here,' he said, 'from your cousin Rachel.'

7

H e gave me the letter. I looked at the handwriting on the folded paper. I don't know what I thought to see. Something bold, perhaps, with loops and flourishes; or its reverse, darkly scrawled and mean. This was just handwriting, much like any other, except that the ends of the words tailed off in little dashes, making the words themselves not altogether easy to decipher.

'She does not appear to know that we have heard the news,' said my godfather. 'She must have left Florence before Signor Rainaldi wrote his letter. Well, see what you make of it. I will give you my opinion afterwards.'

I opened up the letter. It was dated from a hostelry in Plymouth, on the thirteenth of September.

'DEAR MR KENDALL,

'When Ambrose spoke of you, as he so often did, I little thought my first communication with you would be fraught with so much sadness. I arrived in Plymouth, from Genoa, this morning, in a state of great distress, and alas alone.

'My dear one died in Florence on the 20th of July, after a short illness but violent in its attack. Everything was done that could be done, but the best doctors I could summon were not able to save him. There was a recurrence of some fever that had seized him earlier in the spring, but the last was due to pressure on the brain which the doctors think had lain dormant for some months, then rapidly increased its hold upon him. He lies in the Protestant cemetery in Florence, in a site chosen by myself, quiet, and a little apart from the other English graves, with trees surrounding it, which is what he would have wished. Of my personal sorrow and great emptiness I will say nothing; you do not know me, and I have no desire to inflict my grief upon you.

'My first thought has been for Philip, whom Ambrose loved so dearly, and whose grief will be equal to my own. My good friend and counsellor, Signor Rainaldi of Florence, assured me that he would write to you and break the news, so that you in turn could tell Philip, but I have little faith in those mails from Italy to England, and was fearful either that the news should come to you by hearsay, through a stranger, or that it would not come at all. Hence my arrival in this country. I have brought with me all Ambrose's possessions; his books, his clothes, everything that Philip would wish to have and keep, which now, by right, belong to him. If you will tell me what to do with them, how to send them, and whether or not I should write to Philip myself, I shall be deeply grateful.

'I left Florence very suddenly, on impulse and without regret. I could not bear to stay with Ambrose gone. As to further plans, I have none. After so great a shock time for reflection is, I think, most necessary. I had hoped to be in England before this, but was held up at Genoa, for the ship that brought me was not ready to sail. I believe I still have members of my own family, the Coryns, scattered about Cornwall, but knowing none of them I have no wish to intrude upon them. I would much prefer to be alone. Possibly, after I have rested here a little, I may travel up to London, and then make further plans.

'I will await instruction from you what to do with my husband's possessions.

'Most sincerely yours,
'RACHEL ASHLEY.'

I read the letter once, twice, perhaps three times, then gave it back to my godfather. He waited for me to speak. I did not say a word.

'You see,' he said at length, 'that after all she has kept nothing. Not so much as one book, or a pair of gloves. They are all for you.'

I did not answer.

'She doesn't even ask to see the house,' he went on, 'the house that would have been her home had Ambrose lived. That voyage she has just made, you realise, of course, that if things had been otherwise they would have made it together? This would have been her homecoming. What a difference, eh? All the people on the estate to welcome her, the servants agog with excitement, the neighbours calling – instead of which, a lonely hostelry in Plymouth. She may be pleasant or unpleasant – how can I tell, I have not met her. But the point is, she asks nothing, she demands nothing. Yet she is Mrs Ashley. I'm sorry, Philip. I know your views, and you won't be shaken. But as Ambrose's friend, as his trustee, I cannot sit here and do nothing when his widow arrives alone and friendless in this country. We have a guest-room in this house. She is welcome to it until her plans are formed.'

I went and stood by the window. Louise was not absent after all. She had a basket on her arm, and was snipping off the heads of the dead flowers in the border. She raised her head and saw me, waving her hand. I wondered if my godfather had read the letter to her.

'Well, Philip?' he said. 'You can write to her or not, just as you wish. I don't suppose you want to see her, and if she accepts my invitation I shall not ask you over whilst she is here. But some sort of message at least is due from you, an acknowledgement of the things she has brought back for you. I can put that in a postscript when I write.'

I turned away from the window, and looked back at him.

'Why should you imagine I don't wish to see her?' I asked. 'I do wish to see her, very much. If she is a woman of impulse, which she appears to be from that letter – I recollect Rainaldi

64

telling me the same thing – then I can also act on impulse, which I propose to do. It was impulse that took me to Florence in the first place, wasn't it?'

'Well?' asked my godfather, his brows knitting, staring at me suspiciously.

'When you write to Plymouth,' I said, 'say that Philip Ashley has already heard the news of Ambrose's death. That he went to Florence on receipt of two letters, went to the villa Sangalletti, saw her servants, saw her friend and adviser, Signor Rainaldi, and is now returned. Say that he is a plain man, and lives in a plain fashion. That he has no fine manners, no conversation, and is little used to the society of women, or indeed of anyone. If, however, she wishes to see him and her late husband's home – Philip Ashley's house is at the disposal of his cousin Rachel, when she cares to visit it.' And I placed my hand upon my heart, and bowed.

'I never thought,' said my godfather slowly, 'to see you grow so hard. What has happened to you?'

'Nothing has happened to me,' I said, 'save that, like a young war-horse, I smell blood. Have you forgotten my father was a soldier?'

Then I went out into the garden to find Louise. Her concern at the news was greater than my own. I took her hand and dragged her to the summer-house beside the lawn. We sat there together, like conspirators.

'Your house isn't fit to receive anyone,' she said at once, 'let alone a woman like the contessa – like Mrs Ashley. You see, I can't help calling her contessa too, it comes more naturally. Why, Philip, there hasn't been a woman staying there for twenty years. What room will you put her in? And think of the dust! Not only upstairs but in the drawing-room too. I noticed it last week.'

'None of that matters,' I said impatiently. 'She can dust the place herself, if she minds so much. The worse she finds it, the better pleased I shall be. Let her know at last the happy care-free life we led, Ambrose and I. Unlike that villa . . .'

'Oh, but you're wrong,' exclaimed Louise. 'You don't want to

65

seem a boor, an ignoramus, like one of the hinds on the estate. That would be putting yourself at a disadvantage before you even spoke to her. You must remember she has lived on the continent all her life, has been used to great refinement, many servants – they say foreign ones are much better than ours – and she is certain to have brought a quantity of clothes, and jewels too, perhaps, besides Mr Ashley's things. She will have heard so much about the house from him that she will expect something very fine, like her own villa. And to have it all untidy, dusty, smelling like a kennel – why, you would not want her to find it so, Philip, for his sake, surely?'

God damn it, I was angry. 'What the devil do you mean,' I said, 'by my house smelling like a kennel? It's a man's house, plain and homely, and please God it always will be. Neither Ambrose nor I went in for fancy furnishings and little ornaments on tables that come crashing to the ground if you brush your knee against them.'

She had the grace to look contrite, if not ashamed.

'I'm sorry,' she said, 'I did not mean to offend you. You know I love your house, I have a great affection for it and always will. But I can't help saying what I think, as to the way it's kept. Nothing new for so long, no real warmth about it, and lacking – well, lacking comfort, if you'll forgive that too.'

I thought of the bright trim parlour where she made my godfather sit of an evening, and I knew which I would prefer to have, and he too in all probability, faced with the choice of that and my library.

'All right,' I said, 'forget my lack of comfort. It suited Ambrose, and it suits me, and for the space of a few days – however long she chooses so to honour me with her presence – it can suit my cousin Rachel too.'

Louise shook her head at me.

'You're quite incorrigible,' she said. 'If Mrs Ashley is the woman I believe her to be she will take one look at the house and then seek refuge in St Austell, or with us.'

'You're very welcome,' I replied, 'when I have done with her.'

Louise looked at me curiously. 'Will you really dare to question her?' she asked. 'Where will you begin?'

I shrugged my shoulders. 'I can't say until I have seen her. She'll try to bluster her way out, I have no doubt. Or maybe make a great play of emotion, swoon and have hysterics. That won't worry me. I shall watch her, and enjoy it.'

'I don't think she will bluster,' said Louise, 'nor have hysterics. She will merely sweep into the house and take command. Don't forget, she must be used to giving orders.'

'She won't give them in my house.'

'Poor Seecombe! What I would give to see his face. She will throw things at him, if he fails to come when she pulls her bell. Italians are very passionate, you know, very quick-tempered. I have always heard so.'

'She's only half Italian,' I reminded her, 'and I think Seecombe is well able to take care of himself. Perhaps it will rain for three days, and she will be confined to bed with rheumatism.'

We laughed together in the summer-house, like a pair of children, but for all that I was not so light of heart as I pretended. The invitation had been flung on to the air like a challenge, and already I think I had regretted it, though I did not say so to Louise. I regretted it more when I went home and looked about me. Dear heaven, it was a foolhardy thing to go and do, and had it not been for pride I think I would have ridden back to my godfather and told him to send no message from me, when he wrote to Plymouth.

What in the world was I to do with that woman in my house? What indeed should I say to her, what action should I take? If Rainaldi had been plausible, she would be ten times more so. Direct attack might not succeed, and what was it the Italian had said anyway about tenacity, and women fighting battles? If she should be loud-mouthed, vulgar, I thought I knew how to shut her up. A fellow from one of the farms became entangled with such a one, who would have sued him for breach of promise, and I soon had her packing back to Devon, where she belonged. But sugary, insidious, with heaving bosom and sheep's eyes, could

I deal with that? I believed so. I had met with some of these in Oxford, and I always found extreme bluntness of speech, amounting to brutality, sent them back to their holes in the ground with no bones broken. No, all things considered, I was pretty cocksure, pretty confident, that when I had actual speech with my cousin Rachel I should find my tongue. But preparations for the visit, that was the deuce, the façade of courtesy before the salute to arms.

To my great surprise, Seecombe received the idea without dismay. It was almost as if he had expected it. I told him briefly that Mrs Ashley had arrived in England, bringing with her Mr Ambrose's effects, and that it was possible she would arrive for a short visit within the week. His under-lip did not just forward, as it usually did when faced with any problem, and he listened to me with gravity.

'Yes, sir,' he said, 'very right and very proper. We shall all be glad to welcome Mrs Ashley.'

I glanced at him over my pipe, amused at his pomposity.

'I thought,' I said, 'you were like me, and did not care for women in the house. You sang a different tune when I told you Mr Ambrose had been married, and she would be mistress here.'

He looked shocked. This time the nether lip went forward.

'That was not the same, sir,' he said; 'there has been tragedy since then. The poor lady is widowed. Mr Ambrose would have wished us to do what we can for her, especially as it seems' – he coughed discreetly – 'that Mrs Ashley has not benefited in any way from the decease.'

I wondered how the devil he knew that, and asked him.

'It's common talk, sir,' he said, 'all around the place. Everything left to you, Mr Philip, nothing to the widow. It is not usual, you see. In every family, big or small, there is always provision for the widow.'

'I'm surprised at you, Seecombe,' I said, 'lending your ear to gossip.'

'Not gossip, sir,' he said with dignity; 'what concerns the Ashley family concerns us all. We, the servants, were not forgotten.'

I had a vision of him sitting out at the back there, in his room, the steward's room as it was called from long custom, and coming in to chat and drink a glass of bitter with him would be Wellington, the old coachman, Tamlyn, the head gardener, and the first woodman – none of the young servants, of course, would be permitted to join them – and the affairs of the will, which I had thought most secret, would be discussed and puzzled over and discussed again with pursed lips and shaking heads.

'It was not a question of forgetfulness,' I said shortly. 'The fact that Mr Ashley was abroad, and not at home, made matters of business out of the question. He did not expect to die there. Had he come home things would have been otherwise.'

'Yes, sir,' he said, 'that is what we thought.'

Oh, well, they could cluck their tongues about the will, it made no odds. But I wondered, with a sudden flash of bitterness, what their manner would have been to me if, after all, I had not inherited the property. Would the deference be there? The respect? The loyalty? Or would I have been young Master Philip, a poor relative, with a room of my own stuck away somewhere at the back of the house? I knocked out my pipe, the taste was dry and dusty. How many people were there, I wondered, who liked me and served me for myself alone?

'That is all, Seecombe,' I said. 'I will let you know if Mrs Ashley decides to visit us. I don't know about a room. I leave that side of the business to you.'

'Why surely, Mr Philip, sir,' said Seecombe in surprise, 'it will be correct to put Mrs Ashley into Mr Ashley's own room?'

I stared at him, shocked into sudden silence. Then fearing my feelings showed in my face, I turned away.

'No,' I said, 'that won't be possible. I shall be moving into Mr Ashley's room myself. I meant to tell you so before. I decided upon the change some days ago.'

It was a lie. I had not thought of such a thing until that moment.

'Very well, sir,' he said, 'in that case the blue room and the dressing-room will be more suitable for Mrs Ashley.' And he left the room.

Good God, I thought, to put that woman into Ambrose's room, what sacrilege. I flung myself down in my chair, biting the stem of my pipe. I felt angry, unsettled, sick of the whole concern. It was madness to have sent that message through my godfather, madness to have her in the house at all. What in the name of the devil had I let myself in for? That idiot, Seecombe, with his ideas of what was right and what was wrong.

The invitation was accepted. She wrote a letter back to my godfather, not to me. Which, as no doubt Seecombe would have thought, was duly right and proper. The invitation had not come direct from me, therefore it must be returned through the correct channel. She would be ready, she said, whenever it was convenient to send for her, or if not convenient she would come by post-chaise. I replied, again through my godfather, that I would send the carriage for her on the Friday. And that was that.

Friday came all too soon. A moody, fitful sort of day, with gusts of wind. We often had them thus, the third week in September, with the big tides of the year. The clouds were low, scudding across the sky from the south-west, threatening rain before the evening. I hoped it would rain. One of our true downpours, with maybe a gale thrown in for further measure. A west country welcome. No Italian skies. I had sent Wellington off with the horses the day before. He would stay overnight in Plymouth and return with her. Ever since I had told the servants that Mrs Ashley was expected a sort of unrest had come upon the house. Even the dogs were aware of it and followed me about from room to room. Seecombe reminded me of some old priest who, after years of abstinence from any form of religious celebration, suddenly conforms again to forgotten ritual. He moved about, mysterious and solemn, with hushed footsteps – he had even bought himself a pair of soft-soled slippers – and bits of silver I had never seen in my life before were borne into the dining-room and placed on the table, or on the sideboard. Relics, I suppose, of my uncle Philip's day. Great candlesticks, sugar-castors, goblets, and a silver bowl filled – great Joshua – with roses placed as a centre piece.

'Since when,' I said to him, 'have you turned acolyte? What about the incense, and the holy water?'

He did not move a muscle of his face. He stood back, surveying the relics.

'I have asked Tamlyn to bring cut flowers from the walled garden,' he said. 'The boys are sorting them now, out at the back. We shall need flowers in the drawing-room, and in the blue bedroom, in the dressing-room and boudoir.' He frowned at the pantry boy, young John, who slipped and nearly fell, staggering under the load of yet another pair of candlesticks.

The dogs gazed up at me, dejected. One of them crept and hid under the settle in the hall. I went upstairs. Heaven knows when last I had trespassed into the blue room. We never had visitors, and it was connected in my mind with some game of hide-and-seek, long since, when Louise had come over with my godfather one Christmas. I could remember creeping into the silent room and hiding beneath the bed, amongst the dust. I had a dim recollection that Ambrose had once said it was aunt Phoebe's room, and aunt Phoebe had gone away to live in Kent, and later died.

No trace of her remained to-day. The boys, under Seecombe's direction, had worked hard, and aunt Phoebe had been swept away with the dust of years. The windows were open, looking out on the grounds, and the morning sun shone on the well-beaten rugs. Fresh linen, of a quality unknown to me, had been put upon the bed. Had that wash-stand and ewer always been there, I wondered, in the dressing-room adjoining? Did that easy chair belong? I remembered none of them, but then I remembered nothing of aunt Phoebe, who had taken herself to Kent before I was even born. Well, what had done for her would do for my cousin Rachel.

The third room, under the arch, making up the suite, had been aunt Phoebe's boudoir. This too had been dusted, and the windows opened. I dare say I had not entered this room either since those days of hide-and-seek. There was a portrait of Ambrose hanging on the wall above the fireplace, painted when he was a young man. I did not even know of its existence, and he had probably forgotten it. Had it been done by some well-known painter it would have been below with the other family portraits, but sent up here, to a room never used, suggested no one had thought much of it. It was painted three-quarter length, and he had his gun under his arm and carried a dead partridge in his left hand. The eyes looked ahead, into my eyes, and the mouth smiled a little. His hair was longer than I remembered it. There was nothing very striking in the portrait, or in the face. Only one thing. It was strangely like myself. I looked in the mirror, and back again to the portrait, and the only difference lay in the slant of his eyes, something narrower than mine, and in his darker colouring of hair. We could be brothers, though, almost twin brothers, that young man in the portrait and myself. This sudden realisation of our likeness gave an uplift to my spirits. It was as if the young Ambrose was smiling at me saying 'I am with you.' And the older Ambrose, too, felt very close. I shut the door behind me and, passing back once more through the dressing-room and the blue bedroom, went downstairs.

I heard the sound of wheels out on the drive. It was Louise, in the dogcart, and she had great bunches of michaelmas daisies and dahlias on the seat beside her.

'For the drawing-room,' she called, on sight of me. 'I thought that Seecombe might be glad of them.'

Seecombe, passing that moment through the hall with his drove of minions, looked offended. He stood stiffly, as Louise passed into the house carrying the flowers. 'You should not have troubled, Miss Louise,' he said, 'I had made all arrangements with Tamlyn. Sufficient flowers were brought in first thing from the walled garden.'

'I can arrange them, then,' said Louise; 'your men will only break the vases. I suppose you have vases. Or have they been cramming the flowers into jam-pots?'

Seecombe's face was a study in pained dignity. I pushed Louise into the library hurriedly and shut the door.

'I wondered,' said Louise, in an undertone, 'whether you would have liked me to stay and see to things, and be here when Mrs Ashley comes. Father would have accompanied me, but he is still rather unwell, and with this threatening rain I thought it best he remained indoors. What do you say? Shall I stay? These flowers were only an excuse.'

I felt vaguely irritated that both she and my godfather should think me so incapable, and poor old Seecombe too, who had worked like a slave-driver for the past three days.

'Good of you to suggest it,' I said, 'but quite unnecessary. We can manage very well.'

She looked disappointed. She was evidently afire with curiosity to see my visitor. I did not tell her that I had no intention of being in the house myself when she arrived.

Louise looked critically about the room, but made no comment. No doubt she saw many faults, but had the tact to hold her tongue.

'You can go upstairs, if you like, and see the blue room,' I told her, as a sop to disappointment.

'The blue room?' said Louise. 'That's the one facing east, over the drawing-room, isn't it? Then you have not put her in Mr Ashley's room?'

'I have not,' I said. 'I use Ambrose's room myself.'

This insistence that she, and everybody else, should put upon the placing of Ambrose's room at the disposal of his widow added fresh fuel to my rising irritation.

'If you really wish to arrange the flowers, ask Seecombe for some vases,' I said, going towards the door. 'I have a mass of things to do outside, and shall be away about the estate most of the day.'

She picked up the flowers, glancing at me as she did so.

'I believe you're nervous,' she said.

'I am not nervous,' I said, 'I merely want to be alone.'

She flushed and turned away, and I felt the prick of conscience that always came to me after wounding anyone.

'Sorry, Louise,' I said, patting her shoulder, 'don't take any notice of me. And bless you for coming, and bringing the flowers, and for offering to stay.'

'When shall I see you again,' she asked, 'to hear about Mrs Ashley? You know I shall be longing to know everything. Of course, if father is better we shall come down to Church on Sunday, but all to-morrow I shall be thinking and wondering . . .'

'Wondering what?' I said. 'If I have thrown my cousin Rachel over the headland? I might do that, if she goads me hard enough. Listen — just to satisfy you — I will ride over to-morrow afternoon to Pelyn, and paint a vivid picture for you. Does that content you?'

'That will do very well,' she answered, smiling, and went off to find Seecombe and the vases.

I was out all morning and returned about two, hungry and thirsty after my ride, and had some cold meat and a glass of ale. Louise had gone. Seecombe and the servants were in their own quarters, sitting down to their midday dinner. I stood alone in the library, munching my sandwich of meat and bread. Alone, I thought, for the last time. To-night she would be here, either in this room or in the drawing-room, an unknown hostile presence, stamping her personality upon my rooms, my house. She came as an intruder to my home. I did not want her. I did not want her or any woman, with peering eyes and questing fingers, forcing herself into the atmosphere, intimate and personal, that was mine alone. The house was still and silent, and I was part of it, belonging, as Ambrose had done and still did, somewhere in the shadows. We needed no one else to break the silence.

I looked about the room, almost in farewell, and then went out of the house and plunged into the woods.

I judged that Wellington would be home with the carriage not earlier than five o'clock, so I determined to remain without until after six. They could wait dinner for me. Seecombe already had his instructions. If she was hungry, she must hold her hunger until the master of the house returned. It gave me satisfaction to think of her sitting alone in the drawing-room, dressed to the nines, full of self-importance, and no one to receive her.

I went on walking in the wind and rain. Up the avenue to where the four roads met, and eastwards to the boundary of our land; then back through the woods again and northwards to the outlying farms, where I made a point of dallying and talking with the tenants, thus spacing out the time. Across the park and over the westward hills, and home at last by the Barton, just as it grew dusk. I was wet nearly to the skin but I did not care.

I opened the hall door and went into the house. I expected to see the signs of arrival, boxes and trunks, travel rugs and baskets; but all was as usual, there was nothing there.

A fire was burning in the library, but the room was empty. In the dining-room a place was laid for one. I pulled the bell for Seecombe. 'Well?' I said.

He wore his new-found look of self-importance, and his voice was hushed.

'Madam has come,' he said.

'So I would suppose,' I answered, 'it must be nearly seven. Did she bring luggage? What have you done with it?'

'Madam brought little of her own,' he said. 'The boxes and trunks belonged to Mr Ambrose. They have all been put in your old room, sir.'

'Oh,' I said. I walked over to the fire and kicked a log. I would not have him notice for the world that my hands were trembling.

'Where is Mrs Ashley now?' I said.

'Madam has gone to her room, sir,' he said. 'She seemed tired, and she asked you to excuse her for dinner. I had a tray taken up to her about an hour ago.'

His words came as a relief. Yet in a sense it was an anti-climax.

'What sort of journey did she have?' I asked.

'Wellington said the road after Liskeard was rough, sir,' he answered, 'and it was blowing hard. One of the horses cast a shoe, and they had to turn in at the smithy before Lostwithiel.'

'H'm.' I turned my back upon the fire and warmed my legs.

'You're very wet, sir,' said Seecombe. 'Better change your things, or you'll take cold.'

'I will directly,' I answered him, and then, glancing about the room, 'Where are the dogs?'

'I think they followed madam upstairs,' he said, 'at least old Don did, I am not certain of the others.'

I went on warming my legs before the fire. Seecombe still hovered by the door, as if expecting me to draw him in conversation.

'All right,' I said, 'I'll bath and change. Tell one of the boys to take up the hot water. And I'll dine in half an hour.'

I sat down that evening alone to my dinner before the newly polished candle-sticks and the silver rose bowl. Seecombe stood behind my chair, but we did not speak. Silence must have been torture to him, on this night of nights, for I knew how much he longed to comment on the new arrival. Well, he could bide his time, and then let forth to his heart's content in the steward's room.

Just as I finished dinner, John came into the room and whispered to him. Seecombe came and bent over my shoulder.

'Madam has sent word that if you should wish to see her, when you have dined, she will be pleased to receive you,' he said.

'Thank you, Seecombe.'

When they had left the room I did something that I very rarely did. Only after extreme exhaustion, after riding perhaps, or a hard day's shoot, or buffeting about in a summer gale in the sailing boat with Ambrose. I went to the sideboard and poured myself a glass of brandy. Then I went upstairs, and knocked upon the door of the little boudoir.

8

A low voice, almost inaudible, bade me come in. Although it was now dark, and the candles had been lit, the curtains were not drawn, and she was sitting on the window-seat looking out on to the garden. Her back was turned to me, her hands were clasped in her lap. She must have thought me one of the servants, for she did not move when I entered the room. Don lay before the fire, his muzzle in his paws and the two young dogs beside him. Nothing had been moved in the room, no drawers opened in the small secretaire, no clothes flung down; there was none of the litter of arrival.

'Good evening,' I said, and my voice sounded strained and unnatural in the little room. She turned, and rose at once and came towards me. It was happening so quickly that I had no time, no moment for reflection back upon the hundred images I had formed of her during the past eighteen months. The woman who had pursued me through the nights and days, haunted my waking hours, disturbing my dreams, was now beside me. My first feeling was one of shock, almost of stupefaction, that she should be so small. She barely reached my shoulder. She had nothing like the height or the figure of Louise.

She was dressed in deep black, which took the colour from her hair, and there was lace at her throat and at her wrists. Her hair was brown, parted in the centre with a low knot behind, her features neat and regular. The only things large about her were the eyes, which at first sight of me widened in sudden recognition, startled, like the eyes of a deer, and from recognition to bewilderment, from bewilderment to pain, almost to apprehension. I saw the colour come into her face and go again, and I think I was as great a shock to her as she was to me. It would be hazardous to say which of us was the more nervous, which the more ill-at-ease.

I stared down at her and she looked up at me, and it was a moment before either of us spoke. When we did, it was to speak together.

'I hope you are rested,' was my stiff contribution, and hers, 'I owe you an apology.' She followed up my opening swiftly with 'Thank you, Philip, yes,' and moving towards the fire she sat down on a low stool beside it and motioned me to the chair opposite. Don, the old retriever, stretched and yawned, and pulling himself on to his haunches placed his head upon her lap.

'This is Don, isn't it?' she said, putting her hand on his nose. 'Was he really fourteen last birthday?'

'Yes,' I said, 'his birthday is a week before my own.'

'You found him in a pie-crust with your breakfast,' she said. 'Ambrose was hiding behind the screen in the dining-room, and watched you open up the pie. He told me he would never forget the look of amazement on your face when you lifted the crust and Don struggled out. You were ten years old, and it was the first of April.'

She looked up from patting Don, and smiled at me; and to my great discomfiture I saw tears in her eyes, gone upon the instant.

'I owe you an apology for not coming down to dinner,' she said. 'You had made so much preparation, just for me, and must have come hurrying home long before you wanted. But I was very tired. I would have made a poor sort of companion. It seemed to me that it would be easier for you if you dined alone.'

I thought of how I had tramped about the estate from east to west so as to keep her waiting, and I said nothing. One of the younger dogs woke up and licked my hand. I pulled his ears to give myself employment.

'Seecombe told me how busy you were, and how much there is to do,' she said. 'I don't want you to feel hampered in any way by my sudden unexpected visit. I can find my way about alone, and shall be happy doing so. You mustn't make any sort of alteration in your day to-morrow because of me. I just want to say one thing, which is thank you, Philip, for letting me come. It can't have been easy for you.'

She rose then, and crossed over to the window to draw the curtains. The rain was beating against the panes. Perhaps I should have drawn the curtains for her, I did not know. I stood up, awkwardly, in an attempt to do so, but it was too late anyway. She came back beside the fire, and we both sat down again.

'It was such a strange feeling,' she said, 'driving through the park and up to the house, with Seecombe standing by the door to welcome me. I've done it so many times, you know, in fancy. Everything was just as I had imagined it. The hall, the library, the pictures on the walls. The clock struck four as the carriage drove up to the door; I even knew the sound of it.' I went on pulling at the puppy's ears. I did not look at her. 'In the evenings, in Florence,' she said, 'last summer and winter before Ambrose became ill, we used to talk about the journey home. It was his happiest time. He would tell me about the gardens, and the woods, and the path down to the sea. We always intended to return by the route I came; that's why I did it. Genoa, and so to Plymouth. And the carriage coming there with Wellington to bring us back. It was good of you to do that, to know how I would feel.'

I felt something of a fool, but found my tongue.

'I fear the drive was rather rough,' I said, 'and Seecombe told me you were obliged to stop at the smithy to shoe one of the horses. I'm sorry about that.'

'It did not worry me,' she said. 'I was quite happy, sitting beside the fire there, watching the work and chatting to Wellington.'

Her manner was quite easy now. That first nervousness had gone, if it had been nervousness at all. I could not tell. I found now that if anyone was at fault it was myself, for I felt oddly large and clumsy in so small a room, and the chair in which I was sitting might have been made for a dwarf. There is nothing so defeating to ease of manner as being uncomfortably seated, and I wondered what sort of a figure I must cut, hunched there in the damnable little chair, with my large feet tucked awkwardly beneath it and my long arms hanging down on either side of it.

'Wellington pointed out to me the entrance to Mr Kendall's house,' she said, 'and for a moment I wondered if it would be right, and polite, to go and pay him my respects. But it was late, and the horses had been far, and very selfishly I was longing to be — here.' She had paused a moment before saying the word 'here', and it came to me that she had been on the point of saying 'home' but checked herself. 'Ambrose had described it all so well to me,' she said, 'from the entrance hall to every room in the house. He even sketched them for me, so that to-day, I well believe, I could find my way blindfold.' She paused a moment, and then she said, 'It was perceptive of you to let me have these rooms. They were the ones we meant to use, had we been together. Ambrose always intended you to have his room, and Seecombe told me you had moved into it. Ambrose would be glad.'

'I hope you'll be comfortable,' I said. 'Nobody seems to have been in here since someone called aunt Phoebe.'

'Aunt Phoebe fell love-sick of a curate, and went away to Tonbridge to mend a broken heart,' she said, 'but the heart proved stubborn, and aunt Phoebe took a chill that lasted twenty years. Did you never hear the story?'

'No,' I said, and glanced across at her, under my eyes. She was looking into the fire, smiling, I suppose at the thought of aunt Phoebe. Her hands were clasped on her lap in front of her. I had never seen hands so small before on an adult person. They were very slender, very narrow, like the hands of someone in a portrait painted by an old master and left unfinished.

'Well,' I said, 'what happened to aunt Phoebe?'

'The chill left her, after twenty years, at sight of another curate. But by then aunt Phoebe was five-and-forty, and her heart was not so brittle. She married the second curate.'

'Was the marriage a success?'

'No,' said my cousin Rachel, 'she died on her wedding night — of shock.'

She turned and looked at me, her mouth twitching, yet her

eyes still solemn, and suddenly I had a vision of Ambrose telling the story, as he must have done, hunched in his chair, his shoulders shaking, with her looking up at him in just this way, concealing laughter. I could not help myself. I smiled at cousin Rachel, and something happened to her eyes and she smiled back at me.

'I think you made it up upon this instant,' I said to her, instantly regretting my smile.

'I did nothing of the sort,' she said. 'Seecombe will know the story. Ask him.'

I shook my head. 'He would not think it fitting. And he would be deeply shocked if he thought you had told it to me. I forgot to ask you if he brought you anything for dinner?'

'Yes. A cup of soup, a wing of chicken, and a devilled kidney. All were excellent.'

'You realise, of course, there are no women servants in the house? No one to look after you, to hang your gowns, only young John or Arthur to fill your bath?'

'I much prefer it. Women chatter so. As to my gowns, all mourning is the same. I have only brought this and one other. I have strong shoes for walking in the grounds.'

'If it rains like this tomorrow you will have to stay indoors,' I said. 'There are plenty of books in the library. I don't read much myself, but you might find something to your taste.'

Her mouth twitched again and she looked at me gravely. 'I could always polish the silver,' she said. 'I had not thought to see so much of it. Ambrose used to say it turned to mildew by the sea.' I could swear from her expression that she had guessed the array of relics came from a long-locked cupboard, and that behind her large eyes she was laughing at me.

I looked away. I had smiled at her once, I was damned if I would smile at her again.

'At the villa,' she said, 'when it was very hot, we would sit out in a little court there, with a fountain. Ambrose would tell me to close my eyes, and listen to the water, making believe that it was the rain falling at home. He had a great theory, you know,

81

that I should shrink and shiver in the English climate, especially the damp Cornish one; he called me a green-house plant, fit only for expert cultivation, quite useless in the common soil. I was city-bred, he said, and over-civilised. Once I remember I came down to dinner wearing a new gown, and he told me I reeked of old Rome. "You'll freeze in that at home," he said; "it will be flannel next the skin, and a woollen shawl." I haven't forgotten his advice. I brought the shawl.' I glanced up. Indeed she had one, black like her dress, lying on the stool beside her.

'In England,' I said, 'especially down here, we lay great stress upon the weather. We have to, by the sea. Our land isn't very rich, you see, for farming, not as it is up-country. The soil is poor, and with four days out of seven wet we're very dependent on the sun when it does shine. This will take off to-morrow, I dare say, and you'll get your walk.'

''Bove town and Bawden's meadow,' she said, 'Kemp's close and Beef Park, Kilmoor and beacon field, the Twenty Acres, and the West Hills.'

I looked at her astonished. 'You know the names of the Barton lands?' I said.

'Why yes, I've known them by heart now for near two years,' she answered.

I was silent. There seemed nothing I could say in answer. Then, 'It's rough walking for a woman,' I told her gruffly.

'But I have strong shoes,' she answered me.

The foot she thrust out from beneath her gown seemed to me woefully inadequate for walking, clad as it was in a black velvet slipper.

'That?' I asked.

'Of course not, something stronger,' she replied.

I could not picture her tramping about the fields, however much she saw herself. And my ploughman boots would drown her.

'Can you ride?' I asked her.

'No.'

'Can you sit upon a horse if you were led?'

'I might do that,' she answered, 'but I would have to hold on to the saddle with both hands. And isn't there something called a pommel on which one balances?'

She put the question with great earnestness, her eyes solemn, yet once more I was certain there was laughter hidden there and she wished to draw me. 'I'm not sure,' I said stiffly, 'if we have a lady's saddle. I'll ask Wellington, but I have never seen one in the harness room.'

'Perhaps aunt Phoebe used to ride,' she said, 'when she lost her curate. It may have been her only consolation.'

It was useless. Something bubbled in her voice, and I was lost. She saw me laughing, that was the devil of it. I looked away.

'All right,' I said, 'I'll see about it in the morning. Do you think I should ask Seecombe to search the closets and see if aunt Phoebe left a riding-habit too?'

'I shan't need a habit,' she said, 'not if you lead me gently and I balance on that pommel.'

At that moment Seecombe knocked upon the door and entered, bearing in his hands a silver kettle upon a monstrous tray, likewise a silver tea-pot and a canister. I had never set eyes upon the things before, and I wondered from what labyrinth in the steward's room he had come upon them. And for what purpose did he bring them? My cousin Rachel saw the amazement in my eyes. Not for the world would I hurt Seecombe, who placed his offering upon the table with great dignity, but a rising tide of something near hysteria rose in my chest, and I got up from my chair and went over to the window in pretence of looking out upon the rain.

'Tea is served, madam,' said Seecombe.

'Thank you, Seecombe,' she answered solemnly.

The dogs rose, sniffing, thrusting their noses at the tray. They were as amazed as I. Seecombe clicked at them with his tongue.

'Come, Don,' he said, 'come on, all three of you. I think, madam, I had better remove the dogs. They might upset the tray.'

'Yes, Seecombe,' she said, 'perhaps they might.'

Again that laughter in the voice. I was thankful my back was turned to her. 'What about breakfast, madam?' asked Seecombe. 'Mr Philip has his in the dining-room at eight o'clock.'

'I should like mine in my room,' she said. 'Mr Ashley used to say no woman was fit to look upon before eleven. Will that give trouble?'

'Certainly not, madam.'

'Then thank you, Seecombe, and good night.'

'Good night, madam. Good night, sir. Come, dogs.'

He snapped his fingers and they followed him reluctantly. There was silence in the room for a few moments and then she said softly: 'Would you like some tea? I understand it is a Cornish custom.'

My dignity vanished. Holding to it had become too great a strain. I went back to the fire and sat on the stool beside the table.

'I'll tell you something,' I said. 'I have never seen this tray before, nor the kettle, nor the tea-pot.'

'I didn't think you had,' she said. 'I saw the look in your eyes when Seecombe brought them into the room. I don't believe he has seen them before either. They're buried treasure. He has dug for them in the cellars.'

'Is it really the thing to do,' I asked, 'to drink tea after dinner?'

'Of course,' she said, 'in high society, when ladies are present.'

'We never have it on Sundays,' I said, 'when the Kendalls and the Pascoes come to dinner.'

'Perhaps Seecombe doesn't consider them high society,' she said. 'I'm very flattered. I like my tea. You can eat the bread and butter.'

This too was an innovation. Pieces of thin bread, rolled like small sausages. 'I'm surprised they knew how to do this in the kitchen,' I said, swallowing them down, 'but they're very good.'

'A sudden inspiration,' said cousin Rachel, 'and no doubt you will have what is left for breakfast. That butter is melting, you had better suck your fingers.'

She drank her tea, watching me over her cup.

'If you want to smoke your pipe, you can,' she said.

I stared at her surprised.

'In a lady's boudoir?' I said. 'Are you sure? Why, on Sundays, when Mrs Pascoe comes with the vicar, we never smoke in the drawing-room.'

'It's not the drawing-room, and I'm not Mrs Pascoe,' she answered me.

I shrugged my shoulders and felt in my pocket for my pipe.

'Seecombe will think it very wrong,' I said. 'He'll smell it in the morning.'

'I'll open the window before I go to bed,' she said. 'It will all blow out, with the rain.'

'The rain will come in and spoil the carpet,' I said, 'then that will be worse than the smell of the pipe.'

'It can be rubbed down with a cloth,' she said. 'How pernickety you are, like an old gentleman.'

'I thought women minded about such things.'

'They do, when they have nothing else to worry them,' she said.

It struck me suddenly as I smoked my pipe, sitting there in aunt Phoebe's boudoir, that this was not at all the way I had intended to spend the evening. I had planned a few words of icy courtesy and an abrupt farewell, leaving the interloper snubbed, dismissed.

I glanced up at her. She had finished her tea, and put the cup and saucer back on the tray. Once again I was aware of her hands, narrow and small and very white, and I wondered if Ambrose had called them city-bred. She wore two rings, fine stones both of them, on her fingers, yet they seemed to clash in no way with her mourning, nor be out of keeping with her person. I was glad I had the bowl of my pipe to hold, and the stem to bite upon; it made me feel more like myself and less like a sleep-walker, muddled by a dream. There were things I should be doing, things I should be saying, and here was I sitting like a fool before the fire, unable to collect my thoughts or my impressions. The day, so long-drawn-out and anxious, was now over, and I could not for the life of me decide whether it had turned to my advantage or gone against me. If only she had borne some resemblance to the image I had created I would know better what to do, but now that she was here, beside me, in the flesh, the images seemed fantastic crazy things that all turned into one another and then faded into darkness.

Somewhere there was a bitter creature, crabbed and old, hemmed about with lawyers; somewhere a larger Mrs Pascoe, loud-voiced, arrogant; somewhere a petulant spoilt doll, with corkscrew curls; somewhere a viper, sinuous and silent. But none of them was with me in this room. Anger seemed futile now, and hatred too, and as for fear – how could I fear anyone who did not measure up to my shoulder, and had nothing remarkable about her save a sense of humour and small hands? Was it for this that one man had fought a duel, and another, dying, written to me and said, 'She's done for me at last, Rachel my torment?' It was as though I had blown a bubble in the air, and stood by to watch it dance; and the bubble had now burst.

I must remember, I thought to myself, nearly nodding by the flickering fire, not to drink brandy another time after a ten-mile walk in the rain; it dulls the senses and it does not ease the tongue. I had come to fight this woman and I had not even started. What was it she had said about aunt Phoebe's saddle?

'Philip,' said the voice, very quiet, very low, 'Philip, you're nearly asleep. Will you please get up and go to bed?'

I opened my eyes with a jerk. She was sitting watching me, her hands in her lap. I stumbled to my feet, and nearly crashed the tray.

'I'm sorry,' I said, 'it must have been because I was sitting cramped there on that stool, it made me sleepy. I usually stretch my legs out in the library.'

'You took a lot of exercise to-day too, didn't you?' she said.

Her voice was innocent enough and yet . . . What did she mean? I frowned, and stood staring down at her, determined to say nothing. 'If it's fine then to-morrow morning,' she said, 'will you really find a horse for me that will be steady and quiet, so that I can sit up on him and go and see the Barton acres?'

'Yes,' I said, 'if you want to go.'

'I needn't bother you; Wellington shall lead me.'

'No, I can take you. I have nothing else to do.'

'Wait though,' she said, 'you forget it will be Saturday. That's the morning you pay the wages. We'll wait till afternoon.'

I looked down at her, nonplussed. 'Great heavens,' I said, 'how in the world do you know that I pay the wages on Saturday?'

To my dismay and great embarrassment, her eyes grew bright suddenly, and wet, as they had done earlier when she talked of my tenth birthday. And her voice became much harder than before.

'If you don't know,' she said, 'you have less understanding than I thought. Stay here a moment, I have a present for you.'

She opened the door and passed into the blue bedroom opposite, and returned within a moment carrying a stick in her hand.

'Here,' she said, 'take it, it's yours. Everything else you can sort out and see another time, but I wanted to give you this myself, tonight.'

It was Ambrose's walking stick. The one he always used, and leant upon. The one with the gold band, and the dog's head on the top carved in ivory.

'Thank you,' I said awkwardly, 'thank you very much.'

'Now go,' she said, 'please go, quickly.'

And she pushed me from the room, and shut the door.

I stood outside, holding the stick in my hands. She had not given me time even to wish her good night. No sound came from the boudoir, and I walked slowly down the corridor to my own room. I thought of the expression in her eyes as she gave me the stick. Once, not so long ago, I had seen other eyes with that same age-old look of suffering. Those eyes too had held reserve and pride, coupled with the same abasement, the same agony of supplication. It must be, I thought, as I came to my room, Ambrose's room, and examined the well-remembered walking stick, it must be because the eyes are the same colour and they belong to the same race. Otherwise they could have nothing in common, the beggar woman beside the Arno and my cousin Rachel.

9

I was down early the following morning, and immediately after breakfast walked across to the stables and summoned Wellington, and we went together to the harness room.

Yes, there were some half-dozen side-saddles amongst the rest. I suppose the fact was that I had never noticed them.

'Mrs Ashley cannot ride,' I told him. 'All she wants is something to sit upon and to cling on to.'

'We'd better put her up on Solomon,' said the old coachman. 'He may never have carried a lady but he won't let her down, that's certain. I couldn't be sure, sir, of any of the other horses.'

Solomon had been hunted years back, by Ambrose, but now took his ease chiefly in the meadow, unless exercised on the high road by Wellington. The side-saddles were high up on the wall of the harness room, and he had to send for the groom, and a short ladder, to bring them down. It caused quite a pother and excitement, the choice of the saddle; this one was too worn, the next too narrow for Solomon's broad back, and the lad was scolded because the third had a cobweb across it. I laughed inwardly, guessing that neither Wellington nor anybody else had thought about those saddles for a quarter of a century, and told Wellington that a good polish with a leather would set it to rights, and Mrs Ashley would think the saddle had come down from London yesterday.

'What time does the mistress wish to start?' he asked, and I stared at him a moment, taken aback by his choice of words.

'Some time after noon,' I said shortly. 'You can bring Solomon round to the front door, and I shall be leading Mrs Ashley myself.'

Then I turned back to the estate room, in the house, to reckon up the weekly books and check the accounts before the men came for their wages. The mistress indeed. Was that how they looked upon her, Wellington and Seecombe and the rest? I supposed in a sense it was natural of them, yet I thought how swiftly men, especially men-servants, became fools when in the presence of a woman. That look of reverence in Seecombe's eye when he had brought in the tea last night, and his respectful manner as he placed the tray before her, and this morning at breakfast it was young John, if you please, who waited by the side-board and lifted the covers from my bacon, because 'Mr Seecombe,' he said,' has gone upstairs with the tray for the boudoir.' And now here was Wellington, in a state of excitement, polishing and rubbing at the old side-saddle, and shouting over his shoulder to the boy to see to Solomon. I worked away at my accounts, glad to be so unmoved by the fact that a woman had slept under the roof for the first time since Ambrose had sent my nurse packing; and now I came to think of it her treatment of me as I nearly fell asleep, her words, 'Philip, go to bed,' were what my nurse might have said to me, over twenty years ago.

At noon the servants came, and the men who worked outside in the stables, woods, and gardens, and I gave them their money; then I noticed that Tamlyn, the head gardener, was not amongst them. I enquired the reason, and was told that he was somewhere about the grounds with 'the mistress'. I made no observation as to this, but paid the rest their wages and dismissed them. Some instinct told me where I should find Tamlyn and my cousin Rachel. I was right. They were in the forcing ground, where we had brought on the camellias, and the oleanders, and the other young trees that Ambrose had carried back from his travels.

I had never been an expert – I had left that to Tamlyn – and now as I rounded the corner and came upon them I could hear her talking about cuttings, and layers, and a north aspect, and the feeding of the soil, and Tamlyn listening to it all with his hat in his hand and the same look of reverence in the eye that Seecombe had, and Wellington. She smiled at the sight of me and rose to her feet. She had been kneeling on a piece of sacking, examining the shoots of a young tree.

'I've been out since half-past ten,' she said. 'I looked for you to ask permission but could not find you, so I did a bold thing and went down myself to Tamlyn's cottage to make myself known to him, didn't I, Tamlyn?'

'You did, ma'am,' said Tamlyn, with a sheep's look in his eye.

'You see, Philip,' she continued, 'I brought with me to Plymouth – I could not get them in the carriage, they will follow on by carrier – all the plants and shrubs that we had collected, Ambrose and I, during the past two years. I have the lists here with me, and where he wished them to go, and I thought it would save time if I talked over the list with Tamlyn, and explained what everything was. I may be gone when the carrier brings the load.'

'That's all right,' I said. 'You both of you understand these things better than I do. Please continue.'

'We've finished, haven't we, Tamlyn?' she said. 'And will you please thank Mrs Tamlyn for that cup of tea she gave me, and tell her that I do so hope her sore throat will be better by this evening? Oil of eucalyptus is the remedy, I will send some down to her.'

'Thank you, ma'am,' said Tamlyn (it was the first I had heard of his wife's sore throat), and looking at me he added, with a little awkward air of diffidence, 'I've learnt some things this morning, Mr Philip, sir, that I never thought to learn from a lady. I always believed I knew my work, but Mrs Ashley knows more about gardening than I do, or ever will for that matter. Proper ignorant she's made me feel.'

'Nonsense, Tamlyn,' said my cousin Rachel, 'I only know about trees and shrubs. As to fruit – I haven't the least idea how to set about growing a peach, and remember, you haven't yet taken me round the walled garden. You shall do so to-morrow.'

'Whenever you wish, ma'am,' said Tamlyn, and she bade him good morning and we set back towards the house.

'If you have been out since after ten,' I said to her, 'you will want to rest now. I will tell Wellington not to saddle the horse after all.'

'Rest?' she said. 'Who talks of resting? I have been looking forward to my ride all morning. Look, the sun. You said it would break through. Are you going to lead me, or will Wellington?'

'No,' I said, 'I'll take you. And I warn you, you may be able to teach Tamlyn about camellias, but you won't be able to do the same with me and farming.'

'I know oats from barley,' she said. 'Doesn't that impress you?'

'Not a jot,' I said, 'and anyway, you won't find either out on the acres, they're all harvested.'

When we came to the house I discovered that Seecombe had laid out a cold luncheon of meat and salad in the dining-room, complete with pies and puddings as though we were to sit for dinner. My cousin Rachel glanced at me, her face quite solemn, yet that look of laughter behind her eyes.

'You are a young man, and you have not finished growing,' she said. 'Eat, and be thankful. Put a piece of that pie in your pocket and I will ask you for it when we are on the west hills. I am going upstairs now to dress myself suitably for riding.'

At least, I thought to myself as I tucked into the cold meat with hearty appetite, she does not expect waiting upon or other niceties, she has a certain independence of spirit that would seem, thank the Lord, unfeminine. The only irritation was that my manner with her, which I hoped was cutting, she apparently took in good part and enjoyed. My sarcasm was misread as joviality.

I had scarcely finished eating when Solomon was brought round to the door. The sturdy old horse had undergone the grooming of his lifetime. Even his hoofs were polished, an attention that was never paid to my Gypsy. The two young dogs pranced around his heels. Don watched them undisturbed; his running days were over, like his old friend Solomon's.

I went to tell Seecombe we would be out till after four, and when I returned my cousin Rachel had come downstairs and was already mounted upon Solomon. Wellington was adjusting her stirrup. She had changed into another mourning gown, cut somewhat fuller than the other, and instead of a hat she had wound her black lace shawl about her hair for covering. She was talking to Wellington, her profile turned to me, and for some reason or other I remembered what she had said the night before about Ambrose teasing her, how he had told her once that she reeked of old Rome. I think I knew now what he meant. Her features were like those stamped on a Roman coin, definite, yet small; and now with that lace shawl wound about her hair I was reminded of the women I had seen kneeling in that cathedral in Florence, or lurking in the doorways of the silent houses. As she sat up on Solomon you could not tell that she was so small in stature when she stood upon the ground. The woman whom I considered unremarkable, save for her hands and her changing eyes and the bubble of laughter in her voice upon occasion, looked different now that she sat above me. She seemed more distant, more remote, and more – Italian.

She heard my footstep and turned towards me; and it went swiftly, the distant look, the foreign look, that had come upon her features in repose. She looked now as she had before.

'Ready?' I said. 'Or are you fearful of falling?'

'I put my trust in you and Solomon,' she answered.

'Very well, then. Come on. We shall be about two hours, Wellington.' And taking the bridle I set off with her to tour the Barton acres.

The wind of the day before had blown itself up-country, taking the rain with it, and at noon the sun had broken through and the sky was clear. There was a salty brightness in the air, lending a zest to walking, and you could hear the running swell of the sea as it broke upon the rocks fringing the bay. We had these days often in the fall of the year. Belonging to no season they had a freshness all their own, yet with a hint of cooler hours to come and tasting still the aftermath of summer.

Ours was a strange pilgrimage. We started off by visiting the Barton, and it was as much as I could do to prevent Billy Rowe and his wife from inviting us inside the farmhouse to sit down to cakes and cream; in fact it was only by the promise of doing so on Monday that I got Solomon and my cousin Rachel past the byre and the midden and through the gates at all, up on the stubble of the west hills.

The Barton lands form a peninsula, the beacon fields forming the further end of it and the sea running into bays, east and west, on either side. As I had told her, the corn had all been carried, and I could lead old Solomon wherever I pleased, for he could do no damage on the stubble. The larger part of the Barton land is grazing land anyway, and to make a thorough tour of it all we kept close to the sea, and finally brought up by the beacon itself, so that looking back she could see the whole run of the estate, bounded on the western side by the great stretch of sandy bay and three miles to the eastward by the estuary. The Barton farm, and the house itself – the mansion, as Seecombe always called it – lay in a sort of saucer, but already the trees planted by Ambrose and my uncle Philip grew thick and fast to give the house more shelter, and to the north the new avenue wound through the woods and up the rise to where the four roads met.

Remembering her talk of the night before, I tried to test my cousin Rachel on the names of the Barton fields, but could not fault her; she knew them all. Her memory did not mislead her when she came to mention the various beaches, the headlands, and the other farms on the estate; she knew the names of the tenants, the size of their families, that Seecombe's nephew lived in the fish house on the beach, and that his brother had the mill. She did not throw her information at me, it was rather I, my curiosity piqued, who led her on to disclose it, and when she gave me the names, and spoke of the people, it was as a matter of course and with something of wonder that I should think it strange.

'What do you suppose we talked of, Ambrose and I?' she said to me at last, as we came down from the beacon hill to the eastward fields. 'His home was his passion, therefore I made it mine. Would you not expect a wife of yours to do the same?'

'Not possessing a wife I cannot say,' I answered her, 'but I should have thought that having lived on the continent all your life your interests would have been entirely different.'

'So they were,' she said, 'until I met Ambrose.'

'Except for gardens, I gather.'

'Except for gardens,' she agreed, 'which was how it started, as he must have told you. My garden at the villa was very lovely, but this' – she paused a moment, reining in Solomon, and I stood with my hand on the bridle – 'but this is what I have always wanted to see. This is different.' She said nothing for a moment or two, as she looked down on the bay. 'At the villa,' she went on, 'when I was young and first married – I am not referring to Ambrose – I was not very happy, so I distracted myself by designing afresh the gardens there, replanting much of them and terracing the walls. I sought advice, and shut myself up with books, and the results were very pleasing; at least I thought so, and was told so. I wonder what you would think of them.'

I glanced up at her. Her profile was turned towards the sea and she did not know that I was looking at her. What did she mean? Had not my godfather told her I had been to the villa?

A sudden misgiving came upon me. I remembered her composure of the night before, after the first nervousness on meeting, and also the easiness of our conversation, which, on thinking it over at breakfast, I had put down to her own social sense and my dullness after drinking brandy. It struck me now that it was odd she had said nothing last night about my visit to Florence, odder still that she had made no reference to the manner in which I had learnt of Ambrose's death. Could it be that my godfather had shirked that issue and left it to me to break it to her? I cursed him to myself for an old blunderer and a coward, and yet as I did so I knew that it was I myself who was the coward now. Last night, had I only told her last night, when I had the brandy inside me; but now, now it was not so easy. She would wonder why I had said nothing of it sooner. This was the moment, of course. This was the moment to say, 'I have seen the gardens at your villa Sangalletti. Didn't you know?' But she made a coaxing sound to Solomon and he moved on.

'Can we go past the mill, and up through the woods the other side?' she asked.

I had lost my opportunity, and we went on back towards home. As we progressed through the woods she made remarks from time to time about the trees, or the set of the hills, or some other feature; but for me the ease of the afternoon had gone, for somehow or other I had got to tell her about my visit to Florence. If I said nothing of it she would hear of it from Seecombe, or from my godfather himself when he came to dinner on Sunday. I became more and more silent as we drew towards the house.

'I've exhausted you,' she said. 'Here I have been, riding like a queen on Solomon, and you walking all the while, pilgrim fashion. Forgive me, Philip. I've been so very happy. You can never guess how happy.'

'No, I'm not tired,' I said, 'I'm – I'm delighted that you enjoyed your ride.' Somehow I could not look into those eyes, direct and questioning.

Wellington was waiting at the house to help her dismount. She went upstairs to rest before she changed for dinner, and I sat down in the library, frowning over my pipe and wondering how the devil I was to tell her about Florence. The worst of the business was that had my godfather told her of it in his letter it would have been for her to open the subject, and for me to relax and wait for what she said. As things stood at present, the move must come from me. Even this would not have mattered had she been the woman I expected. Why, in heaven's name, did she have to be so different and play such havoc with my plans?

I washed my hands, and changed my coat for dinner, and put into my pocket the two last letters Ambrose had written me, but when I went into the drawing-room, expecting to see her seated there, the room was empty. Seecombe, passing that moment through the hall, told me that 'Madam' had gone into the library.

Now that she no longer sat on Solomon, above me, and had taken off the head-shawl and smoothed her hair, she seemed even smaller than before, and more defenceless. Paler too by candle-light, and her mourning gown darker in comparison.

'Do you mind my sitting here?' she said. 'The drawing-room is lovely in the daytime, but somehow now, at evening, with the curtains drawn and the candles lit, this room seems the best. Besides, it was where you and Ambrose always sat together.'

Now perhaps was my chance. Now to say, 'Yes. You have nothing like this at the villa.' I was silent, and the dogs came in to make distraction. After dinner, I said to myself, after dinner is the time. And I will drink neither port nor brandy.

At dinner Seecombe placed her on my right hand, and both he and John waited upon us. She admired the rose bowl and the candlesticks, and talked to Seecombe as he handed the courses, and all the while I was in a sweat that he should say, 'That happened, madam, or this occurred, when Mr Philip was away in Italy.'

I could hardly wait for dinner to be over and for the pair of us to be alone again, though it brought me nearer to my task. We sat down together before the library fire, and she brought out some piece of embroidery and began to work upon it. I watched the small deft hands and wondered at them.

'Tell me what it is that is bothering you,' she said, after a while. 'Don't deny there is something, because I shall know you are not speaking the truth. Ambrose used to tell me I had an animal's instinct for sensing trouble, and I sense it with you, to-night. In fact, since late afternoon. I have not said anything to hurt you, have I?'

Well, here it was. At least she had opened a way clear for me.

'You've said nothing to hurt me,' I replied, 'but a chance remark of yours confounded me a little. Could you tell me what Nick Kendall said to you in the letter he wrote to Plymouth?'

'Why, certainly,' she said. 'He thanked me for my letter, he told me that you both of you knew already the facts of Ambrose's death, that Signor Rainaldi had written to him sending copies of the death certificate and other particulars, and that you invited me here for a short visit until my plans were formed. Indeed, he suggested that I should go on to Pelyn after leaving you, which was very kind of him.'

'That was all he said?'

'Yes, it was quite a brief letter.'

'He said nothing about my having been away?'

'No.'

'I see.' I felt myself grow hot, and she went on sitting there so calm and still, working at the piece of embroidery.

Then I said, 'My godfather was correct in telling you that he and the servants learnt of Ambrose's death through Signor Rainaldi. But it was not so for me. You see, I learnt of it in Florence, at the villa, from your servants.'

She lifted her head and looked at me; and this time there were no tears in her eyes, no hint of laughter either; the gaze was long and searching and it seemed to me I read in her eyes both compassion and reproach.

10

'Y ou went to Florence?' she said. 'When, how long ago?'
'I have been home a little under three weeks,' I said.
'I went there and returned through France. I spent one
night in Florence only. The night of the fifteenth of August.'

'The fifteenth of August?' I heard the new inflection in her
voice, I saw her eyes flash back in memory. 'But I had only left
for Genoa the day before. It isn't possible.'

'It is both possible and true,' I said; 'it happened.'

The embroidery had fallen from her hands, and that strange
look, almost of apprehension, came back into her eyes.

'Why didn't you tell me?' she said. 'Why have you let me stay
here in the house, four-and-twenty hours, and never breathed a
word of it? Last night, you should have told me last night.'

'I thought you knew,' I said. 'I had asked my godfather to
write it in his letter. Anyway, there it is. You know now.'

Some coward streak in me hoped that we could let the matter
rest, that she would pick up the embroidery once again. But it
was not to be.

'You went to the villa,' she said, as though talking to herself.
'Giuseppe must have let you in. He would open up the gates and
see you standing there, and he would think ... .' She broke off, a
cloud came over her eyes, she looked away from me to the fire.

'I want you to tell me what happened, Philip,' she said.

I put my hand in my pocket. I felt the letters there.

'I had not heard from Ambrose in a long while,' I said, 'not
since Easter, or perhaps Whitsun – I don't recall the date, but I
have all his letters upstairs. I grew worried. And the weeks went
by. Then, in July, the letter came. Only a page. Unlike himself, a
sort of scrawl. I showed it to my godfather, Nick Kendall, and

he agreed that I should start at once for Florence, which I did within a day or two. As I left another letter came, a few sentences only. I have both these letters in my pocket now. Do you want to see them?'

She did not answer immediately. She had turned back from the fire and was looking at me once again. There was something of compulsion in those eyes, neither forceful nor commanding, but strangely deep, strangely tender, as if she had the power to read and understand my reluctance to continue, knowing the reason for it, and so urged me on.

'Not just yet,' she said, 'afterwards.'

I shifted my gaze from her eyes down to her hands. They were clasped in front of her, small and very still. It was easier to speak somehow if I did not look directly at her, but at her hands.

'I arrived in Florence,' I said, 'I hired a carrozza and drove to your villa. The servant, the woman, opened the gate, and I asked for Ambrose. She seemed frightened and called to her husband. He came, and then he told me Ambrose was dead and you had gone away. He showed me the villa. I saw the room where he had died. Just before I left the woman opened a chest and gave me Ambrose's hat. It was the only thing you had forgotten to take with you.'

I paused, and went on looking at the hands. The right fingers were touching the ring on the left hand. I watched them tighten upon it.

'Go on,' she said.

'I went down into Florence,' I said. 'The servant had given me the address of Signor Rainaldi. I went and called upon him. He looked startled at sight of me, but soon recovered. He gave me the particulars of Ambrose's illness and death, also a note to the guardian at the Protestant cemetery should I care to visit the grave, which I did not. I enquired of your whereabouts, but he professed not to know. That was all. The following day I started back on my journey home.'

There was another pause. The fingers relaxed their hold upon the ring. 'Can I see the letters?' she said.

I took them from my pocket and gave them to her. I looked back again at the fire, and I heard the crinkle of the paper as she opened the letters. There was a long silence. Then she said, 'Only these two?'

'Only those two,' I answered.

'Nothing after Easter, or Whitsun, did you say, until these came?'

'No, nothing.'

She must have been reading them over and over, learning the words by heart as I had done. At last she gave them back to me.

'How you have hated me,' she said slowly.

I looked up, startled, and it seemed to me, as we stared at one another, that she knew now all my fantasies, my dreams, that she saw one by one the faces of the women I had conjured all those months. Denial was no use, protestation absurd. The barriers were down. It was a queer feeling, as though I sat naked in my chair.

'Yes,' I said.

It was easier, once said. Perhaps, I thought to myself, this is how a Catholic feels in the confessional. This is what it means to be purged. A burden lifted. Emptiness instead.

'Why did you ask me here?' she said.

'To accuse you.'

'Accuse me of what?'

'I am not sure. Perhaps of breaking his heart, which would be murder, wouldn't it?'

'And then?'

'I had not planned so far. I wanted, more than anything in the world, to make you suffer. To watch you suffer. Then, I suppose, to let you go.'

'That was generous. More generous than I should deserve. Still, you have been successful. You have got what you wanted. Go on watching me, until you've had your fill.'

Something was happening to the eyes that looked at me. The face was very white and still; that did not change. Had I ground the face to powder with my heel, the eyes would have remained, with the tears that never ran down upon the cheeks, and never fell.

I rose from my chair and walked across the room.

'It's no use,' I said. 'Ambrose always told me I would make a rotten soldier. I can't shoot in cold blood. Please go upstairs, or anywhere but here. My mother died before I can remember, and I have never seen a woman cry.' I opened the door for her. But she went on sitting there by the fire, she did not move.

'Cousin Rachel, go upstairs,' I said.

I don't know how my voice sounded, whether it was harsh, or loud, but old Don, lying on the floor, lifted his head and looked up at me, fixing me in his old-wise doggy fashion, and then stretching himself, and yawning, went and laid his head on her feet, beside the fire. Then she moved. She put down her hand and touched his head. I shut the door and came back to the hearth. I took the two letters and threw them in the fire.

'That's no use either,' she said, 'when we both of us remember what he said.'

'I can forget,' I said, 'if you will too. There's something clean about a fire. Nothing remains. Ashes don't count.'

'If you were a little older,' she said, 'or your life had been different, if you were anyone but yourself and had not loved him quite so much, I could talk to you about those letters, and about Ambrose. I won't, though; I would rather you condemned me. It makes it easier in the long run for both of us. If you will let me stay until Monday I will go away after that, and you need never think about me again. Although you did not intend it to be so, last night and today were deeply happy. Bless you, Philip.'

I stirred the fire with my foot, and the embers fell.

'I don't condemn you,' I said. 'Nothing has worked out as I thought or planned. I can't go on hating a woman who doesn't exist.'

'But I do exist.'

'You are not the woman I hated. There's no more to it than that.'

She went on stroking Don's head, and now he lifted it and leant it against her knee.

'This woman,' she said, 'that you pictured in your mind. Did she take shape when you read the letters, or before?'

I thought about it for a moment. Then I let it all come, with a rush of words. Why hold back anything to rot?

'Before,' I said slowly. 'In a sense I was relieved when the letters came. They gave me a reason for hating you. Up till then there was nothing I could go upon, and I was ashamed.'

'Why were you ashamed?'

'Because I believe there is nothing so self-destroying, and no emotion quite so despicable, as jealousy.'

'You were jealous . . .'

'Yes. I can say it now, oddly enough. Right from the start, when he wrote and told me he was married. Perhaps even before there may have been a sort of shadow, I don't know. Everyone expected me to be as delighted as they were themselves, and it wasn't possible. It must sound highly emotional and absurd to you that I should have been jealous. Like a spoilt child. Perhaps that's what I was, and am. The trouble is that I have never known anyone or loved anyone in the world but Ambrose.'

Now I was thinking aloud, not caring what she thought of me. I was putting things into words I had not acknowledged to myself before.

'Was not that his trouble too?' she said.

'How do you mean?'

She took her hand off Don's head, and cupping her chin in her hands, her elbows on her knee, she stared into the fire.

'You are only twenty-four, Philip,' she said, 'you have all your life before you, many years probably of happiness, married no doubt, with a wife you love, and children of your own. Your love for Ambrose will never grow less, but it will slip back into place where it belongs. The love of any son for any father. It was not so for him. Marriage came too late.'

I knelt on one knee before the fire and lit my pipe. I did not think to ask permission. I knew she did not mind.

'Why too late?' I asked.

'He was forty-three,' she said, 'when he came out to Florence

102

just two years ago, and I saw him for the first time. You know how he looked, how he spoke, his ways, his smile. It was your life since babyhood. But you would not know the effect it had upon a woman whose life had not been happy, who had known men – very different.'

I said nothing, but I think I understood.

'I don't know why he turned to me, but he did,' she said. 'Those things can never be explained, they happen. Why this man should love that woman, what queer chemical mix-up in our blood draws us to one another, who can tell? To me, lonely, anxious, and a survivor of too many emotional shipwrecks, he came almost as a saviour, as an answer to prayer. To be strong as he was, and tender too, lacking all personal conceit, I had not met with that. It was a revelation. I know what he was to me. But I to him . . .'

She paused, and drawing her brows together, frowned into the fire. Once again her fingers played with the ring on her left hand.

'He was like someone sleeping who woke suddenly and found the world,' she said, 'all the beauty of it, and the sadness too. The hunger and the thirst. Everything he had never thought about or known was there before him, and magnified themselves into one person who by chance, or fate, call it what you will, happened to be me. Rainaldi – whom he detested by the way, as you probably did too – told me once that Ambrose had woken to me just as some men wake to religion. He became obsessed, in the same fashion. But a man who gets religion can go into a monastery and pray all day before Our Lady on an altar. She is made of plaster anyway, and does not change. Women are not so, Philip. Their moods vary with the days and nights, sometimes even with the hours, just as a man's can do. We are human, that is our failing.'

I did not understand what she meant about religion. I could only think of old Isaiah, down at St Blazey, who turned Methodist and went about bare-headed preaching in the lanes. He called upon Jehovah, and said he and all of us were miserable sinners in the eyes of the Lord, and we must go knocking at the gates of a new Jerusalem. I did not see how this state of things applied to Ambrose. Catholics were different, of course. She must mean that Ambrose had thought of her like a graven image in the Ten Commandments. Thou shalt not bow down to them, nor worship them.

'You mean,' I said, 'that he expected too much of you? He put you on a sort of pedestal?'

'No,' she said, 'I would have welcomed a pedestal, after my rough life. A halo can be a lovely thing, providing you can take it off, now and again, and become human.'

'What then?'

She sighed, and her hands dropped to her side. She suddenly looked very tired. She leant back in her chair, and resting her head against the cushion closed her eyes.

'Finding religion does not always improve a person,' she said, 'waking to the world did not help Ambrose. His nature changed.'

Her voice sounded tired too, and oddly flat. Perhaps if I had been speaking in the confessional, so had she. She lay back in the chair pressing her eyes with the palms of her hands.

'Change?' I said. 'How did his nature change?'

I felt a queer sort of shock in my heart, like the shock that comes to you as a child when you suddenly learn of death, or of evil, or of cruelty.

'The doctors told me later that it was his illness,' she said, 'that he could not help himself, that qualities lying dormant all his life came to the surface at long last, through pain, and fear. But I shall never be sure. Never be certain that it need have happened. Something in me brought out those qualities. Finding me was ecstasy to him for one brief moment, and then catastrophe. You were right to hate me. If he had not come to Italy he would have been living here with you now. He would not have died.'

I felt ashamed, embarrassed. I did not know what to say. 'He might have become ill just the same,' I said, as though to help her. 'Then I would have borne the brunt of it, not you.'

She took her hands away from her face, and without moving looked across at me and smiled.

'He loved you so much,' she said. 'You might have been his son, he was so proud of you. Always my Philip would do this, my boy would do that. Why, Philip, if you have been jealous of me these eighteen months, I think we are quits. Heaven knows I could have done with less of you at times.'

I looked back at her, and slowly smiled.

'Did you make pictures too?' I asked her.

'I never stopped,' she said. 'That spoilt boy, I told myself, always writing letters to him, which I may say he would read extracts from, but never show. That boy who has no faults, but all the virtues. That boy who understands him, when I fail. That boy who holds three-quarters of his heart, and all the best of him. While I hold one-third, and all the worst. Oh, Philip . . .' She broke off, and smiled again at me. 'Good God,' she said, 'you talk of jealousy. A man's jealousy is like a child's, fitful and foolish, without depth. A woman's jealousy is adult, which is very different.' Then she put back the cushion from behind her head, and patted it. She straightened her gown, and sat upright in her chair. 'I would say that, for this night, I have talked to you enough,' she said. She bent forward, and picked up the piece of embroidery that had fallen on the floor.

'I'm not tired,' I said. 'I could go on longer, much longer. That is to say, not speaking perhaps myself, but listening to you.'

'We still have tomorrow,' she said.

'Why only tomorrow?'

'Because I go on Monday. I came for the week-end only. Your godfather, Nick Kendall, has invited me to Pelyn.'

It seemed to me absurd, and altogether pointless, that she should shift her quarters quite so soon.

'There's no need to go there,' I said, 'when you have only just arrived. You have plenty of time to visit Pelyn. You have not seen the half of this yet. I don't know what the servants would think, or the people on the estate. They would be deeply offended.'

'Would they?' she asked.

'Besides,' I said, 'there is the carrier coming from Plymouth, with all the plants and cuttings. You have to discuss it with Tamlyn. And there are Ambrose's things to go through and sort.'

'I thought you could do that by yourself,' she said.

'Why,' I said, 'when we could do it both of us together?'

I stood up from my chair and stretched my arms above my head. I kicked Don with my foot. 'Wake up,' I said, 'it's time you stopped that snoring and went out with the others to the kennels.' He stirred himself, and grunted. 'Lazy old devil,' I said. I glanced down at her, and she was looking up at me with such a strange expression in her eyes, almost as though she saw right through me into someone else.

'What is it?' I asked.

'Nothing,' she answered, 'nothing at all . . . Can you find me a candle, Philip, and light me up to bed?'

'Very well,' I said. 'I'll take Don to his kennel afterwards.'

The candlesticks were waiting on the table by the door. She took hers, and I lighted the candle for her. It was dark in the hall but above, on the landing, Seecombe had left a light to the further corridor.

'That will do,' she said. 'I can find my way alone.'

She stood a moment on one step of the staircase, her face in the shadow. One hand held the candlestick, the other held her dress.

'You don't hate me any more?' she asked.

'No,' I said, 'I told you it was not you. It was another woman.'

'Are you sure it was another woman?'

'Quite sure.'

'Good night, then. And sleep well.'

She turned to go, but I put my hand on her arm and held her back.

'Wait,' I said, 'it's my turn to ask you a question.'

'What is it, Philip?'

'Are you still jealous of me, or was that also some other man, and never me at all?'

She laughed and gave me her hand, and because she stood

106

above me on the stairs there seemed a new sort of grace about her that I had not realised before. Her eyes looked large in the flickering candlelight.

'That horrid boy, so spoilt and prim?' she said. 'Why, he went yesterday, as soon as you walked into aunt Phoebe's boudoir.'

Suddenly she bent, and kissed my cheek.

'The first you have ever had,' she said, 'and if you don't like it, you can pretend I did not give it to you, but that it came from the other woman.'

She walked up the stairs away from me, and the light of the candle threw a shadow, dark and distant, on the wall.

11

We always carried out a strict routine upon a Sunday. Breakfast was later, at nine o'clock, and at a quarter past ten the carriage came to take Ambrose and me to church. The servants followed in the waggonette. When church was over, they returned to eat their midday dinner, later again, at one; and then at four we dined ourselves, with the vicar and Mrs Pascoe, possibly one or two of the unmarried daughters, and generally my godfather and Louise. Since Ambrose had gone abroad I had not used the carriage but had ridden down to church on Gypsy, causing, I believe, some small amount of talk, I know not why.

This Sunday, in honour of my visitor, I gave orders for the carriage to come as of old custom, and my cousin Rachel, prepared for the event by Seecombe when he took her break-fast, descended to the hall upon the stroke of ten. A kind of ease had come upon me since the night before, and it seemed to me, as I looked upon her, that I could in future say to her what I pleased. Nothing need hold me back, neither anxiety, nor resent-ment, nor even common courtesy.

'A word of warning,' I said, after I had wished her a good morning. 'All eyes will be upon you in the church. Even the laggards, who sometimes make excuse to stay in bed, will not remain at home to-day. They will be standing in the aisles, maybe on tip-toe.'

'You terrify me,' she said. 'I shall not go at all.'

'That would be disgrace,' I said, 'for which neither you nor I would ever be forgiven.'

She looked at me with solemn eyes.

'I am not sure,' she said, 'that I know how to behave. I was bred a Catholic.'

'Keep it to yourself,' I told her. 'Papists, in this part of the world, are fit only for hellfire. Or so they tell me. Watch everything I do. I won't mislead you.'

The carriage came to the door. Wellington, with brushed hat and trim cockade, the groom beside him, was swollen with importance like a pouter pigeon. Seecombe, in starched clean stock and his Sunday coat, stood at the front door with no less dignity. It was the occasion of a lifetime.

I handed my cousin Rachel into the carriage and took my place beside her. She had a dark mantle around her shoulders, and the veil from her hat concealed her face.

'The people will want to see your face,' I said to her.

'Then they must want,' she answered.

'You don't understand,' I said. 'Nothing like this has happened in their lives. Not for nearly thirty years. The old people remember my aunt, I suppose, and my mother, but for the younger ones there has never been a Mrs Ashley come to church before. Besides, you must enlighten their ignorance. They know you come from what they term outlandish parts. For all they know Italians may be black.'

'Will you please be quiet?' she whispered. 'I can tell from Wellington's back there, up on the box, that he can hear what you are saying.'

'I shall not be quiet,' I said, 'the matter is of grave importance. I know how rumour spreads. All the countryside will go back to Sunday dinner shaking their heads and saying Mrs Ashley is a negress.'

'I will lift my veil in church, but not before,' she said, 'when I am kneeling. They can look then, if they have the mind, but by rights they should do no such thing. Their eyes should be on their prayer-books.'

'A high bench surrounds the pew, with curtains to it,' I told her. 'Once kneeling there you will be concealed from view. You can even play marbles if you want to. I used to, as a child.'

'Your childhood,' she said; 'don't speak of it. I know every detail. How Ambrose dismissed your nurse when you were three. How he took you out of petticoats and put you into breeches. The monstrous way in which you learnt your alphabet. I am not surprised you played at marbles in the church pew. I wonder you did no worse.'

'I did once,' I said. 'I brought white mice in my pocket and they ran under the seat. They scampered up the petticoat of an old lady in the pew behind. She had the vapours, and had to be removed.'

'Didn't Ambrose beat you for it?'

'Why, no. It was he who set them loose upon the floor.'

My cousin Rachel pointed to Wellington's back. His shoulders had stiffened, and his ears were red.

'You will behave yourself to-day, or I shall walk out of the church,' she said to me.

'Then everyone would think *you* had the vapours,' I said, 'and my godfather and Louise would come rushing to your assistance. Oh, great heaven . . .' I broke off, and clapped my hand on my knee in consternation.

'What's the matter?'

'I've only just remembered. I promised to ride over yesterday to Pelyn to see Louise, and I forgot all about it. She may have waited for me all afternoon.'

'That,' said my cousin Rachel, 'was not very gallant of you. I hope she snubs you well.'

'I shall blame it upon you,' I said, 'which will be the truth. I shall say you demanded to be taken round the Barton.'

'I would not have asked you to do so,' she said, 'had I known you were supposed to be elsewhere. Why did you not tell me?'

'Because I had forgotten all about it.'

'If I were Louise,' she said, 'I would take that in bad part. You could not offer a woman a worse excuse.'

'Louise isn't a woman,' I said, 'she's younger than myself, and I have known her since she ran around in petticoats.'

'That's no answer. She has feelings just the same.'

'Ah well, she will get over them. She will sit next to me at dinner, and I shall tell her how well she arranged the flowers.'

'What flowers?'

'The flowers in the house. The flowers in your boudoir, and in the bedroom. She drove over especially to do them.'

'How very thoughtful.'

'She did not trust Seecombe to do them properly.'

'I don't blame her for that. She showed great delicacy and taste. I liked best of all the bowl on the mantelpiece in the boudoir, and the autumn crocus beside the window.'

'Was there a bowl on the mantelpiece,' I said, 'and another by the window? I did not notice either. But I will compliment her just the same, and hope she does not ask for a description.'

I looked at her, and laughed, and I saw the eyes smile back at me under the veil, but she shook her head.

We had descended the steep hill and turned along the lane, and were now come to the village and the church. As I had thought, there was a gathering of people by the rails. I knew most of them, but there were many besides drawn there by curiosity. There was a sort of pressure amongst them as the carriage drew up before the gate and we alighted. I took off my hat and offered my cousin Rachel my arm. I had seen my godfather do this to Louise a score of times. We walked up the path to the church door, the people staring at us. I had expected to feel myself a fool, and out of my own character, but it was quite otherwise. I felt confident and proud, and oddly pleased. I stared ahead of me, looking neither to right nor to left, and as we passed the men took their hats off to us and the women curtsied. I could not remember them doing this to me alone. It was, after all, a great occasion.

As we entered the church, and the bells were ringing, those people who were already seated in their pews turned round to look at us. There was a scraping of feet amongst the men, and a rustle of skirts amongst the women. We walked up the aisle past the Kendall pew to our own. I caught sight of my godfather, his bushy brows drawn straight together, a thoughtful

111

expression on his face. No doubt he was wondering how I had conducted myself during the past forty-eight hours. Good breeding forbade him to look at either of us. Louise sat beside him, very stiff and straight. She had a haughty air about her, and I supposed I had given her offence. But as I stepped aside to let my cousin Rachel enter the pew first, curiosity proved too much for Louise. She glanced up, stared at my visitor, and then caught my eye. She raised her eyebrows in a question. I pretended not to see, and closed the door of the pew behind me. The congregation knelt in prayer.

It was a queer sensation having a woman in the pew beside me. My memory went right back to childhood, when Ambrose took me first, and I had to stand on a footstool to look over the bench in front of me. I would copy Ambrose, holding the prayer-book in my hands, but very often upside down; and when it came to murmuring the responses I would echo the mumble he made, with no thought as to meaning. As I grew taller I would pull the curtains aside and look out upon the people, watch the parson and the choir boys in their stalls, and later, on holiday from Harrow, sit back with folded arms as Ambrose did, and doze if the sermon proved too long. Now I had come to manhood church had become a period for reflection. Not, I regret to say, upon my failings and omissions, but upon my plans for the forth-coming week; what must be done upon the farmlands or in the woods, what I must say to Seecombe's nephew at the fish-house in the bay, what forgotten order must be passed on to Tamlyn. I had sat in the pew alone, locked in myself, with nothing and no one to distract me. I sang the psalms and gave the responses from long habit. This Sunday was different. I was aware of her beside me all the time. There was no question of her not know-ing what to do. She might have attended a Church of England service every Sunday of her life. She sat very still, her eyes fixed gravely upon the vicar, and when she knelt I noticed that she knelt full upon her knees, and did not sit half upon the seat as Ambrose and I were wont to do. Nor did she rustle, turn her head, or stare about her, as Mrs Pascoe and her daughters always

112

did, from their pew in the side aisle where the vicar could not see them. When we came to sing the hymns she put up her veil, and I saw her lips follow the words, but I did not hear her sing. She lowered the veil again when we sat down to listen to the sermon.

I wondered who had been the last women to sit here in the Ashley pew. Aunt Phoebe possibly, sighing for her curate; or uncle Philip's wife, Ambrose's mother, whom I had never seen. Perhaps my father had sat here, before he went away to fight the French and lose his life, and my own mother, young and delicate, who survived my father, Ambrose told me, a bare five months. I had never thought much about them, or felt the lack of them, Ambrose had answered for them both. But now, looking at my cousin Rachel, I wondered about my mother. Had she knelt there, on that footstool beside my father; had she sat back, and clasped her hands on her lap in front of her, and listened to the sermon? And afterwards, did she drive back home and go to pick me from my cradle? I wondered, sitting there as Mr Pascoe's voice droned on, what it had felt like as a child, being held in my mother's arms. Had she touched my hair and kissed my cheek, and then, smiling, put me back into the cradle? I wished suddenly that I could remember her. Why was it that a child's mind could not return beyond a certain limit? I had been a little boy, staggering after Ambrose, shouting to him to wait for me. Nothing before that. Nothing at all . . .

'And now to God the Father, God the Son, and God the Holy Ghost.' The vicar's words brought me to my feet. I had not heard a word of his sermon. Nor had I planned my week to come. I had sat there dreaming, and watching my cousin Rachel.

I reached for my hat, and touched her arm. 'You did very well,' I whispered, 'but your real ordeal is now before you.'

'Thank you,' she whispered back, 'so is yours. You have to make amends for your broken promise.'

We went out of the church into the sun, and there waiting for us was a little crowd of people, tenants, acquaintances and friends, and amongst them Mrs Pascoe, the vicar's wife, and her daughters, as well as my godfather and Louise. One by one they came up to be presented. We might have been at Court. My cousin Rachel put up her veil, and I made a mental note to tease her about it when we were alone again.

As we walked down the path to the waiting carriages she said to me before the others, so that I could not remonstrate – and I could tell by the look in her eye and the bubble in her voice that she did it purposely – 'Philip, would you not like to conduct Miss Kendall in your carriage, and I will go with Mr Kendall in his?'

'Why certainly, if you prefer it,' I said.

'That seems to me a very happy arrangement,' she said, smiling at my godfather, who, bowing in his turn, offered her his arm. They turned with one accord to the Kendall carriage, and there was nothing for it but to climb into the first one with Louise. I felt like a schoolboy who has been slapped. Wellington whipped up the horses and we were off.

'Look here, Louise, I'm sorry,' I began at once, 'it was quite impossible to get away yesterday afternoon after all. My cousin Rachel wished to see the Barton acres, so I accompanied her. There was no time to let you know, or I would have sent the boy over with a note.'

'Oh, don't apologise,' she said. 'I waited about two hours, but it did not matter. The day was luckily fine, and I passed the time by picking a basket of late blackberries.'

'It was most unfortunate,' I said, 'I'm really very sorry.'

'I guessed something of the sort had kept you,' she said, 'but I am thankful it was nothing serious. I know how you felt about the whole visit, and I was rather fearful that you might do something violent, perhaps have some terrible disagreement, and we would suddenly find her arriving on our doorstep. Well, what happened? Have you really survived so far without a clash? Tell me all.'

I tilted my hat over my eyes and folded my arms.

'All? What do you mean by "all"?'

'Why, everything. What did you say to her, how did she take

114

it. Was she very much aghast by all you said, or did she show no sign of guilt at all?'

Her voice was low, and Wellington could not hear, but for all that I felt irritated, and altogether out of humour. What a place and time to choose for such a conversation, and anyway, why must she catechise me at all?

'We've had little time for talking,' I said. 'The first evening she was tired, and went early to bed. Yesterday was taken up by walking about the place. The gardens in the morning, and the Barton lands in the afternoon.'

'Then you've had no serious discussion whatsoever?'

'It depends what you mean by serious. All I know is that she is a very different sort of person from what I thought she would be. You can see that for yourself, in the brief glimpse you've had of her.'

Louise was silent. She did not lean back against the carriage seat as I did. She sat bolt upright, her hands in her muff.

'She's very beautiful,' she said at last.

I took my legs down from the seat opposite and turned round to stare at her.

'Beautiful?' I said, amazed. 'My dear Louise, you must be mad.'

'Oh, no, I'm not,' replied Louise. 'Ask my father, ask anyone. Didn't you notice how the people stared when she put up her veil? It's only because you are so blind to women that you have not noticed it.'

'I've never heard such nonsense in my life,' I said. 'Perhaps she has fine eyes, but otherwise she is quite ordinary. The most ordinary person I have ever met. Why, I can say what I like to her, I can talk of anything, I don't have to put on any sort of special manner of behaviour in front of her, it is the easiest thing in the whole world merely to sit down in a chair in front of her and light my pipe.'

'I thought you said you had no time to talk to her?'

'Don't quibble. Of course we talked at dinner, and out upon the acres. The point I wish to make is that it required no effort.'

'Evidently.'

'As to being beautiful, I shall have to tell her. She will laugh at that. Naturally the people stared at her. They stared at her because she was Mrs Ashley.'

'That as well. But not entirely. Anyway, whether she be ordinary or not, she seems to have made a great impression on you. Of course she is middle-aged. Quite thirty-five I should say, wouldn't you? Or do you think her less?'

'I haven't the remotest idea, not do I care, Louise. I'm not interested in people's ages. She could be ninety-nine for all I know.'

'Don't be ridiculous. Women don't have eyes like that at ninety-nine, nor that complexion. She dresses well. That gown was excellently cut, so was the mantle. Mourning certainly does not appear drab on her.'

'Great heavens, Louise, you might be Mrs Pascoe. I've never before in my life heard such woman-ish sort of gossip come from you.'

'Nor I such enthusiasm from you, so it's tit-for-tat. What a change in forty-eight hours. Well, one person will be relieved and that's my father. He feared bloodshed, after you saw him last, and who shall blame him?'

I was thankful the long hill had come, so that I could get out of the carriage and walk up it, with the groom, to ease the horses as was our custom. What an extraordinary attitude for Louise to take. Instead of being relieved that my cousin Rachel's visit was passing off so well she appeared quite put out, almost angry. It seemed to me a poor way to show her friendship. When we came to the top of the hill I climbed in again and sat beside her, and we did not say a word to one another the whole way. It was quite ridiculous, but if she made no attempt to break the silence I was damned if I would either. I could not help reflecting how much more pleasant had been the drive going down to church than the return.

I wondered how the other pair had fared in the second carriage. Pretty well, it seemed. When we descended from our carriage and Wellington had turned round to make way for them,

Louise and I stood by the door and waited for my godfather and my cousin Rachel. They were chattering like old friends, and my godfather, generally rather blunt and taciturn, was holding forth upon some subject with unusual warmth. I caught the words 'disgraceful' and 'the country won't stand for it.' I knew then that he was launched upon his favourite subject, the Government and the Opposition. I wagered to myself that he, for his part, had probably not eased the horses by walking up the hill.

'Did you have a pleasant drive?' enquired my cousin Rachel, searching my eye, a tremor at her mouth, and I could swear she knew from our stiff faces how the drive had been.

'Thank you, yes,' said Louise, standing back, allowing her to pass first, in courtesy; but my cousin Rachel took her arm and said, 'Come with me to my room, and take off your coat and hat. I want to thank you for the lovely flowers.'

My godfather and I had barely had time to wash our hands and exchange greetings before the entire family of Pascoe was upon us, and it devolved upon me to escort the vicar and his daughters round the gardens. The vicar was harmless enough, but I could have dispensed with the daughters. As to the vicar's wife, Mrs Pascoe, she had gone upstairs to join the ladies like a hound after quarry. She had never seen the blue room out of dust covers . . . The daughters were loud in praise of my cousin Rachel, and like Louise professed to find her beautiful. It delighted me to tell them that I found her small and entirely unremarkable, and they uttered little squeals of protestation. 'Not unremarkable,' said Mr Pascoe, flipping the head of a hortensia with his cane, 'certainly not unremarkable. Nor would I say, as the girls do, beautiful. But feminine, that is the word, most decidedly feminine.'

'But, father,' said one of the daughters, 'surely you would not expect Mrs Ashley to be anything else?'

'My dear,' said the vicar, 'you would be surprised how many women lack that very quality.'

I thought of Mrs Pascoe and her horselike head, and swiftly pointed out the young palms that Ambrose had brought back from Egypt, which they must have seen a score of times before, thus turning, it seemed to me with tact, the conversation.

When we returned to the house, and entered the drawing-room, we discovered Mrs Pascoe telling my cousin Rachel in loud tones about her kitchen-maid, brought to trouble by the garden boy.

'What I cannot understand, Mrs Ashley, is where it happened? She shared a room with my cook, and as far as we know never left the house.'

'How about the cellar?' said my cousin Rachel.

The conversation was instantly stifled as we came into the room. Not since Ambrose had been home two years before had I ever known a Sunday pass as swiftly. And even when he was there it had dragged many times. Disliking Mrs Pascoe, indifferent to the daughters, and merely suffering Louise because she was the daughter of his oldest friend, he had always angled for the vicar's company alone, with my godfather's. Then the four of us had been able to relax. When the women came the hours had seemed like days. This day was different.

Dinner, when it was served, with the meats upon the table and the silver polished, seemed to spread itself before us like a banquet. I sat at the head of the table, where Ambrose had always sat, and my cousin Rachel at the further end. It gave me Mrs Pascoe as a neighbour, but for once she did not goad me to a fury. Three-quarters of the time her large enquiring face was turned to the other end; she laughed, she ate, she forgot even to snap her jaws at her husband, the vicar, who, drawn out of his shell for possibly the first time in his life, flushed and with eyes afire, proceeded to quote poetry. The entire Pascoe family blossomed like the rose, and I had never seen my godfather enjoy himself so much.

Only Louise seemed silent, and withdrawn. I did my best with her, but she did not, or would not, respond. She sat stiffly on my left hand, eating little and crumbling bits of bread, with a fixed expression on her face as if she had swallowed a marble. Well, if she wanted to sulk, then sulk she must. I was too much entertained myself to worry with her. I sat hunched in my chair, resting my arms on the sides of it, laughing at my cousin Rachel, who kept encouraging the vicar with his verse. This, I thought to myself, is the most fantastic Sunday dinner I have ever sat through, eaten, and enjoyed, and I would have given the whole world for Ambrose to be there, sharing it with us. When we had finished dessert, and the port was put upon the table, I did not know whether I should rise, as I usually did, to open the door, or if, now I had a hostess opposite me, it would be her place to give some signal. There was a pause in the conversation. Suddenly she looked at me and smiled. I smiled back at her in answer. We seemed to hold each other for a moment. It was queer, strange. The feeling went right through me, never before known.

Then my godfather remarked in his gruff deep voice, 'Tell me, Mrs Ashley, does not Philip remind you very much of Ambrose?'

There was a moment's silence. She put down her napkin on the table. 'So much so,' she said, 'that I have wondered, sitting here at dinner, if there is any difference.'

She rose to her feet, the other women too, and I went across the dining-room and opened the door. But when they were gone, and I had returned to my chair, the feeling was with me still.

12

They all went off about six o'clock, as the vicar had to take evensong in another parish. I heard Mrs Pascoe engage my cousin Rachel to pass an afternoon with her during the week, and each of the Pascoe daughters pressed their claims upon her too. One wanted advice upon a water-colour, another had a set of covers to be worked in tapestry and could not decide upon the wools, a third always read aloud to a sick woman in the village every Thursday, could my cousin Rachel possibly accompany her, the poor soul had such a wish to see her. 'Indeed,' said Mrs Pascoe, as we advanced through the hall to the front door, 'there are so many people who desire to make your acquaintance, Mrs Ashley, that I think you can reckon upon engagements every afternoon for the next four weeks.'

'She can do that very well from Pelyn,' said my godfather; 'we are situated handily for visiting. More so than here. And I rather believe we are to have the pleasure of her company within a day or two.'

He glanced at me, and I made haste to reply and squash the idea before further entanglement was possible.

'Not so, sir,' I said, 'my cousin Rachel remains here for the present. Before she becomes involved in any outside invitations she has the whole of the estate to visit. We begin to-morrow by taking tea at the Barton. The rest of the farms must be taken in their turn. Great offence will be given if she does not pay her respects to every one of the tenants in strict precedence.'

I saw Louise look at me wide-eyed, but I took no notice.

'Oh, well, yes of course,' said my godfather, in his turn surprised, 'very right, very proper. I would have suggested conducting Mrs Ashley myself, but if you are prepared to do that is quite another matter. And if,' he went on, turning to my cousin Rachel, 'you find yourself uncomfortable here – Philip will forgive me, I know, for saying this, but they have not been used to entertaining ladies here for many years, as you doubtless know, and things may be a little rough – or if you would like a woman's company, I know my daughter will only be too ready to receive you.'

'We have a guest-room at the vicarage,' said Mrs Pascoe. 'If at any time you should be lonely, Mrs Ashley, always remember it is at your disposal. We should be so happy to have you with us.'

'Indeed, indeed,' echoed the vicar; and I wondered if another tag of poetry was ready on his lips.

'You are all very kind and more than generous,' said my cousin Rachel. 'When I have done my duty here, on the estate, we will talk about it again, shall we? Meanwhile, believe me grateful.'

There was much clatter and chatter and saying of good-byes, and the carriages drove away down the drive.

We went back into the drawing-room. The evening had passed pleasantly enough, heaven knows, but I was glad that they had gone and the house was silent once again. She must have had the same thought, for as she stood a moment, looking around her in the drawing-room, she said, 'I love the stillness of a room, after a party. The chairs are moved, the cushions disarranged, everything is there to show that people enjoyed themselves; and one comes back to the empty room happy that it's over, happy to relax and say, 'Now we are alone again.' Ambrose used to say to me in Florence that it was worth the tedium of visitors to experience the pleasure of their going. He was so right.'

I watched her as she smoothed the covering of a chair, and touched a cushion. 'You don't have to do that,' I told her. 'Seecombe and John and the rest will see to it to-morrow.'

'A woman's instinct,' she said to me. 'Don't look at me; sit down and fill your pipe. Have you enjoyed yourself?'

'I have.' I lay sideways, sprawling on a stool. 'I don't know why,' I added, 'usually I find Sundays a great bore. It's because

121

I'm not a conversationalist. All I had to do to-day was to sit back in my chair and let you do the talking for me.'

'That's where a woman can be useful,' she said; 'it's part of their training. Instinct warns them what to do if conversation flags.'

'Yes, but you don't make it obvious,' I said. 'Mrs Pascoe is very different. She goes on and on until one wants to scream. No man ever got a chance to talk on other Sundays. I can't think what it is you did to make it all so pleasant.'

'So it was pleasant?'

'Why, yes, I've told you so.'

'Then you had better hurry up and marry your Louise, and have a real hostess, not just a bird of passage.'

I sat up on the stool, and stared at her. She was smoothing her hair before the mirror.

'Marry Louise?' I said. 'Don't be absurd. I don't want to marry anyone. And she isn't 'my' Louise.'

'Oh!' said my cousin Rachel. 'I rather thought she was. At least, your godfather gave me that impression.'

She sat down on one of the chairs and took up her embroidery. Just then young John came in to draw the curtains, so I was silent. I was fuming, though. By what right did my godfather make such an assumption? I waited until John had gone.

'What did my godfather say?' I asked.

'I don't remember, specifically,' she said; 'I just think he felt it was an understood thing. He mentioned, driving back from church in the carriage, that his daughter had come over here to do the flowers, and that it had been such a handicap for you, brought up in a household of men; the sooner you married and had a wife to look after you the better. He said Louise understood you very well, as you did her. I hope you apologised for your bad manners on Saturday.'

'Yes, I apologised,' I said, 'but it did not seem to make much difference. I have never met Louise in so vile a humour. By the way, she thinks you are beautiful. And so do the Miss Pascoes.'

'How very flattering.'

'And the vicar does not agree with them.'

'How distressing.'

'But he finds you feminine. Decidedly feminine.'

'I wonder in what way?'

'I suppose in a way different from Mrs Pascoe.'

A bubble of laughter escaped from her, and she glanced up from her embroidery. 'How would you define it, Philip?'

'Define what?'

'The difference in our femininity, Mrs Pascoe's and mine.'

'Oh, heaven knows,' I said, kicking the leg of the stool, 'I don't know anything about the subject. All I know is that I like looking at you, and I don't like looking at Mrs Pascoe.'

'That's a nice simple answer, thank you, Philip.'

I might have said the same about her hands. I liked watching them too. Mrs Pascoe's hands were like boiled hams.

'It's all nonsense about Louise, anyway,' I said, 'so please forget it. I have never considered her as a wife, and don't intend to.'

'Poor Louise.'

'Ridiculous of my godfather to have got such an idea into his head.'

'Not really. When two young people are of the same age, and thrown much together, and like each other's company, it is very natural that onlookers should think of marriage. Besides, she is a nice, good-looking girl, and very capable. She would make you an excellent wife.'

'Cousin Rachel, will you be quiet?'

She looked up at me again, and smiled.

'And another thing you can be quiet about is this nonsense of visiting everybody,' I said, 'staying at the vicarage, staying at Pelyn. What is wrong with this house, and with my company?'

'Nothing, as yet.'

'Well, then . . .'

'I will stay until Seecombe becomes tired of me.'

'Seecombe has nothing to do with it,' I said, 'nor Wellington nor Tamlyn, nor anyone at all. I am the master here, and it has to do with me.'

'Then I must do as I am bid,' she answered; 'that is part of a woman's training too.'

I glanced at her suspiciously to see if she was laughing, but she was looking at her work and I could not see her eyes.

'To-morrow,' I said, 'I shall draw up a list of the tenants, in order of seniority. The ones who have served the family longest will be the first to be visited. We will start with the Barton, as arranged on Saturday. We will set forth at two o'clock every afternoon until there is not a single individual on the estate that you have not met.'

'Yes, Philip.'

'You will have to write a note of explanation to Mrs Pascoe and those girls, explaining you are otherwise engaged.'

'I will do so to-morrow morning.'

'When we have finished with our own people, you will have to stay in the house three afternoons a week, I believe it is Tuesdays, Thursdays, and Fridays, in case you are called upon by the county.'

'How do you know the days?'

'Because I have heard them discussed often enough by the Pascoes and Louise.'

'I see. And do I sit alone here in the drawing-room, or do you sit with me, Philip?'

'You sit alone. They will call upon you, not me. Receiving the county is not part of a man's work.'

'Supposing I am invited out to dinner, may I accept?'

'You will not be invited. You are in mourning. If there is any question of entertaining, we shall do it here. But never more than two couples at a time.'

'Is that etiquette in this part of the world?' she asked.

'Etiquette be blowed,' I answered her. 'Ambrose and I never followed etiquette; we made our own.'

I saw her bend her head lower over her work, and I had a shrewd suspicion it was to hide laughter, though what she was laughing at I could not say. I was not trying to be funny.

'I suppose,' she said, after a moment, 'you would not care to draw up for me a little list of rules? A code of conduct? I could study it here, while I am waiting to be called upon. It would be very unfortunate if I made some social *faux pas*, according to your lights, and so disgraced myself.'

'You can say what you please, to whom you please,' I said; 'all I ask is that you say it here, in the drawing-room. Never allow anyone to enter the library, under any pretext whatsoever.'

'Why? What will be happening in the library?'

'*I* shall be sitting there. With my feet upon the mantel.'

'On Tuesdays, Thursdays, and on Fridays too?'

'Not on Thursdays. On Thursdays I go into town to the bank.'

She held her skeins of silk closer to the candlesticks to examine the colour, and then folded them and wrapped them in her work. She rolled the work into a bundle, and put it aside.

I glanced at the clock. It was early yet. Did she think of going upstairs so soon? I had a sense of disappointment.

'And when the county have finished calling upon me,' she said, 'what happens then?'

'Why, then, you are obliged to return their calls, every single one of them. I will order the carriage every afternoon for two o'clock. I beg your pardon. Not every afternoon. But every Tuesday, Thursday and Friday.'

'And I go alone?'

'You go alone.'

'And what do I have to do on Mondays and on Wednesdays?'

'On Mondays and on Wednesdays, let me see . . .' I considered rapidly, invention failing me. 'Do you sketch at all, or sing? Like the Miss Pascoes? You could practise singing on the Mondays, and draw or paint upon the Wednesdays.'

'I neither sketch nor sing,' said my cousin Rachel, 'and I am afraid you are drawing up for me a programme of leisure for which I am entirely unsuited. If, instead of waiting for the county to call upon me, I call upon them for the purpose of giving them lessons in Italian, that would suit me much better.'

She rose to her feet, having snuffed the candles in the tall stand beside her. I stood up from my stool.

'Mrs Ashley give lessons in Italian?' I said, in mock horror. 'What a disgrace upon the name. Only spinsters give lessons, when they have no one to support them.'

'And what do widows do who find themselves in similar circumstances?' she asked.

'Widows?' I said, not thinking. 'Oh, widows marry again as fast as possible, or sell their rings.'

'I see. Well, I intend doing neither. I prefer giving lessons in Italian.' She patted me on the shoulder and left the room, calling good night over her shoulder.

I felt myself go scarlet. Good God, what had I said? I had spoken without a thought of her condition, forgetting who she was and what had happened. I had fallen into the fun of conversation with her as I might have done with Ambrose in the past, and had let my tongue run away with me in consequence. Remarry. Sell her rings. What in heaven's name could she have thought of me?

How blundering, how unfeeling, how altogether oafish and ill-bred I must have seemed. I could feel the colour mount right up the back of my neck to the roots of my hair. Hell and damnation. No use apologising. It would make too big a business of it. Better to let it go, and hope and pray she would forget. I was thankful nobody else had been present, my godfather, say, to draw me aside and frown at such breach of manners. Or suppose it had been at table, and Seecombe waiting, and young John? Remarry. Sell her rings. Oh, Lord . . . Oh, Lord . . . What on earth could have possessed me? I should not sleep now for the night, I should lie awake and toss and turn, and all the while hear that reply of hers, swift as lightning, 'I intend doing neither. I prefer giving lessons in Italian.'

I called Don, and letting myself out by the side-door I walked out in the grounds. As I walked it seemed to me that my offence grew worse instead of better. Coarse, unthinking, empty-headed lout . . . And what had she meant anyway? Was it possible that she had so little money that she was really serious in what she said? Mrs Ashley give lessons in Italian? I remembered her letter to my godfather from Plymouth. That she planned, after a short rest, to go to London. I remembered what that man Rainaldi had said, that she was obliged to sell the villa in Florence. I remembered, or rather I realised, with the full force of its application, that in Ambrose's will he had left her nothing, nothing at all. Every penny of his property belonged to me. I remembered, once again, the servants' gossip. No provision made for Mrs Ashley. What in the world would they think, in the servants' hall, on the estate, in the neighbourhood, in the county, if Mrs Ashley went about giving lessons in Italian?

Two days ago, three days ago, I would not have cared. She could have starved, that other woman of my fancy, and deserved it. But not now. Now it was different. The whole situation had entirely changed. Something would have to be done about it, and I did not know what. I could not possibly discuss it with her. The very thought made me go scarlet again with shame and embarrassment too. Then, with a sensation of relief, I suddenly remembered that the money and the property were not yet legally mine, and would not become so until my birthday in six months' time. Therefore it was out of my hands. It was the responsibility of my godfather. He was trustee to the estate, and my guardian. Therefore it was for him to approach my cousin Rachel and make some sort of provision for her out of the estate. I would go to see him about it at the first opportunity. My name need not come into the matter. It could seem as though it was just a piece of legal business that would have happened anyway, the custom in this country. Yes, that was the solution. Thank heaven I had thought of it. Italian lessons . . . How shaming, how appalling.

Feeling easier in mind I came back to the house, but I still had not forgotten the original blunder. Remarry, sell the rings . . . I came to the edge of the grass by the east front and whistled softly to Don, who was sniffing in the undergrowth. My footsteps crunched slightly on the gravel path. I heard a voice call down to me, 'Do you often go walking in the woods at night?' It was my cousin Rachel. She was sitting, without a light, at the open window of the blue bedroom. My blunder came upon me with full force, and I thanked heaven she could not see my face.

'At times,' I said, 'when I have something on my mind.'

'Does that mean you have something on your mind to-night?'

'Why, yes,' I answered. 'I came to a serious conclusion walking in the woods.'

'What was it?'

'I came to the conclusion that you were perfectly right to dislike the sound of me, before you saw me, and to consider me, as you did, conceited, pert and spoilt. I am all three, and worse than that besides.'

She leant forward, her arms upon the window-sill.

'Then walking in the woods is bad for you,' she said, 'and your conclusions very stupid.'

'Cousin Rachel . . .'

'Yes?'

But I did not know how to make my apology. The words that had strung themselves so easily to make a blunder in the drawing-room would not come now that I wished the blunder remedied. I stood there below her window, tongue-tied and ashamed. Suddenly I saw her turn and stretch behind her, and then she leaned forward once again and threw something at me from the window. It struck me on the cheek and fell to the ground. I stooped to pick it up. It was one of the flowers from her bowl, an autumn crocus.

'Don't be so foolish, Philip; go to bed,' she said.

She closed her window and drew the curtains; and somehow my shame went from me, and the blunder too, and I felt light of heart.

It was not possible to ride over to Pelyn in the early part of the week, because of the programme I had drawn up for visiting the tenants. Besides, I could hardly have made the excuse of seeing my godfather without taking my cousin Rachel to call upon Louise. On Thursday my opportunity arrived. The carrier came from Plymouth with all the shrubs and plants that she had brought with her from Italy, and as soon as Seecombe gave her

the news of this — I was just finishing my breakfast at the time
— my cousin Rachel was dressed and downstairs, her lace shawl
wound about her head, prepared to go out into the garden. The
door of the diningroom was open to the hall and I saw her pass.
I went out to say good morning.

'I understood,' I said, 'that Ambrose told you no woman was
fit to look upon before eleven. What are you doing downstairs
at half-past eight?'

'The carrier has come,' she said, 'and at half-past eight on the
last morning of September I am not a woman; I am a gardener.
Tamlyn and I have work to do.'

She looked gay and happy as a child might do at the prospect
of a treat.

'Are you going to count the plants?' I asked her.

'Count them? No,' she answered, 'I have to see how many
have survived the journey and which are worth putting in the
soil at once. Tamlyn will not know, but I shall. No hurry for
the trees, we can do that at our leisure, but I would like to see
the plants in right away.' I noticed that she wore upon her hands
an old rough pair of gloves, most incongruous on her neat small
person.

'You are not going to grub about the soil yourself?' I asked
her.

'But of course I am. You'll see. I shall work faster than Tamlyn
and his men. Do not expect me home for any midday meal.'

'But this afternoon,' I protested. 'We were expected at Lankelly
and at Coombe. The farm kitchens will be scrubbed, and tea
prepared.'

'You must send a note postponing the visit,' she said. 'I commit
myself to nothing when there is planting to be done. Good-bye.'
And she waved her hand at me and passed through the front
door on to the gravel drive.

'Cousin Rachel?' I called at her from the dining-room window.

'What is it?' she said over her shoulder.

'Ambrose was wrong in what he said of women,' I shouted.
'At half-past eight in the morning they look very well indeed.'

'Ambrose was not referring to half-past eight,' she called back to me; 'he was referring to half-past six, and he did not mean downstairs.'

I turned back laughing into the dining-room, and saw Seecombe standing at my elbow, his lips pursed. He moved, with disapproval, to the sideboard, and motioned to young John to remove the breakfast dishes. One thing at least about this day of planting, I should not be wanted. I altered my arrangements for the morning, and giving orders for Gypsy to be saddled I was away on the road to Pelyn by ten o'clock. I found my godfather at home and in his study, and without any preamble I broached the subject of my visit.

'So you understand,' I said to him, 'something will have to be done, and right away. Why, if it should reach Mrs Pascoe's ears that Mrs Ashley considers giving lessons in Italian it would be about the county in twenty-four hours.'

My godfather, as I had expected, looked most shocked and pained.

'Oh, disgraceful,' he agreed, 'quite out of the question. It would never do at all. The matter is a delicate one, of course. I must have time to think this out, how to approach the business.'

I became impatient. I knew his cautious legal frame of mind. He would fiddle-faddle with the job for days.

'We have no time to waste,' I said. 'You don't know my cousin Rachel as well as I do. She is quite capable of saying to one of the tenants, in her easy way, 'Do you know of anyone who would like to learn Italian?' And where should we be then? Besides, I have heard gossip already, through Seecombe. Everyone knows that she has been left nothing in the will. All that must be rectified, and at once.'

He looked thoughtful, and bit his pen.

'That Italian adviser said nothing of her circumstances,' he said. 'It is unfortunate that I cannot discuss the matter with him. We have no means of knowing the extent of her private income, or what settlement was made upon her by her previous marriage.'

'I believe everything went to pay Sangalletti's debts,' I said. 'I remember Ambrose said as much in his letters to me. It was one of the reasons why they did not come home last year, her financial affairs were so involved. No doubt that is why she has to sell that villa. Why, she may scarcely have a penny to her name. We must do something for her, and to-day.'

My godfather sorted his papers spread upon the desk.

'I am very glad, Philip,' he said, glancing at me over his spectacles, 'that you have changed your attitude. I was most uncomfortable before your cousin Rachel came. You were prepared to be very unpleasantly rude, and do absolutely nothing for her, which would have caused a scandal. At least you now see reason.'

'I was mistaken,' I said shortly; 'we can forget all that.'

'Well then,' he answered, 'I will write a letter to Mrs Ashley, and to the bank. I will explain to her, and to the bank, what the estate is prepared to do. The best plan will be to pay a quarterly cheque, from the estate, into an account which I will open for her. When she moves to London, or elsewhere, the branch there will have instructions from us here. In six months' time, when you become twenty-five, you will be able to handle the business yourself. Now, as to the sum of money every quarter. What do you suggest?'

I thought a moment, and named a figure.

'That is generous, Philip,' he said, 'rather over-generous. She will hardly need as much as that. Not at the moment, at least.'

'Oh, for God's sake, don't let's be niggardly,' I said. 'If we do this thing, let us do it as Ambrose would have done it, or not at all.'

'H'm,' he said. He scribbled a figure or two on his blotter.

'Well, she should be pleased by this,' he said; 'it should atone for any disappointment with the will.'

How hard and cold-blooded was the legal mind. Scratching away there with his pen at sums and figures, reckoning up shillings and pence, how much the estate could afford. Lord! how I hated money.

'Hurry, sir,' I said, 'and write your letter. Then I can take it

131

back with me. I can ride to the bank also, so that they have your letter too. My cousin Rachel can then draw from them at once.'

'My dear fellow, Mrs Ashley will hardly be as pushed as that. You are going from one extreme to the other.'

He sighed, and drew a sheet of paper before him on the blotter.

'She was correct when she said you were like Ambrose,' he replied.

This time, when he wrote his letter, I stood over him, so that I could be certain what he said to her. He did not mention my name. He talked of the estate. It was the wish of the estate that provision should be made for her. The estate had decided upon the sum to be paid quarterly. I watched him like a hawk.

'If you do not wish to seem mixed up in the affair,' he said to me, 'you had better not take the letter. Dobson has to go your way this afternoon. He can take the letter for me. It will look better.'

'Excellent,' I said, 'and I will go to the bank. Thank you, uncle.'

'Don't forget to see Louise before you go,' he said; 'I think she is somewhere in the house.'

I could have done without Louise, in my impatience to be off, but I could not say so. She was in the parlour, as it happened, and I was obliged to pass the open door from my godfather's study.

'I thought I heard your voice,' she said. 'Have you come to spend the day? Let me give you some cake and fruit. You must be hungry.'

'I have to go at once,' I said, 'thank you, Louise. I only rode over to see my godfather on a business matter.'

'Oh,' she said, 'I see.' Her expression, that had been cheerful and natural at sight of me, turned back to the stiff look of Sunday. 'And how is Mrs Ashley?' she said.

'My cousin Rachel is well, and exceedingly busy,' I said. 'All the shrubs she brought home from Italy have arrived this morning, and she is planting them out with Tamlyn in the forcing ground.'

'I should have thought you would have stayed at home to help her,' said Louise.

I don't know what it was about the girl, but this new inflection in her voice was strangely irritating. I was reminded suddenly of her behaviour in old days, when we would be running races in the garden, and just as I would be happily employed she would for no reason shake her curls and say to me, 'I don't think, after all, I want to play,' and would stand looking at me with this same stubborn face.

'You know perfectly well I am a fool at gardening,' I said, and then, from devilry, I added, 'Haven't you got over your ill-humour yet?'

She drew herself up, and flushed. 'Ill-humour? I don't know what you mean,' she said quickly.

'Oh yes, you do,' I answered. 'You were in a vile humour the whole of Sunday. It was most noticeable. I wonder the Pascoe girls did not remark upon it.'

'The Pascoe girls,' she said, 'like everyone else, were probably far too busy remarking something else.'

'And what was that?' I asked.

'How simple it must be for a woman of the world, like Mrs Ashley, to twist a young man like yourself around her finger,' said Louise.

I turned on my heel and left the room. I could have struck her.

13

By the time I had ridden back along the high road from Pelyn, and across country down into town, and so home again, I must have covered near on twenty miles. I had paused for a draught of cider at the inn on the town quay, but had eaten nothing, and was well-nigh famished by four o'clock.

The clock struck the hour from the belfry on the house and I rode straight to the stables, where as ill luck had it Wellington was waiting instead of the groom.

He clucked his tongue at sight of Gypsy in a lather. 'This won't do at all, Mr Philip, sir,' he said, as I dismounted, and I felt as guilty as I used to do when on holiday from Harrow. 'You know the mare catches cold when overheated, and here you've been and brought her back steaming. She's in no condition to follow hounds, if that's what you've been doing.'

'If I'd been following hounds I'd be away on Bodmin moor,' I said. 'Don't be an ass, Wellington. I've been over to see Mr Kendall on business, and then went into town. I'm sorry about Gypsy, but it can't be helped. I don't think she'll come to harm.'

'I hope not, sir,' said Wellington, and he began running his hands over poor Gypsy's flanks as though I had put her to a steeplechase.

I walked back to the house, and went into the library. The fire was burning brightly, but there was no sign of my cousin Rachel. I rang the bell for Seecombe.

'Where is Mrs Ashley?' I asked, as he entered the room.

'Madam came in a little after three, sir,' he said. 'She and the gardeners have been working in the grounds ever since you left. Tamlyn is in the steward's room with me now. He says he has never seen anything like it, the manner in which the mistress sets about it. He says she's a wonder.'

'She must be exhausted,' I said.

'I was afraid of that, sir. I suggested she should go to bed, but she would not hear of it. "Tell the boys to bring me up cans of hot water. I'll take a bath, Seecombe," she said to me, "and I'll wash my hair as well." I was about to send for my niece, it seems hardly right for a lady to wash her own hair, but she would not hear of that either.'

'The boys had better do the same for me,' I told him; 'I've had a hard day too. And I'm devilish hungry. I want my dinner early.'

'Very well, sir. At a quarter to five?'

'Please, Seecombe, if you can manage it.'

I went upstairs, whistling, to throw my clothes off and sit in the steaming tub before my bedroom fire. The dogs came along the corridor from my cousin Rachel's room. They had become quite accustomed to the visitor, and followed her everywhere. Old Don thumped his tail at me from the top of the stairs.

'Hullo, old fellow,' I said; 'you're faithless, you know. You've left me for a lady.' He licked my hand with his long furry tongue, and made big eyes at me.

The boy came with the can and filled the bath, and it was pleasant to sit there in the tub, cross-legged, and scrub myself, whistling a tuneless song above the steam. As I rubbed myself dry with the towel I noticed that on the table beside my bed was a bowl of flowers. Sprigs from the woods, orchis and cyclamen amongst them. No one had ever put flowers in my room before. Seecombe would not have thought of it, or the boys either. It must have been my cousin Rachel. The sight of the flowers added to my mood of high good humour. She may have been messing with the plants and shrubs all day, but she had found the time to fill the bowl with flowers as well. I tied my cravat and put on my dinner coat, still humming my tuneless song. Then I went along the corridor, and knocked upon the door of the boudoir.

'Who is it?' she called from within.

'It is me, Philip,' I answered. 'I have come to tell you that dinner will be early to-night. I'm starving, and so I should think are you, after the tales I've heard. What in the world have you and Tamlyn been up to, that you have to take a bath and wash your hair?'

That bubble of laughter, so infectious, was her answer.

'We've been burrowing underground, like moles,' she called.

'Have you earth up to your eyebrows?'

'Earth everywhere,' she answered. 'I've had my bath, and now I am drying my hair. I am pinned up and presentable, and look exactly like aunt Phoebe. You may come in.'

I opened the door and went into the boudoir. She was sitting on the stool before the fire, and for a moment I scarcely recognised her, she looked so different out of mourning. She had a white dressing wrapper around her, tied at the throat and at the wrists with ribbon, and her hair was pinned on the top of her head, instead of parted smoothly in the centre.

I had never seen anything less like aunt Phoebe, or aunt anyone. I stood blinking at her in the doorway.

'Come and sit down. Don't look so startled,' she said to me.

I shut the door behind me, and went and sat down on a chair.

'Forgive me,' I said, 'but the point is that I have never seen a woman in undress before.'

'This isn't undress,' she said, 'it's what I wear at breakfast. Ambrose used to call it my nun's robe.'

She raised her arms, and began to jab pins into her hair.

'At twenty-four,' she said, 'it is high time you saw a pleasant homely sight such as aunt Phoebe doing up her hair. Are you embarrassed?'

I folded my arms and crossed my legs, and continued to look at her. 'Not in the slightest,' I said, 'merely stunned.'

She laughed, and holding the pins in her mouth took them one by one, and winding her hair into a roll placed it the way it should go, in the low knot behind. The whole matter only took a few seconds, or so it seemed to me.

136

'Do you do that every day in so short a time?' I asked, amazed.

'Oh, Philip, what a lot you have to learn,' she said to me; 'have you never seen your Louise pin up her hair?'

'No, and I wouldn't want to,' I answered swiftly, with a sudden memory of Louise's parting remark as I left Pelyn. My cousin Rachel laughed, and dropped a hair-pin on my knee.

'A keepsake,' she said. 'Put it under your pillow, and watch Seecombe's face at breakfast in the morning.'

She passed from the boudoir into the bedroom opposite, leaving the door wide open.

'You can sit there and shout through to me while I dress,' she called.

I looked furtively at the little bureau to see if there was any sign of my godfather's letter, but could see nothing. I wondered what had happened. Perhaps she had it with her in the bedroom. It might be that she would say nothing to me, that she would treat the matter as a private one between my godfather and herself. I hoped so.

'Where have you been all day?' she called to me.

'I had to go into town,' I said, 'there were people there I was obliged to see.' I need not say a word about the bank.

'I was so happy with Tamlyn and the gardeners,' she called. 'There were only very few of the plants to be thrown away. There is so much, Philip, you know, still to be done in that plantation; the undergrowth bordering the meadow should be cleared, and a walk laid down, and the whole ground there given up to camellias, so that in less than twenty years you could have a spring garden there that the whole of Cornwall would come to see.'

'I know,' I said; 'that was what Ambrose intended.'

'It needs careful planning,' she said, 'and not just left to chance and Tamlyn. He is a dear, but his knowledge is limited. Why do you not take more interest in it yourself?'

'I don't know enough,' I said, 'it was never my department anyway. Ambrose knew that.'

'There must be people who could help you,' she said. 'You could have a designer down from London to lay it out.'

I did not answer. I did not want a designer down from London. I was pretty sure she knew more about it than any designer.

Just then Seecombe appeared and hovered in the passage.

'What is it, Seecombe, is dinner ready?' I asked.

'No, sir,' he replied. 'Mr Kendall's man, Dobson, has ridden over with a note for madam.'

My heart sank. The wretched fellow must have stayed somewhere drinking on the road to be so late. Now I should be caught for the business of her reading it. How wretchedly ill-timed. I heard Seecombe knock on her open door, and give in the letter.

'I think I will go below and wait for you in the library,' I said.

'No, don't go,' she called, 'I'm ready dressed. We can go down together. Here is a letter from Mr Kendall. Perhaps he invites us both to Pelyn.'

Seecombe disappeared along the corridor. I stood up and wished that I could follow him. Suddenly I felt uneasy, nervous. No sound came from the blue bedroom. She must be reading the letter. Ages seemed to pass. At last she came out of the bedroom, and she stood in the doorway, the letter open in her hand. She was dressed for dinner. Perhaps it was the contrast of her skin against the mourning that made her look so white.

'What have you been doing?' she said.

Her voice sounded quite different. Oddly strained.

'Doing?' I said. 'Nothing. Why?'

'Don't lie, Philip. You don't know how.'

I stood most wretchedly before the fire, staring anywhere but in those searching accusing eyes.

'You have been to Pelyn,' she said; 'you rode over there to-day to see your guardian.'

She was right. I was the most hopeless useless liar. At any rate, to her.

'I may have done,' I said. 'What if I did?'

'You made him write this letter,' she said.

'No,' I said, swallowing, 'I did nothing of the sort. He wrote it of his own accord. There was business to discuss, and it so

138

happened that in talking various legal matters came to the fore, and . . .'

'And you told him your cousin Rachel proposed giving lessons in Italian, isn't that the truth?' she said.

I felt hot and cold and miserably ill at ease.

'Not exactly,' I said.

'Surely you realised I was only joking when I told you that?' she said. If she was joking, I thought, why then must she be so angry with me now?

'You don't realise what you have done,' she said; 'you make me feel utterly ashamed.' She went and stood by the window, with her back to me. 'If you wish to humiliate me,' she said, 'by heaven you have gone the right way about it.'

'I don't see,' I said, 'why you have to be so proud.'

'Proud?' She turned round, her eyes very dark and large, and looked at me in fury. 'How dare you call me proud?' she said. I stared back at her. I think I was amazed that anyone who a moment or two before had been laughing with me could suddenly become so angry. Then, to my own very great surprise, my nervousness went from me. I walked towards her, and stood beside her.

'I shall call you proud,' I said, 'I shall go further, and I shall call you damnably proud. It is not you who is likely to be humiliated but me. It was not a joke, when you said that about giving lessons in Italian. Your answer came far too swiftly for it to be a joke. You said it, because you meant it.'

'And if I did mean it?' she said. 'Is there anything shameful in giving lessons in Italian?'

'In the ordinary sense, no,' I said, 'but in your case, yes. For Mrs Ambrose Ashley to give lessons in Italian is shameful; it reflects upon the husband who neglected to make provision for her in his will. And I, Philip Ashley, his heir, won't permit it. You will take that allowance every quarter, cousin Rachel, and when you draw the money from the bank, please remember that it does not come from the estate, nor from the heir to the estate, but from your husband, Ambrose Ashley.'

A wave of anger, as great as hers, had come over me as I spoke. I was damned if any creature, small and frail, should stand there and accuse me of humiliating her; and I was damned furthermore if she should refuse the money that belonged to her by right.

'Well? Do you understand what I have been saying to you?' I said.

For one moment I thought she was going to hit me. She stood quite still, staring up at me. Then her eyes filled with tears, and pushing past me she went into the bedroom and slammed the door. I walked downstairs. I went to the dining-room and rang the bell and told Seecombe that I thought Mrs Ashley would not be down for dinner. I poured myself out a glass of claret, and sat down alone at the head of the table. Christ! I thought, so that's how women behave. I had never felt so angry, nor so spent. Long days in the open, working with the men at harvest time; arguments with tenants behindhand with their rent or involved in some quarrel with a neighbour which I had to settle; nothing of this could compare to five minutes with a woman whose mood of gaiety had turned in a single instant to hostility. And was the final weapon always tears? Because they knew full well the effect upon the watcher? I had another glass of claret. As to Seecombe, who hovered at my elbow, I could have wished him a world away.

'Is Madam indisposed, sir, do you think?' he asked me.

I might have told him that Madam was not so much indisposed as in a fury, and would probably ring her bell in a moment and demand Wellington and the carriage to take her back to Plymouth.

'No,' I said, 'her hair is not yet dry. You had better tell John to take a tray up to the boudoir.'

This, I supposed, was what men faced when they were married. Slammed doors, and silence. Dinner alone. So that appetite, whipped up by the long day's outing, and the relaxation of the bath-tub, and the pleasure of a tranquil evening by the fire passed in intermittent conversation, watching with lazy ease hands that were white and small against embroidery, had to simmer down.

With what cheerfulness had I dressed for dinner and walked along the corridor, knocked on the boudoir door and found her sitting on the stool in that white wrapper, with her hair pinned on top of her head. How easy the mood we shared, making a kind of intimacy that gave a glow to the whole prospect of the evening. And now, alone at the table, with a beefsteak that might have been shoe-leather for all I cared. And what was she doing? Lying on her bed? Were the candles snuffed, the curtains drawn, and the room in darkness? Or was the mood over now, and did she sit sedately in the boudoir, dry-eyed, eating her dinner off the tray, to make a show for Seecombe? I did not know. I did not care. Ambrose had been so right when he used to say that women were a race apart. One thing was certain now. I should never marry . . .

Dinner over, I went and sat in the library. I lit my pipe, and put my feet up on the fire-irons, and composed myself to that after dinner slumber that can be sweet and consoling upon occasion, but to-night lacked every charm. I had become used to the sight of her in the chair opposite my own, her shoulders turned so that the light fell upon her work, and Don at her feet; now the chair looked strangely empty. Well, to hell with it, that a woman could so disturb the close of day. I got up and found a book upon the shelves, and turned the pages. Then I must have dozed, because when I looked up again the hands of the clock in the corner were a little short of nine. To bed then, and to sleep. No sense in sitting on, with the fire gone out. I took the dogs round to the kennels – the weather had changed, it was blowing and spitting rain – and then bolted up and went to my room. I was just about to throw my coat off on the chair when I saw a note, placed beside the bowl of flowers on the table next to my bed. I went over to the table, and picked up the note and read it. It was from my cousin Rachel.

'Dear Philip,' it said, 'if you can bring yourself to do so, please forgive me for my rudeness to you to-night. It was unpardonable of me to behave so in your house. I have no excuse, except that I am not entirely myself these days; emotion lies too near the surface. I have written to your guardian, thanking him for his letter and accepting the allowance. It was generous and dear of you both to think of me. Good night. Rachel.'

I read the letter twice, and then put it in my pocket. Was her pride spent then, and the anger too? Did these feelings dissolve with the tears? A load went from me, that she had accepted the allowance. I had visualised another visit to the bank, and further explanations, countermanding my first orders; and then interviews with my godfather, and arguments, and the whole business ending most wretchedly with my cousin Rachel sweeping out of the house and taking herself to London, there to live in lodgings giving Italian lessons.

Had it cost her much to write that note, I wondered? The swing from pride to humility? I hated the fact that she had to do so. For the first time since he had died, I found myself blaming Ambrose for what had happened. Surely he might have taken some thought for the future. Illness and sudden death can come to anyone. He must have known that by making no provision he left his wife to our mercy, to our charity. A letter home to my godfather would have spared all this. I had a vision of her sitting down in aunt Phoebe's boudoir and writing me this note. I wondered if she had left the boudoir yet and gone to bed. I hesitated for a moment, and then went along the corridor and stood under the archway by her rooms.

The door of the boudoir was open, the door of the bedroom shut. I knocked upon the bedroom door. For a moment no answer came, and then she said, 'Who is it?'

I did not answer 'Philip.' I opened the door, and went inside. The room was in darkness, and the light from my candle showed the curtains of the bed to be partly drawn. I could see the outline of her form under the coverlet.

'I have just read your note,' I said. 'I wanted to thank you for it, and to say good night.'

I thought she might sit up and light her candle, but she did not do so. She lay just as she was, on her pillows, behind the curtains.

'I wanted you to know also,' I said, 'that I had no idea of patronising you. Please believe that.'

The voice that came from the curtains was strangely quiet and subdued.

'I never thought you had,' she answered.

We were both silent an instant, and then she said, 'It would not worry me to give Italian lessons. I have no pride about that sort of thing. What I could not bear was when you said my doing so would reflect badly upon Ambrose.'

'It was true,' I said, 'but forget it now. We need not think of it again.'

'It was dear of you, and very like you,' she said, 'to go riding over to Pelyn to see your guardian. I must have seemed so ungracious, so completely lacking in gratitude. I can't forgive myself.' The voice, so near to tears again, did something to me. A kind of tightness came to my throat and to my belly.

'I would much rather that you hit me,' I told her, 'than that you cried.'

I heard her move in her bed, and feel for a handkerchief and blow her nose. The gesture and the sound, so commonplace and simple, happening there in the darkness behind the curtains, made me even weaker in the belly than before.

Presently she said, 'I will take the allowance, Philip, but I must not trespass on your hospitality after this week. I think next Monday, if it will suit you, I should leave here and move elsewhere, perhaps to London.'

A blank feeling came over me at her words.

'Go to London?' I said. 'But why? What for?'

'I only came for a few days,' she answered. 'I have already stayed longer than I intended.'

'But you have not met everybody yet,' I said, 'you have not done everything you are supposed to do.'

'Does it matter?' she said. 'After all – it seems so pointless.'

How unlike her it sounded, that lack of spirit in her voice.

'I thought you liked it,' I said, 'going about the estate, and visiting the tenants. Each day we went about it together you

143

seemed so happy. And today, putting in those shrubs with Tamlyn. Was it all show, and were you just being polite?'

She did not answer for a moment, and then she said, 'Sometimes, Philip, I think you lack all understanding.'

Probably I did. I felt sullen and hurt and I did not care.

'All right,' I said; 'if you want to go, do so. It will cause a lot of talk, but no matter.'

'I should have thought,' she said, 'that it would cause more talk if I stayed.'

'Talk if you stayed?' I said. 'What do you mean? Don't you realise that by rights you belong here, that if Ambrose had not been such a lunatic this would have been your home?'

'Oh, God,' she flared out at me in sudden anger, 'why else do you think I came?'

I had put my foot in it again. Blundering and tactless, I had said all the wrong things. I felt suddenly hopeless and inadequate. I went up to the bed, and pulled aside the curtains, and looked down at her. She was lying propped against her pillows, her hands clasped in front of her. She was wearing something white, frilled at the neck like a choir-boy's surplice, and her hair was loose, tied behind with a piece of ribbon, as I remembered Louise's as a child. It shook me, and surprised me, that she should look so young.

'Listen,' I said, 'I don't know why you came, or what were your motives in doing all you have done. I don't know anything about you, or about any woman. All I know is that I like it now you are here. And I don't want you to go. Is that complicated?'

She had put her hands up to her face, almost in defence, as if she thought I meant to harm her.

'Yes,' she said, 'very.'

'Then it is you who make it so,' I said, 'not I.'

I folded my arms and looked at her, assuming an ease of manner I was far from feeling. Yet in a sense by standing there, while she lay in bed, I had her at a disadvantage. I did not see how a woman with her hair loose, becoming a girl again without a woman's status, could be angry.

I saw her eyes waver. She was searching in her mind for some excuse, some new reason why she should be gone, and in a sudden flash I hit upon a master stroke of strategy.

'You told me this evening,' I said, 'that I should have a designer down from London, to lay out the gardens. I know that was what Ambrose always intended to do. The fact remains that I don't know of one, and should go mad with irritation anyway, if I had to have such a fellow about me. If you have any feeling for the place, knowing what it meant to Ambrose, you would remain here for a few months and do it for me.'

The shaft struck home. She stared in front of her, playing with her ring. I had remarked before that when preoccupied this was a trick of hers. I pushed on with my advantage.

'I never could follow the plans that Ambrose used to draw,' I said to her, 'nor Tamlyn either, for that matter. He works wonders, I know, but only under direction. Time and again he has come to me this past year and asked for advice which I have been quite at a loss to give him. If you remained here – just for the autumn, when so much planting needs to be done – it would help us all.'

She twisted the ring back and forth upon her finger. 'I think I should ask your godfather what he feels,' she said to me.

'It does not concern my godfather,' I said. 'What do you take me for, a schoolboy under age? There is only one consideration, whether you yourself desire to stay. If you really want to go, I cannot keep you.'

She said, surprisingly, in a still small voice, 'Why do you ask that? You know I want to stay.'

Sweet heaven, how could I know? She had intimated the exact opposite.

'Then you will remain, for a little while,' I said, 'to do the garden? That is settled, and you won't go back on your word?'

'I will remain,' she said, 'for a little while.'

I had difficulty in not smiling. Her eyes were serious, and I had the feeling that if I smiled she would change her mind. Inwardly, I triumphed.

'Very well, then,' I said, 'I will bid you good night and leave you. What about your letter to my godfather? Do you want me to put it in the post-bag?'

'Seecombe has taken it,' she said.

'Then you will sleep now, and not be angry with me any more?'

'I wasn't angry, Philip.'

'But you were. I thought you were going to hit me.'

She looked up at me. 'Sometimes you are so stupid,' she said, 'that I think one day I shall. Come here.'

I drew closer, my knee touched the coverlet.

'Bend down,' she said.

She took my face between her hands and kissed me.

'Now go to bed,' she said, 'like a good boy, and sleep well.' She pushed me away, and drew her curtains.

I stumbled out of the blue bedroom with my candlestick, light-headed and somehow dazed, as though I had drunk brandy, and it seemed to me that the advantage I had thought to have over her, as I stood above her and she lay on her pillows, was now completely lost. The last word, and the last gesture too, had been with her. The little girl look and the choir-boy surplice had misled me. She was a woman all the time. For all that, I was happy. The misunderstanding was now over, and she had promised to remain. There had been no more tears.

Instead of going immediately to bed I went down to the library once again, to write a line to my godfather and to reassure him that all had gone off well. He need never know of the troublous evening spent by the pair of us. I scribbled my letter, and went into the hall to place it in the post-bag for the morning.

Seecombe had left the bag for me, as was his custom, upon the table in the hall, with the key beside it. When I opened up the bag two other letters fell into my hand, both written by my cousin Rachel. One was addressed to my godfather Nick Kendall, as she had told me. The second letter was addressed to Signor Rainaldi in Florence. I stared at it a moment, then put it back

146

with the other in the post-bag. It was foolish of me, perhaps, senseless and absurd; the man was her friend, why should she not write a letter to him? Yet, as I went upstairs to bed, I felt exactly as if she had hit me after all.

14

The following day when she came downstairs, and I joined her in the garden, my cousin Rachel was as happy and unconcerned as though there had never been a rift between us. The only difference in her manner to me was that she seemed more gentle, and more tender; she teased me less, laughed with me and not at me, and kept asking my opinion as to the planting of the shrubs, not for the sake of my knowledge but for my future pleasure when I should look upon them.

'Do what you want to do,' I told her; 'bid the men cut the hedge-rows, fell the trees, heap up the banks yonder with shrubs, whatever you fancy will do well, I have no eye for line.'

'But I want the result to please you, Philip,' she said. 'All this belongs to you, and one day will belong to your children. What if I make changes in the grounds, and when it is done you are displeased?'

'I shan't be displeased,' I said; 'and stop talking about my children. I am quite resolved to remain a bachelor.'

'Which is essentially selfish,' she said, 'and very stupid of you.'

'I think not,' I answered. 'I think by remaining a bachelor I shall be spared much distress and anxiety of mind.'

'Have you ever thought what you would lose?'

'I have a shrewd guess,' I told her, 'that the blessings of married bliss are not all they are claimed to be. If it's warmth and comfort that a man wants, and something beautiful to look upon, he can get all that from his own house, if he loves it well.'

To my astonishment she laughed so much at my remark that Tamlyn and the gardeners, working at the far end of the plantation, raised their heads to look at us.

'One day,' she said to me, 'when you fall in love, I shall remind you of those words. Warmth and comfort from stone walls, at twenty-four. Oh, Philip!' And the bubble of laughter came from her again.

I could not see that it was so very funny.

'I know quite well what you mean,' I said; 'it just happens that I have never been moved that way.'

'That's very evident,' she said. 'You must be a heartbreak to the neighbourhood. That poor Louise . . .'

But I was not going to be led into a discussion on Louise, nor again a dissertation upon love and matrimony. I was much more interested to watch her work upon the garden.

October set in fine and mild, and for the first three weeks of it we had barely no rain at all, so that Tamlyn and the men, under the supervision of my cousin Rachel, were able to go far ahead with the work in the plantation. We managed also to visit in succession all the tenants upon the estate, which gave great satisfaction, as I knew it would. I had known every one of them since boyhood, and had been used to calling in upon them every so often, for it was part of my work to do so. But it was a new experience for my cousin Rachel, brought up in Italy to a very different life. Her manner with the people could not have been more right or proper, and it was a fascination to watch her with them. The blend of graciousness and cameraderie made them immediately look up to her, yet put them at their ease. She asked all the right questions, replied with the right answers. Also – and this endeared her to many of them – there was the understanding she seemed to have of all their ailments, and the remedies she produced. 'With my love for gardening,' she told them, 'goes a knowledge of herbs. In Italy we always made a study of these things.' And she would produce balm, from some plant, to rub upon wheezing chests, and oil from another, as a measure against burns; and she would instruct them too how to make tisana, as a remedy for indigestion and for sleeplessness – the best nightcap in the world, she said to them – and tell them how the juice of certain fruits could cure almost any ill from a sore throat to a stye on the eyelid.

'You know what will happen,' I told her; 'you will take the place of midwife in the district. They will send for you in the night to deliver babies, and once that starts there will be no peace for you at all.'

'There is a tisana for that too,' she said, 'made from the leaves of raspberries and of nettles. If a woman drinks that for six months before the birth, she has her baby without pain.'

'That's witchcraft,' I said. 'They wouldn't think it right to do so.'

'What nonsense! Why should women suffer?' said my cousin Rachel.

Sometimes, in the afternoons, she would be called upon by the county, as I had warned her. And she was as successful with the 'gentry', as Seecombe called them, as she was with the humbler folk. Seecombe, I soon came to realise, now lived in a seventh heaven. When the carriages drove up to the door upon a Tuesday or a Thursday, at three o'clock of an afternoon, he would be waiting in the hall. He still wore mourning, but his coat was new, kept only for these occasions. The luckless John would have the task of opening the front door to the visitors, then of passing them on to his superior, who with slow and stately step (I would have it all from John afterwards) preceded the visitors through the hall to the drawing-room. Throwing the door open with a flourish (this from my cousin Rachel) he would announce the names like the toast-master at a banquet. Beforehand, she told me, he would discuss with her the likelihood of this or that visitor appearing, and give her a brief resumé of their family history up to date. He was generally right in his prophecy of who would appear, and we wondered whether there was some method of sending messages from household to household through the servants' hall to give due warning, even as savages beat tom-toms in a jungle. For instance, Seecombe would tell my cousin Rachel that he had it for certain that Mrs Tremayne had ordered her carriage for Thursday afternoon, and that she would bring with her the married daughter Mrs Gough, and the unmarried daughter Miss Isobel; and that my cousin Rachel must beware when she talked to Miss Isobel, as the young lady suffered from an affliction of the speech. Or again, that upon a Tuesday old Lady Penryn would be likely to appear, because she always visited her granddaughter upon that day, who lived only ten miles distant from us; and my cousin Rachel must remember on no account to mention foxes before her, as Lady Penryn had been frightened by a fox before her eldest son was born, and he carried the stigma as a birth-mark upon his left shoulder to this day.

'And Philip,' said my cousin Rachel afterwards, 'the whole time she was with me I had to head the conversation away from hunting. It was no use, she came back to it like a mouse sniffing at cheese. And finally, to keep her quiet, I had to invent a tale of chasing wild cats in the Alps, which is an impossibility, and something no one has done.'

There was always some story of the callers with which she greeted me when I returned home, slinking by the back way through the woods when the last carriage had bowled safely down the drive; and we would laugh together, and she would smooth her hair before the mirror and straighten the cushions, while I polished off the last of the sweet cakes that had been put before the visitors. The whole thing would seem like a game, like a conspiracy; yet I think she was happy there, sitting in the drawing-room making conversation. People and their lives had interest for her, how they thought, and what they did; and she used to say to me, 'But you don't understand, Philip, this is all so new after the very different society in Florence. I have always wondered about life in England, in the country. Now I am beginning to know. And I love every minute of it.'

I would take a lump out of the sugar bowl, and crunch it, and cut myself a slice from the seed cake.

'I can think of nothing more monotonous,' I told her, 'than discussing generalities with anyone, in Florence or in Cornwall.'

'Ah, but you are hopeless,' she said, 'and will end up very narrow-minded, thinking of nothing but turnips and of kale.'

I would fling myself down in the chair, and on purpose to try her put my muddy boots up on the stool, watching her with one eye. She never reproved me, and if she had noticed did not appear to do so.

'Go on,' I would say, 'tell me the latest scandal in the county.'

'But if you are not interested,' she would answer, 'why should I do so?'

'Because I like to hear you talk.'

So before going upstairs to change for dinner she would regale me with county gossip, what there was of it – the latest betrothals, marriages, and deaths, the new babies on the way; she appeared to glean more from twenty minutes' conversation with a stranger than I would from an acquaintance after a lifetime.

'As I suspected,' she told me, 'you are the despair of every mother within fifty miles.'

'Why so?'

'Because you do not choose to look at any of their daughters. So tall, so presentable, so eligible in every way. Pray, Mrs Ashley, do prevail upon your cousin to go out more.'

'And what is your answer?'

'That you find all the warmth and entertainment that you need within these four walls. On second thoughts,' she added, 'that might be misconstrued. I must watch my tongue.'

'I don't mind what you tell them,' I said, 'as long as you do not involve me in an invitation. I have no desire to look at anybody's daughter.'

'There is heavy betting upon Louise,' she said; 'quite a number say that she will get you in the end. And the third Miss Pascoe has a sporting chance.'

'Great heaven!' I exclaimed. 'Belinda Pascoe? I'd as soon marry Katie Searle, who does the washing. Really, cousin Rachel, you might protect me. Why not tell these gossips I'm a recluse and spend all my spare time scribbling Latin verses? That might shake them.'

'Nothing will shake them,' she answered. 'The thought that a good-looking young bachelor should like solitude and verse would make you sound all the more romantic. These things whet appetite.'

'Then they'll feed elsewhere,' I replied. 'What staggers me is the way in which the minds of women in this part of the world – perhaps it's the same everywhere – run perpetually upon marriage.'

'They haven't much else to think about,' she said; 'the choice of fare is small. I do not escape discussion, I can tell you. A list of eligible widowers has been given me. There is a peer down in west Cornwall declared to be the very thing. Fifty, an heir, and both daughters married.'

'Not old St Ives?' I said in tones of outrage.

'Why, yes, I believe that is the name. They say he's charming.'

'Charming, is he?' I said to her. 'He's always drunk by midday, and creeps around the passages after the maids. Billy Rowe, from the Barton, had a niece in service there. She had to come back home, she grew so scared.'

'Who's talking gossip now?' said cousin Rachel. 'Poor Lord St Ives, perhaps if he had a wife he wouldn't creep about the passages. It would, of course, depend upon the wife.'

'Well, you're not going to marry him,' I said with firmness.

'You could at least invite him here to dinner?' she suggested, her eyes full of that solemnity that I had learnt now spelt mischief. 'We could have a party, Philip. The prettiest young women for you, and the best-favoured widowers for me. But I think I have made my choice. I think, if I am ever put to it, I will take your godfather, Mr Kendall. He has a fair direct way of speaking, which I much admire.'

Maybe she did it on purpose, but I rose to the bait, exploding.

'You cannot seriously mean it?' I said. 'Marry my godfather? Why damn it, cousin Rachel, he's nearing sixty; and he's never without a chill or some complaint.'

'That means he doesn't find warmth or comfort inside his house as you do,' she answered me.

I knew then that she was laughing, so laughed with her; but afterwards I wondered about it with mistrust. Certainly my god-father was most courteous when he came on Sundays, and they got on capitally together. We had dined there once or twice, and

153

my godfather had sparkled in a way unknown to me. But he had been a widower for ten years. Surely he could not entertain so incredible an idea as to fancy his chance with my cousin Rachel? And surely she would not accept? I went hot at the thought. My cousin Rachel at Pelyn. My cousin Rachel, Mrs Ashley, becoming Mrs Kendall. How monstrous! If anything so presumptuous was passing through the old man's mind I was damned if I would continue inviting him to Sunday dinner. Yet to break the invitation would be to break the routine of years. It was not possible. Therefore I must continue as we had always done, but the next Sunday, when my godfather on the right of my cousin Rachel bent his deaf ear to her, and suddenly sat back, laughing and saying, 'Oh, capital, capital,' I wondered sulkily what it portended and why it was that they laughed so much together. This, I thought to myself, is another trick of women, to throw a jest in the air that left a sting behind it.

She sat there, at Sunday dinner, looking remarkably well and in high good humour, with my godfather on her right and the vicar on her left, none of them at a loss for conversation, and for no good reason I turned sulky and silent, just as Louise had done that first Sunday, and our end of the table had all the appearance of a Quaker meeting. Louise sat looking at her plate, and I at mine, and I suddenly lifted my eyes and saw Belinda Pascoe, with round eyes, gaping at me; and remembering the gossip of the countryside I became more dumb than ever. Our silence spurred my cousin Rachel to greater effort, in order, I suppose, to cover it; and she and my godfather and the vicar tried to cap each other, quoting verse, while I became more and more sulky, and thankful for the absence of Mrs Pascoe through indisposition. Louise did not matter. I was not obliged to talk to Louise.

But when they had all gone my cousin Rachel took me to task. 'When,' she said, 'I entertain your friends, I look to have a little support from you. What was wrong, Philip? You sat there scowling, with a mulish face, and never addressed a word to either neighbour. Those poor girls . . .' And she shook her head at me, displeased.

154

'There was so much gaiety at your end,' I answered her, 'that I saw no point in contributing to it. All that nonsense about "I love you" in Greek. And the vicar telling you that "my heart's delight" sounded very well in Hebrew.'

'Well, so it did,' she said. 'It came rolling off his tongue, and I was most impressed. And your godfather wants to show me the beacon head by moonlight. Once seen, he tells me, never forgotten.'

'Well, he's not showing it to you,' I replied. 'The beacon is my property. There is some old earth-work that belongs to the Pelyn estate. Let him show you that. It's covered thick in brambles.' And I threw a lump of coal upon the fire, hoping the clatter bothered her.

'I don't know what's come over you,' she said; 'you are losing your sense of humour.' And she patted me on the shoulder and went upstairs. That was the infuriating thing about a woman. Always the last word. Leaving one to grapple with ill-temper, and she herself serene. A woman, it seemed, was never in the wrong. Or if she was, she twisted the fault to her advantage, making it seem otherwise. She would fling these pin-pricks in the air, these hints of moonlight strolls with my godfather, or some other expedition, a visit to Lostwithiel market, and ask me in all seriousness whether she should wear the new bonnet that had come by parcel post from London – the veil had a wider mesh and did not shroud her, and my godfather had told her it became her well. And when I fell to sulking, saying I did not care whether she concealed her features with a mask, her mood soared to serenity yet higher – the conversation was at dinner on the Monday – and while I sat frowning she carried on her talk with Seecombe, making me seem more sulky than I was.

Then in the library afterwards, with no observer present, she would relent; the serenity was with her still, but a kind of tenderness came too. She neither laughed at me for lack of humour, nor chided me for sullenness. She asked me to hold her silks for her, to choose the colours I liked best, because she wanted to work a covering for me to use on the chair in the estate office.

And quietly, without irritating, without probing, she asked me questions about my day, whom I had seen, what I had done, so that all sulkiness went from me and I was eased and rested, and I wondered, watching her hands with the silks, smoothing them and touching them, why it could not have been thus in the first place; why first the pin-prick, the barb of irritation to disturb the atmosphere, giving herself the trouble to make it calm again? It was as if my change of mood afforded her delight, but why it should do so I had no remote idea. I only knew that when she teased me I disliked it, and it hurt. And when she was tender I was happy and at peace.

By the end of the month the fine weather broke. It rained for three days without stopping, and there was no gardening to be done, no work for me on the estate, riding to and fro to be soaked to the skin, and all callers from the county were kept within their doors, like the rest of us. It was Seecombe who suggested, what I think the pair of us had both been shirking, that the time was opportune to go through Ambrose's effects. He broached it one morning as my cousin Rachel and I stood by the library window, staring out at the driving rain.

'The office for me,' I had just observed, 'and a day in the boudoir for you. What about those boxes down from London? More gowns to sort, and try upon your person, and return again?'

'Not gowns,' she said, 'but coverings for curtains. I think Aunt Phoebe's eye lacked lustre. The blue bedroom should live up to its name. At present it is grey, not blue at all. And the quilting to the bed has moth, but don't tell Seecombe. The moth of years. I have chosen you new curtains and new quilting.'

It was then that Seecombe entered, and seeing us apparently without employment said, 'The weather being so inclement, sir, I had thought the boys might be put to extra cleaning within doors. Your room needs attention. But they cannot dust there while Mr Ashley's trunks and boxes cover the floor.'

I glanced at her, fearing this lack of tact might wound her, that she might turn away, but to my surprise she took it well.

'You are quite right, Seecombe,' she said; 'the boys cannot

clean the room until the boxes are unpacked. We have left it far too long. Well, Philip, what about it?'

'Very well,' I said, 'if you are agreeable. Let us have the fire lit, and when the room is warm we'll go upstairs.'

I think that both of us tried to conceal our feelings from the other. We forced a sort of brightness into our behaviour and into our conversation. For my sake, she was determined not to show distress. And I, wishing to spare the same for her, assumed a heartiness utterly foreign to my nature. The rain was lashing at the windows of my old room, and a patch of damp had appeared upon the ceiling. The fire, that had not been lit since last winter, burnt with a false crackle. The boxes stood in a line upon the floor, waiting to be opened; and on top of one was the well remembered travel rug of dark blue, with the yellow monogram 'A.A.' in large letters in one corner. I had the sudden recollection of putting it over his knees that last day, when he drove away.

My cousin Rachel broke the silence. 'Come,' she said, 'shall we open the clothes trunk first?'

Her voice was purposely hard and practical. I handed her the keys, which she had left in Seecombe's charge on her arrival.

'Just as you will,' I said.

She put the key in the lock, and turned it, and threw open the lid. His old dressing-gown was on the top. I knew it well. It was of heavy silk in a dark red colour. His slippers were there too, long and flat. I stood there staring at them, and it was like walking back into the past. I remembered him passing into my room while he was shaving of a morning, the lather on his face. 'Look, boy, I've been thinking . . .' Into this room, where we were standing now. Wearing that dressing-gown, wearing those slippers. My cousin Rachel took them from the trunk.

'What shall we do with them?' she said, and the voice that had been hard was lower now, subdued.

'I don't know,' I said; 'it's for you to say.'

'Would you wear them, if I gave them to you?' she asked.

It was strange. I had taken his hat. I had taken his stick. His old shooting coat with the leather at the elbows that he had left behind when he went upon his last journey, that I wore constantly. Yet these things, the dressing-gown, the slippers – it was almost as though we had opened up his coffin and looked upon him dead.

'No,' I said, 'no, I don't think so.'

She said nothing. She put them on the bed. She came next to a suit of clothing. A light-weight suit – he must have worn it in hot weather. It was not familiar to me, but she must have known it well. It was creased from lying in the trunk. She took it out and placed it with the dressing-gown upon the bed. 'It should be pressed,' she said. Suddenly she began lifting the things from the trunk very swiftly and putting them in a pile, one on top of the other, barely touching them.

'I think,' she said, 'that if you don't want them, Philip, the people on the estate here, who loved him, might like to have them. You will know best what to give, and to whom.'

I think she did not see what she was doing. She took them from the trunk in a sort of frenzy, while I stood by and watched her.

'The trunk?' she said. 'A trunk is always useful. You could do with the trunk?' She looked up at me, and her voice faltered.

Suddenly she was in my arms, her head against my chest.

'Oh, Philip,' she said, 'forgive me. I should have let you and Seecombe do it. I was a fool to come upstairs.'

It was queer. Like holding a child. Like holding a wounded animal. I touched her hair, and put my cheek against her head.

'It's all right,' I said, 'don't cry. Go back to the library. I can finish it alone.'

'No,' she said, 'it's so weak of me, so stupid. It's just as bad for you as it is for me. You loved him so . . .'

I kept moving my lips against her hair. It was a strange feeling. And she was very small, standing there against me.

'I don't mind,' I said; 'a man can do these things. It's not easy for a woman. Let me do it, Rachel, go downstairs.'

She stood a little way apart and wiped her eyes with her handkerchief.

158

'No,' she said, 'I'm better now. It won't happen again. And I have unpacked the clothes. But if you will give them to the people on the estate, I shall be grateful. And anything you want for yourself, wear it. Never be afraid to wear it. I shan't mind, I shall be glad.'

The boxes of books were nearer to the fire. I brought a chair and placed it for her, close to the warmth, and knelt beside the other trunks and opened them, one by one.

I hoped she had not noticed – I had barely noticed it myself – that for the first time I had not called her cousin, but Rachel. I don't know how it happened. I think it must have been because standing there, with my arms about her, she had been so much smaller than myself.

The books did not have the personal touch about them that the clothes had done. There were old favourites that I knew, with which he always travelled, and these she gave to me to keep beside my bed. There were his cuff-links, too, his studs, his watch, his pen – all these she pressed upon me, and I was glad of them. Some of the books I did not know at all. She explained them to me, picking up first one volume, then another, and now no longer was the task so sad; this book, she said, he had picked up in Rome, it was a bargain, he was pleased, and that one there, with the old binding, and the other beside it, came from Florence. She described the place where he had bought them, and the old man who had sold them to him, and it seemed, as she chatted to me, that the strain had lifted, it had gone with the tears she had wiped away. We laid the books, one after the other, upon the floor, and I fetched a duster for her and she dusted them. Sometimes she read a passage out to me and told me how this paragraph had pleased Ambrose; or she showed me a picture, an engraving, and I saw her smiling at some well-remembered page.

She came upon a volume of drawings of the lay-out of gardens. 'This will be very useful to us,' she said, and rising from her chair took it to the window to see it better in the light.

I opened another book at random. A piece of paper fell from between the leaves. It had Ambrose's handwriting upon it. It seemed like the middle scrap of a letter, torn from its context and forgotten. '*It's a disease, of course, I have often heard of it, like kleptomania or some other malady, and has no doubt been handed down to her from her spendthrift father, Alexander Coryn. How long she has been a victim of it I cannot say, perhaps always; certainly it explains much of what has disturbed me hitherto in all this business. This much I do know, dear boy, that I cannot any longer, nay I dare not, let her have command over my purse, or I shall be ruined, and the estate will suffer. It is imperative that you warn Kendall, if by any chance . . .*' The sentence broke off. There was no end to it. The scrap of paper was not dated. The handwriting was normal. Just then she came back from the window, and I crumpled the piece of paper in my hand.

'What have you there?' she said.

'Nothing,' I said.

I threw the piece of paper on the fire. She saw it burn. She saw the handwriting on the paper curl and flicker in the flame.

'That was Ambrose's writing,' she said. 'What was it? Was it a letter?'

'It was just some note he had made,' I said, 'on an old scrap of paper.' I felt my face burn in the light of the fire.

Then I reached for another volume from the trunk. She did the same. We continued sorting the books, side by side, together; but the silence had come between us.

15

We had finished sorting the books by midday. Seecombe sent John up to us, and young Arthur, to know if anything needed carrying downstairs before they went off to their dinner.

'Leave the clothes on the bed, John,' I said, 'and put a covering on top of them. I shall want Seecombe to help me make packages of them by and by. Take this pile of books down to the library.'

'And these to the boudoir, Arthur, please,' said my cousin Rachel.

It was her first utterance since I had burnt the scrap of paper.

'It will be all right, will it, Philip,' she asked, 'if I keep the books on gardens in my room?'

'Why, yes, of course,' I answered. 'All the books are yours, you know that.'

'No,' she said, 'no, Ambrose would have wanted the others in the library.' She stood up, and smoothed her dress, and gave John the duster.

'Some cold luncheon is laid below, madam,' he said.

'Thank you, John. I am not hungry.'

I hesitated, standing by the open door, after the boys had disappeared carrying the books.

'Will you not come down to the library,' I asked, 'and help me put away the books?'

'I think not,' she said, then paused a moment, as if to add something, but did not do so. Then she walked along the corridor to her room.

I ate my lunch alone, staring out of the dining-room windows. It was still raining fast. No use attempting to go out of doors, there was nothing to be done. I had better finish the task of sorting the clothes, with Seecombe to help me. It would please him to be asked advice. What should go to the Barton, what to Trenant, what to the East Lodge; everything to be carefully chosen so that no one should take offence at what he had. It would employ the pair of us all afternoon. I tried to keep my mind upon the business; yet, nagging like a pain in the tooth that flares up suddenly and dies again, my thoughts would be wrenched back to the scrap of paper. What had it been doing between the pages of that book, and how long had it lain there, torn, forgotten? Six months, a year, or longer? Had Ambrose started upon a letter to me which never reached its destination; or were there other bits of paper, part of the same letter, which for some unknown reason were still lying between the pages of a book? The letter must have been written before his illness. The writing was firm and clear. Therefore last winter, last autumn possibly . . . I was swept by a kind of shame. What business was it of mine to probe back into that past, to wonder about a letter that had never reached me? It was not my affair. I wished to heaven I had not come upon it.

All afternoon Seecombe and I sorted the clothes, and he put them into packages while I wrote notes of explanation to go with them. He suggested that the parcels should be given out at Christmas, which seemed to me a sound idea, and one that would appeal to the tenants. When we had finished I went downstairs again to the library, and put the books into the shelves. I found myself shaking the leaves of each volume, before I placed it on the shelf; and as I did so I felt furtive, like someone guilty of a petty crime.

'. . . *a disease, of course, like kleptomania, or some other malady . . .'* Why did I have to remember those words? What did Ambrose mean?

I reached for a dictionary, and looked up kleptomania. 'An irresistible tendency to theft in persons not tempted to do it by needy circumstances.' That was not his accusation. His accusation was one of prodigality, of extravagance. How could extravagance be a malady? It was totally unlike Ambrose, the most generous of men, to accuse anyone of such a habit. As I put the dictionary back upon the shelf the door opened, and my cousin Rachel came into the room.

I felt as guilty as if she had caught me in deceit. 'I have just finished putting away the books,' I said, and I wondered if my voice sounded as false to her as it did to me.

'So I see,' she answered, and she went and sat down by the fire. She was ready changed for dinner. I had not realised it was so late.

'We have sorted the clothes,' I said. 'Seecombe was very helpful. We think it a good plan, if you approve, that the things should be given out at Christmas.'

'Yes,' she said, 'so he told me just now. I think it most appropriate.'

I did not know if it was my manner, or hers, but there was a kind of constraint between us.

'It hasn't ceased raining for the day,' I said.

'No,' she answered.

I glanced at my hands, dusty from the books. 'If you will excuse me,' I said, 'I will go and wash, and change for dinner.' I went upstairs, and dressed, and when I came down again dinner was upon the table. We took our places in silence. Seecombe, from long habit, would break in upon our conversation very often, at dinner-time, when he had something that he wished to say, and to-night, when we had nearly finished, he said to my cousin Rachel, 'Have you shown Mr Philip the new coverings, madam?'

'No, Seecombe,' she answered, 'there hasn't yet been time. But if he cares to see them I can do so after dinner. Perhaps John would carry them down to the library.'

'Coverings?' I said, puzzled. 'What covers are they?'

'Don't you remember?' she answered. 'I told you I had ordered coverings for the blue bedroom. Seecombe has seen them, and is very much impressed.'

'Oh, yes,' I said, 'yes, I remember now.'

'I have seen nothing like them in my life, sir,' said Seecombe, 'certainly no mansion in these parts has any furnishings to touch them.'

'Ah, but then the stuff is imported from Italy, Seecombe,' said my cousin Rachel. 'There is only one place in London where it is procurable. I was told of it in Florence. Would you like to see the coverings, Philip, or does it not interest you?'

She put the question to me half hopefully, half anxiously, as though wishing for my opinion, yet fearing I should be bored.

I don't know how it was, but I felt myself go scarlet. 'Why, yes,' I said, 'I shall be pleased to look at them.'

We rose from dinner and went into the library. Seecombe followed us, and in a moment or two he and John brought down the coverings and spread them out.

Seecombe was right. There could be no other furnishings like these in Cornwall. I had seen none like them anywhere, either in Oxford or in London. There were many of them. Rich brocades, and heavy silken hangings. They were the kind of stuffs you might see in a museum.

'There is quality for you, sir,' said Seecombe. His voice was hushed. He might have been in church.

'I thought this blue for the bed-hangings,' said my cousin Rachel, 'and the deeper blue and gold for the curtains, and the quilting for the coverlet. What do you say, Philip?'

She looked up at me, anxiously. I did not know how to answer her.

'Do you not like them?' she said to me.

'I like them very much,' I said, 'but' – I felt myself go red again – 'are they not very dear?'

'Oh, yes, they are dear,' she answered, 'any stuff like this is dear, but it will last for years, Philip. Why, your grandson, and great grandson, will be able to sleep in the blue bedroom, with these coverings upon the bed and these hangings for the curtains. Isn't that so, Seecombe?'

'Yes, madam,' said Seecombe.

'The only thing that matters is whether you like them, Philip,' she asked again.

164

'Why yes,' I said, 'who could help but like them?'

'Then they are yours,' she told me, 'they are a present to you, from me. Take them away, Seecombe. I will write to the place in London in the morning and say we will keep them.'

Seecombe and John folded the coverings and took them from the room. I had the feeling that her eyes were upon me, and rather than meet them I took out my pipe and lit it, taking longer over the job than usual.

'Something's the matter,' she said. 'What is it?'

I was not sure how to answer her. I did not want to hurt her.

'You should not give me a present like that,' I said awkwardly, 'it will cost you far too much.'

'But I want to give them to you,' she said, 'you have done so much for me. It's such a little gift to give, in return.'

Her voice was soft and pleading, and when I glanced up at her there was quite a wounded look about her eyes.

'It's very sweet of you,' I said, 'but I don't think you should do it, all the same.'

'Let me be the judge of that,' she answered, 'and I know, when you see the room finished, you will be pleased.'

I felt wretched, and uncomfortable; not that she should wish to give me a present, which was generous of her and impulsive, and which I would have accepted without thought had it been yesterday. But this evening, since I had read that infernal scrap of letter, I was haunted by the doubt that what she wanted to do for me might turn in some way to her disadvantage; and that in giving way to her I was giving way to something that I did not fully understand.

Presently she said to me, 'That book of gardens is going to be very helpful for our planning here. I had forgotten I had given it to Ambrose. You must look at the engravings. Of course they are not right for this place, but certain features would work in well. A terraced walk, for instance, looking down to the sea across the fields, and on the other side of it a sunken water garden – as they have in one of the villas in Rome where I used to stay.

165

There's an engraving of it in the book. I know just the spot for it, where that old wall used to stand.'

I hardly know how I did it, but I found myself asking her, in a voice at once casual and off-hand, 'Have you always lived in Italy, since you were born?'

'Yes,' she answered, 'did Ambrose never tell you? My mother's people came from Rome, and my father Alexander Coryn was one of those men who find it difficult to settle anywhere. He never could bear England, I think he did not get on very well with his family here, in Cornwall. He liked the life in Rome, and he and my mother suited each other well. But they led a precarious sort of existence, never any money, you know. I was used to it as a child, but as I grew up it was most unsettling.'

'Are they both dead?' I asked.

'Oh, yes, my father died when I was sixteen. Mother and I were alone for five years. Until I married Cosimo Sangalletti. Five fearful years they were too, moving from city to city, not always certain where our next meal would come from. Mine was not a sheltered girlhood, Philip. I was thinking only last Sunday how different from Louise.'

So she had been twenty-one when she married first. The same age as Louise. I wondered how they had lived, she and her mother, until she met Sangalletti. Perhaps they had given lessons in Italian, as she had suggested doing here. Perhaps that was what had made her think of it.

'My mother was very beautiful,' she said, 'quite different from me, except for colouring. Tall, almost massive. And like many women of her type she went suddenly to pieces, lost her looks, grew fat and careless; I was glad my father did not live to see it. I was glad he did not live to see many things she did, or myself either, for that matter.'

Her voice was matter-of-fact and simple, she spoke without bitterness; yet I thought, looking at her there as she sat by my library fire, how little of her I really knew, and how little of that past life of hers I would ever know. She had called Louise sheltered, which was true. And I thought suddenly that the same

166

held good for me. Here I was, twenty-four, and apart from the conventional years at Harrow and Oxford I knew nothing of the world but my own five hundred acres. When a person like my cousin Rachel moved from one place to another, left one home for a second, and then a third; married once, then twice; how did it feel? Did she shut the past behind her like a door and never think of it again, or was she beset with memories from day to day?

'Was he much older than you?' I said to her.

'Cosimo?' she said. 'Why no, only a year or so. My mother was introduced to him in Florence, she had always wanted to know the Sangallettis. He took nearly a year before he made up his mind between my mother and myself. Then she lost her looks, poor dear, and lost him too. The bargain I picked up proved a liability. But of course Ambrose must have written you the whole story. It is not a happy one.'

I was about to say, 'No, Ambrose was more reserved than you ever knew. If there was something that hurt him, that shocked him, he would pretend it was not there, that it had not happened. He never told me anything about your life before you married him, except that Sangalletti was killed fighting, in a duel.' Instead, I said none of this. I knew suddenly that I did not want to know either. Not about Sangalletti, nor about her mother and her life in Florence. I wanted to shut the door on it. And lock it too.

'Yes,' I said, 'yes, Ambrose wrote and told me.'

She sighed, and patted the cushion behind her head.

'Ah, well,' she said, 'it all seems very long ago now. The girl who endured those years was another person. I had nearly ten years of it, you know, married to Cosimo Sangalletti. I would not be young again, if you offered me the world. But then I'm prejudiced.'

'You talk,' I said, 'as if you were ninety-nine.'

'For a women I very nearly am,' she said. 'I'm thirty-five.'

She looked at me and smiled.

'Oh?' I said. 'I thought you more.'

'Which most women would take as an insult, but I as a

167

compliment,' she said. 'Thank you, Philip.' And then, before I had time to frame an answer, she went on, 'What was really on that piece of paper you threw on the fire this morning?'

The suddenness of the attack caught me unprepared. I stared at her and swallowed hard.

'The paper?' I hedged. 'What paper?'

'You know perfectly well,' she said; 'the piece of paper with Ambrose's handwriting upon it, which you burnt so that I should not see.'

I made up my mind then that a half-truth was better than a lie. Although I felt the colour flame into my face, I met her eyes.

'It was a piece torn from a letter,' I said, 'a letter, I think, that he must have been writing to me. He simply expressed himself as worried about expenditure. There was only a line or two, I don't even remember how it went. I threw it in the fire because coming upon it, just at that moment, might have saddened you.'

Rather to my surprise, but to my relief also, the eyes, watching me so intently, relaxed. The hands, holding the rings, fell on her lap.

'Was that all?' she said. 'I wondered so much . . . I could not understand.'

Thank heaven, though, she accepted my explanation.

'Poor Ambrose,' she said, 'it was a constant source of worry to him, what he considered my extravagance; I wonder that you did not hear of it more often. The life out there was so entirely different from the one he knew at home. He never could bring himself to accept it. And then – good heaven, I cannot blame him – I know at the bottom of his heart he bore resentment against the life I had been obliged to lead before I met him. Those frightful debts, he paid them all.'

I was silent, but as I sat watching her, and smoking, I felt easier in my mind, no longer anxious. The half-truth had been successful, and she was speaking to me now without strain.

'He was so generous,' she said, 'those first months. You cannot imagine, Philip, what it meant to me; at last someone I could trust, and, what was more wonderful still, someone I could love

168

as well. I think if I had asked him for anything on earth he would have given it to me. That was why, when he became ill . . .' She broke off, and her eyes were troubled. 'That was why it was so hard to understand, the way he changed.'

'You mean,' I said, 'that he wasn't generous any more?'

'He was generous, yes,' she said, 'but not in the same way. He would buy me things, presents, pieces of jewellery, almost as though he tried to test me in some way; I can't explain it. And if I asked him for any money, some little necessity for the house, something we had to have – he would not give me the money. He used to look at me, with a strange brooding sort of suspicion; he would ask me why I wanted the money, how I intended to use it, was I going to give it to anyone . . . Eventually I had to go to Rainaldi, I had to ask Rainaldi, Philip, for money to pay the servants' wages.'

She broke off again, and looked at me.

'Did Ambrose find out that you did that?' I asked.

'Yes,' she said. 'He had never cared for Rainaldi, I believe I told you so before. But when he knew I went to him for money . . . that was the finish, he could not bear him to come to the villa any more. You would hardly credit it, Philip, but I had to go out furtively, when Ambrose was resting, and meet Rainaldi in order to get money for the house.' Suddenly she gestured with her hands, and got up from her chair.

'Oh, God,' she said, 'I did not mean to tell you all this.'

She went over to the window, and pulled aside the curtain, and looked out at the driving rain.

'Why not?' I asked.

'Because I want you to remember him as you knew him here,' she said. 'You have your picture of him, in this house. He was your Ambrose then. Let it stay like that. The last months were mine, and I want no one to share them with me. You, least of all.'

I did not want to share them with her. I wanted her to close all those doors belonging to the past, one by one.

'You know what has happened?' she said, turning round from

the window and looking at me. 'We did wrong when we opened those boxes in the room upstairs. We should have let them stay there. We were wrong to touch his things. I felt it from the first moment, when I opened the trunk and saw his dressing-gown and the slippers. We have let something loose that was not with us before. Some sort of bitter feeling.' She had become very white. Her hands were clasped in front of her. 'I have not forgotten,' she said, 'those letters that you threw into the fire, and burnt. I pushed the thought of them away, but to-day, since we opened up the trunks, it is just as though I had read them once again.'

I got up from my chair and stood with my back to the fire. I did not know what to say to her as she paced up and down the room.

'He said, in his letter, that I watched him,' she went on. 'Of course I watched him, lest he should do himself some damage. Rainaldi wanted me to have the nuns in from the convent to help me, but I would not; had I done that, Ambrose would have said they were keepers, brought in by me to spy upon him. He trusted no one. The doctors were good and patient men, but more often than not he refused to see them. One by one, he asked me to dismiss the servants. In the end, only Giuseppe remained. He trusted him. He said he had dog's eyes . . .'

She broke off, and turned away. I thought of the servant from the lodge by the villa gate, and his desire to spare me pain. It was strange that Ambrose too had believed in those honest, faithful eyes. And I had only looked upon the servant once.

'There is no need to talk of all that now,' I said to her: 'it does no good to Ambrose, and it only tortures you. As to myself, what happened between you and him is no concern of mine. That is all over and done with and forgotten. The villa was not his home. Nor, when you married Ambrose, was it yours either. This is your home.'

She turned and looked at me. 'Sometimes,' she said slowly, 'you are so like him that I become afraid. I see your eyes, with that same expression, turned upon me; and it is as though, after

170

all, he had not died, and everything that was endured must be endured once more. I could not bear it again, not that suspicion, not that bitterness, going on and on, day after day, night after night.'

As she spoke, I had a clear picture of the villa Sangalletti. I saw the little court, and the laburnum tree as it would be in spring, with yellow blossom. I saw the chair there, with Ambrose sitting in it and his stick beside him. I felt the whole dark silence of the place. I smelt the musty air, I watched the dripping fountain. And for the first time the woman who looked down from the balcony above was not a figment of my imagination, but was Rachel. She looked at Ambrose with the same pleading look, that look of suffering, of supplication. Suddenly I felt very old, and very wise, and full of a new strength I did not understand. I held out my hands to her.

'Rachel. Come here,' I said.

She came across the room to me, and she put her hands in mine.

'There is no bitter feeling in this house,' I said to her. 'The house is mine. Bitterness goes with people when they die. Those clothes are all packed up and put away. They have nothing any more to do with either of us. From now on you are going to remember Ambrose as I remember him. We'll keep his old hat there, on the settle in the hall. And the stick, with the others, in the stand. You belong here now, just as he did, just as I do. We are all three of us part of the place together. Do you understand?'

She looked up at me. She did not take away her hands.

'Yes,' she said.

I felt strangely moved, as if all that I did and said was laid down for me and planned, while at the same time a small still voice whispered to me in some dark cell of matter, 'You can never go back upon this moment. Never . . . never . . .' We stood, holding each other's hands, and she said to me, 'Why are you so good to me, Philip?'

I remembered that in the morning, when she cried, she had rested her head against my heart. I had put my arms about her,

171

for a moment, and laid my face against her hair. I wanted it to happen again. More than anything I had ever known. But to-night she did not cry. To-night she did not come and rest her head against my heart. She just stood there, holding my hands.

'I'm not good to you,' I said; 'I only want you to be happy.'

She moved away and picked up her candlestick to take to bed, and as she went from the room she said to me, 'Good night, Philip, and God bless you. One day you may come to know some of the happiness that I knew once.'

I heard her go upstairs, and I sat down and stared into the library fire. It seemed to me that if there was any bitterness left in the house it did not come from her, nor from Ambrose, but was a seed deep in my own heart, which I should never tell her of and she need never know. The old sin of jealousy I thought buried and forgotten was with me once again. But this time I was jealous, not of Rachel, but of Ambrose, whom hitherto I had known and loved best in the whole world.

16

November and December passed very swiftly, or so it seemed to me. Usually, as the days shortened and the weather worsened, when there would be little to do outside and it grew dark by half-past four, I had found the long evenings in the house monotonous. Never a great reader, and unsociable, so that I did not care to shoot with my neighbours or go out and dine with them, I used to be champing for the turn of the year, when with Christmas behind me and the shortest day gone I could look forward to the spring. And spring comes early, in the west. Even before New Year's Day the first shrubs are in bloom. Yet this autumn passed without monotony. The leaves fell, and the trees were bare, and all the Barton acres lay brown and soggy with the rain, while a chill wind nipped the sea and turned it grey. But I did not look upon it with despondency.

We settled down to a routine, my cousin Rachel and myself, which seldom varied, and it seemed to suit us well. When the weather permitted it, she would spend the morning in the grounds directing Tamlyn and the gardeners about the planting, or watching the progress of the terraced walk we had decided upon, which had necessitated the employment of extra men, besides those who worked in the woods; while I did my usual business about the estate, riding to and fro amongst the farms, or visiting others in the outlying districts, where I held land also. We met at half-past twelve for a brief meal, cold usually, a ham, or pie, with cake. It was the servants' dinner hour, and we waited on ourselves. It would be my first sight of her for the day, for she always took breakfast in her room.

When I was out and about on the estate, or in my office, and heard the clock on the belfry strike noon, followed almost at once by the great clanging bell that summoned the men to their dinner, I would be aware of a rising excitement within me, a quick lifting of the heart.

What I was employed upon would seem, all of a sudden, to lack interest. If I was riding out of doors, in the park, say, or in the woods or the nearby acres, and the sound of the clock and the bell echoed through the air – for it travelled far, and I have heard it three miles distant when the wind was with it – I would turn Gypsy's head for home with impatience, almost as if I feared, by delaying any longer without doors, I might miss one moment of the luncheon hour. And in my office it would be the same. I would stare at the papers on the desk before me, bite on my pen, tilt backwards on my chair; and what I had been writing would become, of a sudden, of no importance whatsoever. That letter could wait, those figures need not be reckoned, that piece of business over in Bodmin could be decided upon another time; and pushing everything aside I would leave the office, and pass through the court-yard to the house and so the dining-room.

She was usually there before me, to give me welcome and wish me a good morning. Often she laid a sprig beside my plate, as a sort of offering, which I would put into my button-hole; or there would be some new cordial for me to taste, one of those herb brews of which she seemed to have a hundred recipes and was forever giving to the cook to try. She had been several weeks with me in the house before Seecombe told me, in deadly secret, behind his hand, that the cook had been going to her every day to ask for orders, and that was the reason why we now fed so well.

'The mistress,' Seecombe said, 'had not wished Mr Ashley to know, lest it should be thought presumptuous of her.'

I laughed, and did not tell her that I knew; but sometimes, for the fun of it, I would remark upon some dish that we were having, and exclaim, 'I cannot think what has come over them in the kitchen. The boys are turning into chefs from France,' and she would answer me in innocence, 'Do you like it? Is it something better than you had before?'

One and all called her 'the mistress' now, and I did not mind it. I think it pleased me and gave me, too, a sort of pride.

When we had eaten luncheon she would go upstairs to rest, or if it was a Tuesday or a Thursday I might order the carriage for her, and Wellington would drive her about the neighbourhood to return the calls that had been made upon her. Sometimes, if I had business on the way, I would ride with her for a mile or so, and then get out of the carriage and let her go her way. She would take great care about her person, when she went calling. Her best mantle, and her new veil and bonnet. I would sit with my back to the horses, in the carriage, so that I could look at her; and, I think to tease me, she would not lift her veil.

'Now to your gossip,' I would say, 'now to your little shocks and scandals. I would give much to become a fly upon the wall.'

'Come with me,' she would answer; 'it would be very good for you.'

'Not on your life. You can tell me all, at dinner.'

And I would stand in the road and watch the carriage bowl away, while from the window blew the wisp of a handkerchief to taunt me. I would not see her again until we dined at five, and the intervening hours become something to be gone through for the evening's sake. Whether I was on business, or about the estate, or talking with people, all the time I had a sense of urgency, an impatience to be done. How was the time? I looked at Ambrose's watch. Still only half-past four? How the hours dragged. And coming back to the house, by way of the stables, I would know at once if she had returned, for I would see the carriage in the coach-house and the horses being fed and watered. Going into the house, passing into the library and the drawing-room, I would see both rooms were empty, and this would mean she had gone up to her rooms to rest. She always rested before dinner. Then I would take a bath, or wash, and change, and go down into the library below to wait for her. My impatience mounted as the hands of the clock drew nearer to five. I would leave the door of the library open, so that I could hear her step.

First would come the patter of the dogs – I counted for nothing with them now, they followed her like shadows – and then the rustle of her gown as it swept the stairs. It was, I think, the moment I loved best in the whole day. There was something in the sound that gave me such a shock of anticipation, such a feeling of expectancy, that I hardly knew what to do or what to say when she came into the room. I don't know what stuff her gowns were made of, whether of stiff silk, or satin, or brocade, but they seemed to sweep the floor, and lift, and sweep again; and whether it was the gown itself that floated, or she wearing it and moving forward with such grace, but the library, that had seemed dark and austere before she entered, would be suddenly alive.

A new softness came to her by candlelight that was not with her in the day. It was as if the brightness of morning and the duller shades of afternoon were given up to purposes of work, of practicality, making a briskness of movement that was definite and cool; and now with evening closed in, the shutters fastened, the weather banished, and the house withdrawn into itself, she shone with a radiance that had lain concealed about her person until now. There was more colour to her cheeks and to her hair, great depth to her eyes, and whether she turned her head to speak, or moved to the bookcase to pick up a volume, or bent to pat Don as he lay stretched out before the fire, there was an easy grace in all she did which gave to every movement fascination. I wondered, in these moments, how I could ever have thought her unremarkable.

Seecombe would announce dinner, and we would pass into the dining-room and take our places, I at the head of the table, she at my right hand, and it seemed to me this had always happened, there was nothing new in it, and nothing strange, and I had never sat there alone, in my old jacket, unchanged, with a book propped up in front of me so that I did not have to talk to Seecombe. Yet, if it had always happened, it would not have seemed stimulating to me, as it did now, with the mere process

176

of eating and drinking becoming, in a sense, a new adventure.

The excitement did not lessen with the passing weeks, rather it increased, so that I would find myself making excuses to be about the house, for the sake of five minutes or so, when I might catch a glimpse of her, thus making an addition to the regular time of midday and evening when we would be together.

She might be in the library, or passing through the hall upon some business, or waiting in the drawing-room for her callers, and she would smile at me and say, in some surprise, 'Philip, what brings you home at such an hour?' causing me to think up some invention. As to the gardens, I who had yawned and kicked my heels in the old days when Ambrose had tried to interest me, I now made a point of being present whenever there should be a consultation in the plantation or upon the terrace walk, and again after dinner, in the evenings, we would look through her Italian books together, compare the engravings and debate, with much argument, what could best be copied. I think if she had suggested we should build a replica of the Roman Forum itself, above the Barton acres, I would have agreed with her. I said yes, and no, and very fine indeed, and shook my head, but I never really listened. It was watching her interest in the business that gave me pleasure, watching her consider thoughtfully between one picture and another, her brows knit, a pen in her hand to mark the page, and then to watch the hands themselves that turned from one volume to another.

We did not always sit below in the library. Sometimes she would ask me to go with her upstairs, to aunt Phoebe's boudoir, and we would spread out the books and plans of gardens upon the floor. I was host in the library down below, but here, in her boudoir, she was hostess. I am not sure I did not like it better. We lost formality. Seecombe did not bother us – by some great measure of tact she had got him to dispense with the solemnity of the silver tea tray – and she would brew tisana for us both instead, which she said was a continental custom and much better for the eyes and skin.

These after-dinner hours passed all too swiftly, and I would hope that she would forget to ask the time, but the wretched clock in the belfry, far too close to our heads to strike ten o'clock and not be noticed, always shattered the peace.

'I had no idea it was so late,' she used to say, rising to her feet and closing the books. I knew this was the signal for dismissal. Even the trick of lingering by the door in conversation did not pass with her. Ten o'clock had struck, and I must go. Sometimes she gave me her hand to kiss. Sometimes she offered me a cheek. Sometimes she patted me upon the shoulder, as she might have done a puppy. Never again did she come close to me, or take my face between her hands as she had done that evening when she lay in bed. I did not look for it, I did not hope for it; but when I had said goodnight and gone back along the corridor to my own room, opened up my shutters and stared out at the silent garden, and heard the distant murmur of the sea breaking in the little bay beneath the woods, I would feel oddly lonely, as a child does when holiday is done.

The evening, which had built itself up, hour by hour throughout the day in fevered fancy, was over now. It would seem long before it came again. And neither my mind nor my body was ready for repose. In the old days, before she had come to the house, I used to doze before the fire in winter after dining, and then, stretching and yawning, clump my way upstairs, happy to roll into my bed and sleep till seven. Now, it was otherwise. I could have walked all night. I could have talked till dawn. To do the first was foolish. To do the second, an impossibility. Therefore I flung myself down in a chair before the open window, and smoked, and stared out across the lawn; and sometimes it was one or two in the morning before I undressed and went to bed, and all I had done was to sit there brooding in my chair, thinking of nothing, wasting the silent hours.

In December the first frosts came with the full moon, and then my nights of vigil held a quality harder to bear. There was a sort of beauty to them, cold and clear, that caught at the heart and made me stare in wonder. From my windows the long lawns dipped to the meadows, and the meadows to the sea, and all of them were white with frost, and white too under the moon. The trees that fringed the lawns were black and still. Rabbits came out and pricked about the grass, then scattered to their burrows; and suddenly, from the hush and stillness, I heard that high sharp bark of a vixen, with the little sob that follows it, eerie, unmistakable, unlike any other call that comes by night, and out of the woods I saw the lean low body creep and run out upon the lawn, and hide again where the trees would cover it. Later I heard the call again, away in the distance, in the open park, and now the full moon topped the trees and held the sky, and nothing stirred on the lawns beneath my window. I wondered if Rachel slept, in the blue bedroom; or if, like me, she left her curtains wide. The clock that had driven me to bed at ten struck one, struck two, and I thought that here about me was a wealth of beauty that we might have shared.

People who mattered not could take the humdrum world. But this was not the world, it was enchantment; and all of it was mine. I did not want it for myself alone.

So like a weather-glass I swung, from moods of exultation and excitement to a low level sometimes of dullness and depression, when, remembering her promise to remain with me for a brief time only, I wondered how much longer she would stay. If, after Christmas, she would turn to me and say, 'Well, Philip, next week I go to London.' The spell of hard weather put a stop to all the planting, and little more could be done now till the spring. The terrace might be completed, for this was better done when dry, but with the plan to follow the men could work without her very well. Any day she might decide to go, and I would not be able to think of an excuse to hold her back.

In old days, at Christmas, when Ambrose had been home, he had given dinner to the tenants on Christmas Eve. I had let it lapse, the last winters of his absence, because when he had returned from travelling he held the dinner on mid-summer day. Now I decided to give the dinner once again, as of long custom, if only for the reason that Rachel would be there.

When I was a child it had been the highlight of my Christmas.

The men used to bring in a tall fir tree about a week before Christmas Eve, and put it in the long room over the coach houses, where we held the dinner. I was not supposed to know that it was there. But when no one was about, generally at midday, when the servants would be eating, I used to go round by the back and climb up the steps to the side-door leading into the long room, and there I would see the great tree, standing in its tub at the far end, and stacked against the wall, ready to place in rows, were the long trestle tables for the dinner. I never helped to decorate until my first holiday from Harrow. The promotion was tremendous. I had never felt so proud. As a little lad I had sat beside Ambrose at the top table, but on my promotion I headed a table of my own.

Now, once again, I gave my orders to the woodmen, in fact I went out myself into the woods to choose the tree. Rachel was all delight. No celebration could have pleased her better. She held earnest consultation with Seecombe and the cook, she visited the larders, and the storage chambers, and the game-house; she even prevailed upon my male household to allow two girls from the Barton to come up and make French pastry under her supervision. All was excitement, and mystery too; because I would have it that she should not see the tree, and she insisted that I must not know what would be put before us for the dinner.

Packages arrived for her, and were whisked away upstairs. When I knocked upon her boudoir door I would hear crackling of paper, and then, an age afterwards it seemed, her voice would answer me, 'Come in.' And she would be kneeling on the floor, her eyes bright, her cheeks flushed, with a covering flung over several objects strewn about the carpet, and she would tell me not to look.

I was back to childhood once again, back to the old fever of standing in my nightshirt tip-toe on the stairs, hearing the murmur of voices from below, and Ambrose coming suddenly from the library and laughing at me, 'Go up to bed, you rascal, I'll flay the hide off you.'

One thing gave me anxiety. What could I give Rachel for a

present? I took a day in Truro, browsing in the bookshops for a book on gardens, but could find nothing. And what was more, the books from Italy she had brought with her were finer than any I could give her. I had no idea what present pleased a woman. My godfather used to buy stuff to make a gown, when he gave anything to Louise, but Rachel wore mourning only. I could not give her that. Once, I remember, Louise had been much delighted with a locket that he had brought from London. She used to wear it of an evening, when she ate Sunday dinner with us. And then the solution came to me.

There must be something, amongst the jewels belonging to my family, that I could give to Rachel. They were not kept at home in the safe, with the Ashley documents and papers, but at the bank. Ambrose had thought it best, in case of fire. I had no knowledge what was there. I had a hazy recollection of going to the bank one day with Ambrose, when I was very young, and of his picking up some necklace and telling me, smiling, that it had belonged to our grandmother, and that my mother had worn it on her wedding-day, but for the day only, as a loan, my father not being in the direct line of succession, and that one day, if I behaved myself well, Ambrose would permit me to give it to my wife. I realised, now, that whatever there was in the bank belonged to me. Or would do, in three months' time; but that was quibbling.

My godfather would know, of course, what jewels there were, but he had gone up to Exeter on business and would not be home until Christmas Eve, when he and Louise were invited to the dinner. I determined to go to the bank myself and demand to see the jewels.

Mr Couch received me with his usual courtesy, and taking me into his private room, facing the harbour, he listened to my request.

'I take it Mr Kendall would have no objection?' he asked.

'Of course not,' I said impatiently, 'the matter is quite understood.' Which was untruthful, but at twenty-four, within a few months of my birthday, to have to ask my godfather for permission to do every little thing was quite ridiculous. And it riled me.

181

Mr Couch sent to the vaults for the jewels. They came up, in sealed boxes. He broke the seal, and, placing a cloth on the desk in front of him, laid the jewels out upon it, one by one.

I had no idea the collection was so fine. There were rings, bracelets, earrings, brooches; and many of the pieces went together, such as a ruby headpiece for the hair and ruby ear-rings to go with it, likewise a sapphire bracelet and pendant and ring. Yet as I looked at them, not liking to touch them even with my finger, I remembered, with disappointment, that Rachel was in mourning, and wore no coloured stones. If I presented her with these, it would be pointless; she would have no use for them.

Then Mr Couch opened the last box, and drew from it a collar of pearls. There were four strands. They fastened round the neck like a band, with a single diamond clasp. I recognised it instantly. It was the necklace that Ambrose had shown me as a child.

'I like this,' I said, 'this is the finest thing in the whole collection. I remember my cousin Ambrose showing it to me.'

'Why, there might be a difference of opinion,' said Mr Couch; 'for my part, I would price the rubies highest. But there is family feeling about the pearl collar. Your grandmother, Mrs Ambrose Ashley, wore it first as a bride, at the Court of St James. Then your aunt, Mrs Philip, had it given to her, as a matter of course, when the estate passed down to your uncle. Various members of the family have worn it on their wedding-day. Your own mother was amongst them; in point of fact, I think she was the last to do so. Your cousin, Mr Ambrose Ashley, would never permit it to go out of the country, when there were weddings elsewhere.'

He held the collar in his hand, and the light from the window fell upon the smooth round pearls.

'Yes,' he said, 'it is a beautiful thing. And no woman has put it on for five-and-twenty years. I attended your mother's wedding. She was a pretty creature. It became her well.'

I put out my hand and took the collar from him.

'Well, I want to keep it now,' I said, and I placed the collar with its wrappings in the box. He looked a little taken aback.

'I do not know if that is wise, Mr Ashley,' he said. 'If this should be lost or mislaid it would be a terrible thing.'

'It won't be lost,' I answered briefly.

He did not seem happy, and I made haste to go, lest he should produce some argument more forceful.

'If you are worried what my guardian will say,' I told him, 'please rest assured. I will make it right with him when he returns from Exeter.'

'I hope so,' said Mr Couch, 'but I had preferred it had he been present. Of course in April, when you come into the property legally, it would not matter if you took the whole collection, and did as you wished with them. I should not advise such a step, but it would be strictly legal.'

I held out my hand to him and wished him a pleasant Christmas and rode home, much elated. If I had searched the whole country I could not have found a better present for her. Thank heaven pearls were white. And it made a bond to think that the last woman to wear them had been my mother. I would tell her that. Now I could face the prospect of Christmas Eve with a lighter heart.

Two days to wait . . . The weather was fine, the frost was light, and there was all the promise of a clear dry evening for the dinner. The servants were much excited, and on the morning of Christmas Eve, when the trestle tables and the benches had been set down the room, and the knives and forks and platters all laid ready, with evergreen hanging from the beams, I asked Seecombe and the lads to come with me and decorate the tree. Seecombe made himself master of the ceremony. He stood a little apart from the rest of us, to give himself a longer view, and as we turned the tree this way and that, and lifted one branch and then another, to balance the frosty fir cones on it and the holly berries, he waved his hands at us, looking for all the world like the conductor of a string sextet.

'The angle does not please me, Mr Phillip,' he said, 'the tree would appear to better advantage if moved a trifle to the left. Ah! too far . . . Yes, that is better. John, the fourth branch on the right is bent. Raise it somewhat. Tch, tch . . . your touch is heavy. Spread out the branches, Arthur, spread them. The tree must seem to be standing as nature placed it. Don't stamp upon the berries, Jim. Mr Philip, let it stay now as it is. One further movement, and the whole is wrecked.'

I had never thought him to possess such a sense of artistry.

He stood back, his hands under his coat-tails, his eyes near closed. 'Mr Philip,' he said to me, 'we have attained perfection.' I saw young John nudge Arthur in the ribs and turn away.

Dinner was set to start at five. The Kendalls and the Pascoes would be the only 'carriage folk', as the expression had it. The rest would come by wagonette or trap, or even on their own feet, those who lived near by. I had written out all the names on pieces of paper, and placed them on the appropriate platters. Those who had difficulty in reading, or who could not read at all, had neighbours who could do so. There were three tables. I was to head one, with Rachel at the further end. The second was headed by Billy Rowe from the Barton, and the third by Peter Johns, from Coombe.

The custom was for all the company to be assembled in the long room, ready seated, soon after five; and when everyone was in place we would walk into the room. When dinner was over, Ambrose and I used to give the people their presents from the tree, always money for the men, and new shawls for the women, and hampers of food for all of them. The presents never varied. Any change of routine would have shocked them, every one. This Christmas, though, I had asked Rachel to give out the presents with me.

Before dressing for dinner, I had sent along to Rachel's room the collar of pearls. I had left it in its wrappings, but had placed a note inside. On the note I had written these words, 'My mother wore this last. Now it belongs to you. I want you to wear it tonight, and always. Philip.'

I had my bath, and dressed, and was ready before a quarter to five.

The Kendalls and the Pascoes would not call for us at the

house; the custom was for them to go straight to the long room, where they chatted with the tenants and helped to break the ice. Ambrose had always considered this a sound idea. The servants would be in the long room also, and Ambrose and I used to walk through the stone passages at the back of the house, and across the court, and out and up the flight of steps to the long room above the coach-houses. Tonight, Rachel and I would walk the passages alone.

I came downstairs and waited in the drawing-room. I felt some trepidation, as I stood there, for never in my life had I given a present to a woman. It might be that it was a breach of etiquette, that flowers only were acceptable, or books, or pictures. What if she should be angry, as she had been over that business of the quarterly allowance, and should imagine, in some queer fashion, that I did this to insult her? It was a desperate thought. The passing minutes were slow torture. At last I heard her footstep on the stairs. No dogs preceded her to-night. They had all been locked early in their kennels.

She came slowly; the familiar rustle of her gown drew near. The door was open, and she came into the room and stood before me. She wore deep black, as I had expected, but I had not seen the gown before. It stood out, away from her, clinging only about the bodice and the waist, and the stuff had a sheen to it as though the light was upon it. Her shoulders were bare. She had dressed her hair higher than usual, the roll of it was looped up and drawn back, showing her ears. Around her neck was the collar of pearls. It was the only piece of jewellery upon her person. It glowed soft and white against her skin. I had never seen her look so radiant, or so happy. Louise and the Pascoes had been right after all. Rachel was beautiful.

She stood there a moment watching me, and then she put out her hands to me and said, 'Philip.' I walked towards her. I stood in front of her. She put her arms about me and held me to her. There were tears in her eyes, but tonight I did not mind. She took her arms from my shoulders, and raised them to the back of my head, and touched my hair.

Then she kissed me. Not as she had done before. And as I stood there, holding her, I thought to myself, 'It was not yearning for home, nor sickness of the blood, nor fever of the brain – but for this, that Ambrose died.'

I kissed her in return. In the belfry the clock struck five. She said nothing to me, nor I to her. She gave me her hand. We went down the dark kitchen passages together, across the court, and so to the long room above the coach-house, where the windows were brightly lit. To the laughing surge of voices and the bright expectant faces.

17

The whole company stood up as we came into the room. The tables were pushed back, there was shuffling of feet, the murmur of voices hushed; the heads of one and all turned round to look at us. Rachel paused a moment on the threshold; I think she had not expected such a sea of faces. Then she saw the Christmas tree at the far end, and gave a cry of pleasure. The pause was broken, and a murmur of sympathy and gladness at her surprise arose from everyone.

We took our places at our respective ends of the top table, and Rachel sat down. The rest of us did the same, and at once a clamour of chat and talk began, with clattering of knives, and moving of platters, and each man jostling his neighbour in laughter and apology. I had for partner on my right Mrs Bill Rowe, from the Barton, sprigged out to beat all comers in her muslins, and I noticed that Mrs Johns of Coombe, upon my left, looked at her in disfavour. I had forgotten, in my desire for protocol, that neither of them 'spoke' to the other. Some rift, dating back to a misunderstanding about eggs on market day, had lasted fifteen years. No matter, I would be gallant to the pair of them and cover all distress. Flagons of cider would come to my assistance, and seizing the nearest jug I helped them, and myself, most liberally, then turned to the bill of fare. The kitchens had done us well. Never, in my long memories of Christmas dinners, had we been offered plenty such as this. Roast goose, roast turkey, sides of beef and mutton, great smoked hams decorated with a frill, pastries and pies of all shapes and sizes, puddings bulging with dried fruits; and between the heavier fare were platters of that delicate fragile pastry, airy as thistledown, that Rachel had concocted with the Barton maids.

Smiles of anticipation and of greed wreathed the faces of the hungry guests, my own amongst them, and already great gusts of laughter came from the other tables, where, undaunted by the immediate presence of the 'master', the broader-tongued among my tenants let themselves go with loosening of belts and collars. I heard Jack Libby, of bibulous eye, utter hoarsely to his neighbour – I think he had already had a glass or two of cider on the road – 'By Gor ... after this lot they could feed us to the crows and we wouldn't feel et.' Little thin-lipped Mrs Johns upon my left pricked at her wing of goose with a fork poised between her fingers like a quill, and the fellow whispered to her, with a wink in my direction, 'Go to it 'm'dear, with thumb and finger. Tear 'un asunder.'

It was then I noticed that each one of us had a small package put beside his plate, the packages addressed in Rachel's handwriting. Everybody seemed to perceive this at the same time, and for a brief moment the food was forgotten, in the excited tearing of the paper. I watched, and waited, before opening my own. I realised, with a sudden ache in my heart, what she had done. She had given every man and woman assembled there a present. She had wrapped them up herself, and enclosed with each a note. Nothing big, or fine, but a little trifle that would please them well. So that was the reason for the mysterious wrappings behind the boudoir door. I understood it all.

When each of my neighbours had fallen to their food again I opened my own. I unwrapped it on my knees, beneath the table, determined that only I myself should see what had been given me. It was a gold chain for my keys, with a disk upon it bearing our initials, P.A.R.A., and the date beneath. I held it for a moment in my hands, then put it, furtively, into my waistcoat pocket. I looked up at her and smiled. She was watching me. I raised my glass to her, she raised hers in reply. God! I was happy.

Dinner proceeded, uproarious and gay. Greasy platters, heaped with food, were emptied, I know not how. Glasses were filled, and filled again. Someone, halfway down the table, began to sing, and the song was taken up and joined by those from the other tables. Boots hummed a measure on the floor, knives and forks beat time upon the platters, bodies swayed to and fro in rollicking rhythmic fashion; and thin-lipped Mrs Johns of Coombe told me that, for a man, my lashes were far too long. I helped her to more cider.

At last, remembering how Ambrose timed his moment to perfection, I rapped long and loud upon the table. The voices died away. 'Those who desire to do so,' I said, 'may go outside, and then return again. In five minutes' time Mrs Ashley and I will give the presents from the tree. Thank you, ladies and gentlemen.'

The pressure to the doors was precisely what I had expected. And with a smile on my lips I watched Seecombe, walking stiff and straight yet treading the ground lest it should give way beneath his feet, bring up the rear. Those who remained pushed the benches and the trestles against the wall. After the presents had been given from the tree, and we had departed, those who were able to do so would take their partners in a dance. High revelry would last until midnight. I used to listen to the stamping, as a boy, from my nursery window. To-night I made my way over to the little group standing by the tree. The vicar was there, and Mrs Pascoe, three daughters and a curate. Likewise my godfather and Louise. Louise looked well, but a trifle pale. I shook hands with them. Mrs Pascoe gushed at me, all teeth, 'You have surpassed yourself. Never have we enjoyed ourselves so much. The girls are quite in ecstasy.'

They looked it, with one curate between three of them.

'I'm glad you thought it went off well,' I said, and, turning to Rachel, 'Have you been happy?'

Her eyes met mine and smiled. 'What do you think?' she said. 'So happy, I could cry.'

I saluted my godfather. 'Good evening to you, sir, and happy Christmas,' I said. 'How did you find Exeter?'

'Cold,' he said shortly, 'cold and drear.'

His manner was abrupt. He stood with one hand behind his back, the other tugged at his white moustache. I wondered if

189

something about the dinner had upset him. Had the cider flowed too freely for his liking? Then I saw him stare at Rachel. His eyes were fixed upon the collar of pearls around her throat. He saw me staring, and he turned away. For a moment I felt back again in the Fourth Form at Harrow, with the master discovering the crib hidden under my Latin book. Then I shrugged my shoulders. I was Philip Ashley, aged four-and-twenty years. And no one in the world, certainly not my godfather, could dictate to me to whom I should, or should not, give Christmas presents. I wondered if Mrs Pascoe had already dropped some fell remark. Possibly good manners would prevent her. And anyway, she could not know the collar. My mother had been dead before Mr Pascoe held the living. Louise had noticed it. That was already plain. I saw her blue eyes waver towards Rachel, and then drop again.

The people came stumping back into the room. Laughing, murmuring, pressing together, they came nearer to the tree, as Rachel and I took our stand before it. Then I bent to the presents, and, reading out the names, gave the parcels to Rachel; and one by one they came to take their gifts. She stood there, before the tree, flushed, and gay, and smiling. It was all I could do to read the names instead of looking at her. 'Thank you, God bless you, sir,' they said to me; and passing on to her, 'Thank you, m'am. God bless you, too.'

It took us the best part of half an hour to give the presents and to say a word to each. When it was over and done with, the last present accepted with a curtsey, a sudden silence fell. The people, standing all together in a great group against the wall, waited for me. 'A happy Christmas to you, one and all,' I said. And back came the shout from the whole lot of them as one, 'A happy Christmas to you, sir, and to Mrs Ashley.'

Then Billy Rowe, his one lock plastered down upon his brow for the occasion, piped up in a high reedy voice, 'Three cheers, then, for the pair of 'en.' And the cheers that echoed through the rafters of the long room nearly shook the boards and brought us all down upon the carriages below. I glanced at Rachel. There

190

were tears now. I shook my head at her. She smiled, and blinked them back, and gave her hand to me. I saw my godfather looking at us with a stiff nipped face. I thought, most unpardonably, of that retort, passed from one schoolboy to another, to silence criticism. 'If you don't like it, you can go . . .' The blast would be appropriate. Instead of which I smiled, and drawing Rachel's hand inside my arm I led her back from the long room to the house.

Someone, young John I should imagine, for Seecombe had been moving as though to a distant drum, had bolted back to the drawing-room between present giving and placed cake and wine in the drawing-room. We were too well-filled. Both remained untouched, though I saw the curate crumble a sugared bun. Perhaps he eats for three. Then Mrs Pascoe, who was surely born into this world, heaven save her, to wreck all harmony with her blabbing tongue, turned to Rachel and said, 'Mrs Ashley, forgive me, I really must comment upon it. What a beautiful pearl collar you are wearing. I have had eyes for nothing else all evening.'

Rachel smiled at her, and touched the collar with her fingers. 'Yes,' she said, 'it is a very proud possession.'

'Proud indeed,' said my godfather drily; 'it's worth a small fortune.'

I think only Rachel and myself noticed his tone of voice. She glanced at my godfather, puzzled, and from him to me, and was about to speak when I moved forward. 'I think the carriages have come,' I said.

I went and stood by the drawing-room door. Even Mrs Pascoe, usually deaf to suggestions of departure, saw by my manner that her evening had reached its climax. 'Come, girls,' she said, 'you must all be tired, and we have a busy day before us. No rest for a clergyman's family, Mr Ashley, on Christmas Day.' I escorted the Pascoe family to the door. Luckily, I had been right in my surmise. Their carriage was ready waiting. They took the curate with them. He crouched like a small bird between two daughters, fully fledged. As they drove away the Kendall carriage drew

191

forward in its turn. I turned back to the drawing-room and found it empty, save for my godfather.

'Where are the others?' I asked.

'Louise and Mrs Ashley went upstairs,' he said; 'they will be down in a moment or two. I am glad of the opportunity to have a word with you, Philip.'

I crossed over to the fireplace and stood there, with my hands behind my back.

'Yes?' I said. 'What is it?'

He did not answer for a moment. He was plainly embarrassed.

'I had no chance to see you before I left for Exeter,' he said, 'or I would have spoken of this before. The fact is, Philip, I have had a communication from the bank that I find decidedly disturbing.'

The collar, of course, I thought. Well, that was my affair.

'From Mr Couch, I suppose?' I said to him.

'Yes,' he answered. 'He advises me, as is very right and proper, that Mrs Ashley is already several hundred pounds overdrawn on her account.'

I felt myself go cold. I stared back at him; then the tension snapped, and the colour flamed into my face.

'Oh?' I said.

'I don't understand it,' he continued, pacing the floor. 'She can have few expenses here. She is living as your guest, and her wants must be few. The only thing that occurs to me is that she is sending the money out of the country.'

I went on standing by the fire and my heart was beating against my ribs. 'She is very generous,' I said, 'you must have noticed that, to-night. A present for each one of us. That cannot be done on a few shillings.'

'Several hundred pounds would pay for them a dozen times over,' he replied. 'I don't doubt her generosity, but presents alone cannot account for an overdraft.'

'She has taken it upon herself to spend money on the house,' I said. 'There have been furnishings bought for the blue bedroom. You can take all that into consideration.'

'Possibly,' said my godfather, 'but nevertheless the fact remains that the sum we decided to give her quarterly has already been doubled, nearly trebled, by the amount she has withdrawn. What are we to decide for the future?'

'Double, treble, the amount we give her now,' I said. 'Obviously what we gave was not sufficient.'

'But that is preposterous, Philip,' he exclaimed. 'No woman, living as she does here, could possibly desire to spend so much. A lady of quality in London would be hard put to it to fritter so much away.'

'There may be debts,' I said, 'of which we know nothing. There may be creditors, pressing for money, back in Florence. It is not our business. I want you to increase the allowance and cover that overdraft.'

He stood before me, with pursed lips. I wanted the matter over, done with. My ears were awake for the sound of footsteps on the stairs.

'Another thing,' he said, uneasily. 'You had no right, Philip, to take that collar from the bank. You realise, don't you, that it is part of the collection, part of the estate, and you have not the right to remove it?'

'It is mine,' I said; 'I can do what I like with my property.'

'The property is not yet yours,' he said, 'for a further three months.'

'What of it?' I gestured. 'Three months pass quickly. No harm can come to the collar in her keeping.'

He glanced up at me.

'I am not so sure,' he said.

The implication in his words drove me to fury.

'Good God!' I said. 'What are you suggesting? That she might take that collar and sell it?'

For a moment he did not reply. He tugged at his moustache.

'Since going to Exeter,' he said, 'I have come to learn a little more about your cousin Rachel.'

'What the devil do you mean?' I asked.

His eyes went from me to the door, then back again.

'It happened that I came across old friends,' he said, 'people you would not know, who are great travellers. They have wintered in Italy and France over a period of years. It seems that they met your cousin when she was married to her first husband, Sangalletti.'

'Well?'

'Both were notorious. For unbridled extravagance, and, I must add, for loose living also. The duel in which Sangalletti died was fought because of another man. These people said that when they learnt of Ambrose Ashley's marriage to the countess Sangalletti they were horrified. They predicted that she would run through his entire fortune within a few months. Luckily, it was not so. Ambrose died before it was possible for her to do it. I am sorry, Philip. But this news has much disturbed me.' Once again he paced the floor.

'I did not think that you would fall so low as to listen to travellers' tales,' I said to him. 'Who are these people, anyway? How dare they have the mischief to repeat gossip of over ten years past? They would not dare to do so before my cousin Rachel.'

'Never mind that now,' he replied. 'My concern now is with those pearls. I am sorry, but as your guardian for another three months I must ask you to desire her to return the collar. I will have it placed in the bank again, with the rest of the jewellery.'

Now it was my turn to pace the floor. I hardly knew what I did.

'Return the collar?' I said. 'But how can I possibly ask her to do that? I gave it to her, tonight, as a Christmas present. It is the last thing in the whole world that I could do.'

'Then I must do it for you,' he answered.

I suddenly hated his stiff stubborn face, his rigid way of standing, his stolid indifference to all feeling.

'I'll be damned if you will,' I said to him.

I wished him a thousand miles away. I wished him dead.

'Come, Philip,' he said, altering his tone, 'you are very young, very impressionable, and I quite understand that you wanted to give your cousin some token of esteem. But family jewels are rather more than that.'

194

'She has a right to them,' I said. 'God knows if anyone has a right to wear the jewels it is she.'

'Had Ambrose lived, yes,' he answered, 'but not now. Those jewels remain in trust for your wife, Philip, when you marry. And that's another thing. That collar has a significance of its own, which some of the older among the tenants at dinner tonight may remark upon. An Ashley, on his marriage, allows his bride to wear the collar on her wedding day, as sole adornment. That is the kind of family superstition which the people about here delight in, and, as I have told you, the older amongst them know the tale. It is unfortunate, and the sort of thing that causes gossip. I am sure that Mrs Ashley, in her situation, is the last person to wish that.'

'The people here tonight,' I said impatiently, 'will think, if they were in a state to think at all, that the collar is my cousin's own possession. I have never heard such rubbish in my life, that her wearing of it might cause gossip.'

'That,' he said, 'is not for me to say. I shall doubtless know only too soon if there is talk. One thing I must be firm upon, Philip. And that is, that the collar is returned to the safety of the bank. It is not yet yours to give, and you had no right whatsoever to go to the bank, without my permission, and bring it from safe custody. I repeat, if you will not ask Mrs Ashley to return it, I shall.'

In the intensity of our discussion we had not heard the rustle of the gowns upon the stairs. Now it was too late. Rachel, followed by Louise, stood in the doorway.

She stood there, her head turned towards my godfather, who was planted in the centre of the drawing-room, confronting me.

'I am sorry,' she said, 'I could not help but overhear what you have said. Please, I don't want either of you to embarrass yourselves on my account. It was dear of Philip to let me wear the pearls tonight, and quite right, Mr Kendall, of you to ask for their return. Here they are.' She raised her hands and unfastened them from her neck.

'No,' I said, 'why the devil should you do so?'

'Please, Philip,' she said.

She took off the collar and gave it to my godfather. He had the grace to look uncomfortable, yet relieved too.

I saw Louise look at me with pity. I turned away.

'Thank you, Mrs Ashley,' said my godfather in his gruff way. 'You understand that this collar is really part of the estate trust, and Philip had no business to take it from the bank. It was a foolish, thoughtless action. But young men are headstrong.'

'I perfectly understand,' she said, 'let us say no more about it. Do you need wrapping for it?'

'Thank you, no,' he answered, 'my handkerchief will do.'

He took a handkerchief from his breast pocket, and placed the collar in the middle of it, with great care.

'And now,' he said, 'I think that Louise and I will say good night. Thank you for a delightful and successful dinner, Philip, and I wish you both a happy Christmas.'

I did not answer. I went out into the hall, and stood by the front door, and handed Louise into the carriage without a word. She pressed my hand in sign of sympathy, but I was too much moved to answer her. My godfather climbed in beside her, and they went away.

I walked slowly back to the drawing-room. Rachel was standing there, gazing down into the fire. Her neck seemed naked without the collar. I stood looking at her without speaking, angry, miserable. At sight of me she put out her arms and I went to her. My heart was too full to speak. I felt like a little lad of ten years old, and it would not have taken much to make me cry.

'No,' she said, her voice tender with the warmth that was so much part of her, 'you must not mind. Please, Philip, please. I am so proud to have worn it for that once.'

'I wanted you to wear it,' I said, 'I wanted you to keep it always. God damn him, and send him to hell.'

'Hush,' she said, 'dear, don't say those things.'

I was so bitter and angry I could have ridden to the bank upon the instant, and gone to the vaults, and brought back every piece of jewellery there, every stone, every gem, and given them

196

to her, and all the gold and silver in the bank as well. I could have given her the world.

'Well, it's spoilt now,' I said, 'the whole evening, the whole of Christmas. Everything is wasted.'

She held me close, and laughed. 'You are like a child,' she said, 'running to me with empty hands. Poor Philip.' I stood away, and looked down upon her.

'I am no child,' I said, 'I am five-and-twenty years, all but three blasted months. My mother wore those pearls on her wedding day, and before that my aunt, and before that my grandmother. Don't you realise why I wanted you to wear them too?'

She put her hands on my shoulders, and kissed me once again.

'Why, yes,' she answered, 'that was why I was so happy, and so proud. You wanted me to wear them because you knew that had I been married here, and not in Florence, Ambrose would have given them to me on our wedding day.'

I said nothing. She had told me, some weeks back, that I lacked perception. To-night, I might have said the same of her. A few moments later, she patted me on the shoulder, and went upstairs to bed.

I felt in my pocket for the gold chain she had given me. That, if nothing else, was mine alone.

18

Our Christmas was a happy one. She saw to that. We rode to the farms on the estate, and to the cottages and lodges, and distributed the clothes that had belonged to Ambrose. And under each roof we were obliged to eat a pie, or taste a pudding, so that when evening came again we were too full to sit ourselves to dinner, but, surfeited, left the servants to finish all the remaining geese and turkey of the night before, while she and I roasted chestnuts before the drawing-room fire.

Then, as though I had gone back in time some twenty years, she bade me shut my eyes, and, laughing, went up to her boudoir and came down again and put into my hands a little tree. This she had dressed in gay fantastic fashion, with presents wrapped in brightly coloured paper, each present an absurdity; and I knew she did this for me because she wanted me to forget the drama of Christmas Eve and the fiasco of the pearls. I could not forget. Nor could I forgive. And from Christmas onwards a coolness came between my godfather and myself. That he should have listened to petty lying gossip was bad enough, but even more I resented his sticking to the quibble in the will which left me under his jurisdiction for three more months. What if Rachel had spent more than we had foreseen? We had not known her needs. Neither Ambrose nor my godfather had understood the way of life in Florence. Extravagant she well might be, but was it so great a crime? As to society there, we could not judge it. My godfather had lived all his life in careful niggardly fashion, and, because Ambrose had never bothered to spend much upon himself, my godfather had taken it for granted that this state of things would continue once the property was mine. My wants were few, and I had no more desire for personal spending than had Ambrose, in his time, but this cheeseparing on the part of my godfather induced in me a sort of fury that made me determined to have my way and use the money that was mine.

He had accused Rachel of frittering away her allowance. Well, he could accuse me of wanton waste about my house. I decided, after the New Year, that I wished to make improvements to the property that would be mine. But not only to the gardens. The terracing of the walk above the Barton fields proceeded, also the hollowing away and preparation of the ground beside it that was to become the sunken water-garden, copied from the engraving in Rachel's book.

I was determined to repair the house as well. Too long, I considered, we had made do with the monthly visitations of Nat Dunn, the estate mason, who crept from ladder to ladder upon the roof and replaced slates, swept off by a gale of wind, smoking his pipe up there the while, his back against a chimney. Now was the time to set the whole roof in order, have new tiles, new slates, new guttering, strengthening also those walls damaged by long years of wind and rain. Too little had been done about the place since the old days, two hundred years ago, when the men of Parliament had wrought such havoc, and my ancestors had been hard put to it to keep the house from falling into ruin. I would make amends for past neglect, and if my godfather pulled a face and drew sums upon his blotter he could go hang himself.

So I went my own way about the business, and before January was out some fifteen to twenty men were working on my roof, or about the building, and inside the house as well, decorating ceilings and walls to my orders. It gave me the greatest satisfaction to picture my godfather's expression when the bills for the work should be submitted to him.

I made the repairs about the house serve as an excuse for not entertaining visitors, thereby putting an end, for the time being, to Sunday dinner. Therefore I was spared the regular visit of the Pascoes and the Kendalls, and saw nothing of my godfather, which was part of my intention. I also had Seecombe spread it, in his jungle fashion, below stairs, that Mrs Ashley found it difficult to receive callers at the moment, owing to there being workmen in the drawing-room. We lived therefore, during those days of winter and early spring, in hermit fashion, greatly to my liking. Aunt Phoebe's boudoir, as Rachel would still insist in naming it, became our place of habitation. There, at the close of day, Rachel would sit, and sew or read, and I would watch her. A new gentleness had come to her manner, since the incident of the pearls on Christmas Eve, which, though warming beyond belief, was sometimes hard to bear.

I think she had no knowledge what it did to me. Those hands, resting for a moment on my shoulder, or touching my head in a caress, as she passed by the chair where I was sitting, talking all the while about the garden or some practical matter, would set my heart beating so that it would not be stilled. To watch her move was a delight, and sometimes I even wondered if she rose from her chair on purpose, to go to the window, to reach upwards to the curtain, to stand there with her hand upon it looking outwards on to the lawn, because she knew my eyes were watching her. She said my name Philip in a manner quite her own. To others, it had always been a short, clipped word, with some emphasis on the final letter, but she lingered on the 'l' slowly, deliberately, in a way that somehow, to my ear, gave it a new sound I liked well. As a lad I had always wished to be called Ambrose, and the wish had remained with me, I think, until the present. Now I was glad that my name went back even farther into the past than his had done. When the men brought the new lead piping to be placed against the walls, to serve as guttering from the roof to the ground, and the bucket heads were in position, I had a strange feeling of pride as I looked up at the little plaque beneath them stamped with my initials P.A. and the date beneath, and lower down the lion that was my mother's crest. It was as though I gave something of myself into the future. And Rachel, standing beside me, took my arm and said, 'I never thought you proud, Philip, until now. I love you the better for it.'

Yes, I was proud . . . but emptiness went with it all the same.

So the work proceeded, in the house and in the grounds; and the first days of spring came, being in themselves a blend of torment and delight. Blackbird and chaffinch sang beneath our windows on first waking, rousing both Rachel and myself from sleep. We talked of it at midday when we met. The sun came to her first, on the eastern side of the house, and with her windows wide drove a slant of light on to her pillow. I had it later, as I dressed. Leaning out, looking over the meadows to the sea, I would see the horses and the plough climb the further hill, with the gulls wheeling about them, and in the pasture lands closer to the house were the ewes and the young lambs, back to back for comfort. Lapwings, on passage bent, came in a little cloud, with fluttering wings. Soon they would pair, and the male soar and tumble in his flight of rapture. Down on the shore the curlews whistled, and the oyster-catchers, black and white like parsons, poked in the seaweed solemnly, for breakfast. The air had a zest to it, salt-tasting, under the sun.

It was on a morning such as this that Seecombe came to me and told me that Sam Bate, up at the East Lodge, who was in bed, poorly, wished very much that I would go and see him, as he had something of importance to give me. He inferred that whatever it was he had was too precious to deliver to his son or to his daughter. I thought little of it. It is always a pleasure amongst country folk to make much mystery over small matters. Nevertheless, in the afternoon, I walked up the avenue to the gates there where the four roads meet, and turned in at the lodge to have a word with him. Sam was sitting up in bed, and lying on the blanket before him was one of the coats that had belonged to Ambrose, which had been given to him on Christmas Day. I recognised it as the light-coloured one I had not known, which Ambrose must have bought for the hot weather on the continent.

'Well, Sam,' I said, 'I am sorry to find you in bed. What is the matter?'

'The same old cough, Mr Philip, sir, that catches me aback every spring,' replied the man. 'My father had it before me, and one spring t'will carry me to the grave, the same as it did him.'

'Nonsense, Sam,' I told him, 'those are old tales they spread, that what a man's father had will kill the son.'

Sam Bate shook his head. 'There's truth in it, sir,' he said, 'and you know it, too. How about Mr Ambrose and his father, the old gentleman your uncle? Brain sickness did for the pair of them. There's no going agin the ways of nature. I've seen the same in cattle.'

I said nothing, wondering, at the same time, how Sam should know what illness it was of which Ambrose had died. I had told no one. It was incredible how rumour spread about our countryside.

'You must send your daughter to ask Mrs Ashley for some cordial to cure your cough,' I said to him. 'She has great knowledge of such things. Oil of eucalyptus is one of her remedies.'

'I will, Mr Philip, I will,' he answered me, 'but first I felt it right to ask you to come yourself, concerning the matter of the letter.'

He lowered his voice, and looked suitably concerned and solemn.

'What letter, Sam?' I asked.

'Mr Philip,' he replied, 'on Christmas Day, you and Mrs Ambrose kindly gave some of us clothes and the like belonging to the late master. And very proud we are, all of us, to have the same. Now this coat that you see here, on the bed, was given to me.' He paused, and touched the coat, with some of the same awe about him still with which he had received it on Christmas Day. 'Now I brought the coat up here, sir, that same night,' Sam continued, 'and I said to my daughter if we had a glass case to put it in we'd do so, but she told me to get along with such nonsense, the coat was meant to wear, but wear it I would not, Mr Philip. T'would have seemed presuming on my part, if you follow me, sir. So I put the coat away in the press, yonder, and took him out now and agin and had a look at it. Then, when this cough seized me, and I lay up here abed, I don't know how it was, but the fancy came upon me to wear the coat. Just sitting up in bed, like, as you see me now. The coat being lightish weight,

202

and easy on my back. Which I did, Mr Philip, for the first time yesterday. It was then I found the letter.'

He paused, and, fumbling under his pillow, drew forth a packet. 'What had happened, Mr Philip, was this,' he said. 'The letter must have slipped down inside the material of the coat and the lining. T'wouldn't have been noticed in the folding of it, or in packing. Only by someone such as me smoothing the coat with my hands for wonder at having it around me. I felt the crackling of it, and made so bold as to open up the lining with a knife. And here it is, sir. A letter, plain as day. Sealed, and addressed to you by Mr Ambrose himself. I know his hand, of old. It shook me, sir, to come upon it. It seemed, if you understand, as though I had come upon a message from the dead.'

He gave the letter to me. Yes, he was right. It was addressed to me, and by Ambrose. I looked down at the familiar handwriting, and felt a sudden wrench at my heart.

'That was wise of you, Sam, to act as you have done,' I said, 'and very proper to send for me in person. Thank you.'

'No thanks, Mr Philip, no thanks at all,' he answered, 'but I thought how maybe that letter had laid there all these months, and should have been in your hands a long time since. But the poor master being dead, made it so wisht, to come upon it. And the same to you on reading it, maybe. And so I thought it best to tell you of it myself, rather than send my daughter to the mansion.'

I thanked him again, and after putting the letter away in my breast pocket talked for a few minutes or so, before I left him. Some intuition, I don't know what it was, made me tell him to say nothing of the business to anyone, not even to his daughter. The reason I gave him was the same that he had given me, respect for the dead. He promised, and I left the lodge.

I did not return at once to the house. I climbed up through the woods to a path that runs above that part of the estate, bordering the Trenant acres and the wooded avenue. Ambrose had been fonder of this walk than any other. It was our highest point of land, saving the beacon to the south, and had a fine view over the woods and the valley to the open sea. The trees fringing the path, planted by Ambrose and his father before him, gave shelter, although not high enough as yet to dim the view, and in May month the bluebells made a cover to the ground. At the end of the path, topping the woods, before plunging to descent and the keeper's cottage in the gully, Ambrose had set up a piece of granite. 'This,' he said to me, half joking, half in earnest, 'can serve me for tombstone when I die. Think of me here, rather than in the family vault with the other Ashleys.'

He little thought, when he had it put in place, that he would not lie in the family vault ever, but in the Protestant cemetery, in Florence. Upon the slab of granite he had scrolled some mention of the lands where he had travelled, and a line of doggerel at the end to make us laugh when we looked at it together. For all the nonsense, though, I believe his heart intended it; and during that last winter, when he was from home, I had often climbed the path up through the woods to stand beside the granite stone, and look down upon the prospect that he loved so well.

When I came to it today I stood for a moment with my hands upon the slab, and I could not bring myself to a decision. Below me the smoke curled from the keeper's cottage, and his dog, left upon a chain while he was absent, barked now and again, at nothing, or maybe because the sound of his own yelps gave him company. The glory of the day had gone, and it was colder. Clouds had come across the sky. In the distance I could see the cattle coming down from the Lankelly hills to water in the marshes under the woods, and beyond the marshes, in the bay, the sea had lost the sun and was slatey grey. A little wind blew shoreward, rustling the trees below me.

I sat down beside the slab, and taking Ambrose's letter from my pocket placed it face downwards, on my knee. The red seal stared up at me, imprinted with his ring and the chough's head. The packet was not thick. It contained nothing. Nothing but a letter, which I did not want to open. I cannot say what misgiving held me back, what cowardly instinct drove me to hide my head like an ostrich in the sand. Ambrose was dead, and the past went with him when he died. I had my own life to make, and my own will to follow. It might be that in this letter there would be some further mention of that other matter I had chosen to forget. If Ambrose had accused Rachel of extravagance, he could now use the same epithet, with more reason perhaps, to me. I should have dispensed more upon the house itself in a few months than he had done in years. I did not feel it was betrayal.

But not to read the letter . . . what would he say to that? If I tore it now to shreds, and scattered the pieces, and never learnt the contents, would he condemn me? I balanced the letter in my hand, this way and that. To read, or not to read; I wished to heaven the choice was not before me. Back in the house, my loyalty was with her. In the boudoir, with my eyes upon her face, watching those hands, that smile, hearing her voice, no letter would have haunted me. Yet here, in the woods beside the slab of granite where we had so often stood together, he and I, Ambrose holding the very stick I carried now, wearing the same coat, here his power was strongest. Like a small boy who prays that the weather shall be fine upon his birthday I prayed God now that the letter should contain nothing to disturb me, and so opened it. It was dated April of the preceding year, and was therefore written three months before he died.

'DEAREST BOY,

'If my letters have been infrequent, it is not because I have not thought of you. You have been in my mind, these past months, perhaps more than ever before. But a letter can miscarry, or be read by others, and I would not wish either of those things to happen; therefore I have not written, or when I have done so I know there has been little in anything I have said. I have been ill, with fever and bad headache. Better now. But for how long, I cannot tell. The fever may come again, and the headaches too, and when in the grip of them I am not responsible for what I say or do. This much is certain.

205

'But I am not yet certain of the cause. Philip, dear boy, I am much disturbed. That is lightly said. I am in agony of mind. I wrote to you, during the winter I think it was, but was ill shortly afterwards and have no recollection what happened to the letter, I may very well have destroyed it in the mood that possessed me. In it, I believe I told you of her fault that caused me so much concern. Whether hereditary or not I cannot say, but I believe so, and believe also that the loss of our child, only a few months on its way, did her irreparable harm.

'This, by the way, I had kept from you in my letters; we were both much shaken at the time. For my part, I have you, and am consoled. But with a woman it goes deeper. She had made plans and projects, as you can imagine, and when, after but four-and-a-half months, it went for nothing, and she was told by her doctor there could not be another, her distress was very great, profounder than my own. I could swear her manner altered from that time. The recklessness with money became progressive, and I perceived in her a tendency to evasion, to lies, to withdrawal from me, that was completely contrary to the warm nature that was hers when we first married. As the months passed I noticed more and more that she turned to this man I have mentioned before in my letters, signor Rainaldi, a friend and I gather a lawyer of Sangalletti's, for advice, rather than to me. I believe this man to have a pernicious influence upon her. I suspect him of having been in love with her for years, even when Sangalletti was alive, and although I do not for an instant believe that she ever thought of him in such a connection up to a short while ago, now, since she has altered in her manner to me, I cannot be so sure. There is a shadow in her eye, a tone in her voice, when his name is said that awakens in my mind the most terrible suspicion.

'Brought up as she was by feckless parents, living a

life, before and even during her first marriage, about which both of us have had reserve, I have often felt that her code of behaviour is different to ours at home. The tie of marriage may not be so sacred. I suspect, in fact I have proof, that he gives her money. Money, God forgive me for saying so, is at the present time the one way to her heart. I believe, if the child had not been lost, none of this would be; and I wish with all my heart that I had not listened to the doctor at the time when he dissuaded travel, but had brought her home. We would have been with you now, and all of us content.

'At times she seems like her true self, and all is well, so well that I feel I have been through some nightmare and wake again to the happiness of the first months of our marriage. Then, with a word or an action, all is lost again. I will come down to the terrace and find Rainaldi there. At sight of me, both fall silent. I cannot but wonder what it is they have been discussing. Once, when she had gone into the villa and Rainaldi and I were left alone, he asked an abrupt question as to my will. This he had seen, incidentally, when we married. He told me that as it stood, and should I die, I would leave my wife without provision. This I knew, and had anyway drawn up a will myself that would correct the error, and would have put my signature to it, and had it witnessed, could I be certain that her fault of spending was a temporary passing thing, and not deep-rooted.

'This new will, by the way, would give her the house and the estate for her lifetime only, and so to you upon her death, with the proviso that the running of the estate be left in your hands entirely.

'It still remains unsigned, and for the reason I have told you.

'Mark you, it is Rainaldi who asked questions on the will, Rainaldi who drew my attention to the omissions of the one that stands at present. She does not speak of it, to me. But do they speak of it together? What is it that they say to one another, when I am not there?

'This matter of the will occurred in March. Admittedly, I was unwell, and nearly blinded with my head, and Rainaldi bringing up the matter may have done so in that cold calculating way of his, thinking that I might die. Possibly it is so. Possibly it is not discussed between them. I have no means of finding out. Too often now I find her eyes upon me, watchful and strange. And when I hold her, it is as though she were afraid. Afraid of what, of whom?

'Two days ago, which brings me to the reason for this letter, I had another attack of this same fever, which laid me low in March. The onset is sudden. I am seized with pains and sickness, which passes swiftly to great excitation of my brain, driving me near to violence, and I can hardly stand upon my feet for dizziness of mind and body. This, in its turn, passes, and an intolerable desire for sleep comes upon me, so that I fall upon the floor, or upon my bed, with no power over my limbs. I do not recollect my father being thus. The headaches, yes, and some difficulty of temperament, but not the other symptoms.

'Philip, my boy, the only being in the world whom I can trust, tell me what it means, and if you can, come out to me. Say nothing to Nick Kendall. Say no word to any single soul. Above all, write not a word in answer, merely come.

'One thought possesses me, leaving me no peace. Are they trying to poison me?

'AMBROSE.'

I folded the letter back into its creases. The dog stopped barking in the cottage garden below. I heard the keeper open his gate and the dog yelp at him in welcome. I heard voices from the cottage, the clank of a pail, the shutting of a door. From the trees on the hill opposite the jackdaws rose in flight, and circled, cawing, and moved in a black cloud to the tops of other trees, beside the marshes.

I did not tear the letter. I dug a hole for it, beneath the slab of granite. I put it inside my pocket-book, and buried the pocket-book, deep in the dark earth. Then I smoothed the place with my hands. I walked away down the hill, and through the woods to the avenue below. As I climbed again, up the back way to the house, I heard the laughter and the chatter of the men as they went home from work. I stood a moment and watched them trudge off across the park. The scaffolding placed against the walls where they had been working all the day looked bleak and bare.

I went in, through the back entrance across the court, and as my feet sounded on the flags Seecombe came out to me from the steward's room, with consternation on his face.

'I am glad you have come, sir,' he said. 'The mistress has been asking for you this long while. Poor Don has had an accident. She is much concerned.'

'An accident?' I said. 'What happened?'

'A great slate from the roof fell on him, sir,' he answered. 'You know how deaf he has become of late, and how loath to leave his place in the sun, outside the library window. The slate must have fallen on his back. He cannot move.'

I went to the library. Rachel was kneeling there on the floor, with Don's head pillowed in her lap. She raised her eyes when I came into the room. 'They have killed him,' she said, 'he is dying. Why did you stay away so long? If you had been here, it would not have happened.'

Her words sounded like an echo to something long forgotten in my mind. But what it was I could not now remember. Seecombe went from the library, leaving us alone. The tears that filled her eyes ran down her face. 'Don was your possession,' she said, 'your very own. You grew up together. I can't bear to see him die.'

I went and knelt beside her on the floor, and I realised that I was thinking, not of the letter buried deep beneath the granite slab, nor of poor Don so soon to die, stretched out there between us, his body limp and still. I was thinking of one thing only. It was the first time since she had come to my house that her sorrow was not for Ambrose, but for me.

19

We sat with Don, through the long evening. I had my dinner, but Rachel would eat nothing. Shortly before midnight he died. I carried him away and covered him, and tomorrow we would bury him in the plantation. When I returned the library was empty, and Rachel had gone upstairs. I walked along the corridor to the boudoir and she was sitting there, with wet eyes, staring into the fire.

I sat beside her and took her hands. 'I think he did not suffer,' I said to her. 'I think he had no pain.'

'Fifteen long years,' she said, 'the little boy of ten, who opened his birthday pie. I kept remembering the story, as he lay there with his head in my lap.'

'In three weeks' time,' I said, 'it will be the birthday once again. I shall be twenty-five. Do you know what happens on that day?'

'All wishes should be granted,' she answered, 'or so my mother used to say, when I was young. What will you wish for, Philip?'

I did not answer her at once. I stared, with her, into the fire.

'I shall not know,' I said, 'until the day comes.'

Her hand, with rings upon it, lay white and still upon my own.

'When I am twenty-five,' I said, 'my godfather has no further control over the property. It is mine, to do with what I will. The pearl collar, the other jewels there in the bank, I can give them all to you.'

'No,' she said, 'I would not take them, Philip. They should remain in trust for your wife, when you marry. I know you have no desire to marry yet, but one day you may change your mind.'

I knew well what I longed to say to her, yet dared not. Instead, I bent down and kissed her hand, then moved away.

'It is only through error,' I said, 'that those jewels are not yours today. And not only the jewels, but everything. This house, the money, the estate. You know that perfectly.'

She looked distressed. She turned from the fire, and leant back in her chair. Her hand began playing with her rings.

'There is no need to discuss that,' she said. 'If there was error, I am used to it.'

'You may be,' I said, 'but I am not.'

I stood up, my back to the fire, looking down upon her. I knew now what I could do, and no one could prevent me.

'What do you mean?' she said, with that same shadow of distress still in her eyes.

'It does not matter,' I answered; 'you shall know, in three weeks' time.'

'In three weeks' time,' she said, 'after your birthday, I must leave you, Philip.'

She had said them at last, the words I had expected. But now that I had a plan formed in my mind they might not matter.

'Why?' I asked.

'I have stayed too long,' she answered.

'Tell me,' I said, 'supposing that Ambrose had made a will leaving the property to you for your lifetime, with the proviso that during that lifetime I looked after the estate and ran it for you, what would you have done?'

Her eyes flickered away from me, back to the fire again.

'How do you mean,' she asked, 'what would I have done?'

'Would you have lived here?' I said. 'Would you have turned me out?'

'Turned you out?' she exclaimed. 'From your own home? Why, Philip, how could you ask me such a thing?'

'You would have stayed then?' I replied. 'You would have lived here in the house, and, in a sense, employed me in your business? We should be living here together, just as we are doing now?'

'Yes,' she said, 'yes, I suppose so. I have never thought. It would be so different, though, you cannot make comparison.'

'How different?'

She gestured with her hands. 'How can I explain to you?' she said. 'Don't you understand that my position, as it is, is untenable, simply because I am a woman? Your godfather would be the first to agree with me. He has said nothing, but I am sure he feels that the time has come for me to go. It would have been quite otherwise, had the house been mine and you, in the sense you put it, in my employ. I should be Mrs Ashley, you my heir. But now, as it has turned out, you are Philip Ashley, and I, a woman relative, living on your bounty. There is a world of difference, dear, between the two.'

'Exactly,' I replied.

'Well then,' she said, 'let's talk of it no further.'

'We will talk of it further,' I said, 'because the matter is of supreme importance. What happened to the will?'

'What will?'

'The will that Ambrose made, and never signed, in which he left the property to you?'

I saw the anxiety deepen in her eyes.

'How do you know of such a will? I never told you of it,' she said.

A lie would serve as an excuse, and I gave it her.

'I have always known there must be one,' I answered, 'but possibly it was left unsigned, and so invalid, from a legal point of view. I go even further, and suggest you have it here amongst your things.'

This was a shot at venture, but it told. Her eyes flashed instinctively towards the little bureau, against the wall, then back to me.

'What are you trying to make me say?' she asked.

'Only confirm that it exists,' I said.

She hesitated, then shrugged her shoulders.

'Very well, yes,' she replied, 'but it alters nothing. The will was never signed.'

'Can I see it?' I asked.

213

'For what purpose, Philip?'

'For a purpose of my own. I think you can trust me.'

She looked at me a long while. She was clearly bewildered, and I think anxious too. She rose from her chair and went towards the bureau, then, hesitant, glanced back at me again.

'Why suddenly all this?' she said. 'Why can't we leave the past alone? You promised we should do so, that evening in the library.'

'You promised you would stay,' I answered her.

To give it me or not, the choice was hers. I thought of the choice that I had made that afternoon beside the granite slab. I had chosen, for better or for worse, to read the letter. Now she must come to a decision too. She went to the bureau, and, taking a small key, opened up a drawer. Out of the drawer she took a piece of paper, and gave it to me.

'Read it, if you wish,' she said.

I took the paper to the candlelight. The writing was in Ambrose's hand, clear and firm, a stronger hand than in the letter I had read that afternoon. The date was November, of a year ago, when he and Rachel had been married seven months. The paper was headed 'Last Will and Testament of Ambrose Ashley.' The contents were just as he had told me. The property was left to Rachel, for her lifetime, passing at her death to the eldest of any children that might be born to both of them, and failing the birth of children, then to me, with the proviso that I should have the running of the same while she should live.

'May I make a copy of this?' I said to her.

'Do what you want,' she said. She looked pale and listless, as if she did not care. 'It's over and done with, Philip, there is no sense in talking of it now.'

'I will keep it for the moment, and make a copy of it too,' I said, and sitting at the bureau I took pen and paper and did so, while she lay in her chair, her cheek resting in her hand.

I knew that I must have confirmation of everything that Ambrose had told me in his letter, and though I hated every word I had to say I forced myself to question her. I scratched away with the pen: copying the will was more a pretext than anything else, and served its purpose so that I did not have to look at her.

'I see that Ambrose dated this November,' I said. 'Have you any idea why he should choose that month to make a new will? You were married the preceding April.'

Her answer was slow in coming; and I thought suddenly how a surgeon must feel, when he probes about the scar of a wound but lately healed.

'I don't know why he wrote it in November,' she said. 'We were neither of us thinking of death at that time. Rather the reverse. It was the happiest time of all the eighteen months we were together.'

'Yes,' I said, seizing a fresh piece of paper, 'he wrote and told me of it.' I heard her move in her chair, and turn to look at me. But I went on writing at the bureau.

'Ambrose told you?' she said. 'But I asked him not to, I feared you might misunderstand and feel, in some way, slighted; it would be very natural if you had. He promised to keep it secret. And then, as it turned out, it made no odds.'

The voice was flat, without expression. Perhaps, after all, when a surgeon probed a scar the sufferer would say dully that he felt no pain. In the letter, buried beneath the granite, Ambrose had said, 'With a woman, these things go deeper.' As I scratched upon the piece of paper I saw that I had written the words, 'It made no odds . . . it made no odds.' I tore up the piece of paper, and began afresh.

'And finally,' I said, 'in the long run, the will was never signed.'

'No,' she said, 'Ambrose left it as you see it now.'

I had done with writing. I folded the will and the copy I had made, and put both of them in my breast pocket, where earlier in the afternoon I had carried his letter. Then I went and knelt beside her chair, and putting my arms about her held her fast; not as I would a woman, but as a child.

'Rachel,' I said, 'why did not Ambrose sign the will?'

She lay quite still, and did not move away. Only the hand that rested on my shoulder tightened suddenly.

'Tell me,' I said, 'tell me, Rachel.'

The voice that answered me was faint and far away, not more than a whisper in my ear.

'I never knew,' she said; 'we did not speak of it again. But I think when he realised that I could not, after all, have children, he lost belief in me. Some sort of faith went, though he never knew it.'

As I knelt there, with my arms about her, I thought of the letter in the pocket book beneath the granite slab, with this same accusation said in other words, and I wondered how it could be that two people who had loved could yet have such a misconception of each other and, with a common grief, grow far apart. There must be something in the nature of love between a man and a woman that drove them to torment and suspicion. 'You were unhappy then?' I asked.

'Unhappy?' she said. 'What do you suppose? I was almost out of my mind.'

And I could see them sitting on the terrace of the villa, with this strange shadow between them, built out of nothing but their own doubts and fears, and it seemed to me that the seeds of this same shadow went back beyond all reckoning and could never more be traced. Perhaps, unconscious of his grudge, he brooded about her past with Sangalletti and before, blaming her for the life he had not shared, and she, with resentment likewise, feared loss of love must go with loss of child-bearing. How little she had understood of Ambrose after all. And what small knowledge he had had of her. I might tell her of the contents of the letter under the slab, but it would do no good. The misunderstanding went too deep.

'So it was all through error that the will was never signed, and put aside?' I said to her.

'Call it error if you like,' she answered, 'it cannot matter now. But soon afterwards, his manner altered and he himself changed. Those headaches, almost blinding him, began. They drove him near to violence, once or twice. I wondered how much could be my fault, and was afraid.'

'And you had no friend?'

'Only Rainaldi. And he never knew what I have told you tonight.'

That cold hard face, those narrow searching eyes, I did not blame Ambrose for mistrusting him. Yet how could Ambrose, who was her husband, have been so uncertain of himself? Surely a man must know when a woman loved him? Yet possibly one could not always tell.

'And when Ambrose fell ill,' I said, 'you no longer asked Rainaldi to the house?'

'I dared not,' she said. 'You will never understand how Ambrose became, and I don't want to tell you. Please, Philip, you must not ask me any more.'

'Ambrose suspected you — of what?'

'Of everything. Of infidelity, and worse than that.'

'What can be worse than infidelity?'

Suddenly she pushed me away, and rising from her chair went to the door and opened it. 'Nothing,' she said, 'nothing in the world. Now go away, and leave me to myself.'

I stood up slowly, and went to the door beside her.

'I am sorry,' I said, 'I did not mean to make you angry.'

'I am not angry,' she answered me.

'Never again,' I said, 'will I ask you questions. These were the last. I give you my solemn promise.'

'Thank you,' she said.

Her face was strained and white. Her voice was cold.

'I had a reason for asking them,' I said. 'You will know it in three weeks' time.'

'I don't ask the reason, Philip,' she said, 'all I ask of you is, go.'

She did not kiss me, or give me her hand. I bowed to her, and went. Yet a moment just before she had permitted me to kneel beside her with my arms about her. Why, in a sudden, had she changed? If Ambrose had known little about women, I knew less. That warmth so unexpected, catching a man unaware and lifting him to rapture, then swiftly, for no reason, the changing mood, casting him back where he had stood before. What trail

217

of thought, confused and indirect, drove through those minds of theirs, to cloud their judgment? What waves of impulse swept about their being, moving them to anger and withdrawal, or else to sudden generosity? We were surely different, with our blunter comprehension, moving more slowly to the compass points, while they, erratic and unstable, were blown about their course by winds of fancy.

Next morning, when she came downstairs, her manner was as usual, kind and gentle; she made no reference to our conversation of the night before. We buried poor Don in the plantation, in a piece of ground apart, where the camellia walk began, and I made a small circle round his grave with stones. We did not talk of that tenth birthday when Ambrose gave him to me, nor yet of the twenty-fifth that was to come. But the following day I rose early, and, giving orders for Gypsy to be saddled, rode to Bodmin. I called upon an attorney there, a man named Wilfred Tewin, who did much of the business for the county but had not hitherto handled Ashley affairs, my godfather dealing with his own people in St Austell. I explained to him that I had come upon a matter of great urgency and privacy, and that I desired him to draw up a document in legal form and language that would enable me to dispose of my entire property to my cousin, Mrs Rachel Ashley, upon the first day of April, when it became mine by law.

I showed him the will that Ambrose had not signed, and I explained to him that it was only through sudden illness, followed by death, that Ambrose had omitted to sign it. I told him to incorporate, in the document, much of what Ambrose had written in the will, that on Rachel's decease the property passed back again to me, and that I should have the running of it in her lifetime. Should I die first the property would go, as matter of course, to my second cousins in Kent, but only at her death, and not before. Tewin was quick to understand what it was I wanted, and I think, being no great friend to my godfather – which was partly the reason I had gone to him – he was gratified to have so important a business entrusted to his care.

'You wish,' he said, 'to put in some clause safeguarding the land? As the draft stands at present, Mrs Ashley could sell what acreage she pleased, which seems to me unwise if you desire to pass it on to your heirs in its entirety.'

'Yes,' I said slowly, 'there had better be a clause forbidding sale. That goes, most naturally, for the house too.'

'There are family jewels, are there not,' he said, 'and other personal possessions? What of them?'

'They,' I replied, 'are hers, to do with as she pleases.'

He read the draft through to me, and I did not think it could be faulted.

'One thing,' he said. 'We have no proviso should Mrs Ashley marry again.'

'That,' I said, 'is not likely to happen.'

'Possibly not,' he answered, 'but the point should be covered just the same.'

He looked at me enquiringly, his pen poised in the air.

'Your cousin is still comparatively a young woman, is she not?' he said. 'It should certainly be taken into account.'

I thought suddenly, most monstrously, of old St Ives in the far end of the county, and the remarks that Rachel had made to me in jest.

'In the case of her re-marriage,' I said quickly, 'the property reverts again to me. That is most definite.'

He made a note upon the paper, and read the draft again.

'And you desire this ready and drawn up, in legal form, by the first of April, Mr Ashley?' he said.

'Please. That is my birthday. On that day the property becomes mine, absolutely. No objection can be put forward from any quarter.'

He folded the paper, and smiled at me.

'You are doing a very generous thing,' he said, 'giving every-thing away the moment it is yours.'

'It would never have been mine to begin with,' I said, 'if my cousin Ambrose Ashley had put his signature to that will.'

'All the same,' he said, 'I doubt if such a thing has ever been

219

done before. Certainly not to my knowledge, or in my lifetime of experience. I gather you want nothing said of this until the day?'

'Nothing at all. The matter is most secret.'

'Very well, then, Mr Ashley. And I thank you for entrusting me with your confidence. I am at your disposal at any time in the future should you wish to call upon me regarding any matter whatsoever.'

He bowed me from the building, promising that the full document should be delivered to me on the thirty-first day of March.

I rode home with a reckless feeling in my heart. I wondered if my godfather would have an attack of apoplexy when he heard the news. I did not care. I wished him no ill, once I was rid of his jurisdiction, but for all that I had turned the tables on him to perfection. As for Rachel, she could not go to London now and leave her property. Her argument of the preceding night would not hold good. If she objected to me in the house, very well, I would take myself to the lodge, and call upon her every day for orders. I would be with Wellington and Tamlyn and the rest, and wait upon her bidding, cap in hand. I think had I been a little lad, I would have cut a caper from sheer love of living. As it was, I set Gypsy at a bank, and nearly took a toss in doing so when I landed with a bump the other side. The March winds made a fool of me; I would have sung aloud, but I could not for the life of me keep to a single tune. The hedgerows were green, and the willows were in bud, and all the honeyed mass of golden gorse in bloom. It was a day for folly and high fever.

When I returned, mid-afternoon, and rode up the carriage-way to the house, I saw a post-chaise drawn up before the door. It was an unusual sight, for always, when people called upon Rachel, they came in their own carriage. The wheels and the coach were dusty, as if from a long journey on the road, and certainly neither the vehicle nor the driver was known to me. I turned back at sight of them, and rode round to the stables, but the lad who came to take Gypsy knew no more than I did of the visitors, and Wellington was absent.

I saw no one in the hall but when I advanced softly towards the drawing-room I heard voices from within, behind the closed door. I decided not to mount the stairs, but to go up to my room by the servants' stairway at the back. Just as I turned the drawing-room door opened, and Rachel, laughing over her shoulder, came out into the hall. She looked well and happy, and wore that radiance about her that was so much part of her when her mood was gay.

'Philip, you are home,' she said. 'Come into the drawing-room – this visitor of mine you shall not escape. He has travelled very far to see us both.' Smiling, she took my arm, and drew me, most reluctantly, into the room. A man was seated there, who at sight of me rose from his chair, and came towards me with his hand outstretched.

'You did not expect me,' he said, 'and I make my apology. But then neither did I expect you, when I saw you first.'

It was Rainaldi.

20

I do not know if I showed my feelings in my face as plainly as I felt them in my heart, but I think I must have done; for Rachel passed swiftly on in conversation, telling Rainaldi that I was always without doors, riding or walking, she never knew where, nor had I fixed hours for my return. 'Philip works harder than his own labourers,' she said, 'and knows every inch of his estate far more than they do.'

She still kept her hand upon my arm, as though to show me off before her visitor, much as a teacher would a sullen child.

'I congratulate you upon your fine property,' said Rainaldi. 'I do not wonder that your cousin Rachel has become so much attached to it. I have never seen her look so well.'

His eyes, the eyes that I remembered clearly, heavy-lidded and expressionless, dwelt upon her for a moment, then turned again to me.

'The air here,' he said, 'must be more conducive to repose of mind and body than our keener air in Florence.'

'My cousin,' I said, 'has her origin in the west country. She has merely returned where she belonged.'

He smiled, if the slight movement of his face could be so called, and addressed himself to Rachel. 'It depends what tie of blood is strongest, does it not?' he said. 'Your young relative forgets your mother came from Rome. And, I may add, you grow more like her every day.'

'In face alone, I hope,' said Rachel, 'not in her figure nor in her character. Philip, Rainaldi declares that he will put up in a hostelry, whatever we can recommend, he is not particular, but I have told him it is nonsense. Surely we can place a room at his disposal here?'

My heart sank at the suggestion but I could not refuse it.

'Of course,' I said. 'I will give orders at once, and send away the postchaise too, as you won't want it further.'

'It brought me from Exeter,' said Rainaldi. 'I will pay the man, and then hire again when I return to London.'

'There is plenty of time to decide upon that,' said Rachel. 'Now that you are here you must stay a few days at least, so that you can see everything. Besides, we have so much to discuss.'

I went from the drawing-room to give orders for a room to be prepared – there was a large bare one on the west side of the house that would do him well – and went slowly upstairs to my own room to bath myself and change for dinner. From my window I saw Rainaldi come out and pay the fellow with the post-chaise, and then with an air of appraisal he stood a moment in the carriage-way, to look about him. I had the feeling that in one glance he priced the timber, reckoned the value of the trees and shrubs, and I saw him, too, examine the carving on the front door and run his hand over the scrolled figures. Rachel must have joined him, and I heard her laugh, and then the pair of them began talking in Italian. The front door closed. They came inside.

I had half a mind to stay up in my room and not descend, to send word to John to bring me my dinner on a tray. If they had so much to talk about they could do it better with me absent. Yet I was host, and could not show discourtesy. Slowly I bathed, reluctantly I dressed, and came downstairs to find Seecombe and John busy in the dining-room, which we had not used since the men had cleaned the panelling and done some repairs about the ceiling. The best silver was laid upon the table, and all the paraphernalia for visitors displayed.

'No need for all this pother,' I said to Seecombe, 'we could have eaten in the library very well.'

'The mistress gave orders, sir,' said Seecombe, on his dignity, and I heard him order John to fetch the lace-edged napery from the pantry, that we did not even use for Sunday dinner.

I lit my pipe, and went out into the grounds. The spring evening was still bright, and twilight would not come for an hour or more. The candles were lighted in the drawing-room, though, and the curtains not yet drawn. The candles were lighted too in the blue bedroom, and I saw Rachel pass to and fro before the windows as she dressed. It would have been an evening for the boudoir had we been alone, I hugging to myself the knowledge of what I had done in Bodmin, and she in gentle mood, telling me of her day. Now there would be none of this. Brightness in the drawing-room, animation in the dining-room, talk between the two of them about things that concerned me not; and over and above this the instinctive feeling of revulsion that I had about the man, that he came on no idle errand, to pass the time of day, but for some other purpose. Had Rachel known that he had arrived in England and would visit her? All the pleasure of my jaunt to Bodmin had left me. The schoolboy prank was over. I went into the house in low spirits, full of misgiving. Rainaldi was alone in the drawing-room, standing by the fire. He had changed from travelling clothes to dinner dress, and was examining the portrait of my grandmother which hung upon one of the panels.

'A charming face,' he said, commenting on it, 'fine eyes, and complexion. You come of a handsome family. The portrait in itself of no great value.'

'Probably not,' I said, 'the Lelys and the Knellers are on the stairs, if you care to look at them.'

'I noticed them as I came down,' he answered. 'The Lely is well placed but not the Kneller. The latter, I would say, is not in his best style, but executed in one of his more florid moments. Possibly finished by a pupil.' I said nothing, I was listening for Rachel's step upon the stair. 'In Florence, before I came away,' he said, 'I was able to sell an early Furini for your cousin, part of the Sangalletti collection, now unfortunately dispersed. An exquisite thing. It used to hang upon the stairs at the villa, where the light caught it to its greatest advantage. You possibly would not have noticed it when you went to the villa.'

'Very possibly not,' I answered him.

Rachel came into the room. She was wearing the gown she

had worn on Christmas Eve, but I saw she had a shawl about her shoulders. I was glad of it. She glanced from one to the other of us, as though to glean from our expressions how we were doing in conversation.

'I was just telling your cousin Philip,' said Rainaldi, 'how fortunate I was to sell the Furini madonna. But what a tragedy that it had to go.'

'We are used to that, though, aren't we?' she answered him. 'So many treasures that could not be saved.' I found myself resenting the use of the word 'we' in such a connection.

'Have you succeeded in selling the villa?' I asked bluntly.

'Not as yet,' answered Rainaldi, 'in fact – that is partly why I came here to see your cousin Rachel – we are practically decided upon letting it instead, for a term of some three or four years. It would be more advantageous, and to let it not so final as to sell. Your cousin may wish to return to Florence, one of these days. It was her home for so many years.'

'I have no intention of going back as yet,' said Rachel.

'No, possibly not,' he replied, 'but we shall see.'

His eyes followed her as she moved about the room, and I wished to heaven she would sit down so that he could not do so. The chair where she always sat stood back a little distance from the candlelight, leaving her face in shadow. There was no reason for her to move about the room unless to show her gown. I pulled a chair forward, but she did not sit.

'Imagine, Rainaldi has been in London for over a week, and did not tell me of it,' she said. 'I have never been more surprised in my life than when Seecombe announced that he was here. I think it was very remiss of him not to give me warning.' She smiled over her shoulder at him, and he shrugged his shoulders.

'I hoped the surprise of a sudden arrival would give you greater pleasure,' he said; 'the unexpected can be delightful or the reverse, it all depends upon the circumstances. Do you remember that time you were in Rome, and Cosimo and I turned up just as you were dressing for a party at the Casteluccis? You were distinctly annoyed with both of us.'

'Ah, but I had a reason for that,' she laughed. 'If you have forgotten, I won't remind you of it.'

'I have not forgotten,' he said. 'I remember too the colour of your gown. It was like amber. Also Benito Castelucci had presented you with flowers. I saw his card, and Cosimo did not.'

Seecombe came in to announce dinner, and Rachel led the way across the hall into the dining-room, still laughing and reminding Rainaldi of happenings in Rome. I had never felt more glum or out of place. They went on talking personalities, and places, and now and again Rachel would put out her hand to me across the table, as she would do to a child, and say, 'You must forgive us, Philip dear. It is so long since I have seen Rainaldi,' while he watched me with those dark hooded eyes, and slowly smiled.

Once or twice they broke into Italian. He would be telling her something, and suddenly search for a word that would not come, and with a bow of apology to me speak in his own language. She would answer him, and as she spoke and I heard the unfamiliar words pour from her lips, so much faster surely than when we talked together in English, it was as though her whole cast of countenance was changed; she became more animated and more vivid, yet harder in a sense, and with a new brilliance that I did not like so well.

It seemed to me that the pair of them were ill-placed at my table, in the panelled dining-room; they should have been elsewhere, in Florence or in Rome, with smooth dark servants waiting on them and all the glitter of a society foreign to me chattering and smiling in these phrases I did not know. They should not be here, with Seecombe padding round in his leather slippers and one of the young dogs scratching under the table. I sat hunched in my chair, damping, discouraging, a death's head at my own dinner, and, reaching for the walnuts, cracked them between my hands to relieve my feelings. Rachel sat with us while we passed the port and brandy. Or rather I passed it, for I took neither, while he drank both.

He lit a cigar, taking one from a case he carried with him, and surveyed me, as I lit my pipe, with an air of tolerance.

'All young Englishmen smoke pipes, it seems to me,' he observed. 'The idea is that it helps digestion, but I am told it fouls the breath.'

'Like drinking brandy,' I answered, 'which can foul the judgement too.'

I was reminded suddenly of poor Don, dead now in the plantation, and how in his younger days, when he had come upon a dog he much disliked, his hackles rose, his tail stood stiff and straight, and with a bound he seized him by the throat. I knew now how he must have felt.

'If you will excuse us, Philip,' said Rachel, rising from her chair, 'Rainaldi and I have much we must discuss, and he has papers with him that I have to sign. It will be best to do it upstairs, in the boudoir. Will you join us presently?'

'I think not,' I said. 'I have been out all day and have letters in the office. I will wish you both good night.'

She went from the dining-room, and he followed her. I heard them go upstairs. I was still sitting there when John came to clear the table.

I went out then, and walked about the grounds. I saw the light in the boudoir, but the curtains were drawn. Now they were together they would speak Italian. She would be sitting in the low chair by the fire, and he beside her. I wondered if she would tell him about our conversation of the preceding night, and how I had taken away the will and made a copy of it. I wondered what advice he gave to her, what words of counsel, and what papers he too brought from his file to show her that she must sign. When they had finished business, did they return again to personalities, to the discussing of people and of places they both knew? And would she brew tisana for him, as she did for me, and move about the room so that he could watch her? I wondered at what time he would take his leave of her and go to bed, and when he did so would she give him her hand? Would he stay awhile, lingering by the door, making an excuse to dally, as I did myself? Or knowing him so well, would she permit him to stay late?

227

I went on walking in the grounds, up to the new terrace walk, down the pathway nearly to the beach and back, up again along the walk where the young cedar trees were planted, and so round and back and round again, until I heard the clock in the belfry strike ten. That was my hour of dismissal: would it be his, as well? I went and stood at the edge of the lawn, and watched her window. The light was still burning in her boudoir. I watched, and waited. It continued burning. I had been warm from walking but now the air was chill, under the trees. My hands and feet grew cold. The night was dark and utterly without music. No frosty moon this evening topped the trees. At eleven, just after the clock struck, the light in the boudoir was extinguished and the light in the blue bedroom came instead. I paused a moment and then, on a sudden, walked round the back of the house and past the kitchens, and so to the west front, and looked up at the window of Rainaldi's room. Relief came to me. A light burnt there as well. I could see the chink of it, though he kept his shutters closed. The window was tight shut as well. I felt certain, with a sense of insular satisfaction, that he would open neither for the night.

I went into the house and up the staircase to my room. I had just taken off my coat and my cravat, and flung them on the chair, when I heard the rustle of her gown in the corridor, and then a soft tapping on the door. I went and opened it. She stood there, not yet undressed, with that same shawl about her shoulders still.

'I came to wish you good night,' she said.

'Thank you,' I answered, 'I wish you the same.'

She looked down at me, and saw the mud upon my shoes.

'Where have you been all evening?' she asked.

'Out walking in the grounds,' I answered her.

'Why did you not come to the boudoir for your tisana?' she asked.

'I did not care to do so,' I replied.

'You are very ridiculous,' she said. 'You behaved at dinner like a sulky schoolboy in need of a whipping.'

'I am sorry,' I said.

'Rainaldi is a very old friend, you know that well,' she said. 'We had much to talk about, surely you understand?'

'Is it because he is such an older friend than I that you permit him to linger in the boudoir until eleven?' I asked.

'Was it eleven?' she said. 'I really did not realise it.'

'How long is he going to stay?' I asked.

'That depends on you. If you are civil, and will invite him, he will stay for perhaps three days. More is not possible. He has to return to London.'

'Since you ask me to invite him, I must do so.'

'Thank you, Philip.' Suddenly she looked up at me, her eyes softened, and I saw the trace of a smile at the corner of her mouth. 'What is the matter,' she said, 'why are you so foolish? What were you thinking of, as you paced about the grounds?'

I might have answered her a hundred things. How I distrusted Rainaldi, how I hated his presence in my house, how I wanted it to be as it was before, and she alone with me. Instead, for no reason save that I loathed all that had been discussed that evening, I said to her, 'Who was Benito Castelucci that he had to give you flowers?'

The bubble of laughter rose within her, and, reaching up, she put her arms about me. 'He was old, and very fat, and his breath smelt of cigars – and I love you much too much,' she said, and went.

I have no doubt she was asleep within twenty minutes of leaving me, while I heard the clock in the belfry chime every hour until four; and falling into that uneasy morning slumber that becomes heaviest at seven was woken ruthlessly by John at my usual hour.

Rainaldi stayed, not for three days but for seven, and in those seven days I found no reason to alter my opinion of him. I think what I disliked most was his air of tolerance towards me. A kind of half-smile played upon his lips whenever he looked on me, as though I were a child to be humoured, and whatever business I had been upon during the day was enquired about and

229

treated like a schoolboy escapade. I made a point of not returning for any midday luncheon, and when I came home and entered the drawing-room in the afternoon, a little after four, I would find the pair of them together, talking their inevitable Italian, which would be broken off at my entrance.

'Ah, the worker returns,' Rainaldi would say, seated, God damn him, in the chair I always used when we had been alone. 'And while he has been tramping about his acres and seeing, no doubt, that his ploughs make the necessary furrows in the soil, you and I, Rachel, have been many hundred miles away in thought and fancy. We have not stirred for the day, except to wander on the new terrace walk. Middle age has many compensations.'

'You are bad for me, Rainaldi,' she would answer; 'since you have been here I have neglected all my duties. Paid no visits, supervised no planting. Philip will scold me for idleness.'

'You have not been idle intellectually,' came his reply. 'We have covered as much ground in that sense as your young cousin has in actual fact upon his feet. Or was it not upon feet today, but in the saddle? Young Englishmen are forever driving their bodies to fatigue.'

I could sense his mockery of me, a cart-horse with a turnip head, and the way Rachel came to my rescue, once more the teacher with her pupil, made me more angry still.

'Surely it is Wednesday,' she said, 'and on Wednesday Philip does not ride or walk, he does his accounts, in the office. He has a good head for figures, and knows exactly what he spends, don't you, Philip?'

'Not always,' I answered, 'and in point of fact today I attended Petty Sessions for a neighbour, and sat in judgement upon a fellow accused of theft. He was let off with a fine, and not imprisoned.'

Rainaldi watched me, with his same air of tolerance.

'A young Solomon as well as a young farmer,' he said. 'I am continually hearing of new talents. Rachel, does not your cousin remind you very much of Del Sarto's portrait of the Baptist? He has much the same arrogance and innocence so charmingly blended.'

'Perhaps,' said Rachel, 'I had not thought of it before. He resembles one person only, to my mind.'

'Ah, that of course,' answered Rainaldi, 'but there is also quite definitely a Del Sarto touch about him. Some time you will have to wean him from his acres here, and show him our country. Travel broadens the mind, and I would like to see him wander in a gallery or a church.'

'Ambrose was bored by both,' said Rachel, 'I doubt if Philip would be any more impressed. Well, did you see your godfather at Petty Sessions? I would like to take Rainaldi to call upon him at Pelyn.'

'Yes, he was there,' I said, 'and sent you his respects.'

'Mr Kendall has a very charming daughter,' said Rachel to Rainaldi, 'a little younger than Philip.'

'A daughter? H'm, indeed,' observed Rainaldi, 'then your young cousin is not entirely cut off from youthful feminine society?'

'Far from it,' laughed Rachel. 'Every mother has her eye upon him within a distance of forty miles.'

I remember glaring at her, and she laughed the more; and passing by me on her way to dress for dinner, she patted my shoulder in the infuriating habit that was hers – aunt Phoebe's gesture, I had called it before now, which delighted her as though I told her so for compliment.

It was upon this occasion that Rainaldi said to me, when she had gone upstairs, 'It was generous of you and your guardian to give your cousin Rachel the allowance. She wrote and told me of it. She was deeply touched.'

'It was the very least the estate owed to her,' I said, and hoped my tone of voice was discouraging to further conversation. I would not tell him what was going to happen in three weeks' time.

'You perhaps know,' said Rainaldi, 'that apart from the allowance she has no personal means whatsoever, except what I

231

can sell for her from time to time. This change of air has done wonders for her, but I think before long she will feel the need of society, such as she has been used to in Florence. That is the real reason I do not get rid of the villa. The ties are very strong.'

I did not answer. If the ties were strong, it was only because he made them so. She had spoken of no ties until he came. I wondered what was the extent of his own personal wealth, and if he gave her money from his own possession, not only what he sold from Sangalletti's estate. How right Ambrose had been to distrust him. But what weakness in Rachel made her keep him as her counsellor and friend?

'Of course,' continued Rainaldi, 'it would possibly be wiser to sell the villa eventually, and for Rachel to have a small apartment in Florence, or else to build something small, up in Fiesole. She has so many friends who have no wish to lose her, I among them.'

'You told me, when we first met,' I said, 'that my cousin Rachel was a woman of impulse. No doubt she will continue to be so, and live where she pleases.'

'No doubt,' answered Rainaldi. 'But the nature of her impulses has not always led her into happiness.'

I suppose by this he wanted to infer that her marriage with Ambrose had been on impulse, and unhappy likewise, and that her coming to England was also impulse, and he was uncertain of the outcome of it. He had power over her, because he had the management of her affairs, and it was this power that might take her back to Florence. I believed that was the purpose of his visit, so to drum it into her, and possibly to tell her also that the allowance the estate paid to her would not be sufficient to maintain her indefinitely. I had the trump card, and he did not know it. In three weeks' time she would be independent of Rainaldi for the rest of her life. I could have smiled, but for the fact that I disliked him too intensely to do so in his presence.

'It must be very strange, with your upbringing, suddenly to entertain a woman in the house, and for many months, as you have done,' said Rainaldi, with his hooded eyes upon me. 'Has it put you out at all?'

'On the contrary,' I said, 'I find it very pleasant.'

'Strong medicine, all the same,' he answered, 'for one young and inexperienced like yourself. Taken in so large a dose, it could do damage.'

'At nearly five-and-twenty,' I replied, 'I think I know pretty well what medicine suits me.'

'Your cousin Ambrose thought so too, at forty-three,' answered Rainaldi, 'but as it turned out he was wrong.'

'Is that a word of warning, or of advice?' I asked.

'Of both,' he said, 'if you will take it the right way. And now, if you will excuse me, I must go dress for dinner.'

I suppose this was his method to drive a wedge between me and Rachel, to drop a word, hardly venomous in itself, yet with sufficient sting to foul the air. If he suggested I should beware of her, what did he hint of me? Did he dismiss me with a shrug, as they sat together in the drawing-room when I was absent, saying how inevitable it was for young Englishmen to be long of limb and lacking in brain, or would that be too easy an approach? He certainly had a store of personal remarks, always ready to his tongue, to cast aspersion.

'The trouble with very tall men,' he said, on one occasion, 'is the fatal tendency to stoop.' (I was standing under the lintel of the doorway when he said this, bending my head to say a word to Seecombe.) 'Also, the more muscular amongst them turn to fat.'

'Ambrose was never fat,' said Rachel swiftly.

'He did not take the exercise that this lad takes. It is the violent walking, riding and swimming that develops the wrong portions of the body. I have noticed it very often, and nearly always amongst Englishmen. Now, in Italy we are smaller boned, and lead more sedentary lives. Therefore we keep our figures. Our diet, too, is easier on the liver and the blood. Not so much heavy beef and mutton. As to pastry . . .' He gestured with his hands in deprecation. 'This boy is forever eating pastry. I saw him demolish a whole pie for dinner yesterday.'

'Do you hear that, Philip?' said Rachel. 'Rainaldi considers that you eat too much. Seecombe, we shall have to cut down on Mr Philip's food.'

'Surely not, madam,' said Seecombe, greatly shocked. 'To eat less than he does would be injurious to health. We have to remember, madam, that in all probability Mr Philip is still growing.'

'Heaven forbid,' murmured Rainaldi. 'If he is growing still at twenty-four one would fear some serious glandular disturbance.'

He sipped his brandy, which she permitted him to take into the drawing-room, with a meditative air, his eyes upon me, until I felt for all the world that I was nearly seven foot, like poor dull-witted Jack Trevose who was hawked about Bodmin fair by his mother for the people to stare at him and give him pennies.

'I suppose,' said Rainaldi, 'that you do enjoy good health? No serious illness as a child that would account for growth?'

'I don't remember,' I answered, 'ever having been ill in my life.'

'That in itself is bad,' he said; 'those who have never suffered from disease are the first to be struck down, when nature attacks them. Am I not right in saying so, Seecombe?'

'Very possibly, sir. I hardly know,' said Seecombe; but as he went from the room I noticed him glance at me in doubt, as if I already sickened for the smallpox. 'This brandy,' said Rainaldi, 'should have been kept for at least another thirty years. It will be drinkable when young Philip's children come of age. Do you remember, Rachel, that evening at the villa when you and Cosimo entertained the whole of Florence, or so it seemed, and he insisted that all of us should be in dominoes and masks, like a Venetian carnival? And your dear lamented mother behaved so badly with prince someone-or-other, I think it was Lorenzo Ammanati, wasn't it?'

'It could have been with anyone,' said Rachel, 'but it was not Lorenzo, he was too busy running after me.'

'What nights of folly,' mused Rainaldi. 'We were all of us absurdly young, and entirely irresponsible. Far better to be staid and peaceful as we are today. I think they never give such parties here in England? The climate, of course, would be against it. But for that, young Philip here might find it amusing to dress himself up in mask and domino and search about the bushes for Miss Kendall.'

'I am sure Louise would ask for nothing better,' answered Rachel, and I saw her eye upon me and her mouth twitch.

I went out of the room and left them, and almost at once I heard them break into Italian, his voice interrogatory, and hers laughing in answer to his question, and I knew they were discussing me, and possibly Louise also, and the whole damned story of the rumours that were supposed to go about the countryside concerning some future betrothal between the pair of us. God! How much longer was he going to stay? How many more days and nights of this must I endure?

Eventually, on the last evening of his visit, my godfather, with Louise, came to dine. The evening passed off well, or so it seemed. I saw Rainaldi putting himself to infinite trouble to be courteous to my godfather, and the three of them, he, Rainaldi, and Rachel, somehow formed themselves into a group for conversation, leaving Louise and me to entertain ourselves. Now and again I noticed Rainaldi look towards us, smiling with a sort of amiable indulgence, and once I even heard him say, *sotto voce*, to my godfather, 'All my compliments upon your daughter and your godson. They make a very charming couple.' Louise heard it too. The poor girl flushed crimson. And at once I began asking her when she was next due to visit London, which I hoped would ease her feelings, but for all I know it may have made it worse. After dinner the subject of London came up once again, and Rachel said, 'I hope to visit London myself before very long. If we are there at the same time' – this to Louise – 'you must show me all the sights, because I have never been there.'

My godfather pricked up his ears at her remark.

'So you are thinking of leaving the country?' he said. 'Well, you have certainly endured the rigours of a winter visit to us in Cornwall very well. You will find London more amusing.' He turned to Rainaldi. 'You will still be there?'

'I have business there for some weeks yet,' replied Rainaldi, 'but if Rachel decides to come up I shall very naturally put myself at her disposal. I am no stranger to your capital. I know it very well. I hope that you and your daughter will give us the pleasure of dining with us, when you are there.'

'We shall be very happy to,' said my godfather. 'London in the spring can be delightful.'

I could have hit the whole bunch of heads together for the calm assumption of their meeting, but Rainaldi's use of the word 'us' maddened me the most. I could see his plan. Lure her to London, entertain her there while he conducted his other business, and then prevail upon her to return to Italy. And my godfather, for his own reasons, would further such a plan.

They little knew I had a plot to fox them all. So the evening passed, with much expression of good-will on every side, and with Rainaldi even drawing my godfather apart for the last twenty minutes or more, to drop more venom of some sort or other, I well imagined.

I did not return to the drawing-room, after the Kendalls had gone. I went up to bed, leaving my door ajar so that I could hear Rachel and Rainaldi as they came upstairs. They were long in doing so. Midnight struck, and they were still below. I went and stood out on the landing, listening. The drawing-room door was open a little, and I could hear the murmur of their voices. Resting my hand upon the banister, to bear my weight, I went halfway down the stairs in my bare feet. Memory flashed back to childhood. I had done this as a lad, when I knew Ambrose was below and had company for dinner. The same sense of guilt was with me now. The voices went on and on. But listening to Rachel and Rainaldi was of no purpose, for they spoke together in Italian. Now and again I caught mention of my name, Philip, and several times that of my godfather, Kendall. They were discussing me or him, or both of us. Rachel had an urgency to her voice that sounded strange, and he, Rainaldi, spoke as though he questioned her. I wondered, with sudden revulsion, if my godfather had told Rainaldi about his travelling friends from Florence, and if, in his turn, Rainaldi talked of this to Rachel.

How useless had been my Harrow education, and the study of Latin and Greek. Here were two persons talking Italian in my own house, discussing perhaps matters that might be of great importance to me, and I could gather nothing from it, save the mention of my own name.

There fell a sudden silence. Neither of them spoke. I heard no movement. What if he had gone towards her, and had put his arms about her, and she kissed him now as she had kissed me on Christmas Eve? Such a wave of hatred for him came to me at the thought that I nearly lost all caution and went running down the stairs to fling the door open wide. Then I heard her voice once more, and the rustle of her gown, drawing nearer to the door. I saw the flicker of her lighted candle. The long session was over at last. They were coming up to bed. Like that child of long ago, I stole back to my room.

I heard Rachel pass along the corridor to her own suite of rooms, and he turn the other way to his. I would never know, in all probability, what they had discussed together all those hours, but at least this was his last night under my roof, and tomorrow I should sleep with an easy heart. I could hardly swallow my breakfast, the next morning, in haste to hurry him away. The wheels of the post-chaise that was to carry him to London sounded on the drive, and Rachel, who I had thought must have said farewell the night before, came down, ready dressed for gardening, to bid him goodbye.

He took her hand, and kissed it. This time, for the sake of common courtesy to me, his host, he spoke his adieus in English. 'So you will write me your plans?' he said to her. 'Remember, when you are ready to come, I shall await you there, in London.'

'I shall make no plans,' she said, 'before the first of April.' And, looking over his shoulder, she smiled at me.

'Isn't that your cousin's birthday?' said Rainaldi, climbing into the postchaise. 'I hope he enjoys it, and does not eat too large a pie.' And then, looking from the window, said as a parting shot to me, 'It must be odd to have a birthday on so singular a date. All Fools Day, is it not? But perhaps, at twenty-five, you will think yourself too old to be reminded of it.' Then he was gone, the post-chaise passing down the drive to the park-gates. I looked across at Rachel.

'Perhaps,' she said, 'I should have asked him to return upon that day, for celebration?' Then, with the sudden smile that touched my heart, she took the primrose she had been wearing in her gown and put it in my button-hole. 'You have been very good,' she murmured, 'for seven days. And I, neglectful of my duties. Are you glad we are alone again?' Without waiting for my answer she went off to the plantation after Tamlyn.

21

The remaining weeks of March passed very swiftly. Each day that came I felt a greater confidence in the future, and grew more light of heart. Rachel seemed to sense my mood, and shared it with me.

'I have never,' she said, 'seen anyone so absurd about a birthday. You are like a child, who finds the world magic when he wakes. Does it mean so much to you to be free of poor Mr Kendall and his care? I am sure you could not have a guardian more kind. What plan, anyway, do you intend to make for the day itself?'

'No plan at all,' I answered, 'except that you have to remember what you said to me the other day. The celebrator of a birthday must be granted every wish.'

'Only up to the age of ten years old,' she said, 'never afterwards.'

'That is not fair,' I said; 'you made no stipulation about age.'

'If we are to picnic by the sea, or sail a boat,' she told me, 'I will not come with you. It is too early in the year to sit upon a beach, and as for climbing in a boat, I know even less about that than I do about a horse. You must take Louise instead.'

'I will not take Louise,' I said, 'and we will go nowhere not fitting to your dignity.' In point of fact, I had not thought about the events of the day itself, I only planned that she should have the document upon her breakfast tray, and the rest I would leave to chance. When the day of the thirty-first of March came, however, I knew that there was something else I wished to do. I remembered the jewels in the bank, and thought what a fool I was not to have recollected them before. So I had two encounters before me, on that day. One with Mr Couch, and the other with my godfather.

I made certain first of Mr Couch. I thought the packages might be too bulky to carry upon Gypsy, and I did not wish to order the carriage for fear Rachel might hear of it and express a desire to come into town upon some errand. Besides, it was an unusual thing for me to do, to go anywhere by carriage. So on some unnecessary pretext I walked into town, and had the groom fetch me in the dog-cart. As ill-luck had it, the whole neighbourhood appeared to be on shopping bent upon that morning, and as a person must either dodge into a doorway or fall into the harbour if he wishes to avoid his neighbour in our port, I was forever skulking behind corners so that I might not come face to face with Mrs Pascoe and her brood of daughters. My very furtiveness must have drawn all eyes upon me, and word gone about the place that Mr Ashley was behaving in singular fashion, running in one door of the fishmarket and out the other, and bobbing into the Rose and Crown before eleven in the morning, just as the vicar's lady from the neighbouring parish came walking down the street. No doubt it would be spread abroad that Mr Ashley drank.

I got myself inside sanctuary at last, within the safe walls of the bank. Mr Couch received me as pleasantly as he had done before.

'This time,' I told him, 'I have come to take all away.' He looked at me in pained surprise.

'You are not, Mr Ashley,' he said, 'intending to remove your banking account to another establishment?'

'No,' I said, 'I was speaking about the family jewels. Tomorrow I shall be twenty-five, and they become my legal property. I wish to have them in my custody when I awake upon my birthday.'

He must have thought me an eccentric, or at best a little odd.

'You mean,' he answered, 'you wish to indulge yourself in a whim for the day only? You did something of the sort, did you not, on Christmas Eve. Mr Kendall, your guardian, brought the collar back immediately.'

'Not a whim, Mr Couch,' I said. 'I want the jewels at home, in my possession. I do not know how I can make it still more clear.'

'I understand,' he said. 'Well, I trust that you have a safe in the house, or at least some place of security where you can keep them.'

'That, Mr Couch,' I said, 'is really my affair. I would be much obliged if you would fetch the jewels right away. Not only the collar this time. The whole collection.'

I might have been robbing him of his own possessions.

'Very good,' he said reluctantly, 'it will take a little time to fetch them from the vaults, and wrap them with even greater care. If you have any other business in the town . . .'

'I have none,' I interrupted. 'I will wait here, and take them with me.' He saw there was no use in delay and, sending word to his clerk, instructed the packages to be brought. I had a carrier for the purpose, which was luckily just large enough to take the whole – as a matter of fact it was a wicker basket that we used at home for carting cabbages, and Mr Couch winced as he put the precious boxes into it, one by one.

'It would have been far better, Mr Ashley,' he said, 'had I sent the packages to the house, in proper fashion. We have a brougham, you know, belonging to the bank, more suitable for the purpose.'

Yes, I thought, and what a clatter of tongues there would have been then. The bank brougham, driving to Mr Ashley's residence, with a top-hatted manager within. Far better the vegetable basket in a dog-cart.

'That is all right, Mr Couch,' I said, 'I can manage very well.'

I staggered from the bank in triumph, bearing the basket upon my shoulder, and ran full tilt into Mrs Pascoe, a daughter on either side.

'Good gracious, Mr Ashley,' she remarked, 'you appear well loaded.'

Holding the basket with one hand, I swept off my hat with a flourish.

'You observe me fallen on evil days,' I said to her. 'I am sunk so low that I needs must sell cabbages to Mr Couch and his clerks. Repairing the roof at home has well nigh ruined me, and I am obliged to hawk my produce about the town.'

She stared at me, her mouth agape, and the two daughters opened their eyes wide. 'Unfortunately,' I said, 'this basketful that I have here is due to another customer. Otherwise I would have pleasure in selling you some carrots. But in future, when you lack vegetables at the rectory, remember me.'

I went off to find the waiting dog-cart, and as I heaved the carrier into it, and climbed up and took the reins, while the groom jumped up beside me, I saw her still staring at me, at the street corner, her face dumbfounded. Now the story would go round that Philip Ashley was not only eccentric, drunk, and mad, but a pauper in the bargain.

We drove home by the long avenue from Four Turnings, and while the boy put away the dog-cart I went into the house the back way – the servants were at dinner – and, going upstairs by their staircase, I tip-toed through to the front and to my room. I looked the vegetable basket in my wardrobe, and went downstairs to eat some lunch.

Rainaldi would have closed his eyes and shuddered. I wrought havoc upon a pigeon pie, and washed it down with a great tankard of ale.

Rachel had been in and waited – she left a note to say so – and, thinking I would not return, had gone up to her room. For this once I did not mind her absence. I think my guilty delight would have shown too plainly on my face.

No sooner had I swallowed my meal than I was off again, this time on horseback, to Pelyn. Safe in my pocket I had the document, which the attorney, Mr Trewin, had sent to me, as he had promised, by special messenger. I also had the will. The prospect of this interview was not as pleasing as that of the morning had been; nevertheless, I was undaunted.

My godfather was at home, and in his study.

'Well, Philip,' he said, 'if I am a few hours premature, no matter. Let me wish you a happy birthday.'

'Thank you,' I said, 'and I would also thank you, in return, for your affection for me and for Ambrose, and for your guardianship over these past years.'

'Which,' he said smiling, 'ends tomorrow.'

'Yes,' I said, 'or rather, tonight, at midnight. And as I do not want to rouse you from your sleep at such an hour, I would like you to witness my signature to a document I wish to sign, which will come into effect at that precise moment.'

'H'm,' he said, reaching for his spectacles, 'a, document, what document?'

I brought the will from my breast pocket.

'First,' I said, 'I would like you to read this. It was not given to me willingly, but only after much argument and discussion. I had long felt such a paper must be in existence, and here it is.'

I passed it to him. He placed his spectacles on his nose and read it through. 'It is dated, Philip,' he said, 'but it is not signed.'

'Quite so,' I answered, 'but it is in Ambrose's hand, is it not?'

'Why, yes,' he replied, 'undoubtedly. What I do not understand is why he never had it witnessed and sent to me. I had expected such a will as this from the first days he was married, and told you so.'

'It would have been signed,' I said, 'but for his illness, and for the fact that he expected, any month, to be home here and give it to you in person. That I know.'

He laid it down on his desk.

'Well, there it is,' he said. 'These things have happened in other families. Unfortunate for his widow, but we can do no more for her than we have done. A will without a signature is invalid.'

'I know,' I said, 'and she did not expect otherwise. As I told you just now, it was only by dint of much persuasion that I retrieved this paper from her. I must return it, but here is a copy.'

I pocketed the will, and gave him the copy I had made.

'What now?' he said. 'Has anything else come to light as well?'

'No,' I answered, 'only that my conscience tells me I have been enjoying something that is not mine by right. Ambrose intended to sign that will, and death, or rather illness in the first place, prevented him. I want you to read this document that I have had prepared.'

And I handed him the scroll that had been drawn up by Trewin at Bodmin.

He read it slowly, carefully, his face becoming grave as he did so, and it was only after a long while that he removed his spectacles and looked at me.

'Your cousin Rachel,' he said, 'has no knowledge of this document?'

'No knowledge whatsoever,' I answered, 'never by word or intimation has she expressed any thought of what I have had put there, and what I intend to do. She is utterly and entirely innocent of my purpose. She does not even know that I am here, or that I have shown you the will. As you heard her say a few weeks ago, she intends to leave for London shortly.'

He sat at his desk, his eyes upon my face.

'You are quite determined upon this course?' he said to me.

'Quite,' I answered him.

'You realise that it may lead to abuse, that there are few safeguards, and that the whole of the fortune due to you eventually, and to your heirs, may be dispersed?'

'Yes,' I said, 'and I am willing to take the risk.'

He shook his head, and sighed. He rose from his chair, looked out of the window, and returned to it again.

'Does her adviser, Signor Rainaldi, know of this document?' he asked.

'Most certainly not,' I said.

'I wish you had told me of it, Philip,' he said. 'I could have discussed it with him. He seemed to me a man of sense. I had a word with him that evening. I went so far as to tell him about my uneasiness as to that overdraft. He admitted that extravagance was a fault, and always had been. That it had led to trouble, not only with Ambrose, but also with her first husband, Sangalletti. He gave me to understand that he, Signor Rainaldi, is the only person who knows how to deal with her.'

'I don't care a jot what he told you,' I said. 'I dislike the man, and believe he uses this argument for his own purpose. He hopes to entice her back to Florence.'

My godfather regarded me once more.

'Philip,' he said, 'forgive me asking you this question, personal I know, but I have known you since birth. You are completely infatuated with your cousin, are you not?'

I felt my cheeks burn, but I went on looking at him.

'I don't know what you mean,' I said. 'Infatuation is a futile and most ugly word. I respect and honour my cousin Rachel more than anyone I know.'

'I have meant to say this to you before,' he said. 'There is much talk, you know, about her being so long a visitor to your house. I go further and say the whole of the county whispers of little else.'

'Let them continue,' I said. 'After tomorrow they will have something else to discuss. The transfer of property and fortune can hardly be kept secret.'

'If your cousin Rachel has any wisdom, and wishes to keep her self-respect,' he said, 'she will either go to London, or ask you to live elsewhere. The present situation is very wrong for you both.'

I was silent. Only one thing mattered, that he should sign the paper.

'Of course,' he said, 'there is, in the long run, only one way out of gossip. And, according to this document, only one way out of the transfer of this property. And that is, that she should marry again.'

'I believe it most unlikely,' I said.

'I suppose,' he said, 'you have not thought of asking her yourself?'

Once again the colour flamed in my face.

'I would not dare to do so,' I said; 'she would not have me.'

'I am not happy about any of this, Philip,' he said. 'I wish now that she had never come to England. However, it is too late to regret that. Very well then, sign. And take the consequences of your action.'

I seized a pen, and put my name to the deed. He watched me with his still, grave face.

'There are some women, Philip,' he observed, 'good women very possibly, who through no fault of their own impel disaster. Whatever they touch, somehow turns to tragedy. I don't know why I say this to you, but I feel I must.' And then he witnessed my signature on the long scroll of paper.

'I suppose,' he said, 'you will not wait to see Louise?'

'I think not,' I replied, and then relenting, 'If you are both at liberty to-morrow evening, why not come and dine, and drink my health upon my birthday?'

He paused. 'I am not certain if we are free,' he said. 'I will at any rate send word to you by noon.' I could see plainly he had little wish to come and see us, and had some embarrassment in refusing my invitation. He had taken the whole matter of the transfer better than I had expected, there had been no violent expostulation, no interminable lecture, but possibly he knew me too well by now to imagine anything of the sort would have had effect. That he was greatly shaken and distressed I knew by his grave manner. I was glad that no mention had been made of the family jewels. The knowledge that they were concealed in the cabbage basket in my wardrobe might have proved the final straw.

I rode home, remembering my mood of high elation the last time I had done so, after visiting the attorney Trewin in Bodmin, only to find Rainaldi on arriving home. There would be no such visitor to-day. In three weeks full spring had come about the countryside and it was warm like May. Like all weather prophets, my farmers shook their heads and prophesied calamity. Late frost would come, and nip the buds in bloom and wither the growing corn beneath the surface of the drying soil. I think, on that last day of March, I would not have greatly cared if famine came, or flood, or earthquake.

The sun was sinking beyond the westward bay, flaming the quiet sky, darkening the water, and the rounded face of the near full moon showed plain over the eastern hills. This, I thought to myself, is how a man must feel when in a state of high intoxication, this complete abandon to the passing hour. I saw things, not in hazy fashion, but with the clarity of the very drunk. The park, as I entered it, had all the grace of fairy tale; even the cattle, plodding down to drink at their trough beside the pool, were beasts of enchantment, lending themselves to beauty. The jackdaws were building high, they flapped and straddled their untidy nests in the tall trees near to the avenue, and from the house and the stables I could see the blue smoke curling from the chimneys, and I could sense the clatter of pails about the yard, the whistling of the men, the barking of the puppies from their kennels. All this was old to me, long-known and loved, possessed from babyhood; yet now it held new magic.

I had eaten too fully at midday to be hungry, but I was thirsty, and drank deep of the cool clear water from the well in the courtyard.

I joked with the boys as they bolted the back doors and closed the shutters. They knew to-morrow was my birthday. They whispered to me how Seecombe had had his likeness painted for me, as a deadly secret, and that he had told them I was bound to hang it upon a panel in the hall with the ancestral portraits. I gave them a solemn promise that it was exactly what I would do. And then the three of them, with much head-nodding amongst themselves and muttering in corners, disappeared into the servants' hall and then returned again, bearing a package. John, as spokesman, gave it me and said, "'Tis from us all, Mr Philip, sir, we none of us can bear wait to give it you.'

It was a case of pipes. It must have cost them all of a month's wages. I shook hands with them, and clapped them on the back, and vowed to each that I had been planning to get the very same myself next time I went to Bodmin or to Truro, and they gazed back at me in great delight, so that like an idiot I could have wept to see their pleasure. In truth, I never smoked any pipe but the one Ambrose had given me when I was seventeen, but in the future I must make a point of smoking all of theirs, for fear of disappointing them.

I bathed and changed, and Rachel was waiting for me in the dining-room.

'I smell mischief,' she said at once. 'You have not been home for the day. What have you been at?'

'That, Mrs Ashley,' I said to her, 'is no concern of yours.'

'No one has set eyes upon you since early morning,' she said. 'I came home to luncheon, and had no companion.'

'You should have lunched with Tamlyn,' I told her. 'His wife is a most excellent cook, and would have done you well.'

'Did you go to town?' she asked.

'Why, yes, I went to town.'

'And did you see anyone of our acquaintance?'

'Why, yes,' I answered, nearly bursting into laughter. 'I saw Mrs Pascoe and the girls, and they were greatly shocked at my appearance.'

'Why so?'

'Because I was carrying a basket on my shoulder, and told them I had been selling cabbages.'

'Were you telling them the truth, or had you been to the Rose and Crown and drunk too much cider?'

'I was not telling them the truth, nor had I been to the Rose and Crown for cider.'

'Then what was it all about?'

I would not answer her. I sat in my chair and smiled.

'I think,' I said, 'that when the moon is fully risen I shall go swimming after dinner. I feel all the energy of the world in myself to-night, and all the folly.'

She looked at me over her glass of wine with solemn eyes.

'If,' she said, 'you desire to spend your birthday in your bed with a poultice on your chest, drinking black currant every hour, nursed – not by me, I warn you, but by Seecombe – go swimming, if you please. I shall not stop you.'

I stretched my arms above my head, and sighed for pure enjoyment. I asked permission to smoke, which she granted.

I produced my case of pipes. 'Look,' I said, 'what the boys have given me. They could not wait till morning.'

'You are as great a baby as they,' she said, and then, in a half-whisper, 'You do not know what Seecombe has in store for you.'

'But I do,' I whispered back, 'the boys have told me. I am flattered beyond measure. Have you seen it?'

She nodded. 'It is perfect,' she said; 'his best coat, the green one, his underlip, and all. It was painted by his son-in-law, from Bath.'

When we had dined we went into the library, but I had not been telling her an untruth when I said I had all the energy of the world. I was in such a state of exultation that I could not rest in my chair, with longing for the night to pass and for the day to come.

'Philip,' she said at last, 'for the sake of pity, go and take your walk. Run to the beacon and back again, if that will cure you. I think you have gone mad, in any case.'

'If this is madness,' I said, 'then I would want to stay that way for always. I did not know lunacy could give such delight.'

I kissed her hand and went out into the grounds. It was a night for walking, still and clear. I did not run, as she had bidden me, but for all that I achieved the beacon hill. The moon, so nearly full, hovered, with swollen cheek, above the bay, and wore about his face the look of a wizard man who shared my secret. The bullocks, sheltering for the night in the lea of the stone wall in the valley's dip, stumbled to their feet at my approach, and scattered.

I could see a light from the Barton, above the meadow, and when I reached the beacon head, and the bays stretched out on either side of me, there were the flickering lights of the little towns along the western coast, and our own harbour lights to the east as well. Yet presently they dimmed, as the candle-light did within the Barton, and there was nothing about me but that light from the pale moon, making a silver track across the sea. If it was a night for walking it was a night for swimming too. No threat of poultices or cordials would keep me from it. I climbed down, to my favourite point where the rocks jutted, and, laughing to myself at this folly most sublime, plunged into the water. God! It was icy cold. I shook myself like a dog, with chattering teeth, and struck out across the bay, returning, after a bare four minutes, back to the rocks to dress.

Madness. Worse than madness. But still I did not care, and still my mood of exultation held me in thrall.

I dried myself, as best I could, upon my shirt, and walked up through the woods, back to the house. The moonlight made a ghostly path for me, and shadows, eerie and fantastic, lurked behind the trees. Where my path divided into two, one taking me to the cedar walk and the other to the new terrace above, I heard a rustle where the trees grew thickest, and suddenly to my nostrils came that rank vixen smell about me in the air, tainting the very leaves under my feet; yet I saw nothing, and all the daffodils, leaning from the banks on either side of me, stayed poised and still, without a breath to stir them.

I came to the house at last, and looked up at her window. It was open wide, and I could not tell if her candle burnt still or if she had blown it out. I looked at my watch. It wanted five minutes to midnight. I knew suddenly that if the boys had not been able to wait to give me my present, neither could I wait to give Rachel hers. I thought of Mrs Pascoe, and the cabbages, and my mood of folly swept me in full force. I went and stood under the window of the blue bedroom, and called up to her. I called her name three times before I had an answer. She came to the open window, dressed in that white nun's robe, with the full sleeves and the lace collar.

'What do you want?' she said. 'I was three parts asleep, and you have woken me.'

'Will you wait there,' I said, 'just a few moments? I want to give you something. The package that Mrs Pascoe saw me carry.'

'I have not Mrs Pascoe's curiosity,' she said. 'Let it wait until the morning.'

'It cannot wait until the morning,' I said, 'it has to happen now.'

I let myself in by the side door, and went upstairs to my room and came down again, carrying the cabbage basket. Round the handles I knotted a great piece of string. I had with me, also, the document, which I placed in my jacket pocket. She was still waiting there, beside the window.

'What in the world,' she called softly, 'have you got carried in that basket? Now, Philip, if this is one of your practical jokes, I will not share it. Have you got crabs hidden there, or lobsters?'

'Mrs Pascoe believes they are cabbages,' I said. 'At any rate, I give you my promise they won't bite. Now, catch the string.'

I threw up the end of the long string to the window.

'Haul away,' I told her, 'with both hands, mind. The basket is some weight.' She pulled, as she was bidden, and the basket bumped and crashed against the wall, and against the wire that was there to hold the creeper, and I stood below, watching her, shaking with silent laughter.

She pulled the basket on to her window-sill, and there was silence.

After a moment she looked out again. 'I don't trust you, Philip,' she said. 'These packages have odd shapes. I know they are going to bite.'

For answer I began to climb up the creeper wire, hand over hand, until I reached her window.

'Be careful,' she called, 'you will fall and break your neck.'

In a moment I was inside the room, one leg upon the floor, the other on the sill.

'Why is your head so wet?' she said. 'It is not raining.'

'I've been swimming,' I answered. 'I told you I would do so. Now, open up the packages, or shall I do it for you?'

One candle was burning in the room. She stood with bare feet upon the floor and shivered.

'For heaven's sake,' I said, 'put something round you.'

I seized the coverlet from the bed and threw it about her, then lifted her and put her amongst her blankets.

'I think,' she said, 'that you have gone raving mad.'

'Not mad,' I said, 'it's only that I have become, at this minute, twenty-five. Listen.' I held up my hand. The clock struck midnight. I put my hand into my pocket. 'This,' I said, laying the document upon the table, by the candlestick, 'you can read at your leisure. But the rest I want to give you now.'

251

I emptied the packages upon the bed and cast the wicker basket on the floor. I tore away the paper, scattering the boxes, flinging the soft wrappings anywhere. Out fell the ruby head-piece and the ring. Out came the sapphires and the emeralds. Here were the pearl collar and the bracelets, all tumbling in mad confusion on the sheets. 'This,' I said, 'is yours. And this, and this . . .' And in an ecstasy of folly I heaped them all upon her, pressing them on her hands, her arms, her person.

'Philip,' she cried, 'you are out of your mind, what have you done?'

I did not answer. I took the collar, and put it about her neck. 'I'm twenty-five,' I said; 'you heard the clock strike twelve. Nothing matters any more. All this for you. If I possessed the world, you should have it also.'

I have never seen eyes more bewildered or amazed. She looked up at me, and down to the scattered necklaces and bracelets and back to me again, and then, I think because I was laughing, she put her arms suddenly about me and was laughing too. We held one another, and it was as though she caught my madness, shared my folly, and all the wild delight of lunacy belonged to both of us.

'Is this,' she said, 'what you have been planning all these weeks?'

'Yes,' I said, 'they should have come with your breakfast. But like the boys and the case of pipes, I could not wait.'

'And I have nothing for you,' she said, 'but a gold pin for your cravat. Your birthday, and you shame me. Is there nothing else you want? Tell me, and you shall have it. Anything you ask.'

I looked down at her, with all the rubies and the emeralds spread about her, and the pearl collar around her neck, and all of a sudden I was serious and remembered what the collar meant.

'One thing, yes,' I said, 'but it isn't any use my asking it.'

'Why not?' she said.

'Because,' I answered, 'you would box my ears, and send me straight to bed.'

She stared up at me, touching my cheek with her hand.

'Tell me,' she said. And her voice was gentle.

I did not know how a man asks a woman to become his wife. There is generally a parent, whose consent must first be given. Or if no parent, then there is courtship, there is all the give and take of some preceding conversation. None of this applied to her and me. And it was midnight, and talk of love and marriage had never passed between us. I could say to her, bluntly, plainly, 'Rachel, I love you, will you be my wife?' I remembered that morning in the garden, when we had jested about my dislike of the whole business, and I had told her that I asked for nothing better than my own house to comfort me. I wondered if she could understand, and remember too.

'I told you once,' I said, 'that I had all the warmth and the comfort that I needed within four walls. Have you forgotten?'

'No,' she said, 'I have not forgotten.'

'I spoke in error,' I said, 'I know now what I lack.'

She touched my head, and the tip of my ear, and the end of my chin.

'Do you?' she said. 'Are you so very sure?'

'More sure,' I answered, 'than of anything on earth.'

She looked at me. Her eyes seemed darker in the candlelight.

'You were very certain of yourself upon that morning,' she said, 'and stubborn too. The warmth of houses . . .'

She put out her hand to snuff the candle, and she was laughing still.

When I stood upon the grass at sunrise, before the servants had wakened and come down to open the shutters and let in the day, I wondered if any man before me had been accepted in marriage in quite so straight a fashion. It would save many a weary courtship if it was always so. Love, and all its trappings, had not concerned me hitherto; men and women must do as best they pleased, I had not cared. I had been blind, and deaf, and sleeping; now, no longer.

What happened on those first hours of my birthday will remain. If there was passion, I have forgotten it. If there was tenderness, it is with me still. Wonder is mine forever, that a woman, accepting love, has no defence. Perhaps this is the secret that they hold to bind us to them. Making reserve of it, until the last.

I would not know, having no other for comparison. She was my first, and last.

22

I remember the house waking to the sunlight, and seeing the round ball of it appear over the trees that fringed the lawn. The dew had been heavy, and the grass was silver, as though touched with frost. A blackbird started singing, and a chaffinch followed, and soon the whole spring chorus was in song. The weather-vane was the first to catch the sun, and gleaming gold against the sky, poised above the belfry tower, it swung to the nor'west and there remained, while the grey walls of the house, dark and sombre at first sight, mellowed to the morning light with a new radiance.

I went indoors and up to my room, and dragging a chair beside the open window sat down in it, and looked towards the sea. My mind was empty, without thought. My body calm and still. No problems came swimming to the surface, no anxieties itched their way through from the hidden depths to ruffle the blessed peace. It was as though everything in life was now resolved, and the way before me plain. The years behind me counted for nothing. The years to come were no more than a continuation of all I now knew and held, possessing; it would be so, forever and ever, like the amen to a litany. In the future only this; Rachel and I. A man and his wife living within themselves, the house containing us, the world outside our doors passing unheeded. Day after day, night after night, as long as we both should live. That much I remembered from the prayer-book.

I shut my eyes, and she was with me still; and then I must have slept upon the instant, because when I woke the sun was streaming into the open window, and John had come in and laid out my clothes upon the chair and brought me my hot water and gone again, and I had not heard him. I shaved and dressed and went down to my breakfast, which was now cold upon the sideboard – Seecombe thinking I had long descended – but hard-boiled eggs and ham made easy fare. I could have eaten anything that day. Afterwards I whistled to the dogs and went out into the grounds, and, caring nothing for Tamlyn and his cherished blooms, I picked every budding camellia I set eyes upon and laid them in the carrier, the same that had done duty for the jewels the day before, and went back into the house and up the stairs and along the corridor to her room.

She was sitting up in bed, eating her breakfast, and before she had time to call out in protest and draw her curtains, I had showered the camellias down upon the sheets and covered her.

'Good morning once again,' I said, 'and I would remind you that it is still my birthday.'

'Birthday or not,' she said, 'it is customary to knock upon a door before you enter. Go away.'

Dignity was difficult, with the camellias in her hair, and on her shoulders, and falling into the tea-cup and the bread-and-butter, but I straightened my face and withdrew to the end of the room.

'I am sorry,' I said. 'Since entering by window I have grown casual about doors. In fact, my manners have forsaken me.'

'You had better go,' she said, 'before Seecombe comes up to take my tray. I think he would be shocked to see you here, for all your birthday.'

Her cool voice was a damper to my spirits, but I supposed there was logic in her remark. It was a trifle bold, perhaps, to burst in on a woman at her breakfast, even if she was to be my wife – which was something that Seecombe did not know as yet.

'I will go,' I said. 'Forgive me. I only want to say one thing to you. I love you.'

I turned to the door and went, and I remember noticing that she no longer wore the collar of pearls. She must have taken it off after I left her in the early morning, and the jewels were not lying on the floor, all had been tidied away.

But on the breakfast tray, beside her, was the document that I had signed the day before.

Downstairs Seecombe awaited me, a package in his hand bound up in paper.

'Mr Philip, sir,' he said, 'this is a very great occasion. May I take the liberty of wishing you many, many happy returns of your birthday?'

'You may, Seecombe,' I answered, 'and thank you.'

'This, sir,' he said, 'is only a trifle. A small memento of many years of devoted service to the family. I hope you will not be offended, and that I have not taken any liberty in assuming you might be pleased to accept it as a gift.'

I unwrapped the paper and the visage of Seecombe himself, in profile, was before me; unflattering perhaps, but unmistakable.

'This,' I said gravely, 'is very fine indeed. So fine, in fact, that it shall hang in place of honour near the stairs. Bring me a hammer and a nail.' He pulled the bell, with dignity, for John to do his errand.

Between us we fixed the portrait upon the panel outside the dining-room. 'Do you consider, sir,' said Seecombe, 'that the likeness does me justice? Or has the artist given something of harshness to the features, especially the nose? I am not altogether satisfied.'

'Perfection in a portrait is impossible, Seecombe,' I answered. 'This is as near to it as we shall get. Speaking for myself, I could not be more delighted.'

'Then that is all that matters,' he replied.

I wanted to tell him there and then that Rachel and I were to be married, I was so bursting with delight and happiness, but a certain hesitation held me back; the matter was too solemn and too delicate to thrust upon him unawares, and maybe we should tell him together.

I went round the back to the office, in pretence of work, but all I did when I got there was to sit before my desk and stare in front of me. I kept seeing her, in my mind's eye, propped up against the pillows, eating her breakfast, with the camellia buds scattered on the tray. The peace of early morning had gone from me, and all the fever of last night was with me once again. When we were married, I mused, tilting back my chair and biting the end of my pen, she would not dismiss me from her presence with such ease. I would breakfast with her. No more descending to the dining-room alone. We would start upon a new routine.

The clock struck ten, and I heard the men moving in the court and in the yard outside the office window, and I looked at a sheaf of bills, and put them back again, and started a letter to a fellow magistrate upon the bench and tore it up again. For no words came and nothing that I wrote made any sense, and it was still two hours to noon, when Rachel would come downstairs. Nat Bray, the farmer from Penhale, came in to see me, with a long tale about some cattle that had strayed into Trenant and how the fault was with his neighbour for not seeing to his fences, and I nodded and agreed, hearing little of his argument, for surely by now Rachel might be dressed, and out about the grounds, talking to Tamlyn.

I cut the luckless fellow short and bid him good day, and, seeing his look of hurt discomfiture, took him to seek the steward's room and have a glass of ale with Seecombe. 'To-day, Nat,' I said, 'I do no business, it's my birthday, I am the happiest of men,' and clapping him on the shoulder left him open-mouthed to make what he would of my remark.

Then I thrust my head out of the window, and called across the court to the kitchen, and asked them to pack a luncheon basket for a picnic, for suddenly I wanted to be alone with her under the sun, with no formality of house or dining-room or silver upon a table, and this order given I walked to the stables to tell Wellington that I wished to have Solomon saddled for the mistress.

He was not there. The coach-house door was wide and the carriage gone. The stable lad was sweeping the cobbles. He looked blank at my enquiry.

'The mistress ordered the carriage soon after ten,' he said. 'Where she has gone I cannot say. Perhaps to town.'

I went back to the house and rang for Seecombe, but he could tell me nothing, except that Wellington had brought the carriage to the door at a little after ten, and Rachel was ready waiting in the hall. She had never before gone driving in the morning. My spirits, pitched so high, flagged suddenly and dropped. The day was all before us and this was not what I had planned.

I sat about, and waited. Noon came and the bell clanged out for the servant's dinner. The picnic basket was beside me, Solomon was saddled. But the carriage did not come. Finally, at two, I took Solomon round to the stable myself and bade the boy unsaddle him. I walked down the woods to the new avenue, and the excitement of the morning had turned to apathy. Even if she came now it would be too late to picnic. The warmth of an April sun would be gone by four o'clock.

I was nearly at the top of the avenue, at Four Turnings, when I saw the groom open the lodge gates and the carriage pass through. I stood waiting, in the middle of the drive, for the horses to approach, and at sight of me Wellington drew rein and halted them. The weight of disappointment, so heavy during the past hours, went at the glimpse of her, sitting in the carriage, and telling Wellington to drive on I climbed in and sat opposite her, on the hard narrow seat.

She was wrapped in her dark mantle, and she wore her veil down, so that I could not see her face.

'I have looked for you since eleven,' I said. 'Where in the world have you been?'

'To Pelyn,' she said, 'to see your godfather.'

All the worries and perplexities, safely buried in the depths, came rushing to the fore-front of my mind, and with a sharp misgiving I wondered what they could do, between them, to make havoc of my plans.

'Why so?' I asked. 'What need to go find him in such a hurry? Everything has been settled long since.'

'I am not sure,' she answered, 'what you mean by everything.'

The carriage jolted in a rut beside the avenue, and she put out her hand in its dark glove to the strap for steadiness. How remote she seemed, sitting there in her mourning clothes, behind her veil, a world away from the Rachel who had held me against her heart.

'The document,' I said, 'you are thinking of the document. You cannot go against it. I am legally of age. My godfather can do nothing. It is signed, and sealed, and witnessed. Everything is yours.'

'Yes,' she said, 'I understand it now. The wording was a little obscure, that was all. So I wished to make certain what it meant.'

Still that distant voice, cool and unattached, while in my ears and in my memory was the other, that had whispered in my ear at midnight.

'Is it clear to you now?' I said.

'Quite clear,' she answered.

'Then there is nothing more to be said on the matter?'

'Nothing,' she replied.

Yet there was a kind of nagging at my heart, and a strange mistrust. All spontaneity was gone, the joy and laughter we had shared together when I gave her the jewels. God damn my godfather if he had said anything to hurt her.

'Put up your veil,' I said.

For a moment she did not move. Then she glanced up at Wellington's broad back and the groom beside him on the box. He whipped the horses to a brisker pace as the twisting avenue turned into the straight.

She lifted her veil, and the eyes that looked into mine were not smiling as I had hoped, or tearful as I had feared, but steady and serene and quite unmoved, the eyes of someone who has been out upon a matter of business and settled it in satisfaction.

For no great reason I felt blank, and in some sense cheated. I wanted the eyes to be as I remembered them at sunrise. I had thought, foolishly perhaps, that it was because her eyes were still the same that she had hidden them behind her veil. Not so, however. She must have sat facing my godfather thus, across the desk in his study, purposeful and practical and cool, no whit dismayed, while I sat waiting for her, in torment, on the front door step at home.

260

'I would have been back before now,' she said, 'but they pressed me to remain for luncheon, and I could not well refuse. Had you made a plan?' She turned her face to watch the passing scene, and I wondered how it was that she could sit there, as if we were two people of casual acquaintance, while it was as much as I could do not to put out my hands to her and hold her. Since yesterday, everything was changed. Yet she gave no sign of it.

'I had a plan,' I said, 'but it does not matter now.'

'The Kendalls dine tonight in town,' she said, 'but will look in upon us afterwards, before returning home. I fancy I made some progress with Louise. Her manner was not quite so frozen.'

'I am glad of that,' I said, 'I would like you to be friends.'

'In fact,' she went on, 'I am coming back again to my original way of thinking. She would suit you well.'

She laughed, but I did not laugh with her. It was unkind, I thought, to make a joke of poor Louise. Heaven only knew, I wished the girl no harm, and that she might find herself a husband.

'I think,' she said, 'that your godfather disapproves of me, which he has a perfect right to do, but by the end of luncheon I think we understood one another very well. The tension eased, and conversation was not difficult. We made more plans to meet in London.'

'In London?' I asked. 'You don't still intend to go to London?'

'Why, yes,' she said, 'why ever not?'

I said nothing. Certainly she had a right to go to London if she pleased. There might be shops she wished to visit, purchases to make, especially now that she had money to command, and yet . . . surely she could wait awhile, until we could go together? There were so many things we must discuss, but I was hesitant to do so. It struck me with full force, suddenly and sharply, what I had not thought of until now. Ambrose was but nine months dead. The world would think it wrong for us to marry before midsummer. Somehow there were problems to the day that had not been at midnight, and I wanted none of them.

'Don't let's go home immediately,' I said to her. 'Walk with me in the woods.'

'Very well,' she answered.

We stopped by the keeper's cottage in the valley, and descending from the carriage let Wellington drive on. We took one of the paths beside the stream, which twisted upward to the hill above, and here and there were primroses, in clumps, beneath the trees, which she must stoop and pick, returning again to the subject of Louise as she did so, saying the girl had quite an eye for gardens and with instruction would learn more, in time. Louise could go to the ends of the earth for all I cared, and garden there to her heart's content; I had not brought Rachel in the woods to talk about Louise.

I took the primroses from her hands and put them on the ground, and spreading my coat under a tree I asked her to sit down upon it.

'I am not tired,' she said. 'I have been sitting in the carriage this past hour or more.'

'And I also,' I said, 'these four hours, by the front door, waiting for you.'

I took off her gloves, and kissed her hands, and put the bonnet and the veil amongst the primroses, and kissed the rest of her as I had wanted to do for long hours past, and once again she was without defence. 'This,' I said, 'was my plan, which you have spoilt by lunching with the Kendalls.'

'I rather thought it might be,' she answered, 'which was one of the reasons why I went.'

'You promised to deny me nothing on my birthday, Rachel.'

'There is,' she said, 'a limit to indulgence.'

I could see none. I was happy once again, with all anxiety gone.

'If,' she remarked, 'this is a path frequented by the keeper we would look a little foolish.'

'And he more foolish still,' I replied, 'when I pay his wages on Saturday. Or will you take that over with the rest? I am your servant now, you know, another Seecombe, and await your further orders.'

I lay there, with my head in her lap, and she ran her fingers

262

through my hair. I shut my eyes, and wished it might continue. To the end of time, nothing but that moment.

'You are wondering why I had not thanked you,' she said. 'I saw your puzzled eyes in the carriage. There is nothing I can say. I always believed myself impulsive, but you are more so. It will take me a little time, you know, to grasp the full measure of your generosity.'

'I have not been generous,' I answered, 'it was your due. Let me kiss you once again. I have to make up for those hours upon the doorstep.'

Presently she said, 'I have learnt one thing at least. Never to go walking with you in the woods again. Philip, let me rise.'

I helped her to her feet, and, with a bow, handed her the gloves and bonnet. She fumbled in her purse, and brought out a small package, which she unwrapped. 'Here,' she said, 'is your birthday present, which I should have given you before. Had I known that I was coming into a fortune, the pearl head would have been larger.' She took the pin and put it in my cravat.

'Now will you permit me to go home?' she said.

She gave me her hand, and I remembered that I had eaten no lunch that day and had now a prodigious appetite for dinner. We turned along the pathway, I thinking of boiled fowl and bacon and the night to come, and suddenly we were upon the granite stone above the valley, which I had forgotten awaited us at the termination of the path. I turned swiftly into the trees, so as to avoid it, but too late. She had already seen it, dark and square among the trees, and letting go my hand stood still and stared at it.

'What is it, Philip,' she asked, 'that shape there, like a tomb-stone, rising so suddenly out of the ground?'

'It is nothing,' I said swiftly, 'just a piece of granite. A sort of landmark. There is a path here, through the trees, where the walking is less steep. This way, to the left. Not past the stone.'

'Wait a moment,' she said, 'I want to look at it. I have never been this way before.'

She went up to the slab and stood before it. I saw her lips

move as she read the words, and I watched her in apprehension. Perhaps it was my fancy, yet it seemed to me that her body stiffened, and she paused there longer that she need have done. She must have read the words twice over. Then she came back and joined me, but this time she did not take my hand, she walked alone. She made no comment on the monument, nor did I, but somehow that great slab of granite was with us as we walked. I saw the lines of doggerel, and the date beneath, and his initials A.A. cut into the stone, and I saw also, which she could not, the pocket-book with the letter buried deep beneath the stone, in the dank earth. And I felt, in some vile fashion, that I had betrayed them both. Her very silence showed that she was moved. Unless, I thought to myself, I speak now, at this moment, the slab of granite will be a barrier between us, and will grow in magnitude.

'I meant to take you there before,' I said, my voice sounding loud and unnatural after so long an interval. 'It was the view Ambrose liked best, on the whole estate. That is why the stone is there.'

'But it was not,' she answered, 'part of your birthday plan to show it to me.' The words were clipped and hard, the words of a stranger.

'No,' I said quietly, 'not part of the plan.' And we walked along the drive without further conversation, and on entering the house she went straight to her room.

I took my bath and changed my clothes, no longer light of heart but dull, despondent. What demon took us to that granite stone, what lapse of memory? She did not know, as I did, how often Ambrose had stood there, smiling and leaning on his stick, but the silly doggerel lines would conjure up the mood that prompted them, half-jesting, half nostalgic, the tender thought behind his mocking eyes. The slab of granite, tall and proud, would have taken on the substance of the man himself, whom, through fault of circumstance, she had not permitted to return to die at home, but who lay many hundred miles away, in that Protestant cemetery in Florence.

Here was a shadow for my birthday night.

At least she knew nothing of the letter, nor would she ever know, and I wondered, as I dressed for dinner, what other demon had prompted me to bury it there, rather than burn it in the fire, as though I had the instinct of an animal, that would one day return to dig it up. I had forgotten all that it contained. His illness had been upon him as he wrote. Brooding, suspicious, with the hand of death so close, he had not reckoned on his words. And suddenly, as though it danced before me on the wall, I saw the sentence, 'Money, God forgive me for saying so, is, at the present time, the one way to her heart.'

The words jumped on to the mirror, as I stood before it brushing my hair. They were there as I placed her pin in my cravat. They followed me down the stairs and into the drawing-room, and they turned from the written words into his voice itself, the voice of Ambrose, deep, well-loved, long known, remembered always – 'The one way to her heart.'

When she came down to dinner she wore the pearl collar round her neck, as though in forgiveness, as though in tribute to my birthday; yet somehow, to my mind, the fact that she wore it made her not closer to me, but more distant. To-night, if only for to-night, I had rather that her neck had been left bare.

We sat down to dinner, with John and Seecombe waiting on us, and the full regalia of the candlesticks and the silver upon the table, and the lace napery too, in honour of my birthday, and there was boiled fowl and bacon as of long custom, from my school-boy days, which Seecombe bore in with great pride, his eye upon me. We laughed, and smiled, and toasted them and ourselves, and the five-and-twenty years that lay behind me; but all the while I felt that we forced our spirits into jollity for the sake of Seecombe and for John, and left to ourselves would fall to silence.

A kind of desperation came upon me, that it was imperative to feast, imperative to make merry, and the solution therefore was to drink more wine, and fill her glass as well, so that the sharper edge of feeling could be dulled and both of us forget the granite slab and what it stood for in our inner selves. Last night I had walked to the beacon head under the full moon, in exultation, sleep-walking, in a dream. To-night, though in the intervening hours I had woken to the wealth of the whole world, I had woken to shadows too.

Muzzy-eyed, I watched her across the table; she was laughing over her shoulder to Seecombe, and it seemed to me she had never looked more lovely. If I could recapture my mood of early morning, the stillness and the peace, and blend it with the folly of the afternoon among the primroses under the tall beech trees, then I would be happy once again. She would be happy too. And we would hold the mood for ever, precious and sacred, carrying it into the future.

Seecombe filled my glass again and something of the shadow slipped away, the doubts were eased; when we are alone together, I thought, all will be well, and I shall ask her this very evening, this very night, if we can be married soon, but soon, in a few weeks perhaps, in a month, for I wanted everyone to know, Seecombe, John, the Kendalls, everyone, that Rachel would bear her name because of me.

She would be Mrs Ashley; Philip Ashley's wife.

We must have sat late, for we had not left the table when there came the sound of carriage wheels upon the drive. The bell pealed and the Kendalls were shown in to the dining-room where we were still seated amidst the confusion of crumbs and dessert and half-empty glasses, and all the aftermath of dinner. I rose, unsteadily I recollect, and dragged two chairs to the table, with my godfather protesting that they had already dined, and only came in for a moment to wish me good health.

Seecombe brought fresh glasses and I saw Louise, in a blue gown, look at me, a question in her eyes, thinking, I felt instinctively, that I had drunk too much. She was right, but it did not happen often, it was my birthday, and time she knew, once and for all, that she would never have the right to criticise me, except as a childhood friend. My godfather should know too. It would put an end to all his plans for her, and put an end to gossip

266

also, and ease the mind of anyone who cared to worry on the subject.

We all sat down again, with buzz of conversation, my godfather, Rachel and Louise already eased to each other's company through the hours spent at luncheon; while I sat silent at my end of the table, scarce taking in a word, but turning over in my mind the announcement I had resolved to make.

At length my godfather, leaning towards me glass in hand and smiling, said, 'To your five-and-twenty years, Philip. Long life and happiness.'

The three of them looked at me, and whether it was the wine I had taken, or my own full heart within me, but I felt that both my godfather and Louise were dear and trusted friends, I liked them well, and Rachel, my love, with tears already in her eyes, was surely nodding her head and smiling her encouragement.

This was the moment then, opportune and fit. The servants were from the room, so the secret could be held amongst the four of us.

I stood up and thanked them, and then with my own glass filled I said, 'I too have a toast I wish you to drink to-night. Since this morning I have been the happiest of men. I want you, godfather, and you Louise, to drink to Rachel, who is to be my wife.'

I drained my glass, and looked down upon them, smiling. No one answered, no one moved, I saw perplexity in my godfather's expression and turning to Rachel I saw that her smile had gone, and that she was staring at me, her face a frozen mask.

'Have you quite lost your senses, Philip?' she said.

I put my glass down upon the table. I was uncertain of my hand, and placed it too near the edge. It toppled over, and shivered in fragments on the floor. My heart was thumping. I could not take my eyes away from her still white face.

'I am sorry,' I said, 'if it was premature to break the news. Remember it is my birthday, and they are both my oldest friends.'

I gripped the table with my hands for steadiness, and there

was a sound of drumming in my ears. She did not seem to understand. She looked away from me, back to my godfather and Louise.

'I think,' she said, 'that the birthday and the wine have gone to Philip's head. Forgive this piece of school-boy folly, and forget it, if you can. He will apologise when he is himself again. Shall we go to the drawing-room?'

She rose to her feet and led the way from the room. I went on standing there, staring at the debris of the dinner table, the crumbs of bread, the spilt wine on the napery, the chairs pushed back, and there was no feeling in me, none at all, but a kind of vacuum where my heart had been. I waited awhile, and then, stumbling from the dining-room before John and Seecombe should come to clear the table, I went into the library, and sat there in the darkness, beside the empty grate. The candles had not been lighted, and the logs had fallen into ash. Through the half-open door I could hear the murmur of the voices in the drawing-room. I pressed my hands to my reeling head, and the taste of the wine was sour on my tongue. Perhaps if I sat still there, in the darkness, I would recover my sense of balance, and the numb emptiness would go. It was the fault of the wine that I had blundered. Yet why should she mind so much what I had said? We could have sworn the pair of them to secrecy. They would have understood. I went on sitting there, waiting for them to go. Presently – the time seemed endless but it may not have been more than ten minutes or so – the voices grew louder and they passed into the hall, and I heard Seecombe opening the front door, bidding them good night, and the wheels drive away, and the clanging and bolting of the door.

My brain was clearer now. I sat and listened. I heard the rustle of her gown. It came near to the half-open door of the library, paused an instant, then passed away; and then her footstep on the stair. I got up from my chair and followed her. I came upon her at the turn of the corridor, where she had paused to snuff the candles at the stair-head. We stood staring at one another in the flickering light.

'I thought you were gone to bed,' she said. 'You had better go, at once, before you do more damage.'

'Now that they are gone,' I said, 'will you forgive me? Believe me, you can trust the Kendalls. They won't give away our secret.'

'Good God, I should hope not, since they know nothing of it,' she replied. 'You make me feel like a backstairs servant, creeping to some attic with a groom. I have known shame before, but this is the worst.'

Still the white frozen face that was not hers.

'You were not ashamed last night at midnight,' I said, 'you gave your promise then, and were not angry. I would have gone at once if you had bidden me.'

'My promise?' she said. 'What promise?'

'To marry me, Rachel,' I answered.

She had her candlestick in her hand. She raised it, so that the naked flame showed on my face. 'You dare to stand there, Philip,' she said, 'and bluster to me that I promised to marry you last night? I said at dinner, before the Kendalls, that you had lost your senses, and so you have. You know very well I gave you no such promise.'

I stared back at her. It was not I who was out of my mind, but she. I felt the colour flame into my face.

'You asked me what I wanted,' I said, 'as a birthday wish. Then, and now, there was only one thing in the world I could ever ask, that you should marry me. What else could I mean?'

She did not answer. She went on looking at me, incredulous, baffled, like someone listening to words in a foreign language that cannot be translated or comprehended, and I realised suddenly, with anguish and despair, that so it was, in fact, between us both; all that had passed had been in error. She had not understood what it was I asked of her at midnight, nor I, in my blind wonder, what she had given, therefore what I had believed to be a pledge of love was something different, without meaning, on which she had put her own interpretation.

If she was ashamed then I was doubly so, that she could have been mistaken in me.

'Let me put it in plain language now,' I said. 'When will you marry me?'

'But never, Philip,' she said, with a gesture of her hand, as if dismissing me. 'Take that as final, and forever. If you hoped otherwise, I am sorry. I had no intention to mislead you. Now, good night.'

She turned to go, but I seized hold of her hand, and held it fast.

'Do you not love me then?' I asked. 'Was it pretence? Why, for God's sake, did you not tell me the truth last night and bid me go?'

Once again her eyes were baffled; she did not understand. We were strangers, with no link between us. She came from another land, another race.

'Do you dare to reproach me for what happened?' she said. 'I wanted to thank you, that was all. You had given me the jewels.'

I think I knew, upon that instant, all that Ambrose had known too. I knew what he had seen in her, and longed for, but had never had. I knew the torment, and the pain, and the great gulf between them, ever widening. Her eyes, so dark and different from our own, stared at both of us, uncomprehending. Ambrose stood beside me in the shadows, under the flickering candlelight. We looked at her, tortured, without hope, while she looked back at us in accusation. Her face was foreign too, in the half light. Small and narrow, a face upon a coin. The hand I held was warm no longer. Cold and brittle, the fingers struggled for release, and the rings scratched, cutting at my palm. I let it go, and as I did so wanted it again.

'Why do you stare at me?' she whispered. 'What have I done to you? Your face has changed.'

I tried to think what else I had to give. She had the property, the money, and the jewels. She had my mind, my body, and my heart. There was only my name, and that she bore already. Nothing remained. Unless it should be fear. I took the candle from her hand and placed it on the ledge, above the stairs. I put my hands about her throat, encircling it; and now she could not move, but watched me, her eyes wide. And it was as though I held a frightened bird in my two hands, which, with added pressure, would flutter awhile, and die, and with release would fly away to freedom.

'Never leave me,' I said, 'swear it, never, never.'

She tried to move her lips in answer, but could not do so, because of the pressure of my hands. I loosened my grasp. She backed away from me, her fingers to her throat. There were two red weals where my hands had been, on either side of the pearl collar.

'Will you marry me now?' I said to her.

She gave no answer, but walked backwards from me, down the corridor, her eyes upon my face, her fingers still to her throat. I saw my own shadow on the wall, a monstrous thing, without shape or substance. I saw her disappear under the archway. I heard the door shut, and the key turn in the lock. I went to my room, and catching sight of my reflection in the mirror paused, and stared. Surely it was Ambrose who stood there, with the sweat upon his forehead, the face drained of all colour? Then I moved and was myself again; with stooping shoulders, limbs that were clumsy and too long, hesitant, untutored, the Philip who had indulged in school-boy folly. Rachel had told the Kendalls to forgive me, and forget.

I flung open the window, but there was no moon to-night and it was raining hard. The wind blew the curtain, and ruffling the almanack upon the mantelpiece brought it to the floor. I stooped to pick it up, and tearing off the page crumpled it, and flung it in the fire. The end of my birthday. All Fools Day was over.

23

I n the morning when I sat to breakfast, looking out upon the blustering windy day with eyes that saw nothing, Seecombe came into the dining-room with a note upon the salver. My heart jumped at the sight of it. It might be that she asked me to call upon her in her room. But it was not from Rachel. The handwriting was larger, rounder. The note was from Louise. 'Mr Kendall's groom has just brought this, sir,' said Seecombe, 'he is waiting for an answer.'

I read it through. 'Dear Philip, I have been so much distressed by what occurred last night. I think I understand what you felt, more so than my father. Please remember I am your friend, and always will be. I have to go to town this morning. If you want someone to talk to, I could meet you outside the church a little before noon. Louise.'

I put the note in my pocket and asked Seecombe to bring me a piece of paper and a pen. My first instinct, as always at the suggestion of any encounter with no matter whom, but more especially upon this morning, was to scribble a word of thanks, and then refuse. When Seecombe brought the pen and paper, though, I had decided otherwise. A sleepless night, an agony of loneliness made me of a sudden yearn for company. Louise was better known to me than anyone. I wrote therefore, telling her I would be in the town that morning, and would look for her outside the church.

'Give this to Mr Kendall's groom,' I said, 'and tell Wellington I shall want Gypsy saddled at eleven.'

After breakfast I went to the office, and cleared up the bills, and wrote the letter that I had started yesterday. Somehow it was simpler to-day. A part of my brain worked in a dull fashion, took note of facts and figures, and jotted them down as if compelled by force of habit. My work accomplished I walked round to the stable, in a haste to get away from the house and all it meant to me. I did not ride by the avenue through the woods, with its memories of yesterday, but straight across the park and to the high road. My mare was very fresh, and nervous as a fawn; starting at nothing she pricked and shied, and backed into the hedgerows, and the tearing wind did its worst to both of us.

The bluster that should have been in February and March had come at last. Gone was the mellow warmth of the past weeks, the smooth sea, and the sun. Great clouds with dragging tails, black-edged and filled with rain, came scudding from the west, and now and again with sudden bursting fury emptied themselves as hail. The sea was a turmoil in the western bay. In the fields on either side of the road the gulls screamed and dipped in the fresh ploughed earth, seeking the green shoots fostered by the early spring. Nat Bray, whom I had dismissed so swiftly the preceding morning, stood by his gate as I passed it, a wet sack hanging about his shoulders to protect him from the hail, and he put up his hand and shouted me good morning, but the sound of his voice carried beyond me, and away.

Even from the high road I could hear the sea. To the west, where it ran shallow over the sands, it was short and steep, turned backwards on itself and curling into foam, but to the east, before the estuary, the great long rollers came, spending themselves upon the rocks at the harbour entrance, and the roar of the breakers mingled with the biting wind that swept the hedgerows and forced back the budding trees.

There were few people about as I descended the hill into the town, and those I saw went about their business bent sideways with the wind, their faces nipped with the sudden cold. I left Gypsy at the Rose and Crown, and walked up the path to the church. Louise was sheltering beneath the porch. I opened the heavy door and we went in together, to the church itself. It seemed dark and peaceful, after the bluster of the day without, yet with it too that chill so unmistakable, oppressive, heavy, and the mouldering churchy smell. We went and sat by the marble recumbent figure of my ancestor, his sons and daughters weeping at his feet, and I thought how many Ashleys were scattered about the countryside, some here, others in my own parish, and how they had loved, and suffered, and then gone upon their way.

Instinct hushed us both, in the silent church, and we spoke in whispers.

'I have been unhappy about you for so long,' said Louise, 'since Christmas, and before. But I could not tell you. You would not have listened.'

'There was no need,' I answered, 'all had gone very well until last night. The fault was mine, in saying what I did.'

'You would not have said it,' she replied, 'unless you had believed it to be the truth. There has been deception from the first, and you were prepared for it, in the beginning, before she came.'

'There was no deception,' I said, 'until the last few hours. If I was mistaken there is no one but myself to blame.'

A sudden shower stung the church windows southward, and the long aisle with the tall pillars turned darker than before.

'Why did she come here last September?' said Louise. 'Why did she travel all this way to seek you out? It was not sentiment that brought her here, or idle curiosity. She came to England, and to Cornwall, for a purpose, which she has now accomplished.'

I turned and looked at her. Her blue eyes were simple and direct.

'What do you mean?' I asked.

'She has the money,' said Louise. 'That was the plan she had in mind before she took her journey.'

My tutor at Harrow, when teaching in Fifth Form, told us once that truth was something intangible, unseen, which sometimes we stumbled upon and did not recognise, but was found, and held, and understood only by old people near their death, or sometimes by the very pure, the very young.

'You are mistaken,' I said, 'you know nothing about her. She is a woman of impulse and emotion, and her moods are unpredictable and strange, God knows, but it is not in her nature to be otherwise. Impulse drove her from Florence. Emotion brought her here. She stayed because she was happy, and because she had a right to stay.'

Louise looked at me in pity. She put her hand upon my knee.

'Had you been less vulnerable,' she said, 'Mrs Ashley would not have stayed. She would have called upon my father, struck a close fair bargain, and then departed. You have misunderstood her motives from the first.'

I could have stood it better, I thought, as I stumbled from the pew into the aisle, if Louise had struck Rachel with her hands, or spat upon her, torn her hair, her gown. That would be primitive and animal. That would be fighting fair. But this, in the quietude of the church, with Rachel absent, was slander, almost blasphemy.

'I can't sit here and listen to you,' I said. 'I wanted your comfort and your sympathy. If you have none to give, no matter.'

She stood up beside me, catching at my arm.

'Don't you see I am trying to help you?' she pleaded. 'But you are so blind to everything, it's no use. If it's not in Mrs Ashley's nature to plan the months ahead, why has she been sending her allowance out of the country week by week, month by month, throughout the winter?'

'How do you know,' I said, 'that she has done that?'

'My father had means of knowing,' she answered. 'These things could not be hidden, between Mr Couch and my father, acting as your guardian.'

'Well, what if she did?' I said. 'There were debts in Florence, I have known that all along. Creditors were pressing to be paid.'

'From one country to another?' she said. 'Is it possible? I would not have thought so. Isn't it more likely that Mrs Ashley hoped to build up something for her return, and that she spent the winter here only because she knew you came legally into your money and your property on your twenty-fifth birthday, which was yesterday? Then, with my father no longer guardian, she could bleed you as she chose. But there was suddenly no need. You made her a present of everything you had.'

I could not believe it possible that a girl I knew and trusted could have so damnable a mind, and speak – that was the greatest hell – with so much logic and plain common sense, to tear apart another woman like herself.

'Is it your father's legal mind speaking in you, or you yourself?' I said to her.

'Not my father,' she said; 'you know his reserve. He has said little to me. I have a judgement of my own.'

'You set yourself against her from the day you met,' I said. 'A Sunday, wasn't it, in church? You came back to dinner and did not say a word, but sat there, at the table, with your face all stiff and proud. You had made up your mind to dislike her.'

'And you?' she said. 'Do you remember what you said about her before she came? I can't forget the enmity you had for her. And with good reason.' There was a creaking movement from the side door near to the choir stalls. It opened, and the cleaner, a little mousy woman, Alice Tabb, crept in with broom in hand to sweep the aisles. She glanced at us furtively, and went away behind the pulpit; but her presence was with us, and solitude had gone.

'It's no use, Louise,' I said, 'you can't help me. I am fond of you, and you of me. If we continue talking we shall hate each other.'

Louise looked at me, her hand dropped from my arm.

'Do you love her, then, so much?' she said.

I turned away. She was younger than myself, a girl, and she could not understand. No one could ever understand, save Ambrose, who was dead.

'What does the future hold now for either of you?' asked Louise.

Our footsteps sounded hollow down the aisle. The shower, that had spat upon the windows, ceased. A gleam of fitful sun lit the halo on St Peter's head in the south window, then left it dim once more.

'I asked her to marry me,' I said; 'I have asked her once, and twice. I shall continue asking her. That's my future for you.'

We came to the church door. I opened it and we stood in the porch again. A blackbird, heedless of the rain, was singing from the tree by the church gate, and a butcher's boy, his tray upon his shoulder, went past it whistling for company, his apron over his head.

'When was the first time that you asked her?' said Louise.

The warmth was with me once again, the candlelight, the laughter. And suddenly no light, and suddenly no laughter. Only Rachel and myself. Almost in mockery of midnight, the church clock struck twelve of noon.

'On the morning of my birthday,' I told Louise.

She waited for the final stroke of the bell that sounded so loud above our heads.

'What did she answer you?' she said.

'We spoke at cross purposes,' I answered; 'I thought that she meant yes, when she meant no.'

'Had she read the document at that time?'

'No. She read that later. Later, the same morning.'

Below the church gate I saw the Kendall groom and the dog-cart. He raised his whip, at sight of his master's daughter, and climbed down from the trap. Louise fastened her mantle and pulled her hood over her hair. 'She lost little time in reading it, then, and driving out to Pelyn to see my father,' said Louise.

'She did not understand it very well,' I said.

'She understood it when she drove away from Pelyn,' said Louise. 'I remember perfectly, as the carriage waited and we stood upon the steps, my father said to her "The re-marriage clause may strike a little hard. You must remain a widow if you wish to keep your fortune." And Mrs Ashley smiled at him, and answered, "That suits me very well."'

The groom came up the path, bearing the big umbrella. Louise fastened her gloves. A fresh black squall came scudding across the sky.

'The clause was inserted to safeguard the estate,' I said, 'to prevent any squander by a stranger. If she were my wife it would not apply.'

'That is where you are wrong,' said Louise. 'If she married you, the whole would revert to you again. You had not thought of that.'

'But even so?' I said. 'I would share every penny of it with her. She would not refuse to marry me because of that one clause. Is that what you are trying to suggest?'

The hood concealed her face, but the blue eyes looked out at me, though the rest was hidden.

'A wife,' said Louise, 'cannot send her husband's money from the country, nor return to the place where she belongs. I suggest nothing.'

The groom touched his hat, and held the umbrella over her head. I followed her down the path and to the trap, and helped her to her seat.

'I have done you no good,' she said, 'and you think me merciless and hard. Sometimes a woman sees more clearly than a man. Forgive me for hurting you. I only want you to be yourself again.' She leant to the groom. 'Very well, Thomas,' she said, 'we will go back to Pelyn,' and he turned the horse and they went away up the hill to the high road.

I went and sat in the little parlour of the Rose and Crown. Louise had spoken true when she told me she had done me no good. I had come for comfort, and found none. Only cold hard facts, twisted to distortion. All of what she said would make sense to a lawyer's mind. I knew how my godfather weighed things in the balance, without allowance for the human heart. Louise could not help it if she had inherited his shrewd strict outlook and reasoned accordingly.

I knew better than she did what had come between Rachel and myself. The granite slab, above the valley in the woods, and all the months that I had never shared. 'Your cousin Rachel,' Rainaldi said, 'is a woman of impulse.' Because of impulse she had let me love her. Because of impulse she had let me go again. Ambrose had known these things. Ambrose had understood. And

278

neither for him, nor for me, could there ever be another woman, or another wife.

I sat a long while in the chill parlour of the Rose and Crown. The landlord brought me cold mutton and some ale, though I was not hungry. Later I went out and stood upon the quay and watched the high tide splashing on the steps. The fishing vessels rocked at their buoys, and one old fellow, seated across a thwart, baled out the water from the bottom boards of his boat, his back turned to the spray that filled it again with every breaking sea.

The clouds came lower than they had before, turning to mist, cloaking the trees on the opposite shore. If I wished to return home without a soaking, and Gypsy without a chill, I had best return before the weather worsened. No one remained now, without doors. I mounted Gypsy and climbed the hill, and to spare myself the further mileage of the high road turned down where the four roads met, and into the avenue. We were more sheltered here, but scarce had gone a hundred yards before Gypsy suddenly hobbled and went lame, and rather than go into the lodge and have the business of removing the stone that had cut into her shoe, and having gossip there, I decided to dismount and lead her gently home. The gale had brought down branches that lay strewn across our path, and the trees that yesterday had been so still tossed now, and swayed, and shivered with the misty rain.

The vapour from the boggy valley rose in a white cloud, and I realised, with a shudder, how cold I had been the livelong day, since I had sat with Louise in the church, and all the while in the fireless parlour at the Rose and Crown. This was another world from yesterday.

I led Gypsy past the path that Rachel and I had taken. Our footmarks were still there, where we had trodden in around the beeches for the primroses. Clumps of them nestled still, dejected, in the moss. The avenue seemed endless, with Gypsy hobbling, my hand upon her bridle guiding her, and the dripping rain found its way down the collar of my coat to chill my back.

When I reached home I was too tired to say good afternoon

to Wellington, but threw him the reins without a word, leaving him staring after me. God knows, after the night before, I had little desire to drink anything but water, but being cold and wet I thought a taste of brandy might bring some sort of warmth to me, however raw. I went into the dining-room and John was there, laying the table for dinner. He went to fetch me a glass from the pantry, and while I waited I saw he had laid three places on the table.

On his return I pointed to them. 'Why three?' I said.

'Miss Pascoe,' he replied, 'she's been here since one o'clock. The mistress went calling there this morning, not long after you had gone. She brought Miss Pascoe back with her. She's come to stay.'

I stared at him, bewildered. 'Miss Pascoe come to stay?' I said.

'That's so,' he answered, 'Miss Mary Pascoe, the one that teaches in the Sunday school. We have been busy getting the pink room ready for her. She and the mistress are in the boudoir now.'

He went on with his laying of the table, and leaving the glass upon the side-board, without bothering to pour the brandy, I went upstairs. There was a note upon the table in my room, Rachel's hand upon it. I tore it open. There was no beginning, only the day, and the date. 'I have asked Mary Pascoe to stay here with me in the house as a companion. After last night, I cannot be alone with you again. You may join us in the boudoir, if you wish, before and after dinner. I must ask you to be courteous. Rachel.'

She could not mean it. It could not be true. How often we had laughed about the Pascoe daughters, and more especially about chattering Mary, forever working samplers, visiting those poor who had rather be left alone, Mary, a stouter, even a plainer edition of her mother. As a joke, yes, Rachel could have invited her as a joke, merely for dinner, so as to watch my glum face at the end of the table – but the note was not written as a joke.

I went out on to the landing from my room, and saw that the door of the pink bedroom was open. There was no mistake. A fire burnt in the grate, shoes and a wrapper were laid out upon a chair, there were brushes, books, the personal paraphernalia of a stranger all about the room, and the further door, usually kept locked, which communicated with Rachel's suite of rooms, was locked no longer, but wide open too. I could even hear the distant murmur of voices from the boudoir beyond. This, then, was my punishment. This my disgrace. Mary Pascoe had been invited to make a division between Rachel and myself, that we might no longer be alone together, even as she had written in her note.

My first feeling was one of such intense anger that I hardly knew how to contain myself from walking along the corridor to the boudoir, seizing Mary Pascoe by the shoulders and telling her to pack and begone, that I would have Wellington take her home in the carriage without delay. How had Rachel dared to invite her to my house on such a pretext, miserable, flimsy, and insulting, that she could no longer be alone with me? Was I then doomed to Mary Pascoe at every meal, Mary Pascoe in the library and the drawing-room, Mary Pascoe walking in the grounds, Mary Pascoe in the boudoir, for evermore the interminable chatter between women that I had only endured through force of habit over Sunday dinner?

I went along the corridor – I did not change, I was still in my wet things. I opened the boudoir door. Rachel was seated in her chair, with Mary Pascoe beside her on the stool, the pair of them looking at the great volume with the illustrations of Italian gardens.

'So you are back?' said Rachel. 'It was an odd day to choose to go out riding. The carriage was nearly blown from the road when I went down to call at the Rectory. As you see, we have the good fortune to have Mary here as visitor. She is already quite at home. I am delighted.'

Mary Pascoe gave a trill of laughter.

'Such a surprise, Mr Ashley,' she said, 'when your cousin came to fetch me. The others were green with envy. I can hardly believe yet I am here. And how pleasant and snug it is to sit here in the boudoir. Nicer even than below. Your cousin says it is your habit to sit here of an evening. Do you play cribbage? I am wild for cribbage. If you cannot play I shall be pleased to teach you both.'

'Philip,' said Rachel, 'has little use for games of chance. He prefers to sit and smoke in silence. You and I, Mary, will play together.'

She looked across at me, over Mary Pascoe's head. No, it was no joke. I could see by her hard eyes that she had done this thing with great deliberation.

'Can I speak to you alone?' I said bluntly.

'I see no need for that,' she answered. 'You are at liberty to say anything you please in front of Mary.'

The vicar's daughter rose hurriedly to her feet. 'Oh, please,' she said, 'I don't wish to make intrusion. I can easily go to my room.'

'Leave the doors wide open, Mary,' said Rachel, 'so that you can hear me if I call.' Her eyes, so hostile, remained fixed on me.

'Yes, certainly, Mrs Ashley,' said Mary Pascoe. She brushed past me, her eyes goggling, leaving all the doors ajar.

'Why have you done this?' I said to Rachel.

'You know perfectly well,' she answered; 'I told you in my note.'

'How long is she to stay?'

'As long as I choose.'

'You will not be able to stand her company for more than one day. You will drive yourself mad, as well as me.'

'You are mistaken,' she said. 'Mary Pascoe is a good harmless girl. I shall not talk to her if I do not wish for conversation. At least I feel some measure of security with her in the house. Also, it was time. Things could not have continued as they had been, not after your outburst at the table. Your godfather said as much before he left.'

'What did he say?'

'That there was gossip about my being here, which your boast of marriage will have done little to improve. I don't know what other people you have chatted to. Mary Pascoe will silence further gossip. I shall take good care of that.'

282

Was it possible that my action of the night before could bring about such change, such terrible antagonism?

'Rachel,' I said, 'this can't be settled in a moment's conversation, with the doors open. I beg of you, listen to me, let me talk to you alone, after dinner, when Mary Pascoe goes to bed.'

'You threatened me last night,' she said. 'Once was enough. There is nothing to settle. You can go now, if you wish. Or stay and play cribbage here with Mary Pascoe.' She turned again to the book of gardens.

I went from the room. There was nothing else to do. This then was my punishment, for that brief moment of the night before, when I had put my hands about her neck. The action, instantly repented and regretted, was unforgivable. This, then, the reward. As quickly as my anger had come, it went, turning, with heavy dullness, to despair. Oh, God, what had I done?

Such a little while ago, so few hours in time, we had been happy. The exultation of my birthday eve, and all the magic, was now gone, frittered away by my own fault. Sitting in the cold parlour of the Rose and Crown it had seemed to me that perhaps, in a few weeks, her reluctance to become my wife might be overcome. If not immediately, then later; if not later, then what matter, so long as we could be together, in love, as on my birthday morning. Hers the decision, hers the choice, yet surely she would not refuse? I had been almost hopeful when I had come into the house. But now the stranger, the third person, misunderstanding all about us still. Presently as I stood in my room, I heard their voices approach the stair, and then the sweep of gowns descending. It was later than I thought, they must be ready dressed for dinner. I knew I could not face the business of sitting with them. They must dine alone. Anyway, I was not hungry; I felt cold and stiff, probably I had taken chill, and would be better in my room. I rang the bell and told John to make my apologies, but I would not be down to dinner, I was going straight to bed. This made a pother, as I feared it might, and Seecombe came up, concern upon his face.

'Unwell, Mr Philip, sir?' he said. 'May I suggest a mustard bath, and a hot grog? It comes of riding out in such weather.'

'Nothing, thank you, Seecombe,' I replied. 'I'm a little tired, that's all.'

'No dinner, Mr Philip? We have venison, and apple pie. It is all ready to serve. Both the ladies are in the drawing-room now.'

'No, Seecombe. I slept badly last night. I shall be better in the morning.'

'I will tell the mistress,' he said, 'she will be much concerned.'

At least by remaining in my room it might give me a chance to see Rachel alone. After dinner, perhaps, she would come up and enquire about me.

I undressed and got into my bed. Undoubtedly I must have caught some sort of chill. The sheets seemed bitter cold, and I threw them off and got between the blankets. I felt stiff and numb and my head throbbed, things most unusual and unknown. I lay there, waiting for them to finish dinner. I heard them pass from the hall into the dining-room, the chatter ceaseless – I was spared that, at any rate – and then, after a long interval, back again to the drawing-room.

Some time after eight o'clock I heard them come upstairs. I sat up in bed and put my jacket round my shoulders. This, perhaps, was the moment she would choose. In spite of the rough blankets I was still cold, and the stiff pain that was about my legs and neck shifted in full measure to my head, so that it seemed on fire.

I waited, but she did not come. They must be sitting in the boudoir. I heard the clock strike nine, then ten, then eleven. After eleven, I knew that she did not intend to come and see me that night at all. Ignoring me, then, was but a continuation of my punishment.

I got out of bed and stood in the passage. They had retired for the night, for I could hear Mary Pascoe moving about in the pink bedroom, and now and then an irritating little cough to clear her throat – another habit she had taken from her mother.

I went along the corridor to Rachel's room. I put my hand upon the handle of the door, and turned it. But it did not open. The door was locked. I knocked, very softly. She did not answer.

I went slowly back to my own room and to my bed, and lay there, icy cold.

I remember in the morning that I dressed, but I have no recollection of John coming in to call me, nor that I breakfasted, nor of anything at all, but only the strange stiffness in my neck and the agonising pain in my head. I went and sat on my chair in the office. I wrote no letters, I saw no one. Some time after midday Seecombe came to find me to tell me that the ladies were awaiting luncheon. I said I wanted none. He came near to me and looked into my face.

'Mr Philip,' he said, 'you are ill. What is it?'

'I don't know,' I said. He took my hand and felt it. He went out of the office and I heard him hurry across the courtyard.

Presently the door opened once again. Rachel stood there, with Mary Pascoe behind her and Seecombe also. She came towards me.

'Seecombe says you are ill,' she said to me. 'What is the matter?'

I stared up at her. Nothing of what was happening was real at all. I hardly knew that I was sitting there, in my office chair, but thought myself to be upstairs in my room cold in my bed, as I had been the night before.

'When will you send her home?' I said. 'I won't do anything to harm you. I give you my word of honour.'

She put her hand on my head. She looked into my eyes. She turned swiftly to Seecombe. 'Get John,' she said. 'Both of you, help Mr Ashley to bed. Tell Wellington to send the groom quickly for the doctor . . .'

I saw nothing but her white face and her eyes; and then over her shoulder, ludicrous somehow, out of place and foolish, the startled, shocked gaze of Mary Pascoe fixed upon me. Then nothing. Only the stiffness, and the pain.

Back in my bed again, I was aware that Seecombe stood by the windows, closing the shutters, drawing the curtains, bringing the room to darkness which I craved. Possibly the darkness would ease the blinding pain. I could not move my head upon the pillow, it was as though the muscles of my neck were taut and rigid. I felt her hand in mine. I said again, 'I promise not to harm you. Send Mary Pascoe home.'

She answered, 'Don't talk now. Only lie still.'

The room was full of whispers. The door opening, shutting, opening once again. Soft footsteps creeping on the floor. Chinks of light coming from the landing, and always this furtiveness of whispers, so that it seemed to me, in the sudden sharp delirium that must be sweeping me, that the house was filled with people, a guest in every room, and that the house itself was not large enough to contain them, they stood shoulder to shoulder in the drawing-room and in the library, with Rachel moving in the midst of them, smiling, talking, holding out her hands. I kept repeating, over and over again, 'Send them away.'

Then I saw the round spectacled face of Dr Gilbert looking down on me; he too, then, was of the company. When I was a lad he had come to treat me for the chickenpox, I had scarce seen him since.

'So you went swimming in the sea at midnight?' he said to me. 'That was a very foolish thing to do.' He shook his head at me as if I were still a child, and stroked his beard. I closed my eyes against the light. I heard Rachel say to him, 'I know too much about this kind of fever to be mistaken. I have seen children die of it in Florence. It attacks the spine, and then the brain. Do something, for God's sake . . .'

They went away. And once again the whispering began. This was followed by the sound of wheels on the drive, and a departing carriage. Later, I heard someone breathing, close to the curtains of my bed. I knew then what had happened. Rachel had gone. She had driven to Bodmin, to take the coach for London. She had left Mary Pascoe in the house to watch me. The servants, Seecombe, John, they had all departed; no one was left but Mary Pascoe.

'Please go,' I said, 'I need no one.'

A hand came out to touch my forehead. Mary Pascoe's hand. I shook it off. But it returned again, stealthy, cold, and I shouted loud to her to go, but it pressed down upon me, hard, gripping like ice, and so to ice it turned, on my forehead, on my neck, clamping me close, a prisoner. Then I heard Rachel whisper in my ear, 'Dear, lie still. This will help your head. It will be better, by-and-by.'

I tried to turn, but could not. Had she not gone to London after all?

I said, 'Don't leave me. Promise not to leave me.'

She said, 'I promise. I will be with you all the time.'

I opened my eyes but I could not see her, the room was in darkness. The shape of it was different, not the bedroom that I knew. It was long and narrow, like a cell. The bedstead hard, like iron. There was one candle burning somewhere, behind a screen. In a niche, on the wall opposite, knelt a madonna. I called loudly 'Rachel . . . Rachel . . .'

I heard footsteps running, and a door opening, and then her hand in mine and she was saying, 'I am with you.' I closed my eyes again.

I was standing on a bridge, beside the Arno, making a vow to destroy a woman I had never seen. The swollen water passed under the bridge, bubbling, brown, and Rachel, the beggar girl, came up to me with empty hands. She was naked, save for the pearl collar round her throat. Suddenly she pointed at the water and Ambrose went past us, under the bridge, his hands folded on his breast. He floated away down the river out of sight, and slowly, majestically, his paws raised stiff and straight, went the body of the dead dog after him.

24

The first thing that I noticed was that the tree outside my window was in leaf. I looked at it, puzzled. When I had gone to bed the buds were barely formed. It was very strange. True, the curtains had been drawn, but I well remembered noticing how tight they were upon my birthday morning, when I leant out of the window and looked out across the lawn. There was no pain now in my head and the stiffness had all gone. I must have slept for many hours, possibly a day or more. There was no reckoning with time, when anyone fell ill.

Surely I had seen him many times, though, old Doctor Gilbert with his beard, and another man as well, a stranger. The room in darkness always. Now it was light. My face felt scrubby – I must be in great need of a shave. I put my hand up to my chin. Now this was madness, for I too had a beard. I stared at my hand. It did not look like mine. It was white and thin, the nails grown to a fine length; too often I broke them, riding. I turned my head and saw Rachel sitting in a chair, near to my bed – her own chair, from the boudoir. She did not know I saw her. She was working upon a piece of embroidery, and wore a gown I did not recognise. It was dark, like all her gowns, but the sleeves were short, above the elbow, and the stuff was light, as though for coolness' sake. Was the room so warm? The windows were wide open. There was no fire in the grate.

I put my hand up to my chin again and felt the beard. It had a pleasant touch to it. Suddenly I laughed, and at the sound she raised her head and looked at me.

'Philip,' she said, and smiled; and suddenly she was kneeling by my side, with her arms about me.

'I have grown a beard,' I said.

I could not stop myself from laughing, for the folly of it, and then, from laughing, turned to coughing, and at once she had a glass with some ill-tasting stuff inside it which she made me drink, holding it to my lips, then putting me back again upon the pillows.

This gesture struck a chord in memory. Surely, for a long while, there had been a hand, with a glass, making me drink, that had come into my dreams, and gone again? I had believed it to be Mary Pascoe, and kept pushing it away. I lay staring at Rachel, and put out my hand to her. She took it and held it fast. I ran my thumb along the pale blue veins that showed always on the back of hers, and turned the rings. I continued thus for quite a time, and did not talk.

Presently I said, 'Did you send her away?'

'Send who?' she asked.

'Why, Mary Pascoe,' I replied.

I heard her catch her breath, and glancing up I saw that her smile had gone and a shadow had come to her eyes.

'She has been gone these five weeks,' she said. 'Never mind that now. Are you thirsty? I have made you a cool drink with fresh limes, sent down from London.' I drank, and it tasted good after the bitter medicine she had given me.

'I think I must have been ill,' I said to her.

'You nearly died,' she answered.

She moved, as though to go, but I would not have it.

'Tell me about it,' I said. I had all the curiosity of someone who has been asleep for years, like Rip van Winkle, to find the world had gone along without him.

'If you want to revive in me all those weeks of anxiety I will tell you,' she answered, 'not otherwise. You have been very ill. Let that be enough.'

'What was the matter with me?'

'I have small regard for your English doctors,' she replied. 'On the continent we call that illness meningite, which here no one knew anything about. That you are alive to-day is little short of a miracle.'

'What pulled me through?'

She smiled, and held my hand the tighter. 'I think your own horse strength,' she answered me, 'and certain things I bade them do. Making a puncture on your spine to take the fluid was but one. Also letting into your blood stream a serum made from the juice of herbs. They called it poison. But you have survived.'

I remembered the cordials that she had made for some of the tenants who had been sick during the winter, and how I had teased her about it, calling her midwife and apothecary.

'How do you know about these things?' I said to her.

'I learnt them from my mother,' she said. 'We are very old, and very wise, who come from Florence.'

The words struck some chord in memory, but I could not recollect just what it was. To think was still an effort. And I was content to lie there in my bed, her hand in mine.

'Why is the tree in leaf outside my window?' I asked.

'It should be, in the second week of May,' she said.

That I had lain there knowing nothing all those weeks was hard to understand. Nor could I remember the events that had brought me to my bed. Rachel had been angry with me, for some reason that escaped me, and had invited Mary Pascoe to the house, I knew not why. That we had been married the day before my birthday was very certain, though I had no clear vision of the church, or of the ceremony; except that I believed my godfather and Louise had been the only witnesses, with little Alice Tabb, the church cleaner. I remembered being very happy. And suddenly, for no reason, in despair. Then falling ill. No matter, all was well again. I had not died, and it was the month of May.

'I think I am strong enough to get up,' I said to her.

'You are no such thing,' she answered. 'In a week, perhaps, you shall sit in a chair, by the window there, to feel your feet. And later, walk as far as the boudoir. By the end of the month we may get you below, and sitting out-of-doors. But we shall see.'

Indeed, my rate of progress was much as she had said. I have never in my life felt such a ninny as the first time I sat sideways on the bed, and put my feet upon the floor. The whole room rocked. Seecombe was one side of me, and John the other, and I as weak as a baby newly born.

'Great heavens, madam, he has grown again,' said Seecombe, with the consternation on his face so great I had to sit down again for laughter.

'You can show me for a freak at Bodmin Fair after all,' I said, and then saw myself in the mirror, gaunt and pale, with the brown beard on my chin, for all the world like an apostle.

'I've half a mind,' I said, 'to go preaching about the country-side. Thousands would follow me. What do you think?' I turned to Rachel.

'I prefer you shaved,' she said gravely.

'Bring me a razor, John,' I said; but when the work was done, and my face bare again, I felt I had lost some sort of dignity and was reduced again to school-boy status.

Those days of convalescence were pleasant indeed. Rachel was always with me. We did not talk much, because I found conver-sation tired me sooner than anything else, and brought back some shadow of that aching head. I liked, more than anything, to sit by my open window, and to make diversion Wellington would bring the horses and exercise them round and round the gravel sweep in front of me, like show beasts in a ring. Then, when my legs were stronger, I walked to the boudoir and our meals were taken there, Rachel waiting upon me and caring for me like a nurse with a child; indeed, I said to her on one occasion, if she was doomed to a sick husband for the rest of her life, she had no one to blame but herself. She looked at me strangely when I said this, and was about to speak, then paused, and passed on to something else.

I remembered that for some reason or other our marriage had been kept secret from the servants, I think to allow the full twelve months to lapse since Ambrose died before announcing it; perhaps she was afraid I might be indiscreet in front of Seecombe, so I held my tongue. In two months' time we could declare it to the world; until then, I would be patient. Each day I think I loved

291

her more; and she, more gentle and more tender than ever in the past months of winter.

I was amazed, when I came downstairs for the first time and went out into the grounds, to see how much had been achieved about the place during my sickness. The terrace walk was now completed, and the sunken garden beside it had now been hollowed away to a great depth, and was ready to be paved with stone and the banks faced. At the moment it yawned, dark and ominous, a deep wide chasm, and the fellows digging there looked up at me, grinning, as I stared down at them from the terrace above.

Tamlyn escorted me with pride to the plantation – Rachel had called in to see his wife, at the nearby cottage – and though the camellias were over, the rhododendrons were still in bloom, and the orange berberis, and leaning to the field below the soft yellow flowers of the laburnum trees hung in clusters, scattering their petals.

'We'll have to shift them though, another year,' said Tamlyn. 'At the rate they're growing the branches lean down too far to the field, and the seeds will kill the cattle.' He reached up to a branch, and where the flowers had fallen the pods were already forming, with the little seeds within. 'There was a fellow the other side of St Austell who died eating these,' said Tamlyn, and he threw the pod away, over his shoulder.

I had forgotten how brief was their flowering time, like every other blossom, also how beautiful; and suddenly I remembered the drooping tree in the little courtyard in the Italian villa, and the woman from the lodge taking her broom, sweeping the pods away.

'There was a fine tree of this kind,' I said, 'in Florence, where Mrs Ashley had her villa.'

'Yes, sir?' he said. 'Well, they grow most things in that climate, I understand. It must be a wonderful place. I can understand the mistress wishing to return.'

'I don't think she has any intention of returning,' I replied.

'I'm glad of that, sir,' he said, 'but we heard different. That she was only waiting to see you restored to health before she went.'

It was incredible what stories were made up from scraps of gossip, and I thought how the announcement of our marriage would be the only means to stop it. Yet I was hesitant to broach the matter to her. It seemed to me that once before there had been discussion on that point, which had made her angry, before I was taken ill.

That evening, when we were sitting in the boudoir and I was drinking my tisana, as had become my custom before going to bed, I said to her, 'There is fresh gossip round the countryside.'

'What now?' she asked, lifting her head to look at me.

'Why, that you are going back to Florence,' I replied.

She did not answer me at once, but bent her head again to her embroidery.

'There is plenty of time to decide about these things,' she said. 'First, you must get well and strong.'

I looked at her, puzzled. Then Tamlyn had not been entirely in error. The idea of going to Florence was there, somewhere in her mind.

'Have you not sold the villa yet?' I asked.

'Not yet,' she answered, 'nor do I intend to sell it after all, or even let it. Now things are changed and I can afford to keep it.'

I was silent. I did not want to hurt her, but the thought of having the two homes was not one that pleased me very well. In fact, I hated the very image of that villa which I held still in my mind, and which I thought by now she hated too.

'Do you mean you would want to spend the winter there?' I asked.

'Possibly,' she said, 'or the late summer; but there is no necessity to talk of it.'

'I have been idle too long,' I said. 'I don't think I should leave this place without attention for the winter, or, in fact, be absent from it at all.'

'Probably not,' she said, 'in fact, I would not care to leave the property unless you were in charge. You might like to pay me a visit in the spring, and I could show you Florence.'

The illness I had suffered had left me very slow of

understanding; nothing of what she said made any sense.

'Pay you a visit?' I said. 'Is that how you propose that we should live? Absent from one another for long months at a time?'

She laid down her work and looked at me. There was something of anxiety in her eyes, a shadow on her face.

'Philip dear,' she said, 'I have said, I don't wish to talk about the future now. You have only just recovered from a dangerous illness, and it is bad to start planning the time ahead. I give you my promise I will not leave you until you are well.'

'But why,' I demanded, 'is there any need to go at all? You belong here now. This is your home.'

'I have my villa too,' she said, 'and many friends, and a life out there – different from this, I know, but none the less I am accustomed to it. I have been in England for eight months, and now feel the need for change again. Be reasonable, and try to understand.'

'I suppose,' I said slowly, 'I am very selfish. I had not thought of it.' I must make up my mind, then, to the fact that she would want to divide her time between England and Italy, in which case I must do the same, and start looking about for a bailiff to put in charge of the estate. The idea of separation was of course preposterous.

'My godfather may know of someone,' I said, speaking my thoughts aloud.

'Someone for what?' she asked.

'Why, to take over here, when we are absent,' I replied.

'I think it hardly necessary,' she said. 'You would not be in Florence more than a few weeks, if you came. Though you might like it so much that you would decide to stay longer. It is very lovely in the spring.'

'Spring be damned,' I said. 'Whatever date you decide upon to go, I shall go too.'

Again the shadow on her face, the apprehension in her eye.

'Never mind that now,' she said, 'and look, past nine o'clock, later than you have been as yet. Shall I ring for John, or can you manage alone?'

'Ring for no one,' I said. I got up slowly from my chair, for my limbs were still most damnably weak, and I went and knelt beside her, and put my arms about her.

'I find it very hard,' I said, 'the solitude of my own room, and you so close, along the corridor. Can we not tell them soon?'

'Tell them what?' she said.

'That we are married,' I replied.

She sat very still in my arms, and did not move. It was almost as if she turned rigid, like something without life.

'Oh, God . . .' she whispered. Then she put her hands upon my shoulders, and looked into my face. 'What do you mean, Philip?' she said.

A pulse somewhere in my head began to beat, like an echo to the pain that had been there the past weeks. It throbbed deeper, ever deeper, and with it came a sense of fear.

'Tell the servants,' I said. 'Then it will be right and natural for me to stay with you, because we are married . . .' But my voice sank away to nothing, because of the expression in her eyes.

'But we are not married, Philip dear,' she said.

Something seemed to burst inside my head.

'We are married,' I said, 'of course we are married. It happened on my birthday. Have you forgotten?'

But when had it happened? Where was the church? Who was the minister? All the throbbing pain returned again, and the room swung round about me.

'Tell me it's true?' I said to her.

Then suddenly I knew that all was fantasy, that the happiness which had been mine for the past weeks was imagination. The dream was broken.

I buried my head against her, sobbing; tears had never come from me like this before, not even as a child. She held me close, her hand stroking my hair, and never speaking. Presently I won command over myself again, and lay down in the chair, exhausted. She brought me something to drink, then sat down on the stool beside me. The shadows of the summer evening played about the room. The bats crept forth from their hiding places in the eaves, and circled in the twilight outside the window.

'It would have been better,' I said, 'had you let me die.'

She sighed, and laid her hand against my cheek. 'If you say that,' she answered, 'you destroy me too. You are unhappy now because you are still weak. But presently, when you are stronger, none of this will seem important. You will go about your work again, on the estate – there will be so much to see to that, from your illness, has been allowed to lapse. The full summer will be here. You can swim again, go sailing in the bay.'

I knew from her voice that she was talking to convince herself, not me.

'What else?' I asked.

'You know very well that you are happy here,' she said; 'it is your life, and will continue to be so. You have given me the property, but I shall always look on it as yours. It will be a sort of trust between us.'

'You mean,' I said, 'that letters will pass between us, from Italy to England, month after month, throughout the year. I shall say to you, "Dear Rachel, The camellias are in bloom." And you will reply to me, "Dear Philip, I am glad to hear it. My rose-garden is doing very well." Is that to be our future?'

I could see myself hanging about the gravel sweep of a morning after breakfast, waiting for the boy to bring the post-bag, knowing full well there would be no letter in it, except some bill from Bodmin.

'I would be back again each summer, very probably,' she said, 'to see that all went well.'

'Like the swallows, who come only for the season,' I replied, 'then take wing again the first week in September.'

'I have already suggested,' she said, 'that you visit me in spring. There is much that you would like in Italy. You have not travelled, save the once. You know very little of the world.'

She might have been a teacher, soothing a fractious child. Perhaps it was thus she looked upon me.

'What I have seen,' I answered, 'gives me a distaste for all the rest. What would you have me do? Potter about a church or a museum, guide-book in hand? Converse with strangers, to broaden my ideas? I would rather brood at home and watch the rain.'

My voice was harsh and bitter, but I could not help it. She sighed again, and it was as though she searched about for some argument to prove to me that all was well.

'I tell you again,' she insisted, 'that when you are better the whole of the future will seem different to you. Nothing is so much changed from what it was. As to the money . . .' she paused, looking at me.

'What money?' I said.

'The money for the property,' she went on. 'All that will be placed on a proper footing, and you shall have enough to run the estate without loss, while I take what I need out of the country. It is all in process of arrangement now.'

She could take every farthing for all I cared. What had any of this to do with what I felt for her? But she went on talking.

'You must continue to make what improvements you feel justified in doing,' she said rapidly. 'You know I shall query nothing, you need not even send me the bills, I can trust your judgement. Your godfather will always be near to give advice. In a little while everything will seem to you just the same as it was before I came.'

The room was deep in twilight now. I could not even see her face for the shadows all about us.

'Do you really believe that?' I said to her.

She did not answer at once. She searched for some excuse for my existence, to pile upon those that she had given me already. There were none, and she knew it well. She turned towards me, giving me her hand. 'I must believe it,' she said, 'or I would have no peace of mind.'

In all the months I had known her she had given me many answers to the questions, serious or otherwise, that I had put to her. Some had been laughing, some evasive, yet each one had some feminine twist to make adornment. This was direct at last, straight from the heart. She must believe me happy, to have peace of mind. I had left the land of fantasy, to her to enter into it. Two persons therefore could not share a dream. Except in darkness, as in make-believe. Each figure, then, a phantom.

'Go back if you will,' I said, 'but not just yet. Give me a few weeks more to hold in memory. I am no traveller, you are my world.'

I sought to evade the future and escape. But when I held her it was not the same; faith was gone, and the first ecstasy.

25

We did not speak again of her departure. It was a bogey, thrust into the background by us both. For her sake I strove to appear light-hearted, without care. She did the same, for me. The summer weather was about us, and I soon grew strong again, at least to all appearance; but sometimes the pain in my head returned again, not with its full force, but stabbing, without warning, and for no good reason.

I did not tell her of it – what was the use? It did not come from physical exertion, or when I was outdoors, but only if I put my mind to thinking. Simple problems brought to me in the estate office by the tenants could even do it, so that a fog would seem to settle on me and I be unable to give them a decision.

More often, though, it would happen because of her. I would be looking at her, as we sat perhaps after dinner outside the drawing-room window, for the June weather enabled us to sit without of an evening until past nine o'clock; and suddenly I would wonder what went on there, in her mind, as she sat drinking her tisana, watching the dusk creep closer to the trees that fringed the lawn. Did she ponder, in her secret self, how much longer she must endure this life of solitude? Did she think, secretively, 'Next week, now he is well, I can safely go?'

That villa Sangalletti, back in Florence, had for me now another shape and atmosphere. Instead of the shuttered darkness I had seen on that one visit I saw it now as brightly lit, with all the windows wide. Those unknown people whom she called her friends wandered from room to room; there was gaiety and laughter, much noise of conversation. A sort of brilliance hung above the place, and all the fountains played. She would move from guest to guest, smiling and at ease, mistress of her domain. This, then, was the life she knew, and loved, and understood. Her months with me were an interlude. Thankfully, she would return to the home where she belonged. I could picture the first arrival, with the man Giuseppe and his wife flinging wide the iron gates to admit her carrozza, and then her happy eager pacing through the rooms she knew so well and had not seen for long, asking her servants questions, receiving their replies, opening the many letters there awaiting her, content, serene, with all the myriad threads of an existence to pick up again and hold that I could never know and never share. So many days and nights, no longer mine.

Presently she would feel my eyes upon her, and would say, 'What is the matter, Philip?'

'Nothing,' I would reply.

And as the shadow passed across her face, doubtful, distressed, I felt myself a burden on her shoulders. She would be better quit of me. I tried to lose my energies, as of old, in the running of the place, in the common tasks of day by day; but it no longer meant the same to me. What if the Barton acres were all dried through lack of rain? I could not greatly care. And if our stock won prizes at the Show, and so were the champions of the county, was this glory? Last year, it might have been. But now, what an empty triumph.

I could see myself losing favour in the eyes of all who looked upon me as their master. 'You are still weak, Mr Ashley, after that sickness,' said Billy Rowe, the farmer at the Barton; and there was a world of disappointment in his voice that I had failed to show enthusiasm for his achievements. It was the same with all the rest. Even Seecombe took me to task.

'You don't seem to pick up as you should, Mr Philip,' he said. 'We were talking of it, in the steward's room, last evening. "What's come to the master?" Tamlyn said to me. "He's whisht as a ghost on Hallowe'en, and looks at nothing." I would advise marsala in the morning. There is nothing like a wine-glass of marsala to restore the blood.'

'Tell Tamlyn,' I said to Seecombe, 'to go about his business. I am perfectly well.'

The routine of Sunday dinner, with the Pascoes and the Kendalls, had not yet been restored, which was a mercy. I think poor Mary Pascoe had returned to the rectory, after I fell ill, with tales that I was mad. I saw her look at me askance, in church, the first morning that I went when I was well; and the whole family eyed me with a sort of pity, enquiring for me with low voices and averted gaze.

My godfather came to see me, also Louise. They too assumed an unaccustomed manner, a blend of cheerfulness and sympathy, suited to a child who had been sick; and I felt they had been warned not to touch upon any subject that might cause me concern. The four of us sat like strangers in the drawing-room. My godfather, I thought, is ill at ease, and wishing he had not come, but feels it to be his duty to call upon me; while Louise, with some odd instinct possessed by women, knows what has happened here and shrinks at thought of it. Rachel, as always, was in command of the situation, and kept the tenor of the conversation on the level that was required. The county Show, the betrothal of the second Pascoe daughter, the warmth of the present weather, the prospect of a change in Government – all these were easy matters. But what if we spoke the things we really thought?

'Get out of England soon, before you destroy yourself and this boy with you,' thus my godfather.

'You love her more than ever. I can see it, by your eyes,' from Louise.

'I must prevent them from making Philip anxious, at all costs,' so Rachel.

And myself, 'Leave me alone with her, and go . . .'

Instead, we clung to courtesy, and lied. Each one of us breathed the easier at the termination of the visit, and as I watched them drive to the park gates, no doubt thankful to be away, I wished I could erect a fence about the property, as in the old enchanted tales of childhood, to keep away all callers, and disaster too.

It seemed to me, though she said nothing, that she planned the first steps towards departure. I would find her, of an evening, sorting through her books, arranging them as people do who wish to make a choice between the volumes they take with them and those they leave behind. Another time she would be sitting at the bureau, putting her papers into order, filling the waste-paper basket with torn scraps and discarded letters, and tying up the rest with bands of tape. All this would stop, once I came into the boudoir, and going to her chair she would take up her work, or sit beside the window; but I was not deceived. Why the sudden desire for making all things straight, unless she was soon to leave the boudoir empty?

It seemed to me the room looked barer than it had before. Trifles were missing. A work-basket that had stood through the spring and winter in one corner, a shawl that had lain over the elbow of a chair, a crayon sketch of the house, presented to her by a caller one winter's day, that used to be on the mantelpiece – all were there no more. It took me back to my boyhood, before I went away for the first time, to school. Seecombe had made a clearance in the nursery, tying my books in bundles that would go with me, and the rest, that were not favourites, were placed in a separate box for the children on the estate. There were coats I had outgrown, which were sadly worn; and I remember he insisted that I should hand them down to smaller boys less fortunate than I, which I resented. It was as though he took the happy past away from me. Now something of the same atmosphere clung to Rachel's boudoir. That shawl, had she given it away because she would not need it in a warmer climate? The work-box, was it dismantled, and now reposing at the bottom of a trunk? No sign, as yet, of actual trunks themselves. That would be the final warning. The heavy footsteps in the attic, the boys descending, boxes borne between them, and a kind of dusty cobweb smell, woven about with camphor. Then I would know the worst, and like the dogs with uncanny sense of change, await the end. Another thing was that she started to go out driving in the morning, which she had not done before. She would tell me she had shopping she wished to do, and business at the bank. These things were possible. I should have thought one journey would have settled them. But three mornings in one week followed upon each other, with one day spaced between, and now yet again, in the week that was upon us, twice she had driven into town. The first time it was a morning. The second, afternoon. 'You have,' I said to her, 'the devil of a lot of shopping of a sudden, and business too . . .'

'I would have done it all before,' she answered, 'but could not do so all the weeks that you were ill.'

'Do you meet anyone as you go about the town?'

'Why, no, not in particular. Yes, now I think of it. I saw Belinda Pascoe and the curate to whom she is engaged. They sent you their respects.'

'But,' I insisted, 'you were away all afternoon. Did you buy up all the contents of the drapers?'

'No,' she said. 'You are really very curious, and prying. Can I not order the carriage when I please, or do you fear to tire the horses?'

'Drive to Bodmin or to Truro if you please,' I said, 'you will find better shopping there, and more to see.'

She did not care for it, then, when I questioned her. Her business must be very personal and private, that she was so reserved.

The next time she ordered the carriage the groom did not go with them. Wellington drove her alone. It seemed that Jimmy had the ear-ache. I had been in the office, and I found him sitting in the stable, nursing his injured ear.

'You must ask the mistress for some oil,' I said to him. 'I'm told that is the remedy.'

'Yes, sir,' he said, disconsolate, 'she promised to see to it for me, by and by on her return. I think I caught cold in it yesterday. There was a fresh wind blowing on the quay.'

'What were you doing on the quay?' I asked.

'We were waiting a long while for the mistress,' he answered, 'so Mr Wellington thought best to bait the horses in the Rose and Crown, and he let me go off and watch the boats in the harbour.'

'Was the mistress shopping then all afternoon?' I asked.

'No, sir,' he replied, 'she didn't shop at all. She was in the parlour at the Rose and Crown, the same as always.'

I stared at him in disbelief. Rachel in the parlour of the Rose and Crown? Did she sit taking tea with the landlord and his wife? For a moment I thought to question him further, then decided against it. It might be he was speaking out of turn, and would be scolded by Wellington for blabbing. All things were kept from me these days, it seemed. The whole household was in league against me, in a conspiracy of silence. 'Well, Jim,' I said, 'I hope your ear will soon be better,' and left him in the stable. But here was mystery. Had Rachel grown so desirous of company that she had to seek it in the town inn? Knowing my dislike of visitors, did she hire the parlour for a morning, or an afternoon, and bid people visit her there? I said nothing of the matter, on her return, but merely asked her if she had passed a pleasant afternoon, and she replied she had.

The following day she did not order the carriage. She told me, at luncheon, that she had letters to write, and went up to her boudoir. I said I had to walk to Coombe, to see the farmer there, which was true enough, and so I did. But I went further. Into the town myself. It was a Saturday, and because of the fine weather many folk were out about the streets, people from the neighbouring market towns, who did not know me by sight, so that I passed amongst them unobserved. I saw no one I knew. The 'quality', as Seecombe termed them, never went into the town of an afternoon, and never on a Saturday.

I leant over the harbour wall, near to the quay, and saw some boys fishing from a boat, getting themselves entangled in their lines. Presently they sculled towards the steps and clambered out. One of them I recognised. It was the lad who helped behind the bar in the Rose and Crown. He had three or four fine bass on a piece of string.

'You've done well,' I said. 'Are they for supper?'

'Not for me, sir,' he grinned, 'they'll be welcome at the inn though, I'll be bound.'

'Do you serve bass now with the cider?' I asked.

'No,' he said, 'this fish is for the gentleman in the parlour. He had a piece of salmon yesterday, from up the river.'

A gentleman in the parlour. I pulled some silver from my pocket.

'Well,' I said, 'I hope he pays you well. Here's this for luck. Who is your visitor?'

He screwed his face into another grin. 'Don't know his name, sir,' he replied, 'Italian, they say he is. From foreign parts.'

And he ran off across the quay, with his fish dangling from the string over his shoulder. I glanced at my watch. It was after three o'clock. No doubt the gentleman from foreign parts would dine at five. I walked through the town, and down the narrow alleyway to the boathouse where Ambrose had kept his sails and gear for the sailing boat he used to use. The small pram was made fast to the frape. I pulled in the pram, and climbed down into it; then paddled out into the harbour and lay off, a little distance from the quay.

There were several fellows pulling to and from the vessels anchored in the channel, to the town steps; and they did not notice me, or if they did cared little, and took me for a fisherman. I threw the weight into the water and rested on my paddles, and watched the entrance of the Rose and Crown. The bar entrance was in the side-street. He would not enter that way. If he came at all, it would be by the front. An hour passed. The church clock struck four. Still I waited. At a quarter before five I saw the landlord's wife come out of the parlour entrance and look about her, as though in search of someone. Her visitor was late for supper. The fish was cooked. I heard her call out to a fellow standing by the boats that were fastened to the steps, but I did not catch her words. He shouted back at her and, turning, pointed out towards the harbour. She nodded her head, and went back inside the inn. Then, ten minutes after five, I saw a boat approaching the town steps. Pulled by a lusty fellow in the bows, the boat itself new varnished, it had all the air of one hired out for strangers, who cared to be rowed about the harbour for their pleasure.

A man, with a broad-brimmed hat upon his head, was seated in the stern. They came to the steps. The man climbed out and gave the fellow money, after slight argument, then turned towards the inn. As he stood for a moment on the steps, before entering the Rose and Crown, he took off his hat and looked about him, with that air of putting a price on all he saw that I could not mistake. I was so near, I could have tossed a biscuit at him. Then he went inside. It was Rainaldi.

I hauled up the weight and pulled back to the boathouse, made the boat fast, walked through the town, and up the rope walk to the cliffs. I think I covered the four miles to home in forty minutes. Rachel was in the library waiting for me. Dinner had been put back because I had not come. She came towards me, anxious.

'At last you have returned,' she said. 'I have been very worried. Where were you, then?'

'Out rowing, in the harbour,' I answered her. 'Fine weather for excursions. Far better on the water than inside the Rose and Crown.'

The startled shock that came into her eyes was all I needed for the final proof.

'All right, I know your secret,' I continued. 'Don't think up any lies.'

Seecombe came in to ask if he should serve dinner.

'Do so, at once,' I said, 'I shall not change.'

I stared at her, saying no more, and we went in to dinner. Seecombe was all concern, sensing something wrong. He hovered at my elbow like a doctor, tempting me to taste the dishes that he proffered.

'You have overtaxed your strength, sir,' he said, 'this will not do at all. We shall have you ill again.'

He looked at Rachel for confirmation, and for backing. She said nothing. As soon as dinner was over, which each of us had barely tasted, Rachel rose to her feet and went straight upstairs. I followed her. When she came to the door of the boudoir she would have closed it against me, but I was too quick for her and

306

stood inside the room, with my back against it. The look of apprehension came to her eyes again. She went away from me, and stood by the mantelpiece.

'How long has Rainaldi been staying at the Rose and Crown?' I said.

'That is my business,' she replied.

'Mine also. Answer me,' I said.

I think she saw there was no hope to keep me quiet, or fob me off with fables. 'Very well then, for the past two weeks,' she answered.

'Why is he here?' I said.

'Because I asked him. Because he is my friend. Because I needed his advice, and, knowing your dislike, could not ask him to this house.'

'Why should you need his advice?'

'That, again, is my business. Not yours. Stop behaving like a child, Philip, and have some understanding.'

I was glad to see her so distressed. It showed she was at fault.

'You ask me to have understanding,' I said. 'Do you expect me to understand deceit? You have been lying every day to me for the past two weeks, and cannot deny it.'

'If I have deceived you, it was not willingly,' she said. 'I did it for your sake only. You hate Rainaldi. If you had known that I was meeting him, this scene would have come the sooner, and you would have been ill in consequence. Oh, God – must I go through this all again? First with Ambrose, and now with you?'

Her face was white and strained, but whether from fear or anger was hard to tell. I stood with my back against the door and watched her.

'Yes,' I said, 'I hate Rainaldi, as did Ambrose. And with reason.'

'What reason, for pity's sake?'

'He is in love with you. And has been, now, for years.'

'What utter nonsense . . .' She paced up and down the little room, from the fireplace to the window, her hands clasped in front of her. 'Here is a man who has stood beside me through every trial and trouble. Who has never misjudged me, or tried

307

to see me as other than I am. He knows my faults, my weaknesses, and does not condemn them, but accepts me at my own value. Without his help, through all the years that I have known him – years of which you know nothing – I would have been lost indeed. Rainaldi is my friend. My only friend.'

She paused, and looked at me. No doubt it was the truth, or so distorted in her mind that, to her, it became so. It made no difference to my judging of Rainaldi. Some of his reward he held already. The years of which, so she just told me, I knew nothing. The rest would come in time. Next month, perhaps, next year – but finally. He had a wealth of patience. But not I, nor Ambrose.

'Send him away, back where he belongs,' I said.

'He will go, when he is ready,' she replied, 'but if I need him he will stay. Indeed, if you try and threaten me again I will have him in this house, as my protector.'

'You would not dare,' I said.

'Dare? Why not? The house is mine.'

So we had come to battle. Her words were a challenge that I could not meet. Her woman's brain worked differently from mine. All argument was fair, all blows were foul. Physical strength alone disarmed a woman. I made one step towards her, but she was at the fireplace, with her hand upon the bell-rope.

'Stay where you are,' she cried, 'or I shall ring for Seecombe. Do you want to be shamed in front of him, when I tell him that you tried to strike me?'

'I was not going to strike you,' I replied. I turned, and opened wide the door. 'All right,' I said, 'call for Seecombe, if you wish. Tell him all that has happened here, between us. If we must have violence and shame, let us have it in full measure.'

She stood by the bell-rope, I by the open door. She let the bell-rope fall. I did not move. Then, tears coming to her eyes, she looked at me and said, 'A woman can't suffer twice. I have had all this before.' And lifting her fingers to her throat she added, 'Even the hands around my neck. That too. Now will you understand?'

I looked over her head, straight at the portrait above the mantelpiece, and the young face of Ambrose staring at me was my own. She had defeated both of us.

'Yes,' I said, 'I understand. If you want to see Rainaldi, ask him here. I would rather that, than that you crept to meet him at the Rose and Crown.'

And I left her in the boudoir, and went back to my room.

Next day he came to dinner. She had sent a note to me at breakfast, asking permission to invite him, her challenge of the night before forgotten no doubt, or expediently put aside, to restore me to position. I sent a note back in return, saying I would give orders for Wellington to fetch him in the carriage. He arrived at half-past four.

It happened that I was alone in the library when he came, and by some error on the part of Seecombe he was shown in to me, and not into the drawing-room. I rose from my chair, and bade him good afternoon. He seemed greatly at his ease, and offered me his hand.

'I hope you are recovered,' he said, in greeting me. 'In fact, I think you look better than I expected. All the reports I had of you were bad. Rachel was much concerned.'

'Indeed, I am very well,' I said to him.

'The fortune of youth,' he said. 'What it is to have good lungs, and good digestion, so that in the space of a few weeks all traces of sickness leave you. No doubt you are already galloping about the countryside on horseback. Whereas we older people, like your cousin and myself, go carefully, to avoid all strain. Personally, I consider a nap in the immediate afternoon essential to middle age.'

I asked him to sit down and he did so, smiling a little as he looked about him. 'No alterations to this room as yet?' he said. 'Perhaps Rachel intends to leave it so, as giving atmosphere. Just as well. The money can be better spent on other things. She tells me much has been already done about the grounds, since my last visit. Knowing Rachel, I can well believe it. But I must see first, before I give approval. I regard myself as a trustee, to hold a balance.'

309

He took a thin cigar from his case, and lit it, still smiling as he did so. 'I had a letter to you, written in London,' he said, 'after you made over your estate, and would have sent it, but that I had the news of your illness. There was little in the letter that I can't say now to your face. It was merely thanking you, for Rachel's sake, and assuring you that I would take great care to see there was no great loss to you in the transaction. I shall watch all expenditure.' He puffed a cloud of smoke into the air, and gazed up at the ceiling. 'That candelabra,' he said, 'was not chosen with great taste. We could do better for you than that, in Italy. I must remember to tell Rachel to make a note of these things. Good pictures, good furniture and fittings, are all sound investments. Eventually, you will find we shall hand the property back to you with double value. However, that's in the distant future. And you by that time, no doubt, with grown sons of your own. Rachel and myself, old people in wheeled chairs.' He laughed, and smiled at me again. 'And how is the charming Miss Louise?' he said to me.

I told him I believed that she was well. I watched him smoking his cigar, and thought how smooth his hands were for a man. They had a kind of feminine quality that did not fit in with the rest of him, and the great ring, on his little finger, was out of place.

'When do you go back to Florence?' I asked him.

He flicked the ash that had fallen on his coat down to the grate.

'It depends on Rachel,' he said. 'I return to London to settle my business there, and then shall either go home ahead of her, to prepare the villa and the servants for her reception, or wait and travel with her. You know, of course, that she intends to go?'

'Yes,' I answered.

'I am relieved that you have not put any pressure upon her to remain,' he said. 'I quite understand, that with your illness you became greatly dependent on her; she told me as much. And she has been anxious to spare your feelings in every way. But, as I explained to her, this cousin of yours is now a man, and not a child. If he cannot stand upon his own feet, he must learn to do so. Am I not right?' he asked me.

'Perfectly.'

'Women, especially Rachel, act always from emotion. We men, more usually though not always so, with reason. I am glad to see you sensible. Perhaps in spring, when you visit us in Florence, you will allow me to show you some of the treasures there. You will not be disappointed.' He blew another cloud of smoke up to the ceiling.

'When you say "we",' I ventured, 'do you use it in the royal sense, as if you owned the city, or is it a legal phrase?'

'Forgive me,' he said, 'but I am so accustomed to acting for Rachel, even to thinking for her, in so many ways, that I can never entirely dissociate myself from her and so fall to using that particular pronoun personal.' He looked across at me. 'In time,' he said, 'I have good reason to believe that I shall come to use it in a sense more intimate. But that' – he gestured, his cigar in hand – 'is in the laps of the gods. Ah, here she comes.'

He stood up, and so did I, when Rachel came into the room; and as she gave her hand to him, which he took and kissed, she made him welcome in Italian. Perhaps it was watching them at dinner, I do not know – his eyes, that never left her face, her smile, her change of manner with him – but I felt, rising within me, a sort of nausea. The food I ate tasted of dust. Even the tisana, which she made for the three of us to drink when dinner was over, had a bitter unaccustomed tang. I left them, sitting in the garden, and went up to my room. As soon as I had gone I heard their voices break into Italian. I sat in the chair by my window, where I had sat during those first days and weeks of convalescence, and she beside me; and it was as though the whole world had turned evil, and of a sudden, sour. I could not bring myself to descend and say good night to him. I heard the carriage come, I heard the carriage drive away. I went on sitting in my chair. Presently Rachel came up and tapped upon my door. I did not answer. She opened it, and entering the room came to my side, and put her hand upon my shoulder.

311

'What is it now?' she asked. There was a sort of sigh about her voice, as if she had reached the limit of endurance. 'He could not have been more courteous, or kind,' she said to me. 'What fault was there to-night?'

'None,' I answered.

'He speaks so well of you to me,' she said, 'if you could only hear him, you would realise that he has a great regard for you. This evening you surely could not take exception to anything he said? If only you could be less difficult, less jealous . . .'

She drew the curtains of my room, for dusk was nearly come. Even in her gesture, the way she touched the curtain, there was impatience.

'Are you going to sit there, hunched in that chair, till midnight?' she asked. 'If so, put a wrap about you, or you will take cold. For my part, I am exhausted and shall go to bed.'

She touched my head, and went. Not a caress. The quick gesture of someone patting a child who has misbehaved, the adult finding herself too lost in tedium to continue scolding, but brushing the whole aside. 'There . . . there . . . For heaven's sake, have done.'

That night fever returned to me again. Not with the old force, but something similar. Whether it was chill or not, caught from sitting in the boat in the harbour twenty-four hours before, I do not know, but in the morning I was too giddy to stand upright upon the floor, and fell to retching and to shuddering, and was obliged to go back to bed again. The doctor was sent for, and with my aching head I wondered if the whole miserable business of my illness was to set in with repetition. He pronounced my liver out of order, and left medicine. But when Rachel came to sit with me, in the afternoon, it seemed to me she had upon her face that same expression of the night before, a kind of weariness. I could imagine the thought within her, 'It is going to start again? Am I doomed to sit here as a nurse to all eternity?' She was more brusque with me, as she handed me my medicine; and when later I was thirsty, and wished to drink, I did not ask her for the glass, for fear of giving trouble.

She had a book in her hands, which she did not read, and her presence in the chair beside me seemed to hold a mute reproach.

'If you have other things to do,' I said at last, 'don't sit with me.'

'What else do you suppose I have to do?' she answered.

'You might wish to see Rainaldi.'

'He has gone,' she said.

My heart was the lighter for the news. I was almost well.

'He has returned to London?' I enquired.

'No,' she answered, 'he sailed from Plymouth yesterday.'

My relief was so intense that I had to turn away my head lest I showed it in my face, and so increased her irritation.

'I thought he had business still to do in England?'

'So he had; but we decided it could be done just as well by correspondence. Matters of greater urgency attended him at home. He had news of a vessel due to sail at midnight, and so went. Now are you satisfied?'

Rainaldi had left the country, I was satisfied with that. But not with the pronoun 'we'; nor that she spoke of home. I knew why he had gone – to warn the servants at the villa to make ready for their mistress. There was the urgency attending him. My sands were running out.

'When will you follow him?'

'It depends on you,' she answered.

I supposed, if I wished, I could continue to feel ill. Complain of pain, and make excuse of sickness. Drag on, pretending, for a few weeks more. And then? The boxes packed, the boudoir bare, her bed in the blue room covered with the dust-sheet that had been upon it all the years before she came, and silence.

'If,' she sighed, 'you would only be less bitter and less cruel, these last days could be happy.'

Was I bitter? Was I cruel? I had not thought so. It seemed to me the hardness was in her. There was no remedy. I reached out for her hand, and she gave it me. Yet as I kissed it I kept thinking of Rainaldi . . .

That night I dreamt I climbed to the granite stone and read the letter once again, buried beneath it. The dream was so vivid that it did not fade with waking, but remained throughout the morning. I got up, and was well enough to go downstairs, as usual, by midday. Try as I would, I could not shake off the desire within me to read the letter once again. I could not remember what it said about Rainaldi. I must know, for certainty, what it was Ambrose had said of him. In the afternoon Rachel went to her room to rest, and as soon as she had gone I slipped away through the woods and down to the avenue, and climbed the path above the keeper's cottage, filled with loathing for what I meant to do. I came to the granite slab. I knelt beside it and, digging with my hands, felt suddenly the soggy leather of my pocket-book. A slug had made its home there for the winter. The trail across the front was sticky. I knocked it off, and opening the pocket-book took out the crumpled letter. The paper was damp and limp, the lettering more faded than before, but still decipherable. I read the letter through. The first part more hastily, though it was strange that his illness, from another cause, could have been, in symptoms, so much similar to mine. But to Rainaldi . . .

'As the months passed,' wrote Ambrose, 'I noticed more and more how she turned to this man I have mentioned before in my letters, Signor Rainaldi, a friend and I gather a lawyer of Sangalletti's, for advice, rather than to me. I believe this man to have a pernicious influence upon her. I suspect him of having been in love with her for years, even when Sangalletti was alive, and although I do not for an instant believe she ever thought of him in such a connection up to a short while ago, now, since she has altered in her manner to me, I cannot be so sure. There is a shadow in her eye, a tone in her voice, when his name is said, that awakens in my mind the most terrible suspicion.

'Brought up as she was by feckless parents, living a life, before and even during her first marriage, about which both of us have had reserve, I have often felt her code of behaviour is different to ours at home. The tie of marriage may not be so sacred. I suspect, in fact I have proof, that he gives her money. Money, God forgive me for saying so, is at the present time the one way to her heart.'

There it was, the sentence I had not forgotten, which had haunted me. Where the paper folded the words were indistinct, until I caught again the word 'Rainaldi.' 'I will come down to the terrace,' Ambrose said, 'and find Rainaldi there. At sight of me, both fall silent. I cannot but wonder what it is they have been discussing. Once, when she had gone into the villa and Rainaldi and I were left alone, he asked an abrupt question as to my will. This he had seen, incidentally, when we married. He told me that as it stood, and should I die, I would leave my wife without provision. This I knew, and had anyway drawn up a will myself that would correct the error, and would have put my signature to it, and had it witnessed, could I be certain that her fault of spending was a temporary passing thing, and not deep-rooted.

'This new will, by the way, would give her the house and the estate for her lifetime only, and so to you upon her death, with the proviso that the running of the estate be left in your hands entirely.

'It still remains unsigned, and for the reason I have told you.

'Mark you, it is Rainaldi who asked questions on the will, Rainaldi who drew my attention to the omissions of the one that stands at present. She does not speak of it, to me. But do they speak of it, together? What is it that they say to one another, when I am not there?

'This matter of the will occurred in March. Admittedly, I was unwell, and nearly blinded with my head, and Rainaldi bringing up the matter may have done so in that cold calculating way of his, thinking that I might die. Possibly it is so. Possibly it is not discussed between them. I have no means of finding out. Too often now I find her eyes upon me, watchful and strange. And when I hold her, it is as though she were afraid. Afraid of what, of whom?

'Two days ago, which brings me to the reason for this letter,

315

I had another attack of this same fever, which laid me low in March. The onset is sudden. I am seized with pain and sickness, which passes swiftly to great excitation of my brain, driving me near to violence, and I can hardly stand upon my feet for dizziness of mind and body. This, in its turn, passes, and an intolerable desire for sleep comes upon me, so that I fall upon the floor, or upon my bed, with no power over my limbs. I do not recollect my father being thus. The headaches, yes, and some difficulty of temperament, but not the other symptoms.

'Philip, my boy, the only being in the world whom I can trust, tell me what it means, and if you can, come out to me. Say nothing to Nick Kendall. Say no word to any single soul. Above all, write not a word in answer, only come.

'One thought possesses me, leaving me no peace. Are they trying to poison me? – AMBROSE.'

This time I did not put the letter back into the pocket book. I tore it piece by piece into tiny shreds, and ground the shreds into the earth with my heel. Each shred was scattered, and then ground, in a separate place. The pocket book, soggy from its sojourn in the earth, I was able to wrench in two with a single twist. I flung each half over my shoulder, and they fell amongst the bracken. Then I walked home. It seemed like a postscript to the letter, that when I entered the hall Seecombe was just bringing in the post-bag, that the boy had fetched from town. He waited while I unlocked it, and there, amidst the few there were for me, was one to Rachel, with the Plymouth mark upon it. I needed but to glance at the thin spidery hand to know that it was from Rainaldi. I think, if Seecombe had not been there, I would have kept it. As it was, there was nothing for it but to give it him to take up to Rachel.

It was ironic, too, that when I went up to her a little later, saying nothing of my walk or where I had been, all her sharpness with me seemed to have gone. The old tenderness had returned. She held out her arms to me, and smiled, and asked me how I felt and if I was rested. She said nothing of the letter she had received. I wondered, during dinner, whether the news it had contained had made her happy; and, as I sat eating, I pictured to myself the framework of his letter, what he had said to her, how he addressed her – if, in short, it were a letter of love. It would be written in Italian. But here and there, though, there might be words I should understand. She had taught me a few phrases. I would know, at any rate, with the first words, the relationship they bore to one another.

'You are very silent. Are you well?' she said.

'Yes,' I answered, 'I am well,' and flushed, lest she should read my mind and guess what I meant to do.

After dinner we went up to her boudoir. She prepared the tisana, as usual, and set it down in its cup on the table by my side, and hers as well. On the bureau lay Rainaldi's letter, half covered by her handkerchief. My eyes were drawn towards it, fascinated. Would an Italian, writing to the woman he loved, keep to formality? Or setting sail from Plymouth, with the prospect of a few weeks' separation, and having dined well, drunk his brandy and smoked his cigar, and smiling in complaisance, would he turn to indiscretion and permit himself the licence of spilling love on paper?

'Philip,' said Rachel, 'you keep your eyes fixed on one corner of the room as though you saw a ghost. What is the matter?'

'I tell you nothing,' I said. And for the first time lied, as I knelt beside her pretending an urgency of longing and of love, so that her questions might be stilled, and that she would forget the letter lying on the desk and leave it there.

Late that night, long after midnight, when I knew she slept – for standing in her room with a lighted candle I looked down on her and saw that it was so – I went back into the boudoir. The handkerchief was still there, the letter gone. I looked in the fire, no ashes in the grate. I opened the drawers of the bureau, and there were her papers all in order, but not the letter. It was not in the pigeon-holes, nor the little drawers beside it. There remained only one drawer, and that was locked. I took my knife and edged it in the crack. Something white showed, from inside the drawer. I went back to the bedroom, took the bunch of keys

317

from the bedside table, and tried the smallest. It fitted. The drawer opened. I put in my hand and pulled out an envelope, but as I did so my tense excitement turned to disappointment, for it was not Rainaldi's letter that I held in my hands. It was just an envelope, containing pods, with seeds. The seeds ran from the pods on to my hands, and spilt upon the floor. They were very small, and green. I stared at them, and remembered that I had seen pods and seeds like these before. They were the same as those that Tamlyn had thrown over his shoulder in the plantation, and that had also covered the court in the villa Sangalletti, which the servant there had swept away.

They were laburnum seeds, poisonous to cattle, and to men.

26

I put the envelope back in the drawer. I turned the key. I took the bunch of keys and replaced it on the dressing-table. I did not look at her, as she lay sleeping in her bed. I went to my room.

I think I was more calm than I had been for many weeks. I went to my washing-stand, and standing there beside the jug and basin were the two bottles of medicine that the doctor had prescribed for me. I emptied the contents from the window. Then I went downstairs, with a lighted candle, and into the pantry. The servants had all gone to their quarters long ago. On the table near the washing-sink stood the tray with the two cups upon it from which we had drunk our tisana. I knew that John was sometimes idle of an evening, and might leave the cups till morning to be washed, as indeed he had. The dregs of the tisana lay in both the cups. I examined both of them by candlelight. They looked the same. I put my little finger into the dregs, first hers, then mine, and tasted. Was there a difference? It was hard to tell. It might be that the dregs from my cup were just a little thicker, but I could not swear to it. I left the pantry, and went again upstairs to my room.

I undressed and went to bed. As I lay there in the darkness I was not aware of anger, or of fear. Only compassion. I saw her as someone not responsible for what she did, besmirched by evil. Compelled and driven by the man who had power over her, lacking, through fault of circumstance and birth, in some deep moral sense, she was capable by instinct and by impulse of this final act. I wanted to save her from herself, and knew not how. It seemed to me that Ambrose was beside me, and I lived again

319

in him, or he in me. The letter he had written, which I had torn in shreds, was now fulfilled.

I believed, in her strange way, that she had loved us both, but we had become dispensable. Something other than blind emotion directed her actions after all. Perhaps she was two persons, torn in two, first one having sway and then the other. I did not know. Louise would say that she had been the second always. That from the very first every thought, every move, had some premeditation. In Florence with her mother, after her father died, had it started then, or even before, the way of living? Sangalletti, dying in a duel, who had never been to Ambrose or myself other than a shadow without substance, had he suffered too? Louise, no doubt, would tell me that he had. Louise would insist that from the first encounter with Ambrose, two years before, she planned to marry him, for money. And when he did not give her what she wanted, planned his death. There was the legal mind. And she had not read the letter I had torn to shreds. What would be her judgement if she had?

What a woman had done once without detection, she can do twice. And rid herself of yet another burden.

Well, the letter was torn; neither Louise nor any one else would ever read it. The contents mattered little to me now. I did not think so much of them as of the last scrap that Ambrose wrote, dismissed by Rainaldi, and by Nick Kendall too, as being the final utterance of a brain diseased. 'She has done for me at last, Rachel my torment.'

I was the only one to know he spoke the truth.

I was back again, then, where I had been before. I had returned to the bridge beside the Arno, where I had sworn an oath. Perhaps, after all, an oath was something that could not be foresworn, that had to be fulfilled, in its own time. And the time was come . . .

Next day was Sunday. Like all the Sundays past, since she had been a visitor to the house, the carriage came to take us both to church. The day was fine and warm. It was full summer. She wore a new dark gown of thin light stuff, and a straw bonnet, and carried a parasol. She smiled good morning at Wellington, and at Jim, and I helped her into the carriage. When I took my seat beside her, and we drove off through the park, she put her hand in mine.

I had held it many times, in love, before. Felt the small size of it, turned the rings upon the fingers, seen the blue veins upon the back, touched the small close-filed nails. Now, as it rested in my hand, I saw it, for the first time, put to another purpose. I saw it take the laburnum pods, in deft fashion, and empty out the seeds; then crush the seeds, and rub them in her palm. I remembered once I had told her that her hands were beautiful, and she had answered, with a laugh, that I was the first to tell her so. 'They have their uses,' she said. 'Ambrose used to say, when I was gardening, that they were workmen's hands.'

Now we had come to the steep hill, and the drag was put upon the rear wheel of the carriage. She touched my shoulder with her shoulder, and putting up her parasol against the sun she said to me, 'I slept so sound last night, I never heard you go,' and she looked at me, and smiled. Though she had deceived me for so long, I felt the greater liar. I could not even answer her, but to keep up the lie held her hand the firmer, and turned away my head.

The sands were golden in the westward bay, the tide far out, the water sparkling in the sun. We turned along the lane that led to the village, and to church. The bells were ringing out across the air, and the people stood around the gate and waited for us to alight from the carriage and pass in before them. Rachel smiled and bowed to all of them. We saw the Kendalls, and the Pascoes, and the many tenants from the estate, and we walked up the aisle to our pew as the organ played.

We knelt in prayer for a brief moment, our faces buried in our hands. 'And what,' I thought to myself, for I did not pray, 'is she saying to her God, if she acknowledges one? Does she give thanks for success in all she has achieved? Or does she ask for mercy?'

She rose from her knees and sat back on the cushioned seat,

opening her prayer-book. Her face was serene and happy. I wished that I could hate her, as I had hated her for many months, unseen. Yet I could feel nothing now but this strange, terrible compassion.

We stood up as the vicar entered, and the service began. I remember the psalm we sang upon that morning. 'He that worketh deceit shall not dwell within my house: he that telleth lies shall not tarry in my sight.' Her lips moved with the words, her voice was soft and low as she sang. And when the vicar mounted the pulpit to preach his sermon, she folded her hands upon her lap and composed herself to listen, and her eyes, serious and intent, lifted to watch his face as he gave out his text, 'It is a fearful thing to fall into the hands of the living God.'

The sun came through the stained glass of the windows and shone upon her. I could see, from my seat, the round rosy faces of the village children, yawning a little as they waited for the sermon to finish, and I could hear the shuffle of their feet, pinched into Sunday boots, longing to be barefoot on the green in play. I wished passionately, for one brief moment, that I might be young again, and innocent, with Ambrose, and not Rachel, beside me in the pew.

'There is a green hill far away, beneath a city wall.' I don't know why we sang that hymn this day; perhaps there had been some festival in connection with the village children. Our voices rose loud and clear in the parish church, and I did not think of Jerusalem, as I was no doubt supposed to do, but only of a plain grave in its corner of the Protestant cemetery in Florence.

When the choir had departed and the congregation were stepping out into the aisles, Rachel whispered to me, 'I believe we should ask the Kendalls and the Pascoes to dine to-day, as we used to do. It has been so long, and they will grow offended.'

I thought a moment, and then nodded briefly. It would be better so. Their company would help to bridge the gulf between us, and occupied in conversation with the guests, used to my silence on these occasions, she would have no time to look at me, and wonder. Outside the church, the Pascoes needed no persuasion, the Kendalls rather more. 'I shall be obliged to leave you,' said my godfather, 'immediately we have dined, but the carriage can return again to fetch Louise.'

'Mr Pascoe has to preach again at evensong,' interrupted the vicar's wife, 'we can take you back with us.' They fell into elaborate plans of transportation, and while they were thus arguing, and arranging how it could best be done, I noticed that the foreman in charge of the workmen who were employed upon the building of the terrace walk and the future sunken garden stood at the side of the path to speak to me, his hat in his hand.

'What is it?' I said to him.

'Excuse me, Mr Ashley sir,' he said, 'I looked for you yesterday, when we were done work for the day, but did not see you, just to warn you, if you should go on the terrace walk, not to stand on the bridgeway we are building across the sunken garden.'

'Why, what is wrong with it?'

'It's only a framework, sir, until we can get working on it Monday morning. The planking looks firm enough to the eye, but it doesn't bear no weight upon it. Anyone stepping on it, thinking to cross to the further side, could fall and break their neck.'

'Thank you,' I said, 'I will remember.'

I turned to find my party had come to their agreement, and as on that first Sunday, which now seemed so long ago, we split into three groups, Rachel and my godfather driving in his carriage, and Louise and I in mine. The Pascoes, in their brougham, followed third. No doubt it had come about like this many times between; yet as we climbed the hill, and I got out and walked, I kept thinking of the first time, nearly ten months before, on that Sunday in September. I had been irritated by Louise that morning, sitting so stiff and proud, and had neglected her from that day forward. She had not wavered, but had stayed my friend. When we topped the hill, and I stepped once more into the carriage, I said to her, 'Did you know that laburnum seeds are poisonous?'

She looked at me, surprised. 'Yes, I believe so,' she said; 'I know

323

that if cattle eat them they die. And children too. What makes you ask? Have you lost cattle at the Barton?'

'No, not yet,' I said, 'but Tamlyn spoke to me the other day about moving the trees that lean from the plantation to the field beneath, because of the seeds falling to the ground.'

'It might be wise to do so,' she replied. 'Father lost a horse once, years ago, eating yew berries. It can come about so quickly, and there is nothing one can do.'

We came along the lane, and to the park gates, and I wondered what she would say if I told her of my discovery of the night before. Would she stare at me in horror, telling me I was mad? I doubted it. I thought she would believe me. This was not the place, though, with Wellington seated on the box and Jim beside him.

I turned my head; the other carriages were following behind. 'I want to talk to you, Louise,' I said to her. 'When your father leaves, after dinner, make some excuse to stay.'

She stared at me, a question in her eyes, but I said no more.

Wellington pulled up before the house. I got out and gave Louise my hand. We stood waiting for the others. Yes, it might have been that other Sunday, in September. Rachel was smiling now, as she smiled then. She was looking up at my godfather, talking as she did so; and I believe they were at politics again. That Sunday, though drawn towards her, she had been a stranger to me still. And now? Now, no part of her was strange. I knew the best, I knew the worst. Even the motives for all she did, baffling perhaps even to herself, I guessed them too. She hid nothing for me now, Rachel my torment . . .

'This,' she said smiling, as we all assembled in the hall, 'is like old times again. I am so happy you have come.'

She embraced the party in a glance, and led the way to the drawing-room. The room, as always, looked its best in summer. The windows were flung wide open, it was cool. The Japanese hortensias, feathery blue, stood long and slender in the vases, and reflected in the mirrors on the walls. Outside the sun beat down upon the lawns. It was very warm. A lazy bumble-bee droned against one of the windows. The visitors sat down, languid, and content to rest. Seecombe brought cake and wine.

'You are all overcome because of a little sun,' laughed Rachel. 'To me, it is nothing. In Italy we have it thus for nine months in the year. I thrive upon it. Here, I will wait upon you all. Philip, remain seated. You are still my patient.'

She poured the wine into the glasses and brought it to us. My godfather and the vicar both stood up, protesting, but she waved them aside. When she came last to me, I was the only one who did not drink.

'Not thirsty?' she said.

I shook my head. I would take nothing from her hands again. She put the glass back upon the tray, and with her own went and sat beside Mrs Pascoe and Louise upon the sofa.

'I suppose,' said the vicar, 'that in Florence now the heat is well-nigh unbearable, even to you?'

'I never found it so,' said Rachel. 'The shutters would be closed early in the morning, which kept the villa cool throughout the day. We adapt ourselves to the climate. Anyone who stirs without in the middle of the day asks for disaster; so we stay within, and sleep. I am lucky, at the villa Sangalletti, in having a little court beside the house that faces north and never has the sun upon it. There is a pool there, and a fountain; and when the air feels used I turn on the fountain; the water dripping has a soothing sound. In spring and summer I never sit anywhere else.'

In spring, indeed, she could watch the buds upon the laburnum tree swell and turn to flower, and the flowers themselves, with drooping golden heads, make a canopy for the naked boy who stood above the pool, holding the shell between his hands. In their turn the flowers would fade and fall, and when high summer came to the villa, as it had come here, in less intensity, the pods upon the branches of the tree would burst and scatter, and the green seeds tumble to the ground. All this she would have watched, sitting in the little court, with Ambrose at her side.

'I would dearly love to visit Florence,' said Mary Pascoe, her eyes round, and dreaming of God knew what strange magnificence, and Rachel turned to her, and said, 'Then you must do so, next year, and come and stay with me. You must all come and stay with me, in turn.' At once we were in the midst of exclamations, questions and expressions of dismay. Must she go soon? When would she return? What were her plans? She shook her head in answer. 'Presently I shall go,' she said, 'and presently return. I act on impulse, and will not confine myself to dates.' Nor would she be drawn into further detail.

I saw my godfather glance at me, out of the corner of his eye; then, tugging his moustache, stare at his feet. I could imagine the thought that was passing through his head. 'Once she has gone, he will be himself again.' The afternoon wore on. At four, we sat to dinner. Once more I was seated at the head of the table and Rachel at the foot, my godfather and the vicar on either hand. Once more there was talk and laughter, even poetry. I sat, much with the same silence that I had at first, and watched her face. Then, it had been with fascination, because unknown. The continuation of conversation, the change of topic, the inclusion of each person at the table, was something that I had never seen a woman do, so it was magic. Now, I knew all the tricks. The starting of a subject, the whisper behind her hand to the vicar, and the laughter of both followed at once by my godfather leaning forward asking, 'Now what was that, Mrs Ashley, what did you say?' and her immediate reply, quick and mocking, 'The vicar will inform you,' with the vicar, blushing red and proud, thinking himself a wit, embarking on a story that his family had not heard. It was a little game that she enjoyed, and we were all of us, with our dull Cornish ways, so easy to handle, and to fool.

I wondered if in Italy her task was harder. I did not think so. Only her company there was more suited to her mettle. And with Rainaldi at her hand to help her, speaking the language she knew best, the talk would sparkle at the villa Sangalletti with greater brilliance than it had ever done at my dull table. Sometimes she gestured with her hands, as though to clarify her rapid speech. When she talked to Rainaldi in Italian, I had noticed she did it even more. To-day, interrupting my godfather in some statement, she did it once again; both hands, so quick and deft, brushing aside the air. Then, waiting for his answer, her elbows resting lightly on the table, the hands folded themselves, were still. Her head was turned to him as she listened, so that from the head of the table, where I sat, I looked on her in profile. She was always a stranger, thus. Those neat clipped features on a coin. Dark and withdrawn, a foreign woman standing in a doorway, a shawl about her head, her hand outstretched. But full-face, when she smiled, a stranger never. The Rachel that I knew, that I had loved.

My godfather finished his story. There was a pause, and silence. Trained now to all her movements, I watched her eyes. They looked to Mrs Pascoe, then to me. 'Shall we go into the garden?' she said. We all rose from our chairs, and the vicar, pulling out his watch, sighed and observed, 'Much as I regret it, I must tear myself away.'

'I too,' remarked my godfather. 'I have a brother sick at Luxilyan, and promised to call and see him. But Louise may stay.'

'Surely you have time to drink your tea?' said Rachel; but it seemed the hour was later than they thought, and at length, after some pother, Nick Kendall and the Pascoes departed in the brougham. Louise alone remained.

'Since there are only the three of us,' said Rachel, 'let us be informal. Come to the boudoir.' And smiling at Louise she led the way upstairs. 'Louise shall drink tisana,' she called, over her shoulder. 'I will show her my method. When her father suffers from insomnia, if ever, this is the remedy.'

We all came to the boudoir and sat down, I by the open window, Louise upon the stool. Rachel busied herself with her preparations.

'The English way,' said Rachel, 'if there can be an English way, which I rather doubt, is to take peeled barley. I brought my own dried herbs from Florence. If you like the taste, I will leave some with you when I go.'

Louise rose from the stool, and stood beside her. 'I heard from

327

Mary Pascoe that you know the name of every herb,' she said, 'and have doctored the tenants here on the estate for many ailments. In old days, the people knew more about these things than they do now. Yet some of the old folk can still charm away warts and rashes.'

'I can charm more than warts,' laughed Rachel. 'Call in at their cottages, and ask them. Herb-lore is very ancient. I learnt it from my mother. Thank you, John.' John had brought up the kettle of steaming water. 'In Florence,' said Rachel, 'I used to brew the tisana in my room, and let it stand. It is better thus. Then we would go out into the court, and sit, and I would turn on the fountain, and while we sipped our tisana the water dripped into the pool. Ambrose would sit there, watching it, for hours.' She poured the water that John had brought into the teapot. 'I have a mind,' she said 'to bring back from Florence, next time I come to Cornwall, a little statue, like the one above my pool. It will take some finding, but I shall be successful in the end. Then we can put him to stand in the middle of the new sunken garden we are building here, and make a fountain too. What do you think?' She turned to me, smiling, and she was stirring the tisana with a spoon in her left hand.

'If you like,' I answered.

'Philip lacks all enthusiasm,' she said to Louise; 'either he agrees to all I say, or does not care. Sometimes I think my labours here are wasted, the terrace walk, the shrubs in the plantation. He would have been content with rough grass, and a muddied path. Here, take your cup.'

She gave the cup to Louise, who sat down on the stool. Then she brought me mine, where I was sitting on the window-sill.

I shook my head. 'No tisana, Philip?' she said. 'But it is good for you, and makes you sleep. You have never refused before. This is a special brew. I have made it double strength.'

'You drink it for me,' I replied.

She shrugged her shoulders, 'Mine is already poured. I like it to stand longer. This must be wasted. What a pity.' She leant over me, and poured it from the window. Drawing back, she put her hand on my shoulder, and from her came the scent I knew so well. No perfume, but the essence of her own person, the texture of her skin.

'Are you not well?' she whispered, so that Louise could not hear.

If all knowledge, and all feeling, could be blotted out, I would have asked it then, and that she should remain, her hand upon my shoulder. No letter torn to shreds, no secret packet locked in a little drawer, no evil, no duplicity. Her hand moved from my shoulder to my chin, and stayed there for a moment in a brief caress, which, because she stood between me and Louise, passed unseen. 'My sullen one,' she said.

I looked above her head, and saw the portrait of Ambrose above the mantelpiece. His eyes stared straight into mine, in youth and innocence. I answered nothing; and moving from me she put back my empty cup on to the tray.

'What do you think of it?' she asked Louise.

'I am afraid,' apologised Louise, 'that it would take me a little time to like it well.'

'Perhaps,' said Rachel; 'the musty flavour does not suit all persons. Never mind. It is a sedative to unquiet minds. To-night we shall all sleep well.' She smiled, and drank slowly from her own cup.

We chatted a little while, for perhaps half an hour or more, or rather she did with Louise; then rising, and putting back her cup upon the tray, she said, 'Now it is cooler, who will walk with me in the garden?' I glanced across at Louise, who, looking at me, stayed silent.

'I have promised Louise,' I said, 'to show her an old plan of the Pelyn estate that I came across the other day. The boundaries are strongly marked, and show the old hill fortress being part of it.'

'Very well,' said Rachel, 'take her to the drawing-room, or remain here, as you please. I shall take my walk alone.'

She went, humming a song, into the blue bedroom.

'Stay where you are,' I said softly, to Louise.

I went downstairs, and to the office, for in truth there was an old plan that I had somewhere, among my papers. I found it, in a file, and went back across the court. As I came to the side door, that led from near the drawing-room to the garden, Rachel was setting forth upon her walk. She wore no hat, but had her sunshade, open, in her hand. 'I shall not be long,' she said, 'I'm going up to the terrace – I want to see if a little statue would look well in the sunken garden.'

'Have a care,' I said to her.

'Why, of what?' she asked.

She stood beside me, her sunshade resting on her shoulder. She wore a dark gown, of some thin muslin stuff, with white lace about the neck. She looked much as I had seen her first, ten months ago, except that it was summer. The scent of the new cut grass was in the air. A butterfly flew past in happy flight. The pigeons cooed from the great trees beyond the lawn.

'Have a care,' I said slowly, 'of walking beneath the sun.'

She laughed, and went from me. I watched her cross the lawn and climb the steps towards the terrace.

I turned back into the house, and going swiftly up the stairs came to the boudoir. Louise was waiting there.

'I want your help,' I said briefly, 'I have little time to lose.'

She rose from the stool, her eyes a question. 'What is it?'

'You remember the conversation that we had those weeks ago, in the church?' I said to her. She nodded.

'Well, you were right, and I was wrong,' I answered, 'but never mind that now. I have suspicious of worse beside, but I must have final proof. I think she has tried to poison me, and that she did the same to Ambrose.' Louise said nothing. Her eyes widened in horror.

'It does not matter now how I discovered it,' I said, 'but the clue may lie in a letter from that man Rainaldi. I am going to search her bureau here, to find it. You learnt a smattering of Italian, with your French. Between us, we can reach some translation.'

Already I was looking through the bureau, more thoroughly than I was able to do the night before by candlelight.

'Why did you not warn my father?' said Louise. 'If she is guilty, he could accuse her with greater force than you?'

'I must have proof,' I answered her.

Here were papers, envelopes, stacked neatly in a pile. Here were receipts and bills that might have alarmed my godfather had he seen them but meant little to me, in my fever to discover what I sought. I tried again the little drawer that held the packet. This time it was not locked. I pulled it open, and the drawer was empty. The envelope had gone. This might be an added proof, but my tisana had been poured away. I went on opening the drawers, and Louise stood beside me, her brows knit with anxiety. 'You should have waited,' she said. 'It is not wise. You should have waited for my father, who could take legal action. What you are doing now is what anyone might do, a common thief.'

'Life and death,' I said, 'do not wait for legal action. Here, what is this?' I tossed her a long paper, with names upon it. Some of them in English, some Latin, some Italian.

'I am not sure,' she answered, 'but I think it is a list of plants, and herbs. The writing is not clear.'

She puzzled over it, as I turned out the drawers.

'Yes,' she said, 'these must be her herbs and remedies. But the second sheet is in English, and would seem to be notes on the propagation of plants; species after species, dozens of them.'

'Look for laburnum,' I said.

Her eyes held mine an instant, in sudden understanding. Then she looked down once more to the page she held in her hands.

'Yes, it is here,' she said, 'but it tells you nothing.'

I tore it from her hands and read, where her finger pointed. 'Laburnum Cytisus. A native of south Europe. These plants are all capable of being increased by seeds, and many of them by cuttings and layers. In the first mode, the seeds should be sown, either in beds or where the plants are to remain. In spring, as about March, and when of sufficient growth, transplanted into nursery rows, to remain till of a proper size for being planted in the situations where they are to grow.' Beneath was an added note of the source from where she had taken the information:

331

The New Botanic Garden. Printed for John Stockdale and Company, by T. Bousley, Bold Court. Fleet Street. 1812.

'There is nothing here about poison,' said Louise.

I continued searching the desk. I found a letter from the bank. I recognised the handwriting of Mr Couch. Ruthless and careless now, I opened it. 'Dear Madam, We thank you for the return of the Ashley collection of jewels, which, according to your instruction, as you are shortly to leave the country, will remain with us in custody until such time as your heir, Mr Philip Ashley, may take possession of them. Yours faithfully, HERBERT COUCH.'

I put the letter back, in sudden anguish. Whatever Rainaldi's influence, some impulse of her own directed this action.

There was nothing else of any matter. I had searched thoroughly each drawer, raked every pigeon-hole. Either she had destroyed the letter, or carried it upon her. Baffled, frustrated, I turned again to Louise. 'It is not here,' I said.

'Have you looked through the blotter?' she asked, in doubt.

Like a fool, I had laid it on the chair, never thinking that so obvious a place could hide a secret letter. I took it up, and there, in the centre, between two clean white sheets, fell out the envelope from Plymouth. The letter was still inside. I pulled it from its cover, and gave it to Louise. 'This is it,' I said, 'see if you can decipher it.'

She looked down at the piece of paper, then gave it back to me. 'But it isn't in Italian,' she said to me. 'Read it yourself.'

I read the note. There were only a few, brief lines. He had dispensed with formality, as I had thought he might; but not in the manner I had pictured. The time was eleven of the evening, but there was no beginning. 'Since you have become more English than Italian, I write to you in your language of adoption. It is after eleven, and we weigh anchor at midnight. I will do all you ask of me in Florence, and perhaps more beside, though I am not sure you deserve any of it. At least, the villa will be waiting for you, and the servants, when you at last decide to tear yourself away. Do not delay too long. I have never had great faith in those impulses of your heart, and your emotions. If, in the end, you cannot bring yourself to leave that boy behind, then bring him with you. I warn you though, against my better judgement. Have a care to yourself, and believe me, your friend, Rainaldi.'

I read it once, then twice. I gave it to Louise.

'Does it give you the proof you wanted?' she asked.

'No,' I said.

Something must be missing. Some postscript, on a further scrap of paper, that she had thrust into another sheet of the blotter. I looked once more, but there was nothing. The blotter was clean, save for one folded packet lying on the top. I seized it, and tore away the wrapping. This time it was not a letter, nor a list of herbs or plants. It was a drawing of Ambrose. The initials in the corner were indistinct, but I supposed it was by some Italian friend, or artist, for Florence was scribbled after the initials, and the date was the month of June, of the year he died. As I stared at it, I realised it must be the last likeness ever taken. He had aged much, then, after leaving home. There were lines about his mouth I did not know, and at the corners of his eyes. The eyes themselves had a haunted look about them, as though some shadow stood close to his shoulder and he feared to look behind. There was something lost about the face, and lonely too. He seemed to know disaster was in store. Though the eyes asked for devotion, they pleaded for pity too. Underneath the drawing, Ambrose himself had scribbled some quotation in Italian. 'To Rachel. Non ramentare che le ore felici. Ambrose.'

I gave the drawing to Louise. 'There is only this,' I said. 'What does it mean?'

She read the words aloud, then thought a moment. 'Remember only the happy hours,' she said slowly. She gave it back to me, and the letter from Rainaldi too. 'Did she not show it you before?' she asked.

'No,' I answered.

We looked at one another in silence for a moment. Then Louise said, 'Can we have misjudged her, do you think? About the poison? You see yourself, there is not any proof.'

'There never will be any proof,' I said. 'Not now. Not ever.'

I put the drawing back upon the bureau, and the letter too.

'If there is no proof,' said Louise, 'you cannot condemn her. She may be innocent. She may be guilty. You can do nothing. If she be innocent, and you accused her, you could never forgive yourself. You would be guilty then, not her at all. Let's leave this room, and go down into the drawing-room. I wish now we had not meddled with her things.'

I stood by the open window of the boudoir staring out across the lawn.

'Is she there?' asked Louise.

'No,' I said, 'she has been gone nearly half an hour, and has not returned.'

Louise crossed the room and stood by my side. She looked into my face. 'Why is your voice so strange?' she said. 'Why do you keep your eyes fixed there, on those steps leading to the terrace walk? Is anything the matter?'

I brushed her aside and went towards the door.

'Do you know the bell rope on the landing beneath the belfry,' I said to her, 'the one that is used at noon to summon the men to dinner? Go now, and pull it hard.'

She looked at me, puzzled. 'What for?' she asked.

'Because it is Sunday,' I said, 'and everyone is out, or sleeping, or scattered somewhere; and I may need help.'

'Help?' she repeated.

'Yes,' I said, 'there may have been an accident, to Rachel.'

Louise stared at me. Her eyes, so blue and candid, searched my face.

'What have you done?' she said; and apprehension came upon her, conviction too. I turned, and left the room.

I ran downstairs, and out across the lawn and up the path to the terrace walk. There was no sign of Rachel.

Near to the stones and mortar and the stack of timber above the sunken garden the two dogs were standing. One of them, the younger, came towards me. The other stayed where he was, close to the heap of mortar. I saw her foosteps in the sand and lime, and her sunshade, still open, tipped upon its side. Suddenly the bell rang out from the clock-tower on the house. It went on and on, and the day being still and calm the sound of it must have travelled across the field, down to the sea, so that men fishing in the bay would have heard it too.

I came to the edge of the wall above the sunken garden, and saw where the men had started work upon the bridge. Part of the bridge still remained and hung suspended, grotesque and horrible, like a swinging ladder. The rest had fallen to the depths below.

I climbed down to where she lay amongst the timber and the stones. I took her hands and held them. They were cold.

'Rachel,' I said to her, and 'Rachel' once again.

The dogs began barking up above, and louder still came the sound of the clanging bell. She opened her eyes, and looked at me. At first, I think in pain. Then in bewilderment. Then finally, so I thought, in recognition. Yet I was in error, even then. She called me Ambrose. I went on holding her hands until she died.

They used to hang men at Four Turnings in the old days.

Not any more, though.

VIRAGO MODERN CLASSICS

The first Virago Modern Classic, *Frost in May* by Antonia White, was published in 1978. It launched a list dedicated to the celebration of women writers and to the rediscovery and reprinting of their works. Its aim was, and is, to demonstrate the existence of a female tradition in literature, and to broaden the sometimes narrow definition of a 'classic' which has often led to the neglect of interesting books. Published with new introductions by some of today's best writers, the books are chosen for many reasons: they may be great works of literature; they may be wonderful period pieces; they may reveal particular aspects of women's lives; they may be classics of comedy, storytelling, letter-writing or autobiography.

'The Virago Modern Classics list is wonderful. It's quite simply one of the best and most essential things that has happened in publishing in our time. I hate to think where we'd be without it'
Ali Smith

'A continuingly magnificent imprint'
Joanna Trollope

'The Virago Modern Classics have reshaped literary history and enriched the reading of us all. No library is complete without them'
Margaret Drabble

'The writers are formidable, the production handsome. The whole enterprise is thoroughly grand'
Louise Erdrich

'The Virago Modern Classics are one of the best things in Britain today'
Alison Lurie

Good news for everyone writing and reading today'
Hilary Mantel

'Masterful works'
Vogue

DAPHNE du
MAURIER

Introduced by Sally Beauman

'Last night I dreamt I went to Manderley again . . .'

Working as a paid companion to a bitter elderly lady, the timid
heroine of Rebecca learns her place. Life is bleak until, on a trip
to the South of France, she falls in love with Maxim de Winter,
a handsome widower whose proposal takes her by surprise.
Whisked from Monte Carlo to Manderley, Maxim's isolated
Cornish estate, the young bride begins to realise that she barely
knows her husband at all. And the memory of Rebecca, his dead
wife, is kept alive by the forbidding Mrs Danvers . . .

An international bestseller that has never gone out of print,
Rebecca is the haunting story of a woman consumed by love
and the struggle to find her identity.

'One of the most influential novels of the twentieth century,
Rebecca has woven its way into the fabric of our culture with
all the troubling power of myth or dream. A stunning book'
Sarah Waters

'This chilling, suspenseful tale is as fresh and readable as it
was when it was first written' *Daily Telegraph*

'*Rebecca* will live for ever, because du Maurier touches a fearful
nerve, buried deep in the unconscious'
Kate Saunders, *The Times*

THE BIRDS
AND OTHER STORIES

DAPHNE du
MAURIER

Introduced by David Thomson

'A masterpiece' *Guardian*

'How long he fought with them in the darkness he could not tell, but at last the beating of the wings about him lessened and then withdrew . . .'

A classic of alienation and horror, 'The Birds' was immortalised by Hitchcock in his celebrated film. The five other chilling stories in this collection echo a sense of dislocation and mock man's sense of dominance over the natural world.

'Of all the many short stories du Maurier wrote, "The Birds" is the masterpiece . . . there is an intense and exhilarating fusion of feeling, landscape, climate, character and story. She wrote exciting plots, she was highly skilled at arousing suspense, and she was, too, a writer of fearless originality'
Patrick McGrath, *Guardian*

'One of the last century's most original literary talents'
Daily Telegraph

DAPHNE du
MAURIER

Introduced by Sarah Dunant

'*Jamaica Inn* is a first-rate page-turner' *The Times*

After the death of her mother, Mary Yellan crosses the
windswept Cornish moors to Jamaica Inn, the home of her
Aunt Patience. There she finds Patience a changed woman,
downtrodden by her domineering, vicious husband Joss
Merlyn. The inn is a front for a lawless gang of criminals,
and Mary is unwillingly dragged into their dangerous world
of smuggling and murder. And, despite herself, she is
powerfully attracted to a man she dares not trust. Before
long Mary will be forced to cross her own moral line to
save herself.

'A brilliantly executed thriller' *Vogue*

The
SCAPE-GOAT

DAPHNE du MAURIER

Introduced by Lisa Appignanesi

'Someone jolted my elbow as I drank and said, "*Je vous demande pardon*," and as I moved to give him space he turned and stared at me and I at him, and I realised, with a strange sense of shock and fear and nausea all combined, that his face and voice were known to me too well. I was looking at myself.'

By chance, two men – one English, the other French – meet in a provincial railway station. Their resemblance is uncanny, and they spend the evening talking and drinking. When John, the Englishman, wakes the next morning, he realises that his French companion has stolen his identity and disappeared. So John steps into the Frenchman's shoes, and faces a variety of perplexing roles – as owner of a chateau, director of a failing business, head of a fractious family, and master of nothing.

'What a magnificent thriller this is'
New York Times Book Review

'She wrote exciting plots, she was highly skilled at arousing suspense, and she was, too, a writer of fearless originality'
Guardian

The
LOVING SPIRIT

DAPHNE du MAURIER

Introduced by Michèle Roberts

Janet Coombe longs for adventure and the freedom of the sea. She feels herself pulled fast under its spell, but in her heart she knows she must sacrifice her dreams; she is a woman, and her place is in the home. So she marries Thomas, a boat-builder, and her restless spirit is passed down through her son, and through him to his children's children.

In her acclaimed debut, Daphne du Maurier weaves a compelling tale of heartbreak, courage and love that knows no bounds. *The Loving Spirit*, an inimitable blend of romance, history and adventure, established her reputation as one of the finest writers of her generation.

'She wrote exciting plots, she was highly skilled at arousing suspense, and she was, too, a writer of fearless originality'
Guardian

'A rapturous celebration of the beauties of the Cornish landscape' Michèle Roberts

'Du Maurier creates on the grand scale . . . a rich vein of humour and satire, observation, sympathy, courage, a sense of the romantic are here' *Observer*

virago

To buy any of our books and to find out more
about Virago Press and Virago Modern Classics,
our authors and titles, as well as events and
book club forum, visit our websites

www.virago.co.uk
www.littlebrown.co.uk

and follow us on Twitter

@ViragoBooks

To order any Virago titles p & p free in the UK,
please contact our mail order supplier on:

+ 44 (0)1832 737525

Customers not based in the UK should contact
the same number for appropriate postage
and packing costs.